THE CARLUCCI FILE

BY
GLENN LAUER

authorHOUSE

AuthorHouse™
1663 Liberty Drive, Suite 200
Bloomington, IN 47403
www.authorhouse.com
Phone: 1-800-839-8640

© 2008 Glenn Lauer. All rights reserved.

No part of this book may be reproduced, stored in a retrieval system, or transmitted by any means without the written permission of the author.

First published by AuthorHouse 10/29/2008

ISBN: 978-1-4389-1722-1 (sc)

Printed in the United States of America
Bloomington, Indiana

This book is printed on acid-free paper.

1

Whenever I sat across the desk from Melvin C. Croup, every joke and cliché I ever heard about lawyers would come to mind. It wasn't because I had any general dislike for the profession. I liked attorneys just fine, as long as they were working for me and winning. I guess in Melvin's case it was because he seemed to personify the very essence of the lawyers described in those parables and clichés. Maybe the fact that my only experience with Melvin Croup had come from working *for* him, instead of the other way around might have had something to do with, too.

Today, several of those jokes ran through my mind as I tried to suppress a smile while sitting in his office. Any other man would have looked intimidating standing behind their JFK replica desk, perfectly framed by all their diplomas, credentials, and politico-celebrity photos mounted on the wall behind them, but Melvin's five-foot, six-inch frame and severely receding hairline just didn't make the cut. Instead, the term comical came to mind.

He did have a reputation as a tenacious arbitrator and it was well deserved. He was a monument of contention, never conceding an inch or giving up a dime without arguing his opponent into the ground. I had even heard a story how he had argued his way out of a car jacking, despite a gun being put to his head during the crime. I envisioned the hapless crook left in the wake of Melvin's disputation, standing in the middle of Wilshire Blvd scratching his head while wondering what had just happened. I empathized, because I knew what it felt like.

Begrudging, I had to admit that Melvin was the best-kept secret of his law firm and I suspected the only reason he wasn't a full partner was because of his name. Bartholomew, Howard and Sloan just didn't have the same ring to it with Croup tacked onto the end of it. It sounded like a disease. In fact, I think it *was* a disease. Melvin was certainly a disease. All I knew for sure was that if I ever needed an attorney, I'd call him, but working for him was a completely different situation all together. Today he was swimming in his element, ranting over my simple financial request as if I'd asked him to cut off his right arm.

Despite my rambling thoughts about his abilities as I mentally held his voice on 'mute', I couldn't help but watch him in hypnotic fascination. Part of it had to do with this perpetual expression of pain he carried on his face, as if he had just been dipped in burning oil or nailed to a cross. Accompanying this look of despair, his body language mimicked those amateurish thespians doing their rendition of a long, slow and painful death in the old silent movies. With all my experience working for him, I had yet to see him in action in an actual court case. If his present act was any indication, I figured I could sell tickets outside the courtroom and make a fortune.

Forcing myself back to the moment, I started wondering why the hell I was sitting in this lunatic's office in the first place. Maybe I was the lunatic. Reluctantly, I took him off mute and immediately regretted it. His voice was like fingernails across a chalkboard, perfectly matching his expression and begged the age-old question: which had come first. Waving his arms wildly as he argued his case, I wasn't sure which he resembled most, an insane symphony conductor or a Saturday morning cartoon character.

"That's all it is, just a simple locate." He seemed to be finally winding down. "A couple of days in and out, a walk in the park. I don't understand what the big deal is?"

"If that's all it is, you shouldn't mind paying me up front." I turned on a broad façade of a smile as I calmly repeated the request that had set off his tirade.

"Jesus, Jack, have you heard one word I've said?" He was beginning to remind me of my ex-wife. Next question. "It's a short vacation. A couple of days snooping around the place, you find the guy and check him out, and then you're back home. One, two, three, easy as pie. You don't need the money up front for that. I could do it on pocket change."

"Pocket change to you is rent for me." I nodded towards his trousers. "But if you've got it in loose bills, dig it out now so I can get started."

"For Christ's sake, you know what I mean." His exasperated tone was starting to signal some fatigue. He needed to do less networking and more exercising at his overpriced athletic club.

"Look, Melvin." Despite his insistence that I call him Mel, I always used his full name. I suspected the hazing he got over it as a kid had ultimately led him into the field of law. He probably figured if he couldn't beat up his tormentors he could sue them till they bled. Now an experienced barrister, he was good at bleeding people dry. I'd only been in his office ten minutes and I was already down a pint. Still, I pushed on with my request. "As if this isn't any big news for you, you've stiffed me for the last two jobs I've done for you. I should be charging you double my regular fee, just to get back some of what you owe me."

"Jeez, Jack, you're really busting my balls here." He shook his head and collapsed into his chair, arms flailing over the side rails like a boxer who'd been beaten into his own corner. It might have worked if it weren't for my knowledge of his net worth.

"I feel your pain, Melvin, I really do." I tossed some condescending empathy into my reply. "It must be a real bitch deciding whether to go home to your Beverly Hills estate, the ranch in Saugus, or your Malibu condo each night. Tell me, which ones have wives and which ones are just mistresses?"

Melvin rocked back in his leather desk chair and stopped talking long enough to acknowledge my comment. I wasn't sure which was more deafening, his ranting or the blissful silence, but the look on his face told me I'd struck a nerve. I'd discovered his ownership of the three very pricey residences in and around the Los Angeles area and knew at least one of them was furnished, and I'm not talking sofas and chairs. He should have paid me in the first place. I didn't take too well to being stiffed and always got curious when it happened.

"You don't want to go there, Jack." He tried to look threatening. "That's not funny."

"Our last conversation wasn't funny, either, Melvin." I shot back, emphasizing his name. Physically, he was about as menacing as a Girl Scout. "After all the shouting we did, I thought we'd come to a very loud and clear understanding that I was through working for you as a private investigator and you were through hiring me so you could not pay me for my work."

"So we argued." He argued. "We always argue."

"I'm not signing on without my total fee up front." I shook my head in resolution.

"OK, if that's your only problem, you can have your double fee." He struck a pose, leaning over his desk with that same pained expression on his face, as if he were trying to pass a kidney stone the size of a baseball.

"That'll be fine." I agreed calmly with a wary look. " Then I'll take the customary half up front and get started."

"Why did I even call him?" He threw his hands up with the question, looking around his office as if some unseen person would answer him. "Why do I even bother?"

"That's what's troubling me." I answered for him. "If I didn't know better, I'd say you were trying to send me out to take down some Russian Mob boss, or something else that would equate to my suicide."

"Would I do that to you?" He was pleading again. "After all we've been through?"

"Melvin." I responded with a tired sigh. "You have a whole phone book full of PIs, half of which I'm sure you haven't cheated out of their fee yet. Why me?"

"OK." He sighed and buried his chin in mock defeat. "I'll mail the front half of your fee to your house this afternoon."

"You'll give me a check for it right now, along with traveling expenses, so I can go by your bank and cash it." I sternly admonished with a pointed finger. I knew he'd ultimately stiff me for the other half, but at least I'd get my original fee up front like I'd demanded in the first place. "I won't so much as pack a toothbrush until I have that cash in my hand."

"Jeez, all right, already." He shook his head as he labored heavily to extract a pen from the holder of his desk set.

Picking up a typewritten sheet of paper along with the pen, he made a few notations on it before sliding it over to me. A bit too quickly, he seemed to immerse himself in other work on his desk, leaving me on my own to browse his standard contract with the adjusted fee. It gave me a moment to pause and reflect. I promised myself I'd 'never' work for this shyster again. Croup was so tight you could shove a piece of coal up his ass in the morning and have a diamond by five that afternoon. Nonetheless, I reluctantly penned my signature next to his. It seemed lately that 'never' came around in perfect sync with bill collectors.

I placed the contract back on the desk and watched Melvin immediately press a buzzer on his desk without even looking up. One of his secretaries materialized like magic, plucked the contract off his desk and vanished. My newest client left his busywork long enough to pull a large checkbook from his desk drawer and start writing in it. He spoke as he wrote the draft.

"You can pick up a copy of your contract and the case file on the way out. There's full instructions with the history and all the background, including the individual you've been assigned to locate." He seemed to be talking more to himself as he wrote.

"Who's your client?" I asked offhandedly as I watched him.

"Lloyds of London." He stated simply without looking up.

"What?" I almost choked my response. How could someone overstate the trivial so convincingly and then in the next sentence understate the effects of a nuclear exchange? The answer should have been obvious, but it took me a few moments to catch up.

"You know," He looked up and smiled like a Chinaman who'd just sold a rickshaw for the price of a Mercedes. "That insurance company over in England."

"I suppose you're going to show me where it is on the globe, next?"

He handed the check to me and shrugged the best apology he was capable of.

"If you come up with something, anything, I promise you'll get the back half of your fee this time."

I leaned forward, half out of my seat to take the check, still too stunned to respond. As I sunk back into the armchair, dumbly examining it, I realized for once the little weasel had left me speechless. It was an insurance job. Not just any insurance job, because Lloyds of London wasn't just any insurance company. I wanted to quadruple my fee and double that amount again, but had already signed the contract.

It was common knowledge that the England based insurance

company paid handsomely for recovered assets and the percentages on even their smallest claims could pay for my retirement two lifetimes over. For Melvin, an attorney's fee from Lloyds could finance a fourth mansion and a second or third mistress. The prospect forced me to ponder the status of his libido. He had to have a real set on him to blindside me like this, cause right now I felt like reaching over the desk and popping him like an irritating pimple. Instead, I stared back and forth from him to the check, searching for a comeback. I couldn't find the words and that really pissed me off, because I was known for my comebacks.

"I'll arrange for your flight and hotel expenses, rental car, the usual." He continued with a wave of his hand, now avoiding eye contact as he rocked back and spun in his chair around to examine his glory wall. He looked up at the mementoes as if taking stock in himself.

"You know I don't fly." I stated flatly while staring at the back of his head.

"Driving will take too long and double the hotel fees." He repeated the limp hand gesture.

"No, it won't, because I know you'll put me up in motels with single digit numbers behind the names. In any case, you'll spend a third of what a decent hotel would cost you if I flew." I found some ground and started running in a louder voice. "For what I'm sure you're charging Lloyds in daily expenses, you could buy a whole God Damn chain of motels, so I don't want to hear another word out of you about it. Just rent me a decent full sized car and hope I don't run you down with it."

"Of all the P.I.s in town, I get an Aerophobic maniac." He spun around and shook his head in disappointment at me. "And one with a temper, no less."

"Well, I'm glad you're not afraid of flying." My voice ebbed, but my expression conveyed the message clear enough. "Because I'm about to throw you out the window over there. What is this, the twelfth floor?"

"Jack, take it easy." He went a bit pale, as he held up his hands in mock surrender. "We're just talking business here."

"That's right." I replied with a stiff jaw. "And if you don't like the terms of our agreement, have your Houdini secretary bring back the contract and I'll tear it up right now. I'm sure there's a dozen other firms within walking distance that would pay better on this same claim, not to mention actually compensate me for my work.

"All right." He conceded, again a bit too quickly. "Cash the check and I'll have a rental dropped off at your place within an hour. Just get on the road as soon as you can. OK? Timing is everything here. I have a dozen other investigators in the field and this has to go off like clockwork."

I fell silent as I started to get the bigger picture. Melvin was shotgunning the case, hiring a full spread of private investigators out to work and compartmentalizing them to get the best price on fees while still getting the quickest results possible. It must have been a huge claim to activate so many investigative resources. I knew Melvin was cunning, but this was taking it to a whole new level.

I got up a bit too quickly for his comfort and he reacted by sinking back in his chair, trying not to look at the window. I could see all his childhood fears surfacing as his pained expression turned to one of shear terror. For a second, I almost felt sorry for him. My demeanor relaxed a bit and I continued with more of a resigned tone as I stuffed his check in my pocket.

"Where's the case?" I almost didn't want to know.

"Lone Tree, Nevada."

"Oh, boy." My voice went flat with sarcasm. "Gambling."

"Eh, yeah, I guess." He shrugged uneasily.

"Well, I can't wait." I continued in monotone.

"Good." He tried to pretend I was serious and anxiously gestured towards the door. "Miss Timberlake will have the file. She's the tall blonde receptionist on the right as you're leaving."

"Can I take her with me?" My continued monotone in deadpan seemed more unnerving to him than my overt threats, but this comment broke the mood and he relaxed.

"In your dreams, Hollister." He shook his head with a nervous laugh. His standard expression of pain returned as he waved me off.

"Can't blame me for trying." I headed for the door.

"Yeah, yeah." He leaned forward again and resumed his paperwork as I left the office.

Miss. Timberlake was tall as promised and quite exotic looking. I thought she had the makings of a perfect traveling companion. A few pounds lighter and she could be runway material, but fashion models were anorexic and not to my taste. Miss Timberlake was, but that put her way out of my league. She was the stereotypical California blonde and I was the rough-cut, out of work PI. Those kinds of match-ups only worked in Hollywood films, definitely not in real life, even in tinsel-town real life. Still, I had to keep in practice and since I already knew the outcome, it was easier to roll play.

"I'm headed for one of Nevada's gambling Mecca's." I raised my eyebrows as I approached her at the reception counter. "I could use a co-pilot."

"I'm busy." She responded almost immediately with an icy 'as if' look.

"You peeked at my fee, didn't you?" I frowned in mock defeat.

"I didn't have to." She looked me up and down, acknowledging my everyday dress code of jeans, sandals, and a tie-dye T-shirt.

"Ouch." I replied as I left character. "Apparently you've never seen Bill Gates come out of a Board meeting."

She shook her head in dismissal and put the case file on the countertop before walking away. I hefted it in both hands, looking after her with fresh eyes. She wasn't a receptionist, she was a female weightlifter disguised as a beautiful blonde. The file was a good six inches thick and weighed as much as a Honda Civic.

It was a hot and muggy afternoon in LA, even in the damp shade of the law building's rear parking structure. I labored under the tonnage of the file as I stumbled to my minivan. Opening the passenger door, I plopped the large binder down on the seat and it bounced twice. Looking over the interior of the vehicle, I was glad I was getting a rental. This box with four wheels didn't have too many miles left in it. Of course, I had chosen the older model soccer-mom wagon for its economic range of operation, height for viewing over traffic, ease of handling, and its anonymity as a mobile surveillance platform. Plus, it provided more living space between evictions.

Walking around to the driver's door, I got in and sat, pondering the bulging three-ring binder next to me. It would take less time to handle the case than it would to read the file for it. I started to seriously consider letting my junior partner drive me to Lone Tree so I could review the data on the way there. It would mean splitting the fee three ways: a third for me, a third for my assistant, and a third for the landlord, but it might work. I dismissed the option as I pulled into traffic. He'd miss his paper route and tomorrow was a school day. Besides, his mom would never let him go.

The lunch hour rush was just starting to ebb and it would take the rest of the afternoon to go by Melvin's bank, drive back to my apartment to pack, collect the rental car, and finally head out of town. I suddenly realized I had no idea where Lone Tree was within the state of Nevada. It would be too much to expect it to be a subdivision of Las Vegas. I made a mental note to query the computer for directions before I left town. I was going into this thing completely blind and that raised the hackles on the back of my neck. I'd learned from experience not to ignore that feeling.

All I knew for sure was that Lloyds of London was looking for someone thought to be in Lone Tree, NV. If I was lucky, I'd just knock on a few doors, find this person, and give Croup my report. I shook my head as Melvin's image came back to haunt me like my Ex's alimony. Under his employ and with my luck, a ten-foot tall Hungarian would answer the door and snap me like a twig. I started having doubts and worked my hand across the back of my neck to smooth the raised hairs.

I strained the van's anemic power plant as I crossed over the 405 and headed towards Venice Beach. Melvin's bank had a branch office just down the street from my humble flop pad. I still might have time to make it before all the freeways turned into eight-lane parking lots.

2

 In the shade of a gas pump-island in Elko, Nevada, I finally got a peek at the thick file Melvin had bestowed upon me the day before. I was refueling in the small town situated about half way between Reno and Salt Lake City, preparing for the last leg of my journey due south to Lone Tree. As towns went, Elko was quaint and fashionable in a cowboy sort of way. My Internet query had told me it was known to be a haven for motorcycle riders and legalized prostitution, so I kept an eye out for my ex-brother-in-law.

 I would've been happy to take refuge from the heat inside the truck stop, but their small rest area had been overrun by a throng of octogenarians. The nickel slots that dominated that space were ringing from their loose change while the tour bus idled outside. From their frantic activity, I suspected they were all good Methodists slamming that one last injection of gambling-fever before completing their odyssey home from Reno. Between the incessant clanging of the slot machines and the suspense of which one would win their parking change back first, I opted to take my coffee and ninety-nine cent hot dog outside. If only Miss Timberlake knew what she was missing.

 So, in temperatures hovered near the century mark, I stood in the shade of the gas island canopy next to my rental, listening to the softer dinging from the pump filling the tank while draining my expense account. I'd pushed the drive time to get here, because of Melvin's insistence that I get to Lone Tree and 'be in place' in two days time. What that meant, I had no idea, but figured the answer must lie somewhere in the file that now weighted down the hood of my car.

Heavy reading was not my forte, but with all the class of a top-notch PI, I stuffed the hot dog halfway in my mouth and opened the huge binder for a better understanding of why I was here.

The first few pages really threw me, because they looked like they belonged in a textbook for art students. There were lots of pages with pictures of famous paintings, all with headers that read Musee du Louvre. I knew nothing about artwork. In fact, until I followed a surveillance subject into an art gallery about a year ago, I thought all painters worked off black felt. The captions on some of the photos had names like Peter Paul Rubens, Raphael and Titan. A couple of the paintings looked familiar and were labeled Rembrandt and Leonardo De Vinci. I leafed past the art seminar, trying to get to the meat of the accompanying reports, but so far they were in unreadable French.

Further along in the file, the headings on the reports got more intriguing, even with the language barrier. The word 'Interpol', that little International police force who monitors such alien activity as unlicensed video reproduction, was emblazed over the file pages. That got my attention, because the agency was about the most powerful investigative body outside of the big three, Russia, China and good old USA. Since there was never a Frenchman around to translate when you needed one, I dug deeper into the file in an attempt to find something I could actually understand. Unfortunately, the gas nozzle clunked off before I could find even one report in English.

I stared at the gas hose, cataloging what I'd seen so far, and then thumbed the pages of the file back to the pictures in the front. I was at least heartened to see the French used our numerical system for dates. If they'd used Roman numerals, I would have really been screwed. The lead page had been faxed at one time or another and the information was imprinted along the top edge. It was an International fax number and it was dated August 21, 1997. I studied the paintings in the photos again and started praying they had nothing directly to do with this case.

I looked up and watched a car drive by on the highway, turning south on 225. That was my turn off as well, my last change of direction towards Lone Tree. I thought of the dot on my road map that indicated Elko. That mark was small enough and Lone Tree didn't even rate a dot. It was merely tiny lettering next to a little squiggly line that represented a two-lane highway, hopefully a paved one. I looked at my current surroundings and wondered if a town could actually be smaller. I envisioned a two-sided sign with 'Welcome to Lone Tree, population minus six' on either side of it. A sub-caption came to mind for a town motto, 'Don't blink, you'll miss us'.

I closed the cover of the file and looked down the two-lane blacktop shimmering in the mid-afternoon heat. It just didn't compute. What did any artwork beyond some Indian cave markings have to do with a nothing town in the middle of nowhere? I checked my watch. By not flying, I had pushed my travel time and now had to get into Lone Tree before nightfall. I promised myself to give the time needed to assimilate the case file information before getting any further into the investigation. I suspected I'd be up all night reading.

At least I wasn't going in completely clueless. There had been a large sealed envelope with my name on it tucked inside the case binder. I had opened it on my last gas stop out of curiosity. I suspected the main file had been mass reproduced for the multiple investigators Melvin had working on other parts of it. The whole affair was all very cryptic and James Bond to me, but at least the contents of the envelope had been written in English.

The envelope contained the briefest of information and a couple of photos of a specific target assigned for me to locate, a man who went by the name of Raymond DeLaCosta. It appeared that he owned tons of acreage in and around Lone Tree, if the accompanying assessor's report could be taken seriously. There wasn't much else in the way of documentation or background information, just the assessor's description of land and a couple of black and white pictures of DeLaCosta getting out of a late model Hummer. The second photo was a blow up of the first; giving me a better facial view of the man. He looked to be in his mid-fifties with prematurely gray hair. Judging from his comparison to the vehicle, he wasn't particularly tall and judging by the size of his midsection, not very athletic.

I grunted from what I'd assimilated so far, but without anything more specific, the case was still leaving me in the dark. What was the connection between Raymond DeLaCosta in Bumfuck, Nevada and the Musee Du Louvre in Paris, France? After stuffing the remains of the hot dog in my mouth, I hung up the nozzle and collected my receipt.

Toting the heavy binder in one hand with my coffee in the other, I walked around and got in behind the wheel. The hot dog and two-day-old coffee were already starting to give me as much heartburn as the case was. I started the car and headed south on 225.

The road quickly took me out of town and became deserted, not leaving much to look at besides the sagebrush. At least I guessed that's what it was. I wasn't a botanist and really didn't care what it was past the fact it was dense enough in spots to use as a blind from the highway, should I be caught short on restroom facilities. That made me wonder if there were any rattlesnakes out here and how long I'd live if I got bit in the backside while squatting behind a bush. About an hour south of Elko, I was so busy pondering what I'd look like face down on a hospital gurney with my snake bitten derriere elevated, I completely missed the red and blue lights behind me.

The siren chirped and that got my attention. Spotting the strobes, I did what every red-blooded American did when the cops pulled them over; I looked at the speedometer. My big Dodge rental had a nice ride and it quickly told me I was in trouble. I had no idea what the speed limit was, but had no doubts that I was about to find out. I pulled over and stopped.

There was only one deputy in the car, or at least that's what I thought he must be. I knew what the NHP drove and this wasn't it. Since we were well out of Elko, a city cop wasn't a strong possibility, either. The man got out of the car and I nodded to myself in affirmation. He was wearing a cowboy hat and boots, with Levis that sported a western style gun-belt. The only semblance of a uniform was his tan shirt, complete with badge and arm patches. I watched him make his sloppy approach in the side-view mirror and shook my head. Was that actually a single-action revolver on his hip? I had to suppress a laugh from the whole picture and looked for spurs on the old broken down boots. He must have been pissed when the Sheriff told him he couldn't patrol the back roads on horseback.

I rolled down my window and bit my lip so we wouldn't start off on the wrong foot, 'Hoooowdy Paaaardner'.

"Good afternoon, Deputy." I think my lip was bleeding. "Damn hot out there today, isn't it?"

"It's a warm one." He drawled with a nod of the head. "You know what the speed limit is here?"

"I sure don't." I shook my head in ignorance, noting the nametag on his shirt, 'Turley'. "The last sign I saw was back in Elko."

"Well, you were doing a good deal over the un-posted state limit." He rubbed his chin as he took in the car and its contents. "About 15 mph over."

"Un-posted state limit?" I knew most all states had a standard limit if no signs were posted, but didn't know what Nevada's was and thought pleading stupid might get me off with a warning.

"Yep." He offered an encyclopedia of information. "Can I see your license and registration, please?"

"Of course." I dug the license out of my billfold and rummaged through the center console of the car where I'd stashed the rental papers. "This is a rental, so I'm not sure where the registration is."

"All the way up from Los Angeles, huh?" He hadn't looked at my license or seen any paperwork yet. That meant he must have run the plate before he put his red and blues on.

I hesitated and looked at him, driver's license in hand. He stared back. I had to give him credit for not wearing a pair of cliché Ray Bans, those goggle sunglasses that all stereotypical cops wore. I had gone through the same phase, but very quickly. I caught myself and could see a thin smile of professional recognition cross his face. I handed him the license. He may have been a hick, but he wasn't dumb. He knew a colleague when he saw one.

"Where you headed?" He studied my driver's license.

"Lone Tree." I answered.

Curiously, he nodded as if he'd known the answer before he even pulled me over. He kept looking at the license as he talked.

"You with that other feller?"

"What feller?" I couldn't help mimicking his drawl.

"Stopped another feller just like you a day or so ago, goin the same place and just about as fast." He still didn't look up. "He was ex-law enforcement, too."

"Really." I nodded, having no idea who he was talking about.

"He said he had worked for one of those counties you got down there." He searched his memory. "San Bernardino, I think it was."

"Huh." It was my turn to be over-informative.

"Where'd you work?"

"I'm ex-LAPD." I stated simply and showed him my old badge and ID. "Early retirement."

"Bringin out the big guns, huh?" He said more to himself and finally looked up from the license. "You packin?"

"I have a firearm in the trunk." I was careful not to mention the 45 auto under my seat. Don't ask, don't tell.

"Anything else in the way of firearms?" He was fishing.

"I don't have an Uzi or sniper's rifle, if that's what you mean." Misdirection amounted to denial without directly lying.

"Mind if I have a look?" He stood back from my driver's door to let me out.

"Not at all." I shrugged and got out of the car.

He followed me back to the trunk and I opened it. I took note that we were about the same size and weight, but his creeping gray and deeper facial lines told me he had a few years on me. His attitude and mannerisms suggested he was a retread, possibly a city cop who'd relocated to the country to play Marshal Dillon. It would explain an older guy way out here in the middle of nowhere, working on a new pension.

"Where?" He nodded at the assortment of traveling items I always took on road trips.

"Uh, that one over there." I pointed to the smaller nylon carry-case next to my sleeping bag.

He leaned in and retrieved it, balancing it on the lip of the compartment as he unzipped the bag and searched through it. He pulled the handgun out, holster and all.

"357 magnum." He frowned in contemplation. "Thought all you city boys carried them automatics."

"I'm from the old guard." I acknowledged for the benefit of his obvious preference. "I like the wheel guns."

"Me too." He smiled slightly and then seemed to consider something in the way of options for a few moments. He kept examining the gun as he finally spoke. "Mind if I hang onto this while you're in Lone Tree?"

"Why?" I shook my head. "I'm not carrying it illegally, am I?"

"Nope, not really." He looked up at me.

"I'm not following you." I shrugged with a shake of the head.

"Lone Tree is sort of a different kind of place." He seemed to want to explain, but couldn't find the right words. He pushed on, trying to do the best he could. "Since you can't legally carry a concealed weapon in the state of Nevada, you'd have to leave this in your hotel room."

"Sounds fair enough." I shrugged. "I can leave it in the room."

"You haven't seen the hotel in Lone Tree." It was a statement, not a question and the singularity of the word immediately arrested my attention.

"Well, I can leave it in the trunk then." I was trying to get a sense of where he was going with this.

"But your car would be parked out front." He countered.

I just looked at him with a quizzed expression on my face, waiting for him to explain.

"Your call, Mr. Hollister, but I'd be happy to hold onto your firearm while you stay there." He continued without one. "Our office is in Elko and you could pick it up on your way out. I'd just be holding it in safekeeping, give you a receipt and all."

"Is this place really that light-fingered?" I cocked my head, looking to see if he was actually serious.

"Let's just say I'd rather keep it in safekeeping than be making out another stolen firearm report." He seemed completely serious. "Think there's enough guns in that town already."

"In all due respect, if Lone Tree's that kind of town, I'd rather not be the only unarmed person in it."

"It'll only piss them off if they know you're packin." He said completely straight-faced.

"I'll have to take my chances." I nodded with a wary look of concern. "But I appreciate the offer."

Being unarmed in the type of town he was describing was the type of suicide I had suspected Melvin Croup of placing me in when I took the assignment in the first place. I suddenly wished I did have an Uzi in the trunk, maybe two, one for each hand.

"Your call, like I said." He pulled the heavy revolver out of the holster and wrote down the serial number on the back of the ticket book he was carrying. Once done, he re-holstered it and tucked the whole rig back into the case. As he did so, he noticed the two boxes of ammunition in the bag. "You do come prepared, I'll say that."

"You never know." I studied him for a moment, suddenly aware that an extra gun on my side might come in handy on this trip. "Traveling around the country, you never know when you might come across a state patrol guy or deputy sheriff who's in the middle of something he might need some help with. You guys are always spread pretty thin out here."

He looked at me hard, studying my face, but seemed to buy my philosophy. He carefully packed the carrying case back in the trunk and shut the lid.

"I appreciate the thought, Mr. Hollister." He nodded with that slight smile again. "Knowin someone's got my back out here, and all."

We walked back to the open driver's door and I got back in with a new sense of camaraderie. He followed, closing the door behind me and leaning over as he glanced into the car's interior.

"Huh." He grunted.

"What?" I looked up at him.

"That's a mighty big notebook?" He nodded at the case file on the passenger's seat.

"Just some light reading." I knew this deputy could add and therefore was fishing for the reason I was going to Lone Tree. I tried not to sound too sarcastic, as to not offend my newfound friend.

"Funny." He said curiously.

"What?" Don't you love men's conversations?

"That other feller had the same notebook." He straightened. "You sure you two aren't together?"

"I'm sure." It was my turn to look curious. "When did you say you stopped him?"

"Just a couple of days ago." He reflected. "Just down the road a piece."

"You remember his name?"

"Carl something." He rubbed his chin again. "Stapleton, I think it was."

"Did he give you his firearm for safekeeping?"

"Nope." He shook his head. "Can't say as I blame you guys, but if you knew Lone Tree like I do, you'd reconsider the offer."

"How much time do you spend there on any given day?"

The Carlucci File

"Not a minute more than I have to." He replied dead serious.

I paused and looked at the road ahead of me. What the hell was I getting into? I looked back at the deputy and could tell he was reading my mind. He was nodding ever so slightly with that same stupid expression on his face. I broke off from our mutual train of thought and got back to why we were sitting in the middle of nowhere.

"Uh, well look, I'm sorry." I shook my head. "I mean about the speed. I'm not used to these big cars. I have a beat up minivan back in LA that can't get out of its own way."

"I thought you boys made the big bucks down there?" He looked a little surprised.

"We do." I shrugged again. "And my ex really enjoys her Caddy."

For the first time, the deputy smiled enough to show nicotine-stained teeth. He nodded and handed me back my license, sharing the moment common only to divorced men. In my case, men who married beautiful women who could never seem to balance a checkbook, but knew your exact worth to the penny when it came time for the split. After a moment, he came back to his concerns.

"Look, Mr. Hollister. I'm not sure what's going on down there in Lone Tree, but I wouldn't stay too long." Now, he was worrying me. "It's not a healthy place."

"I appreciate the advice." I really was sincere in the reply. I waved my driver's license in the open window. "And the break on the ticket. I'll watch the speedometer closer."

"No problem." He put his finger to the brim of his hat. "If you see that Carl feller, you might want to hook up with him for some mutual back watching yourself. You know what I mean?"

"I'll look for him." I promised and wasn't kidding.

"Have a good one." He waved slightly and headed back to his car.

I waited for him to turn his cruiser around and head back to whatever billboard he was using as a speeder's blind. When his car was just a dot on the horizon, I looked at the empty road in front of me. Not one car had passed us during the whole time we'd been talking. I really was in the middle of nowhere. And who was Carl Stapleton? I looked down at the case file and thought about reading the whole damn thing before I drove another mile closer to my destination. I consulted my watch and it had different ideas. It told me sunset was coming and I needed to find a room before dark. I thought for a second and decided the watch was right, I did need to find a room before dark. I wanted to study the layout of this place before the sun went down.

I put the car in gear and pulled back onto the highway. For the next hour, I continually rubbed the back of my neck, trying to soothe those hackles.

3

About an hour later, the highway started winding down one of those canyons with shear walls on either side. The rushing water that had originally carved it out a couple of million years ago had now receded to a smaller tributary that looked promising for some fly fishing. The highway held a more direct line down the ancient riverbed, crossing the stream here and there over small bridges, while the water snaked its own path through the ever-widening canyon. The riverbank's soil, enriched over the millennium, brought denser foliage that marked the wandering stream with large poplars whose leaves were just beginning to turn a golden brown with the season.

The drive was just becoming enjoyable when I rounded a bend and saw the sign, 'Lone Tree Inn 1 mile'. The mile went by quick and if I hadn't slowed down, I actually might have missed it as I had joked of earlier. As it turned out, even the two-sided sign I had envisioned for it had been optimistic. There was no dedication for it as a town at all. No little green sign declaring Lone Tree with any population or elevation like you'd expect to see. It was just a few structures that seemed to have sprouted up along with the poplars and other riverbed fauna. It was really more of a rest stop like you'd see in the old black and white movies of yore.

The hotel itself was a two-story affair, kind of a cube shaped structure comprised of thick stucco, supporting a wrap-around porch and upstairs balconies. A red tile roof capped the Southwest style architecture and with the shade trees and stream running along behind it, the whole effect was one of a classic 19th Century hacienda. Unfortunately, it looked like it hadn't been cared for since the same time period. There was a smaller, separate combination gas station slash diner next to it of similar structural design, though kept in better condition. In actuality, it reminded me of some Route 66 stop, built in the early 50's about the time America had first discovered touring in cars, then deserted a few years later with the advent of the super-slab.

There were a few cars parked in front of the inn, all of them older with one exception, a newer sedan not unlike my own rental. Slowing down more, I caught a glimpse of a couple of shabby looking cabins on the opposite side of the stream behind the hotel, partially hidden in the tree line. A dirt service road just this side of the hotel crossed over a corrugated bridge to them and then kept going until it disappeared into the mesa wall. I immediately recognized the roofline of the hotel from my pictures of DeLaCosta standing outside his Hummer. The inn had provided the backdrop for the photos and I figured they must have been taken from the opposite side of the highway, perhaps out of a car window. I almost stopped as I took in the layout, but saw no signs of life other than the cars parked out in front of the inn.

It was too much to expect that any more of Lone Tree lay beyond the ramshackle inn and diner, but I kicked the gas pedal and passed the meager offerings, continuing on for five miles in desperate hope that a Denny's and Motel 6 would pop up out of nowhere. Nothing of the sort materialized, but the short drive further down the canyon road did offer a sense of the local topography or lay of the land, if you like. A few more bends south, I reached a portion of highway that afforded a spectacular view of nature's own, but little else. I pulled over, taking in the vista for a few minutes, while weighing my options. There didn't seem to be many left at this point, so with a sigh, I made a U-turn and doubled back. I was apparently stuck with the one hotel and gas station.

The inn came back into view and I immediately noticed one of the cars was now missing. I hadn't made any mental notes on them individually, except for the one obvious rental, but I knew whatever the missing car was hadn't passed me so it must have driven back in the direction of Elko. I entertained a fleeting thought of chasing it to make sure, but didn't know why? The road only ran two ways and there were no rumors of aliens abducting parked cars in front of old hotels. So, in the absence of hovering spacecraft, I fought the strange urge to give chase and turned in, making a U-turn up to the pumps at the gas station. I had enough fuel to easily get to whatever real civilization lay north or south, but thought topping off the tank would be an innocuous way to make an entrance.

'Oh, hi. I was just touring the Nevada Nowhere and thought I'd drop in for some home made chili and a cup of DeLaCosta, I mean coffee.'

'Sure. Why don't you stay the night and sleep with my daughter?'

'Oh, that's a tempting offer. Why don't you just tell me what DeLaCosta's up to and why the Sheriff never stops here?'

'Oh, well DeLaCosta's a myth and the Sheriff has already slept with my daughter.'

'Sounds like my kind of girl, the perfect candidate for my next ex. Why sure, I'll spend the night.'

I shut off my imagination and then the car. Before getting out, I slid the 45 auto from under the seat and into my rear waistband. No sense in taking unnecessary chances. Checking to make sure my shirt fully bloused over it, I stood outside the car's door while inspecting the gas pumps and getting my bearings. The sun was setting behind the mesas to the west, but there was still ample light in the dusk of a cloudless sky. The air was starting to cool and the breeze that had followed me down the canyon carrying some relief from the hot day. Being from LA, I normally didn't trust air I couldn't see or cut with a knife, but I took a deep breath and decided this could be a nice place. I thought about the stream and how the fishing was, and then wondered why the hell I cared, since I didn't fish?

Making a few more notes to myself, I walked towards the diner's entrance. The pumps were old enough not to accept credit cards or have electric shut offs, so the diner's cashier had to do double duty for both the gas station and the eatery. There was an old soda machine out front that was nearly empty, but seemed to be working. Next to it, a pay phone was mounted on the wall just above a dust free wooden bench, so I figured it probably worked, too. I put a mental asterisk next to that observation, since my cell phone had told me hours ago there was no service here.

I started to step up to the diner's entrance, but noticed a couple of automotive service bays attached to the building just beyond. I detoured to give it a look. They were locked up and the countless coats of paint sealing the large wood bay door to its frame told me it wasn't just closed for the day. The door sported a mosaic of smaller windows, also partially smeared over by the sloppy paint jobs, but they did afforded at least a glimpse inside. I cupped my hands against the outside light, but it was still too dark inside to make out much more than a partially covered tow-truck. It looked like a Mack with running boards, old enough to be my Great-Grandfather's.

With nothing appearing suspicious past the antiquity of the place, I stretched while commencing a 180 survey to summarize. Beyond the service bay there was a small collection of junked cars, almost lost in nature's reclamation of overgrowth. The highway was somewhat elevated, with only vacant landscape dropping off into sagebrush on the opposite side of Lone Tree's layout. The opposing cliff walls of the canyon lay about a quarter-mile beyond. Continuing my scan, I stepped away from the building and took another look at the inn. The parked rental and other cars didn't tell me much past the obvious. They all looked innocent enough. I turned and backed up a bit more and looked up at the front of the hotel, but no activity could be seen. Both the front porch and balcony above were empty.

Curiously, my arrival wasn't generating any particular interest. No extras from the next remake of Deliverance came out to offer full service or a shotgun salute. I remembered Deputy Turley's words and wondered if he'd been pulling my lariat. Glancing around one more time, I turned back to the diner's entrance.

Inside, I was met with the unmistakable aroma of old cooking grease and the strong odor of enamel nail polish. A young woman languished behind the register, inspecting her self-inflicted manicure with the open bottle next to her on the counter. What was it with dark purple nail gloss? A second look revealed an early 20ish waitress who wasn't particularly unattractive. There was a natural sort of beauty under there someplace, hidden beneath gobs of black hair that escaped from the hasty ponytail on top of her head. I remembered when they used to be in back, but maybe I was dating myself. Her dark eyes and smeared eyeliner didn't brighten her expression, or her apparent mood. I could have easily put her in any major mall, one of those 'goth' types that usually turned out in full-metal piercing. She looked up and regarded me with distain. I had to give her some credit for at least matching her lipstick with the nail polish.

"Hi." I tried to smile.

"Anywhere's fine." She frowned in a bored tone and went back to digging at her cuticles.

I anguished for her, another customer. Life must have been hell for her here, having to wait on three of us a year. I tried to maintain the weak smile and looked beyond her perch. There were only five booths; all arranged next to the windows with the curtains drawn. The diner was typical of it genre, with malt-shop style stools running down a serving counter opposite the booths. Behind the counter, there were the usual array of toasters, microwaves and a large commercial coffee maker. A pass-through above the appliances provided delivery for the seriously greasy food from the short-order style kitchen in back. The diner as a whole was grimy, without being outright filthy. Maybe I missed my calling and should have been a restaurant critic. Since I was convinced the coffee I was used drinking could actually kill germs, I figured I'd try theirs, but that would probably be about it.

There was only one other customer. He was sitting in the last booth with his back to the wall, strategically giving him full view of anyone entering, a covered position at the end of the counter, and if all else failed, an escape route through the kitchen. In the manner of pure cop tradition, he had my seat. I couldn't see his face because he had a newspaper propped up with both hands in front of him, but whoever he was, he had a courageous spirit. An empty plate sat on the table in front of him with only the small remains of a sandwich scattered across it. He either enjoyed jumping out of airplanes without a parachute or had the stomach of a cast iron boiler. A coffee cup sitting next to the empty plate was the only encouraging aspect of the whole table setting, but it stood full and untouched.

I walked his way, looking for the next best seat. I was about to sit in the booth just up from him, when he lowered the paper and looked up at me. He wasn't at all what I expected to find in a place like this, but he did have that cop familiar look. I immediately suspected he was my mysterious counterpart. His face seemed to confirm it when lit up like a six-year-old on Christmas morning.

"Thank God, You must be John Hollister." He slammed the paper down and would have leapt to his feet if he could, but the cramped booth and his ample spare tire would only let him motion to the seat across from him.

"Must I?" I took the seat opposite him. "Actually, I go by Jack."

"Carl Stapleton." He announced with a sigh of relief and an extended hand, as if he were on the Titanic and I'd just pulled up in a lifeboat.

"I heard you were in town." I took the hand. It was a firm and vigorous handshake, belying his slightly pale complexion and pudgy physique. I wondered why he was calling me by my proper name, since I hadn't heard it, in like forever. "The question is who sent you here?"

"That little cock-sucker Croup." From his tone and use of adjectives, I surmised he knew Melvin. "I sent for back up two days ago. This is as fast as he could send someone?"

"This isn't exactly around the corner from Wilshire Terrace." I couldn't understand why he wasn't using my nickname. It was all Melvin ever called me. "Why didn't he tell me about you?"

"Little prick." Carl tossed the paper aside and reached into his lap. The Berretta 9mm that came up over the lip of the table so fast I lost my breath. Melvin Croup had evidently pushed yet another P I over the edge and I immediately stopped wondering about names and disclosures. Gratefully, he put the gun down on the table in front of him. "I've been wrapped around this thing since the first day I got here."

"What is this place, Nevada's version of Beirut?" I only breathed again after he left the gun lying on the table.

"Don't let Lorene over there throw you into a false sense of security." He warned. "You haven't seen the hotel yet."

"So what's the deal?" I cocked my head and fell silent as I heard footsteps behind me.

"Coffee?" Lorene was at our booth and looking down at me.

"If you've got some, sure." I tried the smile again.

"Of course we got coffee." She rolled her eyes and exhaled heavily. "This *is* a restaurant."

"If you say so." The smile weakened.

"Do you want a menu?" She dangled the cafe's single sided fare in front of me as if I was a fish and it was on a hook. I wasn't biting.

"No, just coffee."

She shuffled around to the inside of the counter and walked away. I looked at Carl and he just gave me a knowing look.

"Welcome to the case from hell." He nodded.

I looked down to where the gun sat, suddenly aware that Lorene must've seen it, but she hadn't. Carl had slid the newspaper over it. He was quick, I had to give him that.

"So, what's the deal here?" I took the opportunity of Lorene's absence to see if I could get a quick version of the case without staying up all night reading.

"I was hoping you'd be able to tell me." He countered. "You have anymore information linking DeLaCosta to the Paris heist?"

"I haven't read the Encyclopedia Britannica Melvin gave me yet, no." I shook my head. "I was hoping you'd be able to shed some quick light on this. What heist?"

"You mean you don't have any idea where DeLaCosta stands in this thing?"

"Only that I'm supposed to find him and watch him tomorrow. What thing?"

"Tomorrow, huh?" He ignoring my simple questions and fell into deep thought.

"Have you found any signs of this guy even being here, I mean besides the photographs?"

"Photographs?" He looked at me with a confused expression.

"Of DeLaCosta." I gave him a confused look. "Didn't you get the same black and white pictures in your case file?"

"Yeah." His expression didn't change.

"They were taken right outside this place." I studied his face. He *was* a PI, right?

"Oh, those pictures." He seemed to wake up. "I thought maybe you'd gotten more on him."

"Nope, just the same ones I expect he gave you, too."

Lorene again interrupted us. She put the coffee mug down in front of me and collected Carl's empty plate.

"Anything else for you guys?" She looked at his full coffee cup. "Want a fresh cup?"

"No, this is fine." Carl smiled up at her. "You can put this gentlemen's coffee on my tab, too, OK Lorene?"

"Big spender." She quipped and shuffled away with the plate towards the kitchen. "I'll be closing up soon."

"As if anyone would notice." I commented under my breath.

"I tell you, it's the case from hell."

"This is all there is to the place?"

"I've been trapped in here for two days waiting for you." He shook his head. "This is the only place I've felt safe. I'd be sleeping in this booth if she'd let me."

"I take it the hotel isn't the Ritz, then?"

"I'd be out of here in a heartbeat, but I could really use the money."

"I hear you there." I nodded. "If you can squeeze it out of that little bastard at all."

"Look," He bypassed the prospect of not getting paid and pursued the heart of the case with almost feverish anxiety. "Are you sure Melvin didn't give you anymore information on this guy, or the case?"

"I got the case file thrown in my lap just like you did." I shook my head. "The rest of the time till now has been spent getting here. I only got a glimpse of the file and the envelope with DeLaCosta's information inside it."

"Shit." He shook his head with a sense of finality. "I guess you're in the dark as much as I am."

"That's a fact." I sipped from the mug and grimaced, pointing to the cup with my free hand. "Now that's a cup of coffee. I didn't know they could age it in casks for thirty years before serving it."

"Get used to it." Carl shook his head.

I put the coffee cup down with a sense of finality, before speaking my mind.

"I'm this close to getting out of here and telling Melvin where he can stick my fee."

"I wouldn't blame you if you did." Stapleton's face lit up. "I'm thinking I'd be two heartbeats behind you."

"What about the money you need so badly?"

"I don't know." Now, he turned indecisive and somewhat confused again.

"Well," I relaxed a bit. "I guess we should at least stay the one night. It's getting dark and whatever's supposed to go down is supposed to go down tomorrow."

"You might change your mind after you see the hotel." He put the Berretta back down somewhere in his waistband and folded his paper up. "We better get you settled in if your mind is set on staying."

"You afraid they won't have any vacancies left?" I had to smile at his sudden sense of urgency. "How many rooms do they have in that dump?"

"Ten." He said confidently, but then rethought a moment after looking up at me. "I think there's ten. I did a hasty count the first night I was here."

"Well, I only see two other cars outside, besides your rental." I tried the coffee again and put it back down on the table, unable to take another sip. "So I think we're safe on the vacancy. The coffee's another matter entirely. It tastes like Drano."

Carl got up and threw a ten-dollar bill on the table. We thanked Lorene as we passed her at the register, but I wasn't sure why. Outside, Carl followed me to the car and started to help me with the bags. I noticed it was finally starting to get dark outside.

"That's alright." I waved him off. "I'm only grabbing these two here."

"Looks like a gun case." Carl nodded to the smaller carry-case that held the magnum. "Hope you brought plenty of ammo."

"I did." I nodded and grabbed my bag and the carry-case.

An afterthought drove me to open up the nylon clothes duffle and stuff the carry-case deep inside it, so it wouldn't look conspicuous. If Carl could guess what was in the smaller case, so could the hotel staff.

"Good idea." Carl read my mind as he watched with approval. "These guys can smell the law a mile away. Think they're a bunch of ex-cons."

"What the hell are they doing here?" I asked as we started towards the hotel entrance.

"Damned if I know." He shrugged.

We walked through the door and I almost gagged. The lobby smelled like a back alley in downtown Los Angeles. The place was old, dingy and flee-bitten, reminding me of a flop pad for hardcore drug addicts or the tenured homeless. I wondered immediately if we could convince Lorene to let us stay in the restaurant all night. The diner's kitchen grill looked like an operating room compared to this place. Reluctantly, I followed Carl up to the hotel desk.

"Uh, can you fix my friend here up with a room for the night?" Carl peered over at the clerk who was half asleep in a chair behind the registrar's counter.

"Huh?" He looked up from his magazine and regarded us with vacant, bloodshot eyes.

"A room?" Carl repeated, looking somewhat nervous.

"Shit, I guess." He grunted and got up, tossing an old issue of Biker Magazine aside. I was surprised his sweat-stained undershirt hadn't glued him to the chair's backrest.

"How much?" I asked, noticing the colorful collection of tattoos exposed on his bare arms and upper chest.

"Shit, I guess forty bucks will do her." He scratched his shaggy buzz-cut as he looked me up and down. "You a cop?"

"You a criminal?" I looked back at him as I peeled two twenties out of my billfold. The weight of the 45 in the small of my back was suddenly very comforting.

"Shit, no." He lied through his teeth as he shook his head.

"Then why would you care?" I smiled my Melvin Croup smile, as blatantly false as the answer he'd given. The tats were mostly of the prison variety, but I didn't want to fully agitate him so early in the evening.

"Shit, guess you gotta point." He smiled sheepishly and glanced at Carl as he handed me a key. "Number five will work, just up the stairs."

"Much obliged." I took the key and started following Carl towards the staircase.

As we walked up the first flight, I caught the light from another room in back of the clerk's desk. Three men were playing pool on a table that barely had any felt left on it. They looked as ratty as the clerk, two with shoulder length hair, the other with a shaved head, all sporting scruffy beards, crusty jeans, and variety of professional and prison body art. All three stopped in mid-game, cue sticks poised in their hands as they watched us climb the staircase. I felt like Little Red Riding Hood on the Ho Chi Ming Trail at three in the morning. Saying nothing, I continued up the stairs in Carl's wake.

"This is it." He stopped halfway down the second floor hallway and nodded to the '5' on the door. It had been painted over so many times it was barely visible. "I'm just down there, in number 2."

"If you ask me, this whole place is a number two." I shook my head and unlocked the door, noting that it would probably open without a key, or even turning the knob. It had been kicked in so many times there was barely a frame left to hold it in place.

"No argument there." Carl laughed a bit. "I'll be in my room if you need me."

"OK." I walked inside and found the light switch.

I immediately decided there was no way I was laying down on the bed. I remembered my sleeping bag sitting in the trunk of the rental and debated whether or not to go down and get it. Now I wished I'd brought a camping style hammock to stretch right across this whole cesspool. I heard Carl's door close down the hall and wondered if his room was any better. I thought about the sleeping bag and debated some more whether I wanted to journey down those stairs again or not. I began to appreciate Carl's state of mind over this whole situation. I looked at the bed again and debated some more, then remembered the case file I'd left on the passenger seat of the car.

"Shit." I spat in frustration, shaking my head and then nodding in reflection. In more than one way I was most definitely in a huge pile of it.

4

The room was spinning down into a black abyss, consuming me in an overpowering feeling of helplessness. I was hanging onto the bed frame, laying face up with arms and legs spread like De Vinci's Vitruvian Man, as the entire room spun down into nothingness. I passed the first floor of the hotel and I saw the desk clerk and the three men playing pool. They stopped to watch as I descending past them. Enveloped in darkness, it seemed like I was tumbling down a well and they were looking over the edge after me, the only witnesses to my peril.

My eyes popped open and I gasped for breath as if I'd just surfaced from the well water. Covered with sweat, I blinked and felt my arms to make sure I was now fully awake from the nightmare. My stomach was churning with acute nausea and I felt disoriented, dizzy and light-headed. It overwhelmed me and I rolled over, vomiting into the toilet. I was already on the bathroom floor, but at the moment had no idea why or how I'd even gotten there. My stomach retched and my brain swam in a sea of confusion. How long had I been on the floor in here and how many times had I thrown up?

My stomach seemed to finally be empty and on reflect, my hand reached for the flush handle. I looked at it in the dim bathroom light and stopped. Instead of depressing the handle, I rolled back and propped myself up with my back on the bathtub next to the commode. The porcelain felt cool on my back and my body temperature was elevated enough that I could feel it right through my clothes. I'd felt this way before, when I had a bad case of the flu or food poisoning, but this was different somehow. The spinning head seemed to be more prevalent and it was throbbing with pain.

Unable to explain why I felt like I did, I tried to think of what I'd eaten the day before. I knew the hot dog I ate in Elko was a cheapie, but if it had been bad I would have been tossing it up on the side of the road when Deputy Turley found me, instead of speeding down it. I tried to force my thoughts past the returning nausea and re-visit my movements from the day before. The only other food I'd eaten had been snacks and bottled water I always stocked up on for my business trips. Both were sealed and it was highly unlikely any of it was bad.

I peered out into the main room and tried to push my way through the fog. Jeez, maybe a spider had bitten me while I'd been sleeping on the bed. I felt over my body, but could find no swelling or itchy spots. I looked around the bathroom and then back out into the main room where my sleeping bag lay rumpled on the bed over my nylon traveling duffle. From my angle on the bathroom floor, the bag was lending extra bulk to the crumpled bedding and it almost looked like I was still in it. For a moment, I wondered if I was still dreaming.

The thought of the sleeping bag triggered my memories of the prior evening and it all came back in a rush. I had decided to go back down to the car and get it, along with the case file. I recalled creeping to the back of the hotel where I found a door to the rear balcony and the stairway down to the streamside deck below. I even remembered pausing to look at the two small cabins across the creek, sitting quietly in the dark night. On the way back up, I also remembered seeing the two Harley choppers parked on the lower patio, under the balcony.

After grabbing the bag and the file without incident, I'd come back and spread the sleeping bag out on top of the bed and climbed into it. Because the lock on the door was such a joke, I'd kept my travel bag containing the magnum close on the bed next to me. I had then opened the file and started to read, but after a while had drifted off to sleep. Sometime later, I must've awakened in response to the waves of nausea and somehow dragged the book into the bathroom with me. I remembered starting out leaning over the john, but must've ended up on the floor trading a fitful sleep with bouts of vomiting.

I looked around the bathroom and found the file in the corner behind the door. It had all come back now, but the reason for the sickness was still puzzling me. I struggled up to my knees and put my head over the sink while turning on the faucet. Cupping my hand, I filled it with water and drank, rinsing my mouth and spitting out the rest. I repeated the movement a couple of times and took the last of it and put it on my forehead. I was starting to feel better now.

Sitting back on the floor against the wall, my attention again fell on the case file. I remembered getting deeper into it the night before and finally finding a few reports in English. Some items connected the famous museum in Paris had turned up missing from a nearby warehouse. As far as I could determine, the file amounted to an all points bulletin on these items. Pictures of large cardboard tubes and suggestions on other means of transporting their contents had been discussed at length, as if it were more a smuggling case than a theft.

I still wasn't sure what items they were talking about, but the paintings in the front of the binder kept creeping into my brain and the tubing seemed to support the idea. Obviously, they weren't talking about the actual famous paintings in the museum, were they? Those were on display and none of them could ever turn up 'missing', at least not without the whole world knowing about it. So, what was this case all about? Were there other paintings by those famous artists that weren't on display? I was reaching into the corner for the large notebook to find out when I heard a creaking noise.

My hand froze in midair and I stiffened. I had no idea what time it was, but it seemed very dark everywhere but in the dim light of the bathroom. My hand diverted to the light switch and turned it off. The world plunged into the blackness of my nightmare and the disorientation and nausea began to return. I closed my eyes tight and reopened them, working on quelling the sick feeling while regaining some semblance of night vision. At the moment, I was more concerned about vomiting again than whatever was making the noise.

The noise came again and I changed my mind. The creaking sound was sporadic, but was definitely coming from the hallway and moving down it from the direction of the main staircase. I knew the sound all too well, having experienced it with great aggravation on my way to and from the car earlier in the evening. The floorboards in this place were like piano keys. They practically gave the listening audience a concert every time you walked down the hall. At the moment, these errant boards weren't singing the theme from the Great Escape, but more like something from I Know What You Did Last Summer, or in my case, last night.

What was really disconcerting was I could hear the floorboard squeak on the depression, then a few seconds later on the release, like someone was freezing every time they hit a noisy spot in the floor. It wasn't a good sign, any more than it was when they stopped in front of my door. Staring into the blackness of the main room, I could only see the bed and nightstand from where I sat in the bathroom. My heart was pounding loud enough that I was sure whoever was outside the door could hear it. Unconsciously, I held my breath in the following moments of pure silence.

Another familiar creaking noise finally broke the stillness. It was the hinges on my door. A rush of cool air washed over my face, invading the stale atmosphere of the room. It carried just a hint of a faintly familiar smell, but didn't change the fact that someone was standing in my open doorway. The draft was carrying their scent, but no lights were on in the hallway, so darkness still ruled over the room.

A shot of adrenalin ran through my veins as my attention leapt to the carrying case on the bed. My loaded revolver was still in the travel duffle covered by the sleeping bag. My 45 auto must have been loose in the bed somewhere too. I couldn't remember exactly where, but knew it was no longer in my waistband. My mind raced to think of something to defend myself with, but I couldn't move a muscle or take my eyes off he main room. I fought against the surge of adrenalin as I strained in the dark for more sensory intake.

A flash of light broke the void of perception, then another only seconds behind it. The auditory didn't reach me till a mille-second later, but I couldn't put the two together at first. The sound was like an arrow hitting a bulls-eye target on an archery range. A third flash, followed by the same sound came again. This time, the fraction-second of light burned an image onto the back of my brain. In its aftermath, I saw floating particles of dust and feathers in the air, just above the bed. I held my breath with all nausea and confusion gone in an instant while I waited for what would come next.

After a few moments of agonizing silence, the squeaking hinges pierced the room again and the breeze of cool air died with the sound of the door closing. The wood flooring outside in the hallway came alive with the cadence of quicker footsteps as they doubled back towards the stairs. When they finally faded, I exhaled as slowly as I could. The adrenalin was giving me body shakes, but the light-headed feeling and nausea were now completely gone.

My muscles eased as I processed the experience and took deep, deliberate breaths to slow my heartbeat and dissipate the effects of the natural drug. I had never seen anyone use a gun with a silencer on it, but something way back in my brain was whispering to me, 'till now'.

I crept to the far side of the bed on my hands and knees and found my 45 lying on the floor next to it. It must have slipped off when I got up to go to the bathroom. I ran a check on it by Braille in the darkness, removing the magazine and emptying the chamber. Blowing into the action to clear any dust, a mindless habit I'd obtained. I put the weapon back into working order and left the hammer back and the safety off.

Putting the gun carefully onto the bed, I felt over the mattress and covers in the dark. I found nothing amiss on the bed or in the sleeping bag, but running my hands over the travel bag revealed a hole in the nylon. I stuck my finger into it, judging it to be bigger than 22 caliber but not as big as my 45. I slid back onto the floor, grabbing my gun as I came to rest against the wall on the far side of the room.

I had just been shot at. 'Duh, you really think so?' I loved it when I answered myself. 'I just got here' I reasoned. 'Nobody knew me. It usually took at least an hour of knowing me before someone wanted to shoot me.'

My thoughts immediately went to the guys playing pool earlier, but ricocheted away from them at the thought of a silencer. The hardware seemed a bit advanced for bikers. That only left DeLaCosta, but how could he know I was even here? He might have figured out Carl was here, but Stapleton checked in two days ago. Why hadn't anyone shot at him? Nothing connected to DeLaCosta made any sense, so my mind bounced back the local residents. The motorcycles on the rear porch might be a bigger part of the picture than I thought. I tried to back off from the whole scenario and eliminate DeLaCosta entirely. What would make sense about this place if only a bunch of bikers were involved?

Perhaps they were all wanted by the law. I'd come across small hole-in-the-wall enclaves of criminals that banded together in a concentrated place of their own. In the city, they weren't as well defined as this, but it was a possibility. The fact that Deputy Turley didn't stop into the diner for some apple pie and dazzling repartee with Lorene seemed to support the notion. But there was something else that had been bothering me since I arrived. I just couldn't put my finger on. I backed my mind up to the time of my arrival and went over what I had seen. It would come to me. No, it wasn't what I *had* seen; it was what I *hadn't* seen.

Every canyon with a decent stream I'd ever driven down had at least a couple of cars parked alongside the road: fisherman. That's what was missing. I didn't fish, but that didn't mean others didn't. This place did have a paved road going through it, so why weren't there any anglers wading into the water for some fly fishing? It was only a couple of hours out of Elko here, so why wasn't anyone using the road at all? Something, or somebody, had been discouraging them. I noticed the window above me and braved a peek outside. It didn't face the front, but gave me a twilight view of the highway snaking up the canyon. The sky was pretty spectacular, but that was the only positive mark I could give the place right now.

My thoughts turned to Carl Stapleton down the hall. Nothing of what I'd heard or seen seemed to point to his room. My gunman had come up from the front and left the same way. Perhaps a second assailant had crept up the back stairs and given him a similar welcome. But, if this was the blanket treatment for all new arrivals, he still should've been shot two days ago. Perhaps they'd learned I was on the way and waited till I got here to do us both at once. I wanted to go down to his room and check on the other PI, but I had no idea where my antagonist was and knowing the condition of the floor, suspected the whole hotel would know that I was still alive and kicking if I went walking all over the singing floorboards.

I decided there was little I could do until daybreak, but stay quietly in my room. No, actually there was something I could do. I engaged the safety on the gun and put it back in my waistband, then got off the floor and dug into my night bag. I retrieved the magnum and slid it under the mattress for insurance, then grabbed a penlight from my shaving kit. Creeping quietly back into the bathroom, I gathered up the case file and stepped over the lip into the bathtub. Quietly closing the curtain with only a slit at the end to spy out of, I reclined in the cramped quarters and made it my new bed for the night.

The Carlucci File

Slowly, I started from the beginning of the file and worked back, paying close attention to all the reports, in English or otherwise, to get a sense of what the case was about. I looked for any words I could recognize in French and scoured the contents for specifics.

As I started reading again, even paying the closest attention to detail I still wasn't coming up with much. There were some outstanding items that had been reported missing on an inventory sheet, but there were no specifics as to what they were. It had been shortly after the transfer of these items from one secure inspection area to a warehouse they were normally stored in. The security hadn't been terribly tight, so either the items weren't that valuable or someone was going to great lengths to make the transfer low key as to not bring attention to them.

Both the holding area and the warehouse seemed to be very secured locations, but no mention of vaults was made anywhere in the files. It seemed like the authorities were conducting an under the radar investigation into the matter. No actual theft was even being mentioned. It was all very curious. Lloyds of London didn't insure items of little value, yet security on whatever was missing seemed to be gravely lacking. What was most interesting was that the identity of the items in question seemed to be the biggest secret of all. How could a policing organization investigate a crime or even go looking for something if they didn't know specifically what was missing?

About halfway through the files, with nothing other than cryptic notes on the movement of the missing items just before their disappearance, the case file took a bizarre turn. It seemed to become one huge dossier and just about every high-stakes thief on the European continent. French, German, Spanish, Italian, and English names dominated the files, with fingerprints and mug shots, known associates, and past criminal endeavors. It was a who's-who of jewel and artwork thieves. They were laid out in alphabetical order, so I thumbed down to the D's looking for my target. He wasn't there. I skimmed through the bulk of the remaining binder, but no faces leapt out at me.

I closed the book and stored it under my bent knees in the bathtub. Putting the 45 in my lap as the only blanket I'd have for the rest of the night, I rested my head against the shower wall and closed my eyes. I couldn't sleep, but needed to process all this information. 'What information' I had to ask myself. Croup had given me nothing but a photograph and DeLaCosta wasn't even in the file. All the criminals were Europeans. This was Nevada. That was just a tad off the Continental map for this case.

Still, it seemed I was in the middle of something more sophisticated than a biker reunion. So where was this DeLaCosta? He certainly wasn't here in Lone Tree. The picture of him was taken here, but I'd seen no sign of anything but this fee-bag hotel for two hours north and quite a few miles south. I'd had a pretty good view down from where I'd turned around, but had I gone far enough? There had to be something else out there somewhere. The file said he owned a lot of property here, so maybe his farmhouse or ranch house, whatever, was further south.

I had to get some form of rest before the sun came up. Someone thought I was already dead, but what about my body? I guessed the grave detail would be along sooner or later and they'd discover I wasn't ready for it yet. And what about Carl? I decided I wouldn't know till morning. If they had visited him and he wasn't puking his guts out in the bathroom like I had been, he was probably dead by now. Maybe the sandwich Lorene had served him had already beaten the gunman to the task. Maybe they were all working together.

My mind leapt from the diner's food to the coffee Lorene had served me. It had been undrinkable, but I had still taken a couple of sips. I wondered if that amount was all that was needed to make me sick, or worse? That begged the question, was it bad by accident, or by design? I made a mental note to look around the diner's kitchen in the morning. Was I getting paranoid that everyone in the this place was trying to kill me? It would appear that bullets from silenced handguns seemed to have that effect on me.

I couldn't decide what was more disconcerting; that Lorene had possibly poisoned me, or that I wouldn't be able to drink any more coffee for the remainder of the trip. I thought about Croup drinking his Starbucks every morning with that pained expression on his. Wouldn't it be ironic if it wasn't *his* coffee that was laced with the cyanide?

5

I was up just before daybreak and repacking my duffel on the newly perforated bed. I wasn't happy. Besides the small fact that someone had tried to kill me the night before, the fool had also put holes in some of my favorite jeans and shirts. Now, after braving a quick shower and shave, I was packing what few usable clothes I had left into the duffel while debating whether I should just throw everything in the car and head towards Elko or stay on the case. I had to admit, even though I had no idea what Lone Tree or DeLaCosta was all about, I was intrigued that someone really didn't want me here, that is, on the planet.

It was hard not to miss the next sound of footsteps coming up the stairs towards my room. Stealthy they weren't. I could hear them approaching with their heavy motorcycle boots and even the crust on their never-washed jeans could be heard against the morning silence. Someone was finally showing up to remove my body. It was no wonder this place smelled so bad if it always took them this long to remove their corpses. As they arrived at my door, I made sure I was facing it from the opposite side of the bed with my hands buried deep in my duffel.

The door flung open and I only wished I had a camera to capture the expressions on their faces. It was the billiard parlor trio from the night before, Larry, Moe, and Curley Joe, Curley Joe being the bald-headed one, of course. Who could forget any of them?

"I'm sorry, did you miss me?" I smiled at the thought of their new nicknames.

They stared back dumbfounded and clearly didn't seem to know what to do next.

"Hey," I kept the smile on my face. "Do you guys now when the diner opens, cause I'm famished?"

They slowly looked at one another, but it was obvious they weren't physically equipped or mentally prepared to try another attempt on my life. The tallest of the three, the one I'd soon dub as Moe for his sparkling repartee, finally shrugged as the others turned to leave.

"Shit, man." He drawled like a southern Klansman. "We thought you was checked out."

"Not yet." I smiled. I didn't expect him to get the metaphor, but couldn't resist throwing it out anyway. "I'd prefer to be the one to choose when and where that might happen, of you know what I mean?"

"Yeah, I guess." He didn't, but did a half-ass job of pretending he did before shrugging and turned to leave, closing the door behind them.

I listened to their biker boots as they retreated back down the stairs. At least they weren't shoving each other like school kids and arguing, 'I thought you shot him', 'No, I thought *you* shot him'. When they'd left the second floor, I pulled my hands out of the bag and flipped the safety back onto the cocked 45. Tucking it back into my rear waistband, I gave the room one last look while thinking what I'd do next. I was hungry and the only food I trusted was in the trunk of my rental. Trail mix and bottle water would have to do it, but first I had to check on Carl.

I left my door unlocked, why bother, and walked down the hall to number 2. Knocking softly and getting no reply, I tried the door and it opened easily, even though the lock was engaged. Security at the Lone Tree Hotel didn't seem to be a priority. The room was empty and the bed unmade. No signs of anyone using the room, past the tossed bed, was blatantly evident. I walked over to the bathroom and peeked inside, but found nothing. I was about to leave when I noticed something on the bed. Taking a closer look, it appeared to be a small amount of dried blood.

I looked for holes in the mattress that might match mine, but found none. The blood was up where the pillow would usually be, so I surmised that Carl hadn't met his fate in the same manner as was intended for me. In fact, the blood could've simply been from a nosebleed. Naw, I wasn't buying my own argument. Carl Stapleton had simply vanished and that wasn't a good sign. Walking out into the hallway, I looked towards the rear balcony where I'd crept back and forth to my car the night before. I walked to the back door that was outfitted with a window and looked out, thinking it would be a good escape route.

The three brain-dead bikers, including the one who'd actually uttered a few syllables, were walking into one of the cabins across the stream. I watched for a few minutes, but they didn't come back out. Whether they were loading shotguns or just cutting up the remains of Carl Stapleton I had no idea, but I wasn't about to stick around and find out. Good health being the better part of curiosity, I doubled back to my room, retrieved the magnum from under the mattress and threw everything I had left into the perforated duffel. Shouldering it, I exited the room and headed down the main stairs to the hotel desk.

The clerk gave me a curious look, but said nothing. Perhaps the silencer had been for his benefit, but I couldn't understand why. I hefted the travel bag in front of me.

"You know you must have moths here." I tried to smile. "Everything I brought in here last night has holes in it now."

"Really?" His tone told me he was probably in the dark on the whole shoot'em up thing.

"I seemed to have misplaced my friend." I lowered the duffel and spoke slowly so I wouldn't have to repeat myself. "The man in number 2?"

"He checked out." There was that same vacant smile on his face.

"Did he leave anything?" I shook my head a bit. "Note, forwarding address, next of kin?"

"Nope." He shook his head. "Just checked out."

"Did you see him leave?"

"Nope. He was just gone this morning."

"Well, I'm just going to get some more moth food from the trunk of my car." Decision made, I thumbed towards the door and started backing in the same direction. "You know, I've got to recommend this place to triple-A, but you're going to need a couple of slot machines in here. People will think they're in Mississippi instead of Nevada. Now, don't go away, cause I'll be right back."

I was half running for the car, but stopped in my tracks two steps off the porch. The front of the Lone Tree Hotel and the diner was strangely vacant of any rentals. There were still a couple of cars, but none for me to run to. I looked around the parking lot in dismay. Without really knowing why, I numbly walked to the edge of the highway and looked up and down the deserted road. Nothing.

Sighing heavily, I walked back towards the diner. The door was unlocked so I walked into the empty cafe, finding Lorene in the usual position, doing her usual thing.

"Morning Lorene. Can I get some change from you?"

"Sure." She looked up from her nails and opened the register.

"How's the breakfast rush? I couldn't help but notice the line out the door."

She frowned and exchanged my dollar for some coins.

"Keep the griddle hot. I'll be right back." I promised.

I went to the phone and checked for a dial tone. Incredibly, there was one. I slid the change in and dialed the operator. She connected me.

"Elko County Sheriff's Office." The dispatcher had a pixy voice. I pictured a petite blonde.

"Hi, I'd like to report a stolen car." I thought about mentioning the small side tidbits that someone had tried to perforate me in the middle of the night and my partner had disappeared, but who'd believe it?

"Your location, Sir?"

"I'm in Lone Tree." Maybe Deputy Turley would?

"Wait one moment, please." She answered. "I'll connect you to the deputy in that area."

"Really?" I exclaimed. It seemed too simple. "You can do that?"

"Yes, Sir." She droned. "One moment."

Another phone rang, like we were starting a conference call.

"What's up, Cheryl?" I recognized the deputy's voice.

"We have a report of a stolen vehicle in Lone Tree, Mitch." I thought I detected just a trace of 'another dumb-ass stayed in that dump last night' in her voice.

"Are you sure?" He asked.

"The gentleman's on the phone now." She replied. "Sir, this deputy will help you. Go right ahead."

She hung up and Turley didn't say anything at first.

"Deputy Turley, this is Jack Hollister." I jumped in, thinking there might be a problem with the connection.

"Jack who?" He hesitated a long moment. "Oh, Mr. Hollister. The big city cop with that big shiny sedan."

"No, the big city *ex*-cop who is now *without* the big shiny sedan."

"You didn't lose it, did you?" He said, almost accusingly.

"Something like that." I admitted. "There last night at eight, gone this morning."

"Was the magnum still in the trunk?"

"I had it with me in my room."

"That's good." He sounded a bit relieved. "That's a nice gun."

"Family heirloom." I offered in defeated sarcasm.

"Well, I have your license plate writ down here someplace from our chat yesterday, so I'll run the rest on the computer." He advised with a slight drawl of the old west. "We'll have her on the hot sheet within the hour."

"You didn't happen to see it go by last night?"

"I'm on the day shift."

"You don't know who works the night shift?"

"There ain't no night shift, son."

"Somehow I was afraid you'd say that." I shook my head. "Can you at least come by and give me a lift into Elko?"

"Not supposed to, really." There was a pause. "But guess I can swing by."

"I'd appreciate it." I said gratefully. "I'm feeling a bit marooned out here at the moment and I'm not sure when the next stage coach comes through."

"Give me about a hour on that." He advised. "I've got another situation here and as soon as I'm done, we'll get you taken care of."

"Thanks, I'll be waiting in the diner." I hung up the phone and looked around.

There was no sign of life anywhere. Reluctantly, I re-entered the restaurant.

"Did you want something to eat?" Lorene asked as if she were afraid I'd say yes.

"No, I'm good." I waved her off and looked around.

"How about some coffee?" I could tell she was just trying to be polite and she actually managed a smile with the offer. "On the house."

"Tell you what." I studied her out of the corner of my eye. "Have one with me."

"OK." Her smiled widened. "I didn't think you'd be here this morning."

"Oh, why is that?" I eyed her suspiciously as we ambled to the counter. From there, she walked around to the coffee maker as I took one of the stools.

"Cause nobody ever seems to stay the whole night." She retrieved the pot from under the maker and poured two cups. It smelled fresh and steaming hot.

"Doesn't that seem a bit odd to you?" I took the cup from her and nodded thanks.

"Well, the boys over there can be a bit scary to regular folk, so I figure most the tourists just decide to leave early."

"Do they actually leave or just check out?" I asked casually more to myself.

"Huh?" She scrunched her face and noticed my cup wasn't moving anywhere near my lips. "You want cream and sugar with it?"

"This is fine." I smiled and continued to hold it while watching her. "Did you happen to see the man I was talking to here yesterday leave this morning?"

"No." She looked at me with a curious expression. "Is he a friend of yours?"

"First time I'd ever seen him." I started to drink the brew out of reflex, but caught myself. Instead, I smelled it while studying the waitress. "You take sugar and cream?"

"No, I like it strong and black, too." She smiled as if she'd somehow suddenly found a soul mate and happily sipped from the cup without a second thought.

We settled in at the counter, her leaning against it on her side and me on the stool in front of her, elbows propped up with the cup in both hands. I sipped the brew, continuing to inhale the aroma for anything suspicious. It tasted nothing like the sludge she'd served the day before. I looked around the diner, noticing something was missing.

"Where's your cook?"

"I'm it." She looked around. "I'm not much good, but I'm OK with breakfast stuff."

"Tell you what." I suggested. "Have you eaten anything yet?"

"Uh uh." She looked a bit hesitant as she shook her head.

"If the makings are back there and it's OK with you, I'll whip something up for us." I put the cup down on the counter.

"Do that and it's on the house, too." She nodded her head forcefully once and smiled widely. The attractive young woman under the Goth veneer was trying to break out and I could see she did have her moments. I had to smile back. She might not have been the sharpest kid around, but I was starting to like her.

"Done deal." I left my seat and we walked back to the kitchen.

Lorene lingered in the corner at first, content to watch as I found what I needed and fired up the grill. Within a half-hour, bacon and eggs were sizzling on it. She eventually jumped in, putting some bread in the toaster and soon she was talking a mile a minute about everything of little importance and giggling at my responses.

"So, what brings you out to this place, Lorene?" I offered the question as offhandedly as I could, while I divided the scrambled eggs and bacon onto two plates.

"I wish I knew." She shook her head and followed me to the back table with silverware where I took Carl's old seat and she sat across from me. "My dad brought me out here a few years ago after my mom died, but I can't wait to go back."

"Back where?"

"Vegas." She nodded. "I was born there, you know?"

"Really." I nodded and we began to eat. "What happened that you ended up here?"

"My dad lost everything, pretty much, so we packed up and brought what we had left out here." She shook her head and rolled her eyes. "He always had this stupid dream about becoming a cowboy, like those dirt ranchers you see in the movies? He finally got his dream, because all we got now is dirt. Lots of just plain dirt."

"Sorry to hear that." I frowned for empathetic effect and then pushed on, since she seemed to be opening up. "So, what's the story on the guys from the hotel?"

"They're all nuts." Lorene made circles with her index finger around her ear. "Bunch of bikers comin and goin all the time. Sometimes they party and get drunk. Lots of guns over there, like they think they're the Wild Bunch or something."

"They never bother you?" I was half into the meal and my intended questioning was really starting to sound like normal conversation.

"Naw." She shook her head. "They bring they're own girls out with them usually. I'm gone by the time they really get goin anyway, so they never bother me."

"Seems kind of weird to me." I made a face. "They don't even eat here?"

"Benny, the hotel clerk comes over sometimes, but he's the only one who's there all the time. The others come and go so much I figure they must get everything in Elko." She changed the subject. "So where're you from?"

"LA." I said with a shrug.

"I been there once a long time ago." Her eyes lit up a bit. "That street with all the stars in it, all along the sidewalk and then that place with the footprints and hands in the cement. I used to get in trouble for doing that when I was little. Did it when they paved our old street and put in the sidewalk out front."

"Are they still there?" I smiled at her.

"Yeah, think so." She looked at me as her face suddenly brightened. "I guess them big stars got nothing on me."

"I think you're right." We were laughing when I heard the car drive up. I put down my cup and reached for the curtain next to the window. "That must be my ride back to town."

I opened the curtain and a small shock ran down my spine. It was a bright yellow Hummer with very dark window tinting. The photos I had of it were in black and white, so I couldn't be absolutely positive it was DeLaCosta, but how many Hummers were in Lone Tree? How many *cars* were in Lone Tree? I closed the curtain and looked at Lorene.

"Looks like some customers are coming."

She seemed to recognize the sound of the heavy duty SUV, because all trace of mirth left her face.

"I better take care of these." She left my plates, but gathered up any and all evidence that we'd ever sat together and hurried back into the kitchen.

The diner's screen door opened and DeLaCosta walked in. Much to my surprise, he wasn't alone. An extremely attractive woman walked in just behind him. I immediately decided they didn't match as a couple. She appeared a bit young and too innocent looking to be romantically involved with him. Their mannerisms also supported my initial impressions as their posture and demeanor seemed to further imply they were together by happenstance rather than by desire or even mutual arrangement.

She immediately stole my attention with her eyes, wide and expressive, yet black as night. Her hair was also jet-black and long, flowing over her shoulders in large soft curls. She was wearing form-fitting jeans and a clean white blouse that contrasted with her light olive complexion. I sensed she was well educated, smart and maybe just a bit naïve in some ways. To her credit, she seemed unpretentious and curious, rather than aloof and blasé. I had to pry my eyes off her to give DeLaCosta his own assessment.

He was right out of the pictures I had on him in the file. What the photos couldn't convey was his domineering confidence. It seemed to telegraph that he owned everything within a hundred square miles, which in fact, the assessor said he did. He was dressed as if he'd just come from shopping on Rodeo Drive, a silk shirt with open, wide collar and dress slacks. The shoes and belt matched and looked like genuine alligator. His jewelry looked expensive, but tasteful, along with his custom sunglasses.

Watching their entrance, everything about them screamed class, or maybe just good breeding. Even though the woman's style was toned down somewhat, to say they both looked out of place for Lone Tree was a gross understatement.

I sensed no immediate danger, so I picked up my coffee mug and sipped from it in an attempt to appear apathetic to their arrival. I caught a glimpse of Lorene peering anxiously out of the order window from the kitchen as they leisurely walked my way.

DeLaCosta reached the table and lowered his sunglasses on the bridge of his nose. The woman leaned on one of the stools further back and gave me the same casual inspection I'd given her.

"Mr. Hollister," DeLaCosta smiled as if I was a new business associate. "May I call you Jack?"

I stared back at him for a few seconds before flashing my Melvin

Croup smile and replying.

"Mr. DeLaCosta, may I call you Ray?"

DeLaCosta seemed taken back for a few moments, but then laughed and removed the sunglasses from his face, pointing them at me as he spoke.

"I like that." He mused as he motioned to the opposite seat that Lorene had just fled from. "May I join you?"

"No doubt it's your diner anyway, so please." I nodded.

"Raymond DeLaCosta." He put his hand out in a gesture signaling he wanted to start over again.

"Jack Hollister." I obliged and accepted the handshake. After all, a little thing like trying to kill me in my sleep shouldn't prevent us from being civilized.

"Sweetie?" He turned slightly towards his beautiful female companion without actually looking at her. "Could you pour us some coffee? It smells like Lorene made some fresh."

"Of course." Her voice was soft and alluring with a hint of a European accent. I couldn't help but follow her movements back to the coffee maker behind the counter. She saw Lorene in the kitchen and greeted her like an old friend. "Hey, Lori Girl."

It seemed clear DeLaCosta was getting her out of earshot so we could talk freely, but I wasn't ready for the serious stuff yet.

"Sweetie." I looked back at DeLaCosta, who was studying my interest in the woman with a wary expression. "That's a unique name."

"My niece, Anna." He announced bluntly. "Her mother is visiting our native country at the moment, so I'm looking after her."

"She seems old enough to look after herself." I sipped my coffee.

"My sister is of the old world." He explained. "And it's traditions."

"What old world are we talking about?"

"Florence." He offered, as if it should have been obvious.

"Italy." I observed with a nod and raised eyebrows. "Wow, you don't look Italian."

"Things are seldom what they appear." He shot a smile with the quip.

"Some things are." I shot back with my own.

"So, welcome to Lone Tree, Mr. Hollister." DeLaCosta leaned back, as if he'd passed the soup and salad and was ready for the meat and potatoes. He had retreated from using my first name, so I figured his opening line was just to let me know he knew who I was. "Anything in particular you're searching for here in our quaint little village?"

"Oh, just passing through looking for some real estate." My smile turned coy. "Have you seen any?"

He smiled back and nodded slightly before continuing. I suspected he was going to get to the point soon, but maybe wanted to feel me out a bit first.

"Are you enjoying your stay at the hotel?" The look in his eyes was suggesting something, possibly to make sure I knew who owned the bullets that were buried in the woodwork upstairs.

"I'm doing fine." My smile faded a bit. "Sadly, my luggage was assassinated during the night. I suspect a neighboring Samsonite roll-a-long might have been overcome with professional jealousy and shot it several times."

"A quick wit and not easily intimidated." He slammed the table and let out a short laugh. "I like you."

"Enough to give me my car back?"

"Your car?" He recovered and acted surprised. "Was it stolen?"

"My prime suspect would have to be the Samsonite, probably running in panic after killing my duffel." I telegraphed my suspicion that he was responsible for every calamity that had befallen me since I arrived. "What I'm trying to figure out is how it's driving the car from the trunk."

"You know, I can't imagine how you survived even one night staying in that flee infested hotel." He shook his head in mock disgust.

"Luck had a lot to do with it." I nodded and fell silent at the approach of Anna. She put a cup in front of DeLaCosta and filled it from the coffee pot before topping off my own.

"Thank you, my dear." He motioned to me. "May I present Mr. Hollister?"

"Mr. Hollister." She nodded at me and I detected just the slightest curtsy in her posture, that hint of formal upbringing. From a distance, she was captivating, but up close she was nothing less than stunning. There were significant signs of her recent departure from a youthful beauty to a truly stately woman, but they only gave testimony that she would be stealing men's hearts no matter what age she'd live to be.

"Please, call me Jack, and thank you." I smiled, lifting my cup to her as we locked eyes for a few seconds.

"A pleasure." She smiled a bit and I seemed to detect both a glimmer of hope and sadness in them. She left us to return the coffee pot.

I turned back to the man sitting across from me, who seemed strangely intrigued by my interest in his niece. It forced me to block all thoughts of her and get to the matter at hand. If he wanted meat and potatoes, I'd give them to him.

"So, you know my name and undoubtedly what room I was in last night. Unless you want to keep doing this dance and recite my shoe size, why don't we get down to it?"

"If I may be so bold." I detected just a hint of a foreign accent now, as I sensed his manner changing from curiosity to congeniality. "Since you've clearly been dispatched to find me and watch me for the day, why don't you be my guest and do it first hand in more comfortable surroundings. I'd be happy to put you up for the night."

"A tempting offer, Mr. DeLaCosta." I nodded and glanced over to Anna who was now talking to Lorene. "But a bit disconcerting, since you seem to know as much, if not more, about why I'm here than I do."

"Does that bother you?"

"When it concerns attempts on my life, it bothers me a lot. It also bothers me that last night there was two of us and now I seem to be all alone."

"I understood that you were replacing Mr. Stapleton and that he left early this morning to catch a flight out of Reno for home."

"Again, your information seems to be disturbingly better than mine." I gave him a wary look. "From my only conversation with him, I didn't get that impression at all."

"Please." He changed the subject. "Spend the day with me. I'm sure your car will turn up, probably in Elko where no doubt one of those ruffians next door borrowed it to go buy more liquor."

"Or ammunition." I added with an upturned eyebrow and sip from my coffee cup.

"In the meantime, I'd be happy to tell you whatever you'd like to know about myself, or those mysterious disappearances in Paris."

"Should I bring my case file, or do you want to tell me what's in it from memory?"

"Whatever you like." He took a drink from his own coffee cup and set it down with a slight frown. "Please accompany me and my niece, so we can have a proper café."

As if on cue, I heard another car pull up out front. I was praying it was Deputy Turley. In the time it took us to head for the front register, he breached the door and we all met near the entrance.

"Mr. DeLaCosta." Turley nodded and then turned to Anna with his forefinger and thumb on the brim of his hat. His demeanor changed not unlike my own when she had first walked through the door. "Anna."

She frowned a bit and nodded back. I took that as a footnote that there was some kind of history there.

"Deputy Turley." DeLaCosta greeted him in the same manner he'd greeted me, but didn't ask if he could call him Mitch. I guess that meant I was one up on the deputy for being invited to the next poker game.

"Always a pleasure to see you." He nodded respectfully at them both and then looked back at me. "Did you want that ride back to Elko, Mr. Hollister?"

"Mr. DeLaCosta has graciously extended an invitation to his residence." I smiled half seriously. "You've been there, no doubt?"

"Yeah, sure." He looked from DeLaCosta and back to me with a bit of puzzlement on his face.

"I wouldn't want to overstay my welcome there." I tried to convey my meaning, but wasn't sure I was getting through. "So, you think I could take a rain check on that ride till tomorrow afternoon, say around five or so?"

"Sure, I guess." He seemed more eager to do it for DeLaCosta than for me, so I made it sound that way.

"No need." DeLaCosta shook off the notion. "I'd be happy to drive Mr. Hollister to Elko tomarrow, or even Anna could bring him back."

"Just in case the DeLaCostas get tied up, I'd appreciate it if you dropped by anyway." I interjected while staring at Turley. He finally seemed to get my message.

"I'll do that." He said, staring at me with half understanding and a nod. "Just in case."

The conversation seemed to be lost on Anna, although it was

obvious she knew something was going on a bit out of the ordinary. I could feel her physical warmth, as she stood close to my side in the cramped foyer of the diner. It was distracting to say the least.

"Well." DeLaCosta clapped his hands and looked at me with a semi-serious look on face. "Now that we're settled on travel arrangements, let me show you my humble pueblo."

"Why not?" This seemed to be the morning for understatements.

6

We mounted up in DeLaCosta's Hummer and started out from the diner, but I almost jumped out when he took an immediate left turn up the service road that went towards the cabins behind the hotel. In near panic, I watched Deputy Turley take off towards Elko without a second glance our way. This looked like it was going to be a very short ride and I couldn't understand why the deputy didn't notice which way we were going.

I started to move my hand around to the back of my waistband, but stopped when DeLaCosta drove by the ramshackle structures and continued on up the dirt road. Looking back through the rear window, my heart recovered a bit, but I was still concerned about our present course. The road was unpaved and it led straight for the cliffs of the canyon wall. I had no idea what could be out there other than a local dump for Lone Tree, or possibly their local version of Boot Hill.

I looked to Anna for some clue as to what was happening, but she sat coolly in the front passenger's seat, as if they'd just gone to the grocery store for a few odds and ends and were now taking the boring drive home. Nothing from her manner signaled anything was out of place. I looked out both side windows and then forward, between them through the windshield. As we got closer to the mesa, I noticed the road didn't end at the cliffs, but went through a narrow slit cut into it, probably by erosion. I wanted to say something, but didn't know how exactly to put it, so I waited. If Anna wasn't concerned, I decided irrationally that I shouldn't be.

We squeezed through the slit and I was amazed to find a narrow path that led off to one side. The hidden easement was very tight and constricted, but passable as long as one had a stout four-wheel-drive vehicle. We ascended at an alarming rate up the narrow drive, winding through the interior of the mesa, clawing our way in low gear, four-wheel-drive towards the summit. The ground was like all the volcanic earth in this area, a red clay that looked solid as concrete when dry, but I guessed might become a slippery sort of slime when it got wet in weather. I decided if it rained hard enough, it would be a death-defying stunt to come back down in any conveyance, akin to going over Niagara Falls in a barrel.

"Hell of a driveway you got here." I nodded, trying to look unimpressed as I broke the silence. "Who comes down to get your paper every morning?"

"It took several months to excavate this path down to the highway." DeLaCosta turned tour guide. "Before, it was a steep ravine that provided natural run off from the top. I only widened it and took a bit more dirt out. The only other way to get to the house takes over an hour longer and over much rougher terrain. I paid a small fortune for the power lines that took that route."

"I'd suspect it cost a small fortune to have this cut out as well."

"I'm planning on paving it next summer." He seemed to agree with a nod as he worked hard on the steering wheel to keep the vehicle from scraping the sides of the ravine.

"Wouldn't it have been more convenient to just choose a different site for your house?"

"Convenience didn't enter into my choice." He shook his head and as he nearly yelled over the straining motor. "Not for this home. I chose it from the back of a horse, by the way."

Anna smiled with him, but didn't look at either of us or offer anything to the conversation. I studied them both from the backseat sitting next to my duffel, aware of the case file and my extra firearm inside. Strangely, my only thoughts were of my future attire and what clothes were left in the bag that didn't have bullet holes in them.

It was darker in the shade of the narrows going up the road, but ahead I finally started seeing some bright sunlight. Suddenly, we broke onto the top of the mesa. The vegetation was a bit thinner without the lush water supply from the stream, but the view in every direction was to say the least, spectacular. Our elevation was slightly lower than most of the distant mountains around us, but it still gave a vantage point for landscapes hundreds of miles in any direction. Without the canyon walls that surrounded Lone Tree, the stream and other waterways could be seen all the way out till they vanished into the horizon.

"I think I see what you mean." Now I was trying not to sound awestruck.

"I thought you'd appreciate it." DeLaCosta nodded with a broader smile.

At first, we seemed to be alone on the flat tabletop of a small mountain, but now a couple of bumps began to loom before us with erect sides that cast shadows in the early day sun. The color of them looked identical to the red clay earth we were still driving on, but they looked slightly out of place in comparison to the rest of the terrain. The tire grooves in the ground were acting as almost an automatic pilot for the Hummer's steering and since they were heading straight to them, I surmised it was our destination. After a short distance, we drove between two low pillars of large red clay brick and found ourselves in a sort of courtyard.

The appearance of the house from outside was one of a very old adobe dwelling, like something the earliest settlers might have lived in. Although the outside surfaces were clay brick that seemed to slant in as they rose to the roofline, the deeply inset windows and clay roof were strictly southwest in design and construction. The windows looked double paned and modern, as did the red tiles that capped the structure, which were similar to the ones on the hotel only in much newer condition.

I spotted the second building of like construction a bit further back and off to one side. It had wide sliding doors that yawned open in the growing heat of the day. Smaller side doors led off to stalls on either side of it. A dappled gray popped its head out of one of the stalls and greeted us with a whinny. I suspected it was Anna's.

As we made a turn to come up abreast of the front entrance to the house, a middle-aged man came out and walked out to greet us. Behind him, a slightly plump Hispanic woman emerged, but waited at the entry's threshold. The man opened the door for Anna and she exited the SUV without giving him a second look. Instead, she greeted the woman with a wide smile.

"Maria, any calls while we were out?"

"No, Seniorita." She shook her head with an apologetic look. "No calls."

"Tony, this is Mr. Hollister. He'll be staying the night." I looked over to see DeLaCosta giving further instructions to the man over the hood of the Hummer. "Please see that he's made to feel comfortable."

"Of course, Sir." The man looked over and our eyes met in recognition of each other.

Of all the men I'd met or even run across so far on this trip, along with all the others thrown in from my last dozen cases, I immediately sensed this man was by far the most dangerous. He was a bit older than myself, tall, with close-cut salt and pepper hair, wearing casual slacks and a polo shirt. Well groomed and extremely fit without being obviously so, he conveyed a commanding presence. He could've substituted for DeLaCosta quite easily in his demeanor, except for his rigid posture. The idea of a General's Aid popped into the back of my mind as I assessed his household position.

But that wasn't the instant danger I felt as his gaze casually fell upon me. It was the innate look in his eyes and what they conveyed. They were gray and cold as the bottom of the Artic Ocean with absolutely nothing compassionate behind them. Without looking anywhere but straight at me, I sensed he knew I was right-handed, a passable shot, and that I'd taken life before. My impression back was that he was gifted left-hander, could put my eye out at a hundred yards with a pistol, and had killed several times over during his own lifetime.

The difference between us was I'd taken life out of necessity to save others, mainly my partner's and my own, and that I'd done so with instant remorse. Without having had my hand forced by the complex circumstances that gave me no other option, I never would have done so. But with this man, I instinctively knew he'd taken life without so much as blinking an eye. More importantly, I sensed he recognized this vast difference between us, as if he instinctively knew I'd hesitate that fraction of a second before pulling the trigger. In doing so, he had immediately sensed the edge he had over me.

All this passed in the briefest moment, from just a few moments of making eye contact and exchanging nods. In the next second, he was asking me if I needed any help with my bag, as if he were a harmless valet. Suspecting that if he picked it up, he'd not only know there was a loaded gun in it, but what brand, model and how many rounds of ammunition were with it, I passed on the offer and hoisted it myself.

"Thanks, I've got it."

"As you wish, Mr. Hollister." Bowing away just slightly, I suspected he knew why I'd declined the offer. I really hated it when everyone knew what everyone else was thinking, and this house was loaded with such people. What bothered me most was that it wasn't coming from clairvoyance, but from experience. Tony extended an open hand towards the house entrance. "If you'll follow me, I'll show you to your room."

The inside of DeLaCosta's humble pueblo was anything but rustic. The floors were Tarantine with accent tiles set sporadically into the smooth troweled plaster walls. Exposed beams accented the overhead portions of construction while ceiling fans turned in slow motion. A massive peasant style fireplace provided a sort of structural centerpiece for the great-room, set in more smooth plaster and framed in tile. The freestanding hearth separated the living room on one side from the open dining room and bar on the other.

The white plaster finish bounced enough sunlight that the interior of the house looked more like a covered patio, but the thick earthen walls and tile kept it all cool as a cave. On the opposite side of the main area, two large sliders provided access to what looked like a tiled deck out back. One slider lay off the living room with a completely open terrace while the other was adjacent the dining room, protected by a trellised canopy.

I took in the simple beauty of the place with its southwest decor before following Tony down a hallway. We stopped at one of the first rooms with an open door and I peered into a traditional looking bedroom, outfitted with natural wood furnishings and its own bath. The ceiling fan was already turning above the bed.

I walked by Tony and into the room, but turned as he started to leave, voicing what had been going through my head since I first laid eyes on him.

"You haven't been out doing some late night practicing with your silencer lately, have you, Tony?"

He turned back and gave me a look that he knew that I knew,

that… whatever.

"No, Sir." He said with the thinnest of smiles.

"Just wondering." I cocked my head a bit. "You kind of have that look like you've used one a time or two."

"Not for sometime now, Sir." Somehow, I really wanted to believe him, but those holes in my duffel made it hard to.

"Mr. DeLaCosta would have you join him on the veranda for a cafe."

"Sounds like a man after my own heart." I nodded and he left.

I closed the door and threw my duffel on the bed, sighing to myself.

"I just hope he doesn't have any plans to actually cut it out."

- - - - -

I found my host on the open terrace just outside the living room, sitting with his back to the house, coffee in hand. I noticed it was a very small cup.

"Quite an impressive view, Mr. DeLaCosta." I walked up behind him and stood next to an identical chair next to his. It was still early enough that we were both in the shade.

"Please, call me Ray." He smiled up at me and motioned to sit. "The Mr. This and Mr. That gets a little old and this is not the proper setting for such formalities."

"Sounds OK to me." I sat down.

"It is a wondrous view, is it not?" He was looking out at the vista before us. "I never tire of sitting here in the morning and evening, just looking at it and filling myself with its intoxicating aroma and solitude.

I paused a few moments to take it all in. The expanse and contrast of colors were admittedly breathtaking, a 180-degree panorama of what we'd been treated to on our approach to the house. But here we were close enough to the edge that I could see down to the nearby canyon floors. On the opposing mesa wall, at only a moderate distance, the rare sight of a tall slender waterfall seemed to have dictated the building site and positioning of the patio, just for a view of it. The wind-twisted mesquite and sparse sage provided proximate framing for a landscape that could not have been painted any better into a mural of the classic old west.

"This is truly amazing." I admitted as I settled in. Whether his relaxed manner was infectious, or this place was already getting to me, I felt at ease.

Maria was at my side before I knew it and set a cafe identical to DeLaCostas on the wide armrest of my chair. I nodded thanks and carefully picked up the tiny cup. It looked delicate enough to break just by just looking at it.

"One of the traditions I brought with me from the old country." Ray nodded at the cup. "Do you like cappuccino?"

"I like coffee." I assured him. "I'm just not used to drinking it in such small amounts."

Ray smiled as he watched me take a sip. The brew had the same effect as my fifth cup of the day, as if I'd chugged them all at once. I recoiled and regarded the drink before looking back at my host.

"That'll wake you up in the morning." I smiled my approval.

"I'm glad you like it. It's made the old way, not like you get in those fancy coffee places you have in your bigger cities." He seemed pleased and sipped his own, looking back at the view. "How long were you a policeman?"

"I did my twenty and got out early." I followed his gaze and spoke offhandedly. "How long have you been in this country?"

"I was born here, in upstate New York." He nodded. "I'm a citizen, but I lived in my family's native country for many years as a boy and then off and on in my adulthood. I came back just enough to keep my citizenship here."

"See much of France during your 'on and off' periods?"

"Not so much France, but I did travel extensively at times. I particularly liked Greece. It has such a warm climate and friendly people."

"What did you think of Paris?" We were both looking at the view as we talked.

"No need to rush, Jack." He smiled without looking over. "We have the whole day and evening and I'll be as frank and open with you as the circumstances will allow."

"Circumstances?"

"Well, you have been assigned to spy on me, which would under normal circumstances make you an adversary of sorts."

"So, you don't want to tell me anything that you couldn't let me leave with?"

"Something like that." He smiled at my directness.

"Well, I'm in favor of that." I nodded. "I wouldn't want to end up being part of your cactus garden."

"Good. Then we are in agreement." He sipped from the cup and sighed as he looked around. "This is the only way to start the day."

"Kind of a hard place to find, don't you think?" I was thinking on a different level than my host, or maybe not. "It almost gives the appearance of a hideout."

"You mean am I here by choice or by necessity." He finally glanced over at me. "To be candid, a little of both, but not for the reasons you suspect."

"Then why?" I prodded.

"You have a knack for straying directly into that area I mentioned earlier." He gave a short laugh. "You must have been a very good detective."

"I just somehow know people." I admitted and let my previous question drop. "So, can you tell me how you know so much about this case I'm working on?"

"I make it a point to always know what concerns me, and anything where my name comes up concerns me."

"Funny, cause I didn't see your name in the file at all."

"You haven't examined it closely enough, yet."

"What do you know about this thing going on in France?"

"I know certain artifacts have gone missing from the Concierge le Paris, a holding warehouse for the Louvre. These items went missing in 1997 and there's been a feverish search for them ever since."

"By the authorities?"

"Not really." He shook his head. "More from private resources, namely the insurance company and the management of the museum itself."

"I thought I saw INTERPOL's name on some of the paperwork in the file?"

"They've been contacted and their resources have been tapped, but only to help in these other entities recover what's gone missing. INTERPOL is much better at working confidentially with their victims than your domestic agencies."

"So, is this a crime we're talking about here or not?"

"In the strictest sense, yes, but there are mitigating subtleties involved."

"Subtleties?"

"The items are quite confidential and if not misrepresented, their intrinsic value is only what they'd be worth to the original owners."

"Did I ever tell you how much I hate riddles?"

"It will make sense as time goes on." He looked at me straight faced. "But for now, if you'll excuse me, I have some work to do."

"You work from here?"

"Just because I live in the middle of nowhere, doesn't mean I'm retired, Jack." He chuckled a bit with outstretched arms. "I have many ongoing enterprises that need constant attention."

"And Tony?" I got up with him, cup still in hand. "Is he your secretary?"

"My secretary is shopping in Rome right now with my sister." His smile suggested she was a bit more than his secretary. His thoughts strayed and seemed to dismiss my question. "While I'm engaged in my business affairs, Anna has arranged some diversion to keep you occupied."

"Anna?" I was a bit surprised, even more so when all thoughts of the case I was there to work disappeared from my mind.

"Yes." He looked me up and down, as if he was appraising more than my appearance. "If you have any clothes conducive to equestrian activities, I'd suggest you employ them before meeting her in the stables."

"Sure." I had no idea where Raymond DeLaCosta had received his education, but it obviously wasn't in the Brooklyn public school system.

"We'll chat some more later." He started to walk back inside the house. "There's still plenty of time and I'm curious to learn what the significance of this date has in your assignment."

"Will you let me know when you find out?" I followed behind him, now only slightly interested in what he was saying. "I wouldn't mind knowing myself."

I caught a glimpse of Tony out of the corner of my eye, sitting at the bar and drinking coffee from a regular sized cup as he watched me walk through the house. His presence sent a chill down my spine and made me wonder how far he'd be riding behind Anna and me on this apparent outing she was planning. Whoever DeLaCosta was, he seemed to rate some heavy artillery for protection. Tony wasn't a valet or personal secretary. His actions and vigilance suggested something more akin to a bodyguard, which made sense, given his perceived abilities. The whole setup was becoming quite unnerving, but at least the living conditions were a vast improvement over the Lone Tree Inn.

I went back to my room and started digging out more clothes, trying to find some that weren't aerated. In doing so, I grabbed the soft gun case and pulled it out. I hefted it in my hand, noticing it was much lighter than the last time I'd handled it. Opening the case, I removed the holstered magnum and looked deeper. All the ammunition was gone. I pulled the revolver out of the holster and it was also empty. Someone had removed the bullets. I dug down to the bottom of the duffel and found my hiking boots. Checking inside them, I felt the security of my extra magazines for the 45 and the comforting weight of the rounds they contained.

If it weren't for the automatic I was almost never without, I would've been defenseless. DeLaCosta was apparently being very cautious or Tony was just being very efficient. Probably, it was a little of both. In any case, if either one of them tried anything and there was any slack at all in their attempt, they'd be in for a surprise. I shoved the gun case and its contents under the bed, since Tony had rendered it no more useful than a doorstop, and continued my search for some suitable clothes. I couldn't wait to see what Anna had in store for me. I pictured an unbroken stud that would throw me off the mesa's cliff.

7

I found the pueblo's wrangler in the barn, standing with her back to me as she brushed out the gray that had greeted us on our arrival. Anna was still wearing the snug fitting jeans with boots and the white blouse, but her hair was now pinned up under a tan cowboy hat with a thin leather chinstrap. The mare told her I'd arrived by pinning her ears and shifting her weight. Anna turned and looked me up and down, immediately noticing my thick denims had some new ventilation.

"You have holes in your jeans." She smiled at the small tears in the pant legs. "Can I offer you another pair?"

"Is there a western store up here somewhere?" I looked around in mock surprise.

"Tony is about your size." She looked at me as if she was appraising more than my waist and inseam. It wasn't an all-together bad feeling. "I think they'd fit."

"I'd just as soon leave Tony out of everything we say and do for the next few hours, if that's all right with you?"

"He's OK." She said in almost a dismissing tone. "He's apparently a big fan of the cinema. Maria talks about all the pictures of movie ads he has in his room, although she's the only one allowed in his room and that's just for cleaning it. He's been with my uncle for many years now."

"I'll take your word for it." I noticed a seasoned bay gelding tided up on the other side of the breezeway. He looked like a veteran who'd seen it all and wasn't eager to do much more than pull a carriage around Central Park. Anna had done a good job picking him out for me, as I had still never mastered the true art of equestrianism.

"Are you sure you don't want some better pants." She walked over to me and stuck her finger in a couple of the holes, finding more of them than she'd first seen. "These holes look pretty nasty."

"It could've been worse." I assured her. "I could've been in the jeans when they were made."

"You have a strange sense of humor, Mr. Hollister." She straightened and smiled a bit while searching my eyes for whatever women look for in them. "I'm not used to... how do you call it?"

"Sarcasm is the word you're probably looking for." I searched back in hers, not sure just what she was doing up here or what part she had in all this. "I come by it honestly. I was a cop for a lot of years, in LA. If that won't do it to you, nothing will."

"Do what?" Her eyebrows furrowed a bit, but her intoxicating smile remained.

"Make you cynical."

"You must tell me more." She returned to her brushing, but at a slower, more tentative pace, as if she were in no hurry and was ready to hear my memoirs.

"Not much to tell, I'm afraid." I walked over to the gelding, stroking his neck to let him know I wasn't going to shoot him and eat him for dinner. I found another brush and started cleaning off his neck, back and hindquarters.

"You know horses, Mr. Hollister." She watched me as I began to collect the fine hair and red dust off the gelding's back, sweeping them down and off the area the saddle pad would go.

"Just enough to be dangerous on one, I'm afraid." I kept brushing. "I worked in a friend's stable for several years when I was a teenager. I know ground work, but didn't ride enough to become very good."

"Joey will take care of you." She nodded. "He's older, much more mature than some of the others here."

"Guess he's a good match for me, then." I noticed we were being watched quite intently by a few of the other residents. The majority of the stable inhabitants looked like quarter horses. One in particular seemed quite upset by our activities and by the size of his jaws I took him to be the stud of the outfit. "Is the black one Ray's?"

Anna turned and looked at the horse I was indicating. She took a few seconds to answer.

"Yes," She looked back at the gray and kept brushing. "That's Politico."

"Ray must be a good rider."

"He doesn't ride enough to do Politico justice." She shook her head, probably completely unaware of the pun she'd just uttered. "He is of fine stock, but he sits too much. He only gets the proper exercise when I visit and ride him myself."

"You visit your uncle a lot, then?" I sensed a distance between them, more so than I'd first estimated.

"Not as much as I'd like to." She looked around her before returning to her work. "It is so beautiful in this part of your country."

"You were born in Italy, then?"

She paused in her brushing and looked over at me.

"He said you would ask many questions." She put the grooming tool down and removed a saddle pad from a nearby rack.

"Besides being naturally curious, it's also my job to be inquisitive." I followed her lead, finding the tack intended for use next to my mount.

"Are you curious about my uncle, or about me?" She hefted a western style saddle and swung it over the mare.

"Well," I positioned the pad and imitated her technique with the saddle as I heaved it over my own horse. "Truth be told, I'm curious about your uncle, but you're just plain fascinating."

"What do you find so fascinating about me?" She started cinching down the saddle and putting the reins on.

"Your obvious beauty." I shrugged as I continued to follow her lead. "But even more, the way you handle it. The way you act as if you don't possess any at all. That fascinates me."

"Beauty is cheap in your country." She commented as she completed preparations for the ride.

"Amen to that." I intoned. "The true jewels of this world are the late bloomers."

"The late what?" She stopped and looked at me.

"Bloomers." I repeated. "The girls who start out plain and grow into their looks."

"Oh." She returned to her work. "I thought you were talking about women's, uh, you know."

"Bloomers?" I laughed a bit. "Not the underwear, the bloomers like in the garden. Late bloomers like a flower that waits till just the right time to open up."

"That's a wonderful way of putting it." She looked over at me with a fresh expression, but I was too busy getting my mount ready to fully notice it.

"Where are we riding?"

"I thought I'd show you some spots further into the canyon, around the waterfall."

"Sounds good." I unhooked the stirrup off the saddle horn and moved the lead rope, dropping it over the gelding's neck so I could bit him up with the reins provided.

"You surprise me with your knowledge of horses, Mr. Hollister." She nodded approval as she walked over and checked the cinch on the saddle. "It makes it much easier when I don't have to do it all."

"I'm here to make whatever happens as easy as possible and still get the job done." I smiled at her. "I'm hoping your uncle will let me continue along those lines."

"Let's leave my uncle here with Tony and the house." She finished with her tack check and mounted the gray. "Let's pretend it is just you and I up here in the wilderness."

"I couldn't think of a better way to spend the day, Ms…." I paused and looked up at her. "What *is* your last name?"

"Just Anna, Mr. Hollister." She nodded. "Please, just call me Anna."

"I will if you'll stop calling me Mr. Hollister."

"OK, Mr. Jack." She smiled in recognition of what she'd been doing, but still couldn't drop the 'Mr.'.

The other horses made sure everyone within a half a mile knew we were leaving. The stud made the biggest scene, stamped his feet and charging up and down in his stall. It must've been the most exercise he'd gotten in a few weeks, if Anna was telling me the truth about Ray's riding habits.

"You'd think we were taking his one true love from him." I commented as I turned in the saddle.

"Males are all so possessive." She shook her head. "It must be some sort of natural hormone in all of you."

"Seen a lot of possessiveness in your travels?" I looked back at her, understanding how easily she could've come to the conclusion.

"It is such a waist of time." She shook her head a bit and started concentrating on our direction.

"Ever been married?" I pulled my ball cap out of my rear pocket, screwing it tight over my scalp. It was getting hotter, but a breeze was at least keeping the air moving.

"No." That sadness came over her face, the same expression I'd noticed in the diner when we were introduced. "Engaged once."

"What happened?"

"He crashed his car and died two days later in the hospital." She shook her head. "Men and their egos. He loved fast cars and loved to drive them as fast as he could."

"Sorry to hear that." I offered. "So he was the reckless playboy type?"

"No." She looked at me as if I hadn't heard what she was saying. "He spun his car at La Mans in the 24 hours. He was a professional race car driver."

"Oh." I felt like a horse's ass and out classed, all at once. "I misunderstood."

"He loved it, much more than I think he ever loved me." She reflected and looked over at me. "And you're right about the playboy part, but I think I still would have married him."

"So he wasn't the possessive type?"

"That's what I loved about him." She smiled at some distant memory long put to rest. "He treasured my attention, but was never jealous."

"Good qualities." I nodded without really understanding.

"Are you married?" She looked over at me.

"Me?" I did a quick double take. "No. I was, but it didn't work out."

"Why not?"

"Irreconcilable differences." I intoned the words on the decree ending the formal relationship. "I wanted to make money and she wanted to spend it."

"That's not so bad." She smiled.

"No, except that her spending outpaced my income three to one." I shook my head.

"Where is she now?" Her smile remained.

"Working her way up the command structure of my old department." I nodded. "Last I heard she was living with a Deputy Chief."

"Maybe it was for the best, then." She offered. "Like my engagement."

"You think if he hadn't crashed you would have ended up unhappy in the marriage?"

"His death was tragic and devastated me." She shook her head with a frown. "But as time passed, I realized he would have wanted a death just like the one he met with. Almost like a death wish in a way. If he had survived, he would have eventually lost his skills with age and become very depressed and miserable. Racing was his life and I don't think I could have substituted for his one true love."

"You never know." I gently argued. "He might have gotten over it and learned to love you even more than his fast cars."

"That might have been even more difficult for me." She turned introspective.

I shook my head and held my tongue. Women. We were now riding down the crest of a ridge with a shear drop on one side. On the other, it seemed to slope off gradually and angle down towards the canyon floor in the opposite direction, some miles out from us. I sensed this was the alternate route to highway, since a line of wood power poles flanked us on that side and disappeared down into the distance. There was no discernible road, but shallow tracks in the red clay here and there amid the large jagged rocks hinted at some use by trucks or four-bys.

"Was this the original route that the construction guys used while building the house?"

"Yes." She snapped back from her melancholy. "The highway is over those two lower ridges down there."

"I see what your uncle was saying about the terrain." I was inspecting the uneven ground with lots of rocky crags here and there, making for very slow going using the best of four wheel drive trucks and vehicles.

"It took a very long time for the workers to get everything up here." She agreed and nodded off to the steeper side of the ridge as she changed the subject. "We'll cut down into the canyon just up here a bit."

"Sure not much out here." I looked off in the direction I thought the highway was. Nothing was moving except for a few birds circling in the sky.

"No, but that's why my uncle chose it." Anna angled her mare closer to the cliff. "He relishes his solitude."

"Is your horse's name Pegasus?" I remarked as I watched her tightrope on the edge of what looked like a precipice.

"No, why?" She giggled.

"Cause she's going to need wings if you fall off this ridge."

"Have faith." She reassured as she took the lead.

The canyon wall beneath the ridge was steep, but there was what amounted to a goat path down the face of it. I'd never trusted horses, having learned just how big their brains physically were, but I was gaining a clearer appreciation that the larger portion of it must have been designed to tell them exactly where to put their feet on any particular piece of ground. I'd been on rides like this one, but not very many. If the horse slipped, it would be a very long and steep slide to the bottom. I tried to let old Joey have full rein and just relax in the saddle.

For what seemed like an eternity to me, we switched back and forth as we made our way down the face of the ridge. At the bottom, we continued to let our mounts have their head as we traversed some very rocky terrain. Finally, we were on the canyon floor and the ground turned to more of a sandy texture. I heard the faint sound of water crashing over the rocks and figured we were close to our destination.

"You became very quiet back there." She slowed her pace to allow me to ease up to her side.

"Fear does that to me." I admitted as I wiped the palms of my hands on my jeans.

"Most men would never admit such a thing." She was looking at me very intently. "So strange to find a man so open and honest."

"I've heard that most men babble like idiots, spouting all kinds of truths when they think they're about to die."

"I have heard that, also." The tone of her reply seemed more distant to our conversation.

"So." My curiosity machine started up again. "You're not married, been engaged once, like riding horses off of cliffs, and you're from Italy. What else?"

"What do you want to know?" Her accent reminded me of an old movie with Sophia Loren, except Anna's finely sculptured features were much less classic Italian than her pattern of speech.

"Well, what line of work is your family in?" I had other questions in mind, but too intimate for our fresh relationship, so I kept them more general.

"My father was a businessman for many years before his death." Her sadness resurfaced momentarily, but rebounded. "He left my mother very well off, but of course it is our family's business and it is quite wealthy."

"You're very close to your mother."

"Yes," She looked over at me with another surprised look, before looking away again. "And no."

"What was it your father did?" I was growing more curious.

"Wine." She nodded with an answer that came almost too quickly. "Our family has vast vineyards and it makes and sells the wine under many labels around the world."

"Sounds impressive." I admitted, but noticed how she seemed to be referring to her family as almost a separate entity. The family was 'it', not 'we' or 'our'. "You must be a connoisseur of fine wines, then."

"I know a good one when I taste it, but a connoisseur?" She smiled broadly and shook her head. "I think not."

"You have a beautiful smile, Anna." I admired her openly. "An honest, open face."

"Thank you." She turned away and I thought I saw a blush come to her cheeks.

"Does that make you uncomfortable?"

"A bit, yes." She glanced at me before turning away again. She shifted the conversation to our whereabouts. "We are here."

We rounded a outcropping in the canyon's face and before us was a gentle waterfall, feeding a crystal clear pool in the stream. Further back, some hundred yards, the tall waterfall seen from the pueblo's terrace crashed down on the rocks, producing a fine mist that cooled the air and gave off a sweet scent like it was falling rain. The vegetation was again thicker with a brace of large poplars, their golden leaves glistened in the breeze and lightly feathering down on us. Predominantly, there was sand, rock and water making up the canyon's floor.

Anna stopped and dismounted, taking the nylon halter from the

The Carlucci File

saddle horn, putting it over the reins and tying the gray to a fallen tree branch at the stream's edge. I again mimicked her procedure and then followed her on foot upstream to the small pool.

"Take your shoes off and lets cool off." She sat on a rock next to the water's edge and pulled her boots off along with her hat. Her hair cascaded around her shoulders.

"Sure, why not." I unlaced my hiking boots and gratefully noticed there were no holes in them. I stuck my cap back in my jeans pocket. "You come here often?"

"Most often." She nodded as she pulled off her socks and rolled up her pant legs. "When I'm alone, I swim when it is warm like this. The water is delicious."

"Sounds like a great idea." I acknowledged as I looked around.

The stream flowed over the rocks and continually refreshed the pool, then continued downstream over smaller rapids to form back into a stream. Looking around, I acknowledged the seclusion the canyon walls offered.

"We should have worn our suits under our jeans."

"I never bring one." She smiled a bit wickedly and pinned me with a look.

For the second time this week, someone had left me speechless. I just looked back, trying to conjure the image she was describing.

"Do I shock you?" Her expression changed a bit to reflect a challenge of sorts.

"No." I looked around us, trying not to be so obvious. "And yes."

"You were married?" She kept looking at me. "So, you have made love before?"

"I know a good woman when I'm with one." I turned back and challenged her gaze. "But a connoisseur? I think not."

"Bravo." Her laughed lightly and a wide smile followed. It doubled her natural beauty. "Lets cool our feet."

"I thought you'd never ask." All thoughts of DeLaCosta, Tony and the holes in my jeans evaporated as I followed her into the shallows of the pool.

The water was cool and refreshing. Our pant legs were getting soaked but neither of us cared. Wading just a bit deeper, we stopped before the rocks gave way to the swimming end of the shaded oasis.

"It would be nice to take a swim." She was smiling wickedly again and looking over at me, like she was actually considering it. "But I think not."

"Tease." I smiled and grabbed her hand as she teetered off balance for a moment.

"Well, there's the next best thing." She regained her balance and pulled her hand away. Bending down, she scooped a handful of water up and splashed me with it.

"Hey." I returned the gesture and soon we were like kids waging an all out water fight.

We were almost totally soaked by the time she held up her hands, laughing and calling for a schoolyard truce. Her hair was wet enough that it was curling and sticking to her face. I held up my hands to honor her decree and we both giggled at our childlike behavior. It felt good to laugh openly and the company felt even better.

She brushed the hair from her cheeks the best she could, but some stayed glued to it. I reached out and gently pulled it away and smoothed the water droplets off her face with my fingers. Her giggling turned to quiet smile as we stood face to face, now looking at each other with a growing, inexplicable warmth. I cradled her face in my hand and swept the last of the water and hair off her cheek with my thumb. Slowly, our smiles disappeared and closed the distance to our lips as they parted in anticipation.

A small inch away from a kiss, we stopped, exploring each other's eyes in almost magnetic physical attraction and emotional trepidation. Still, we froze in time, as if mutually agreeing that anticipation was more precious than consummation. I couldn't begin to guess how many hearts she had broken with just a look. Still, with only the deafening waterfall as a backdrop, we stood and just stared at one another.

Who Anna was and why I was here finally came rushing over me like a cold shower. The recognition came to my eyes and she saw it, reflecting it back in her own. That familiar sadness returned to them. It was the same sorrow, almost melancholy, I'd seen several times now. I wanted to rip it out of her, but knew it was part of the fabric that made her who she was.

"You see me." Her expression turned and a trace of true wonder passed over it, as if I'd recognized something in her that went unnoticed by most others.

"I see you." I replied softly, still unwilling to release her face from my hand. "Like so many things in this world, I don't understand, but I do see."

"What do you see?" She asked softly, in a tone that said it was more of a search for self than a test.

I searched for just the right word, not wanting to sound like either a poet or biographer. I wanted to express it accurately, without using whole paragraphs.

"Loneliness." I finally stated. "As if the world is at your feet, but they can't even see you, or reach you."

"My life is rich and full, Mr. Jack." She nodded faintly. "But the deepest part of me has been buried under it. I have no one to share it with."

I nodded slowly, but didn't know what to say. We're all who we are and there's no 'fixing' us. There's just living with each other and trying to love each other's faults as much as each other's virtues.

"Thank you for touching me." She put her hand over mine on her face, but it was clear she wasn't talking about anything physical. "I don't want you to go away, not so soon."

"I'm not sure…."

"I just want to spend more time with you." She cut me off. "The men of my social position are vain and shallow. They see nothing of me, but you do."

"I understand." I pulled her face close to mine and we rested our cheeks on each other's shoulders.

Standing on separate boulders beneath the water's surface, we formed a bridge to one other, being careful not to embrace any further down than our shoulders. What part of her was resting against me felt warm and inviting, but going any further didn't seem natural for what we'd experienced so far. So, I pulled back, kissing her cheek as we righted ourselves.

Rather than let the moment drop like a hasty mistake, we let it slowly evaporate, unwinding our mutual explorations and desires and return to the cool air and moisture enriched environment.

"We should probably start back." She said hesitantly. "Before Uncle becomes concerned."

I nodded agreement and we let go of each other. Without further conversation, we put ourselves back in riding habit and remounted our horses. Anna led the way back to the goat path and we slowly ascended the canyon wall. I decided going up was a lot less nerve racking than going down, but I still had to concentrate on relaxing, lest old Joey feel my anxiety and misstep for both of us. I tried to keep my eyes and mind on my beautiful riding companion and what had transpired during our outing. It wasn't hard to do.

We finally broke onto the ridge and even the horses registered their relief by snorting and sneezing with a lighter gait and deeper breathing.

"Do they know they're going home, or what?" I laughed a little as they picked up their pace without cue.

"Of course." She reined in her gray and came back along side of me.

"Maria is making a big dinner I especially planned for you." She smiled widely.

"I'm honored." I didn't know what else to say.

"I'm happy." Her smile widened.

I was looking into her eyes again like a schoolboy when something caught my eye. I looked off in the direction of where Anna said the highway was.

"Anna, does your uncle run any livestock, like cattle or anything?"

"No." She thoughtfully shook her head. "Just the horses."

"And they're all accounted for, right?"

"Yes, of course." She assured.

"Funny." I kept looking at the ridge below us.

"What?" She finally looked off in the same direction.

"Those birds are still circling in the same place." I mused.

"I see what you are now saying." She used her hand to further shade her face from the sun and stood in her saddle. "It is still some miles down the ridge, closer to the highway."

"Well." I dismissed the curious sight. "Something's dead out there. Probably a coyote."

"Probably." She nodded slightly.

We let the horses pick up the pace, but only slightly. It was nearing late lunch or early dinner. Either way, maybe DeLaCosta had discovered what was so special about today in regards to the case. I realized I was caring less and less about it, ceasing to care who had discovered the mysteries surrounding some mystery in France and what effect it could possibly have on a handful of people in the middle of Nevada. I was hungry, and not just for food.

8

We found Raymond DeLaCosta sitting in the main room across from Tony. Off to their far side, a wide-screen TV was on the CNN Channel with the volume barely audible. There was no conversation, but their expressions conveyed some seriousness towards what they might have been discussing before our arrival. My immediate thoughts concerned Tony and whether he had followed Anna and I on our ride. Anna's smile vanished as well, noticing a change of mood immediately.

"Uncle, what is it?" Her brow furrowed, as if the bad news might involve her immediate family.

Her question seemed to break the spell between the two men and DeLaCosta looked up at me, then to Anna.

"Nothing, my dear." He seemed remotely aware of the news channel still droning on at low volume behind him and took advantage of it. "Just a bad day on the stock market."

"It will recover, yes?" Her smile returned and she turned to me. "I will see how Maria is doing with supper."

I nodded with a weak smile, knowing DeLaCosta was lying about the market report, and watched Anna retreat to the kitchen. The aroma of something definitely Italian was cooking in the other room. It was invading the entire house, with lots of tomato and mozzarella, making my stomach growl and realize breakfast had been hours ago. Trying to ignore it, I walked the short distance to where the two men sat and studied their faces. As expected, Tony's was completely unreadable and DeLaCosta just looked like he was deep in thought.

"May I join you?" I took a wild guess that they had discovered the particulars of 'the day' assigned to me as part of the case.

When they didn't immediately answer, I felt a slight chill of regret, as if DeLaCosta had decided inviting me up here had been a mistake. I took the initiative and laid it out for them.

"I take it something's come up." I walked closer, making sure I was out of earshot from the ladies in the kitchen. "Something about why I'm here?"

They exchanged looks, as if they were wordlessly debating just how much to tell me. The sound of the bullets ripping through my duffel came back to haunt me and I imagined those same slugs tearing through my body. DeLaCosta broke the silence with a deep sigh and forced smile. He rose from the sofa and extended an open hand towards the slider Anna and I had just come through.

"Would you join me on the terrace for a glass of wine before we eat, Mr. Hollister?"

"Sure." I looked sideways at him and acknowledged the fact that we were back to last names. Not a good sign. "As long as we stay away from the edge of the cliff."

"Please." He ignored my edgy sense of humor and waited for me to walk in front of him. As I started towards the door, I heard him speak to Tony. "A merlot, perhaps, if you would."

I was hoping the phrase wasn't some kind of code for Tony to collect his gun and shovel.

"Certainly." Tony answered and walked off towards the kitchen.

"Maria is preparing a special supper for your visit." DeLaCosta said to my back as we walked outside. "It should be ready shortly."

"It smells delicious." I nodded and breathed a bit easier at his tone. We took our respective chairs from our earlier conversation in the day. I kept pushing the nervous sarcasm to make the point that I was less than comfortable. "I hope I'm still around to join you when it's ready."

"My current predicament does concern your presence, but nothing here should endanger your well being." DeLaCosta settled into the chair. "At least for now."

Tony was so quick with the refreshment that I didn't have time to ask a question, not that I had formulated one to ask, yet. He placed a couple of stemmed glasses on our respective armrests and filled them halfway with a bottle he placed on the small table between us. He excused himself and we sat quietly for a few moments while DeLaCosta swished the wine around in the glass, watching the liquid as it coated the inside surface of the crystal.

"That seems like good news." I eyed him over the glasses. "For now. Can I ask what was being discussed before Anna and I came into the room?"

"Of little matter for the moment."

"Nothing to do with why I'm here?" I watched him closely for any signs of might indicate deception, but couldn't read his face. He seemed quite aware that I was studying him, so I backed off and regarded the bottle label. "I understand your family's in the wine business. This must be from a private collection."

"Yes, it is." DeLaCosta seemed to embrace my minor distraction and regarded the glass of wine in his hand. "Wine has always provided a satisfying diversion from my daily difficulties."

"Really." I looked around us. "I wouldn't think a man of your means in retirement would have any problems."

"My business concerns were thought to be behind me, but it seems of late that they're catching up with me."

"How far behind you are they now?" I asked, thinking of Carl Stapleton. "What businesses are we talking about, if not the wine industry?" I sipped from my glass. Surprisingly, I found the wine sweet, with a slight dryness to balance it out.

"Various interests." DeLaCosta flipped his hand in a nonchalant manner.

"Are you a man whose interests include art?" I put the wine glass down.

"I have resources in the art world." DeLaCosta turned his own glass on the table between us, looking at it as he spoke. "That is perhaps why my information has come up relevant to your investigation."

"I haven't found you anywhere in my file."

"You haven't looked hard enough." He smiled over at me.

"Did Carl Stapleton find you in it?" I cocked my head towards him.

"Mr. Stapleton wasn't up to the task." Ray said curtly while giving me an appraising look. "I surmise you've been dispatched because your employer thinks that you are."

"If it involves surviving this whole mess, I'm hoping I am, too."

"Time will tell." He replied, again almost offhandedly.

He let the comment hang in the air as we fell silent. I didn't know what game he was playing, but wanted to tell him whatever it was, I didn't like his version of 'sudden death'. After a few minutes had passed, I noticed that he seemed to want to say something. Even with his cool veneer, he appeared anxious to get something off his chest. I decided to reopen our dialogue with a neutral comment.

"What label does your family bottle under?" I examined the smoky green bottle next to the glasses we were sipping from.

"My family is in wine, Jack, but I have dabbled a bit in the art of brokering." He suddenly confessed

"The art of brokering, or brokering art?" I turned the phrase, but then put what I thought was the proper label on it. "You mean you're a fence?"

"I prefer broker. Someone who finds a buyer for something available for sale, then takes a small commission on the transaction."

"If that something has been stolen and you know about it, then it's its fencing." We both understood the terms being tossed out. I just wanted him to know I was clear on them.

"To my fault, sometimes what I broker is more on the gray market."

"The gray market, or the black market?"

"Gray, black, whatever the market may bear. A fence is usually someone with limited knowledge of what he's dealing with. I offer artistic expertise and often know more about what I'm dealing with than those I offer it to." DeLaCosta seemed nervous about his disclosure and now it was his turn to comment off the subject. "How do you find the wine?"

"It tastes great, but honestly, I classify wine by how it's packaged, in a bottle or in a box." I put the glass down, as if to take it off the subject list, and looked at my host. He'd gone this far. It was time to pull whatever else I could out of him. "So, what happened today?"

"There was news concerning certain artifacts that disappeared from the Louvre in France and that an active search has been undertaken for them."

"Certain artifacts?" I cocked my head. "Maybe disappearing around

The Carlucci File

August of '97?"

"They were a collection of forged paintings, Jack." He looked at me with the blunt statement. "Yet still, they were extremely rare, nearly indiscernible from the real works."

"All this fuss over a bunch of fakes?" My thoughts raced over the contents of the file. "That's hard to believe, unless someone thought they'd somehow devalue the originals."

"Unlike forged currency, the originals of these paintings are very much out of circulation." DeLaCosta corrected. "Quite simply, your client, Lloyds of London, has divulged this information to hopefully start a panic among the thieves and numerous people who may have handled or ended up with these forgeries, all in the hope of securing their return."

"Which would include 'brokers'." I frowned at him, wondering how he knew who my client's client was.

"It's ready." Anna was standing in the doorway, beaming with pride.

"It should sit and collect, all the ingredients, before we eat it." He admonished Anna gently. It seemed he was now as anxious to talk to me, as I was to listen.

"It's not wine, Uncle." Anna teased. "We can eat the salad while it 'collects'."

"The wonders of the feminine mystique transcend logic, do they not?" DeLaCosta shook his head as we simultaneously rose from our chairs.

"Amen." I glanced up at Anna and found that same wicked look in her eyes.

Dinner was a delicious distraction from the conversation we'd just finished. If DeLaCosta had one of these fake paintings and wanted to give it up, I'd be happy to take it in for him, case closed. I felt more comfortable knowing he'd had me sent out to do his bidding and Deputy Turley's comrades could investigate whatever had happened to Carl Stapleton. At least it was comforting to know I wasn't among the suspects in his death.

Salad was served up, followed by a main course of lasagna without equal. The only thing close had come from a small forgotten restaurant in Little Italy I'd found on a trip back east. There was the usual pasta and bread, but I tried to take only sample portions of everything but the main dish that I just couldn't resist. I wondered how native Italians could keep from eating themselves into oblivion on this stuff, much less into obesity. I decided I'd need a crane to get out of my house if I had a cook as good as Maria and recipes as good as the DeLaCostas.

Anna hardly looked at me throughout the meal and for some reason it was killing me. If I had a vulnerable spot anywhere in my armor of sarcasm, it was for unpretentious beauties who had their own deep seeded vulnerabilities. She was a grown woman, but something deep in her eyes displayed all the characteristics of an innocent child left at a bus stop, as if her emotional security had never kept up with her physical growth. Lonely and homeless, little understood by those who should understand her and less understood by those who used her for their own vanities, she seemed lost. There was an innate sense of attraction I couldn't define, but couldn't deny.

'Uncle Ray' kept my attention divided, talking about vineyards and the wine country of his youth. Tony joined us at the table, but kept his attention focused on the food and only nibbled, apparently aware of the pitfalls of eating too much, as well. I'd fully expected to see him running up and down the driveway several times tomorrow morning, no doubt as part of some physical regime. I was jealous. My idea of running these days was to the refrigerator for a beer during a football halftime.

DeLaCosta's post supper regime was to watch the sunset from his terrace, an activity that was growing much more to my liking as well. We adjourned once again to our chairs with cigars and brandy snifters while the women cleaned up. I didn't want to admit it, but my host was beginning to grow on me. It was obvious he was a man of means, but in his own element he also seemed unpretentious and pleasant to be around. Tony was like a venomous reptile that always seemed to be perched right off my shoulder, but aside from watching closely, he never made a threatening move.

"Do you like cigars, Jack?" My host was starting out on trivial subjects again, but I figured soon enough he'd get around to finishing what he started before dinner.

"I've never smoked much." I admitted. "But I love the aroma these are giving off."

"I have few of the real pleasures of life," He held the tobacco product out to inspect it. "But what few I retain, I guard very fervently."

"I could understand that." I nodded and took in the scenery. "I'd suspect this place you've carved out for yourself up here is one of them."

"This house and what it contains has been the pride and joy of my life." He agreed with a touch of sadness as he watched the sun set behind a nearby mesa.

"That usually is a good thing." I looked at him. "You make it sound like your going to give it up."

"I'm afraid I'm going to have to do just that." He nodded slowly.

"Why?"

"Because it's time."

We watched together as the world seemed to turn blood red with the land and sky blended into one another. Soon, the atmosphere turned to a deep royal blue in stark contrast with the cliffs below it. Stars began to appear until the night sky was soon a thick black blanket, perforated by millions of tiny lights. My thoughts turned from boyhood camping trips with my folks to Anna and what it would feel like to make love to her under such a sky. She was a distraction I couldn't ignore and one too dangerous to contemplate at the moment. A bug-light hidden just under the trellised patio came on from a timer and started zapping intermittently.

"An enterprising thief," DeLaCosta started tentatively and I knew he'd finally decided to tell me the whole story. "Someone you already have a picture of in your file, stumbled across a piece of inside knowledge concerning a shipment in transit from a showing in Rome back to the Louvre in Paris. He had no idea what the items were, except that they were unguarded and being sent by common carrier. He hastily assembled a team of professionals in his field to carry out the interception. Most of these professionals are also in your file, but I'm unsure as to their exact identity and number."

"Sounds like the stuff movies are made from."

"Perhaps, but this particular project only required minimal deception and skill, literally, just being in the right place at exactly the right time with the information they had was all that was needed." I watched him nod as he puffed on the stogy. Its burning tip glowed brighter in the night air.

"Still, you have to admire an artful thief, almost as much as an artful broker." I eyed him in the darkness.

"Quite literally, the best in each field was put into play, if only because the prize seemed so promising." He ignored my taunt and nodded in agreement, before pushed on with his story. "But this project involved an inside man and a blind snatch. They had no idea what they were stealing."

"A bunch of fake paintings?" I shook my head, thinking of what he'd told me before dinner.

"What they found in the crates were twelve of what seemed to be a collection of some of the rarest, nearly priceless paintings you could imagine." Ray nodded solemnly in the darkness. "Paintings that only a very small circle of ultra rich collectors would be willing to pay for, even though they'd have to lock them up in private vaults where only they could view them. Works that could never be shared at their cocktail parties or even to their most trusted friends, lest they be discovered."

"But these were fakes?" I asked again.

"Not your typical forgeries, as I commented on before dinner." Ray held up a finger. "For as long as there's been famous paintings in museums, there have been rumors of echoes."

"Echoes?" I frowned. "What's an echo?"

"Whenever a priceless piece of artwork, be it canvas, sculpture, even porcelain and jewelry is publicly moved, it is rumored that a decoy shipment of the same item is sometimes put into play." He paused to let his explanation sink in. "It is said there are artists that painstakingly duplicate great pieces of art and they are so good, only the most rigorous of tests can disavow their authenticity.

"How?" I interrupted.

"For paintings, one of the easiest ways is to date the materials used through a regime of tests. Only a very few art experts are left that can look at a masterpiece and judge it's authenticity by mere visual examination." Ray paused to explain, before continuing. "It is rumored that these echoes are commissioned by whoever owns the real piece, in this case the Louvre, to do just such work."

"The museum pays someone to paint fakes?" It didn't make sense. "Why?"

"It is speculated that these echoes are put into play, sometimes conspicuously transported while the actual artwork goes by unmarked courier with only minimal physical protection. Sometimes, as in this case, it's the other way around. Most of the time, those transporting it wouldn't know if their shipments are the real items or not. It's even been suggested that echoes themselves go on display in given exhibits." Ray nodded. "If the museum believes the real artwork is at risk in any given display, they may substitute an echo and rope the viewing audience far enough away that no one can tell. It's an age old shell game that most professional thieves believe has been going on for many years."

"That must've really bummed them out." I chuckled.

"But they didn't know they were echoes at first." Ray shook his head sadly. "They almost fainted when they first opened the containers."

"I'll bet." I reveled in the irony from a cop's point of view. "How'd they finally find out?"

"They split their prize amongst them, as they usually do, and trotted off to their respective brokers."

"Meaning, one of them came to you."

"Correct." Ray put the cigar in his mouth and puffed on it. "Three of the paintings were given to me to find buyers for."

"Did you?"

"Eventually, yes, but I sold them for what they actually were." He hesitated, before shrinking in his seat and twitching slightly. "Well, two of them, at least."

"That sounds a bit ominous."

"When I was approached and inspected the articles, I naturally undertook some necessary tests to authenticate them for my own piece of mind." He flicked the ashes off his stogy and ignored my comment. "I learned what they were and informed my… uh.. provider of my findings. Between us, we decided to get what we could for them, which wasn't much, and go on with our lives."

"But not all three." I could see something more was coming.

"I had a client," He sighed deeply. "Someone who had been looking for one particular artist's work for many years." Ray shook his head. "One of the.. uh… forgeries was a work by this artist. My client leapt at the opportunity to pay top dollar for what he was sure was the real artwork."

"So, you paid your thief the same amount as you did the others, took the price of a real artwork from the client and then 'retired'." I nodded in understanding.

"That would be an astute assessment."

"One thing's buggin me, thought. This all happened nearly ten years ago." I mused. "Why'd it take so long for them to go public with it?"

"I can only speculate that the museum did all they could do quietly, keeping the theft quiet to keep the existence of their echoes from getting out, until their insurance carrier came around to inspect them." Ray shrugged. "Lloyds of London's tactics are much more aggressive." Ray shook his head. "And deceptive."'

"Why would they care about the echoes?" I asked. "Their fakes."

"It's true that Lloyds interest in the them is peripheral to insuring the real artwork, but echoes are considered an invaluable tool in keeping the real works safe and are probably insured themselves. Without them, the premiums on the real paintings could quite literally triple."

"So these fakes are really pretty valuable." I concluded. "Maybe even worth a finder's fee."

"The door has been left wide open for their quiet return." Ray said softly. "And a modest fee has been proposed through my intermediaries. Since I got wind of what was happening, only a short month ago, I've been quietly retrieving the two echoes for the price given. With the finder's fee, I suspect I'll brake even on them."

"I suspect this is a no-questions-asked return arrangement?"

"You would suspect correctly." Ray nodded.

"And what about the third painting?" I looked around the patio. "The reason I suspect you're up here in the first place?"

"That one might be a problem." He nodded conspicuously.

"The person you sold it to is probably going to believe it's a forgery now. "I guessed. "I suspect he might have seem today's news broadcast as well and come looking for you."

"He may have been looking for me for quite some time now." Ray agreed. "That's why I'm out here and have Tony as a constant companion."

"Your dream home is starting to look more like a hideout every minute."

"That photo you no doubt have in your file is the real problem."

"I didn't take it" I assured him.

"That's what I'm worried about." His eyes glowed brighter with the reflection of the bug zapper arcing with another kill. "Someone did, and if you found me with it, that means someone else could too."

We both looked away into the night, puffing our cigars and thinking our separate thoughts. A halo was forming in the eastern sky and it looked like the moon would soon make its appearance. There were no big city lights up here to spoil the view of the night sky or the moonrise. I glanced back towards the slider and imagined, more than saw Tony lurking in the darkness. Now, his presence made sense. For myself, I decided I needed to look at the file again.

9

I decided to sequester myself in my room until I knew a lot more of what the file could tell me about the heist in France. I wanted to believe DeLaCosta, but all this fuss over some forgeries? Even if they were of famous paintings, this was just too much trouble for such a meager prize. Besides, I'd been so long in a job where everyone you came across lied, after a while you had a hard time believing anything anyone told you. Even a layman could see something wasn't gelling and the best way to find out was to research the facts with some independent study. The only facts I had at hand was the case file.

I winced as I pulled out the 45 automatic I thought must now be putting a permanent imprint in the small of my back. Wedging it just slightly between the mattress and box springs on the far side of the bed, I proceeded to lay the file out on the comforter and began meticulously studying it. Passing the pages that dealt with the disappearance of the painting in foreign languages, I pressed on into the dossiers of possible participants. Some had detailed backgrounds, mostly jewel and art thieves that had been caught or heavily suspected at one time or another.

Most had heavy European names, either French, German and quite a few English. There was a spattering of American possibilities, but I was surprised by how few. I thought this was rather disproportionate to a lot of very good thieves I knew of, or had heard about in the states, but if the heist had been as impromptu as Ray suggested, perhaps only more local professionals were on hand to answer the call. I noticed all the dates of the passport activity next to the suspects were centered around Paris on just a few dates in August of 1997.

The passport photos for the ones most suspected accompanied the data, along with all known aliases. It seemed unusual to see so many of them traveling under assumed names. That piqued my curiosity and I started looking at the pictures more than the names as I scanned through the dossiers. I was noticing something else as I read. The suspected thieves in the front of the section were very well traveled. Even in the short time-span delineated in the files, they were all over the place, France, Italy, Spain, the U.S., even Russia and parts of the Mid-east.

I looked up and outside the small slider on the opposite wall of my room to reflect on what I was learning. The sliding glass door was open, but the screen let the fresh canyon air drift in. There was a small patio just on the other side, but it faced a different direction than the large terrace and patio servicing the main rooms. The night was eerie and deathly quiet, except for occasional light breeze. The half moon still gave the sky the deepest of blue-black hues and it made the patio surface visible in its bluish light.

I looked back at the thick binder. There was no indication in the file as to just how many echoes had been stolen, but it was plain after ten years of quietly searching, nothing had surfaced, at least till now. The items could be anywhere, or everywhere for that matter. I pressed on in hopes of getting some feel for the case, outside of what Raymond DeLaCosta was telling me. Knowledge was power and although I was beginning to like my host, something about him still seemed off, like he wasn't telling me everything he knew.

I kept digging until I finally reached a portion of the file that dealt with known accomplices, perhaps including those who might be interested in helping these thieves convert their goods to less traceable assets. There were so many, almost a half-dozen were listed to each page with thumbnail photos and very fine print. Their dossiers included probably residences and places known to be staying at the time of the theft, along with passport activity around the same dates. I switched back and forth from the data on the suspected thieves, comparing them to the possible fences and quickly got the idea that this latter list had been compiled on the basis of the former's destinations immediately following the dates in August.

I studied each face and their passport data on every page, noticing how many had ended up in the states sometime around the dates of interest. On the eleventh page, I stopped and stared at the passport photo. The hair was long and black and the face was much thinner, but the features were unmistakable. Ray DeLaCosta had once been Dimitri Zontos, supposedly a Greek national traveling under a U.S. passport. He had actually flown to the French Riviera on one of the suspected dates in August of '97 and then to New York shortly afterward.

I quickly made note of the dates involved and compared them to the suspected thieves. Three lined up as possible and one was right on the money. They had arrived from different origins of travel and departed in opposite directions, both on the exact same dates. I studied the photo of the thief, a Frenchman with a dozen a.k.a.s.

I returned to DeLaCosta's file and scanned the skimpy data for more, but there wasn't much. There was a history of many other meetings with dozens of other suspected thieves and fences, but no arrest record. His name had also come up several times in connection with other high profile thefts and he'd been questioned on them. The passport had been issued only ten years earlier, but had nothing in it after his trip to New York, almost immediately after he left the Riviera. The last entry on his file listed the whereabouts of Zontos as 'unknown'. At some point after Zontos had vanished, Raymond DeLaCosta had sprung up. My guess was from someone selling new identities in New Jersey.

It appeared that Ray wasn't lying about laying low. The best forged IDs for starting a new life came from America, the great melting pot where people routinely started new lives. You could buy a whole new identity on the streets of New York or Los Angeles for bargain prices, a new life that included birth certificates and even open credit card accounts. The identities were mostly stolen from the deceased and therefore discoverable, but there were a few artists who did their homework and used crib deaths, therefore virtually giving the purchaser a whole new life with even a documented history that would be much harder to trace. All you needed was the price of admission.

I memorized everything on the Zontos file before closing the binder and turning out the light. The moonlight immediately invaded the room with a bluish shadow through the open slider that stretched across the floor. I lay down on top of the bed, staring at the rotating fan above me. DeLaCosta was a player, that was a given. At some point he must've become bored with the family business and decided to strike out into something more adventurous. He seemed more than well off to begin with to do this for the money, but wealthy people could get mixed up in all kinds of stuff. The expression 'more money than common sense' was frequent in my repertoire of quotes.

My eyes drooped, watching the fan rotate and give off faint shadows of the reflecting moonlight on the ceiling above it. There was only one clue I could think of that could lead me to DeLaCosta's real identity. The one true fact I knew about was undeniable, because it came not from Ray, but from Anna. The way DeLaCosta handled the wine and the bottle label confirmed their family must actually be in the business. The fastest, easiest way to find Ray and Anna's family lay not thirty feet from me. Somewhere in the house, there was an office for Ray and it had to be equipped with a computer.

I was formulating some half-assed plan to access the Internet when my eyes closed and I fell into an exhaustive sleep. My dreams bounced off hotels of self-induced nightmares to the soft touch and scent of Anna. I wanted to fold myself into her just rest for as long as I could. The scent grew so strong I began to swim in it and I started to feel her warm touch. Her hair brushed over my face as she pressed her body against me. The weight interrupted my breathing cycle. I finally awoke and opened my eyes.

For a second, I thought I was still dreaming, because a curtain of dark hair brushed either side of my face and I was looking straight up into Anna's coal-black eyes. They seemed to pierce my own in the shadow of moonlight stretching across the floor behind her. She was straddling me on the bed, supporting her weight with her arms on either side of my shoulders.

"Anna?" I whispered.

"Shh." Was the only reply, but it was unmistakably no longer a dream.

She leaned down and we openly kissed, passionate and eagerly. It felt as if we'd spent years making love with only our eyes from across a room, unable to touch each other until this moment. I reached up and drew her down on top of me. She was wearing only a shear robe, open in the front and like her hair, draping to each side of me.

Between the two of us, our clothes were shed and kicked off the bed, my jeans and shirt joining her shear lingerie as we slipped under the sheets. Our lovemaking went the way of all passion long overdue. The exploration was less tentative and more intense, as if we were trying to fulfill needs of a lifetime all in one night, but knowing no matter how hard we tried, it wouldn't be possible. Out of breath from our feverish pace, we silently gasped for air, hoping we wouldn't wake others in the house. Several times I had to cover Anna's mouth as she quietly screamed, coming to her pleasure while biting my fingers with tears in her eyes. I nearly passed out as I came to my own pleasure while trying not to make any noise.

The inherent danger of our liaison wasn't lost on me. I had no idea what the discovery of our lovemaking might bring, but as much as I longed for this beautiful woman, I felt my own pleasure strangely heightened by the prospect. For over an hour, we clawed and clung to one another, leaving the bed surrounded by discarded clothes, rumpled bedding, and strewn pillows. Finally, drenched by our combined perspiration and exhaustive releases, we slipped from our union and lay with our arms and legs intertwined.

As we caught our breath, I again stared at the ceiling fan, trying to regain my optical focus and bring the blood back to more cerebral duties. I tried to remember anytime in my life when I had felt such intense passion for someone. Nothing seemed to even come close. I could hear Anna's breathing subsiding and becoming more regular, but felt her heart still pounding in her chest against my side. My own was doing the same and I inhaled and exhaled deeply to restore oxygen to the blood supply.

I felt her breath against my neck as she nuzzled and gently kissed me on it.

"Thank you." She whispered and seemed to drift off into a deep sleep.

I became concerned that we'd be discovered if we slept together the entire night, but somehow ceased to care. I reached into my imagination as to how DeLaCosta might react, but the strange image of him in the diner that morning rushed by my brain. It seemed he'd almost enjoyed the attention I was giving her. Attention was one thing, making love to her was another and my concern renewed. Still, I couldn't move myself to suggest she leave. Actually, just the opposite was true.

My eyes flickered, begging me for sleep in an all in state of exhaustion. Blissful exhaustion. I wondered what a life with this woman would be like. Troubled by the aspect of it and even more troubled by the denial of it, I grew restless. My body ached for sleep, but my mind raced. My thoughts conjured a large wedding, with Anna's faceless mother and DeLaCosta standing in the front row. Ray's eyes were boring right through me, telling me it wouldn't last. My mind bounced off the thought and begged the question again, what would he do if he discovered his niece was in my bed?

'Probably drag your sorry ass out into the wilderness and blow your head off.' Came the semi-conscious answer. Dead in the wilderness. Worm food, but not before the buzzards had their fill. My eyes popped open and I stared straight ahead. Shit.

I looked over to the rare beauty I could scarcely believe was lying next to me, her breath regular and even as she slept in my arms.

"Anna?" I whispered.

"Umm." She stirred ever so slightly.

"You think we can go for another ride tomorrow morning?"

She moved closer and sleepily looked at me in the darkness, her wicked smile renewing on her lips.

"I'd love to go for a swim with you, my love."

I kissed her openly and passionately, now torn between what I really wanted and what was disturbing me on way too many levels. I decided I'd let the morning take care of itself. I pulled her closer and drifted off to sleep.

~ ~ ~ ~

My eyes opened as my heart skipped a beat, maybe two or three. The room was still bathed in moonlight and I had no idea how long I'd been asleep. I was lying on my side, looking out the open slider with Anna spooning behind me. Had I just heard the door to my bedroom behind us open? Was I dreaming again, or did I detect a rush of air flowing through the room that previously hadn't been there? My body tensed as my senses went hyperactive. I could almost hear someone else breathing in the doorway.

I apparently wasn't alone in the feeling. I felt Anna behind me stiffen as well. She was awake and seemed fully alert. I felt her arms and legs slowly engulf me, reaching around to grasp me as if she were preparing to climb on top of me again. Her muscles were tight, but her breathing had all but stopped, like she was holding her breath.

My hand slid to the edge of the bed and over it, fingering its way to the 45 auto. The hand searched and explored, but found nothing.

The gun was gone.

Now we were collectively holding our breath, waiting in the night for what would come next. My body froze, but my eyes searched the full range of their orbits for some clue, or something, anything to defend ourselves with. For the longest time everything seemed suspended in time. Nothing but the cool rush of fresh air flowing in from the slider and out the bedroom door could be felt. The breeze quietly sang as it hissed through the screen door. Inexplicably, I tried to breathe in the scent of the intruder to see if it matched the hotel shooter, but the draft was going the wrong way and there was no scent.

Finally, the door closed. As if the intruder realized we were both awake and only wanted us to know we hadn't been dreaming, he allowed the door latch to click shut. The draft ceased and the screen door's song fell silent. I waited but there were no footsteps to tell me if someone had left or was still standing outside the door. I gave it a very long count before rolling over the embracing Anna full on, drawing her head onto my shoulder and wrapping my arms tightly around her.

"Who…?" I barely whispered, but she covered my mouth with her fingers before I could finish.

"Shh." Came the hushed reply. "It was Tony. It's alright."

"Why…?" I muffled through her fingers, but she tightened them and cut me off again.

"It's OK." Her hand wrapped around my neck tightened and she drew herself closer. "Nothing can happen to you. I won't let it."

Who was protecting who, here? Did I need protection? Just what was going on? The only thing I could come up with was thinking somehow it had to be related to DeLaCosta's primary linage.

"What's your name, Anna?" I said as if I was comforting her instead of the other way around. "Your last name?"

"Giamoro." She whispered.

"Your maiden name. No, I mean your mother's maiden name."

There was the longest silence, until I wasn't sure if she had heard me or if her non-response amounted to a refusal.

"Carlucci." She said so quietly I could hardly hear it.

"Carlucci?" I whispered back.

"Shh. Go to sleep." She snuggled and relaxed in my arms, as if a great weight had been lifted from her shoulders.

Carlucci? I struggled to make sense of it. It was Italian, as was Giamoro, but neither rang any bells for me. Why was it such a big secret? I mentally shrugged and tried to go back to sleep. I gave the whole disclosure the Valley Girl's double 'V' sign for 'What everrrr'. This cloak and dagger stuff was starting to get old. I wanted to grab Anna and just drive off towards home in Ray's Hummer. The hell with everything, DeLaCosta, the case, the hotel, the stolen rental, the silencer in the night, the missing Carl Stapleton, and most all Melvin Croup.

No, I decided it would be worth one quick side trip to run by the shyster's office and punch his lights out. 'A walk in the park, one, two, three, easy as pie.' I had his pie. I was going to shove it right up his....

Anna stirred and held on tighter. My anger melted and I kissed her forehead. Why was the best in life always tied to the worst? And where was my 45 auto? I felt like James Bond's failed apprentice, James Stupid. Anna may have just saved my life by being with me. The flash of realization begged more questions. Had she curled around me to show Tony I was her lover and not to harm me, or was she merely shielding me from a silenced gunshot and protecting her lover? The circular thinking kept my mind racing.

Naw, I was starting up my paranoid machine again and it had to stop. Anna wanted to be with me and clearly showed it. Her passion was honest and real and it was paranoia to believe anything that intense could be contrived and acted out. Still, I wrestled with the notion, until once again fatigue overcame me and drifted back to sleep.

10

The next morning I rolled over in bed and Anna wasn't there. I didn't know whether to feel relieved we hadn't been caught or disappointed that we couldn't greet the new day together. Her scent still lingered on the pillows, so at least I knew I hadn't been dreaming. It wasn't much past daybreak, but it seemed late from the smells and voices coming from other parts of the house. Food was cooking and there was conversation coming from somewhere in the house. Nothing sounded out of place. In fact, it all felt strangely warm and comfortable, like a Christmas family visit with all the relatives.

But first things being first, I felt around for the automatic handgun that had somehow grown legs in the middle of the night. Even after sliding off the bed and searching under it, there was nothing but the revolver case. I even opened it, numbly hoping for the best, but the magnum was alone and still sadly devoid of ammunition. Shaking my head in dismay, I finally showered and shaved, then dressed before proceeding into the main room. It was empty, but Maria was humming in the kitchen, cooking bacon and eggs on a large stove. She only nodded as I detoured through, looking for the others.

"Great dinner last night."

"Gracias." She flashed a grin for only a moment and then it was gone.

Looping back through the main room, it was still empty, but voices were drifting in from the terrace. Anna's voice was distinguishable and melodic, but I couldn't understand a word she was saying. DeLaCosta replied in the same language that now sounded distinctively Italian. Although their words were completely lost on me, the tone seemed subdued and casual. I opened the screen and joined them, noticing a slight chill in the early morning air.

"Good morning, Mr. Hollister." Anna looked up and smiled in an expression of polite distance.

She was sitting in the chair I'd used the day before, wearing her cowboy hat and a pink shirt under a light buckskin jacket. Her jeans were loose fitting, with long pant legs that bunched up at her small boots, almost hiding them. I got the feeling this was her usual riding attire and she seemed at home in it. A glass of orange juice sat on her armrest and I noticed Ray, dressed much like the day before, was drinking a Bloody Mary.

"Mr. Hollister." Ray turned in his chair, as if slightly surprised to see me. "How are you this morning?"

"Lately, it seems every morning I'm able to wake to is a good one." I eyed my host.

"Did you sleep well?" He either didn't get it, or ignored the innuendo as he motioned to a third chair across from them.

"Very." I glanced at Anna and caught the slightest hint of that wicked grin on her lips. She kept it in check as she watched her uncle continue.

"Maria is making breakfast and I understand you two are going to do a bit more riding this morning." Ray seemed upbeat and relatively happy for some reason.

Maria emerged from the house with a glass of orange juice and a cup of coffee. She placed them on either armrest of my chair before I could even get settled into it.

"Thank you, Maria." I smiled and this time she giggled a bit before disappearing back into the kitchen. I looked at my hosts and shook my head. "Was that a great meal last night of what?"

"My ma-ma's recipe." Anna offered.

"Never had better." I admitted.

"Did Anna show you the waterfall from the canyon's rim?" Ray chimed in.

"You really have some spectacular scenery out here." My hand automatically went for the coffee as I dodged the question.

"It makes me so happy that you are going to give Politico a stretch of his legs." Ray announced buoyantly. "Alas, I've been so busy with other matters that he's grown, how do you call it, barn sour."

"Politico?" I froze with the cup in my hand and looked over at Anna.

"I told Uncle how good you are with horses and how much you admired Politico." Anna's true smile was having the damnedest time hiding behind mischievous eyes. They were practically dancing under her hat brim. "He insisted you give him some well needed exercise."

"How nice." I offered with an anxious smile. I wondered if a horse had ever been listed as a deadly weapon in an assault. I decided being tied to a stud like Politico would easily compare to having the brake lines cut on your car. I tried to beg off the offer as articulately as possible. "You know, as much as I'd like to, I couldn't. Such a fine horse needs a real master to appreciate it. I'm way too inexperienced."

"Nonsense." Ray waved off my concerns. "He's a bit high spirited, but once you run him out a bit, he'll calm right down."

"What county does he usually slow down in?" I replied in a tone more openly anxious.

Anna's smile finally broke out and it was so beautiful I almost forgot about Death Wish II snorting and stamping his feet out in the stable.

"Do not concern yourself, Mr. Hollister." She leaned toward me with the reply. "Politico will not leave Jezebel, so you will not leave me."

"Jezebel is the gray?" I hoped.

"Of course." Anna laughed a bit. "Did I not tell you yesterday?"

"You might have, but I might have forgotten." Slightly relieved, I calmed down a bit without knowing why. I looked over at Ray and changed the subject. "Was that Italian I heard you speaking as I came outside?"

"We often converse in our family's language." Ray chuckled a bit. "We slide into it without even realizing sometimes, especially with Anna being born in Florence."

"Really." I looked over at Anna, but she was watching her uncle. "I didn't know."

"I'm surprised." Ray gave Anna a glance before looking back to me. "That's usually the first thing she tells new acquaintances."

"Oh, well, we spent most of yesterday talking horses." I shrugged off any nagging suspicions he might have.

Breakfast came and we moved to the table under the trellised patio. Afterward, the tiny cups of cappuccino were passed out. I was growing fond of the drink and the company I was keeping as well. DeLaCosta was a gracious host and with Anna there, the whole family Christmas vacation visit scenario drifted through my mind. I wondered what Anna's mother was like. The small talk was a bit strange, since DeLaCosta wouldn't bring up the case in front of Anna and of course Anna couldn't bring up our current events in front of her uncle. So instead, we chatted about Ray's plans for the house and seasonal changes in the weather.

"Where's Tony?" I noticed he'd missed roll call.

"He's in the exercise room." Ray explained. "He spends an hour or two in there just about every morning."

"Admirable." I nodded, but they didn't get the slight edge in my reply.

"After your outing today, I was wondering if we might have a quiet word?" Ray looked at me in all seriousness.

This time it was Anna who froze a fraction of a second. I assumed from the look in Ray's eyes that it had something to do with the case, but whether he was oblivious to what had gone on last night between Anna and myself, I couldn't be sure.

"I've already saddled the horses." Ann seemed to think otherwise as she cut off any reply and downed her cappuccino. "We should start before the day becomes too hot."

"Sure." I drained my own small cup and excused myself. "I'll just grab my cap and meet you at the barn in a couple of minutes."

I took one last mad look around my room for the 45, but even after propping the whole mattress up, I couldn't find it. I knew Anna was waiting, so I finally grabbed my old ball cap and rushed out the door. In the hallway, I almost physically ran into Tony. He was walking from the back of the house, sweating from his exercise with a towel around his neck. He was still wearing a clean white T-shirt over his dress slacks and had another polo shirt in his hands. I wondered if the guy ever took a real day off.

We both stopped just short of colliding and made instant eye contact. I still couldn't read those opaque vacant holes of his. Having always prided myself in 'reading' people that way, I guessed that's what disturbed me so much about him. Of course on my side, my eyes were demanding 'where's my 45 auto, the bullets to my revolver, my car, and where's Carl Stapleton?'

There were no answers coming back in his expression. He didn't speak a word or twitch an eyelash as we just looked at each other for one or two very long moments. Finally, he must have remembered some vague instruction from DeLaCosta and became a veritable chatterbox of greetings.

"Mr. Hollister."

Now, I couldn't shut the guy up.

"Tony." My inflection mentally repeated my questions.

He nodded and backed a half step so I could pass in front of him.

"No, by all means." I backed a full step and bowed slightly, giving him the hall.

He returned the gesture and continued on ahead of me. We parted at the main room and I went out the slider, catching a glimpse of DeLaCosta sitting in his office at his computer. He looked completely absorbed in something and didn't even glance up as I passed by. I figured whatever he wanted to talk about wasn't that important and sighed a bit in relief. It made me wonder just what Tony told his boss and what he didn't.

I again found Anna in the barn, this time doing final tack checks on Politico and Jezebel.

"Was I that bad last night that you're already trying to kill me?" I walked up behind her.

"No, my love." She turned and wrapped her arms around my neck, pulling me down to her lips.

Damn. She could've strapped me to a really pissed off Brahma bull right now and I wouldn't have cared. I hated when that happened. I returned her embrace and we kissed long and passionately before our lips finally parted.

"Uncle would have been suspicious if we'd just repeated the same ride as yesterday." She explained. "He has been charged to watch over me while my ma-ma is away."

"And what has Tony been charged with?" I eyed her.

"With my Uncle's protection, of course." She said quietly.

"So, he thought he was protecting your uncle by coming to my room last night?"

"He... he was protecting me." She hesitated with a reply of obvious deception. "My uncle's obligations are his obligations."

"But he was too late?" I let it go and tightened my embrace around her waist.

"He was too late the moment I saw you in the diner." The wicked smile was back.

I had a comeback for that somewhere, but it got lost in another long kiss. We stood there in the middle of the barn, unwilling to move except to consider the clean empty stall just next to us. Politico, bless his black heart, reminded us why we were there. He sidestepped and nearly pulled the railing off the stall as he jerked back on his halter. Repeating the movement a few more times, the deafening pounding of the railing his head-line was tied to forced us apart to attend to our mounts.

"Show off." I approached Politico, calming him with my hands up in surrender, as if asking him not to kill me the second I got on his back. I looked over my shoulder at Anna, who was just getting on her gray. "First time I've ever looked for a seatbelt on a saddle."

"Do not worry." She reassured me. "As long as Jezebel is by his side, he will behave."

"So, I guess that means we're stuck with each other." I smiled as I mounted up.

"Now that I have you, you won't get away so easily." She smiled.

I reined in Politico a bit and was surprised at his reaction. He calmed right down and paid attention.

"You must have put an aggressive bit in his mouth this morning." I commented as Anna collected her own reins.

"I don't want anything to happen to you." She smiled more openly. "He hasn't had anything in his mouth but food for some time now. I'm hoping he'll quiet down before he gets used to it."

"I would have voted for a stud chain." I nodded and we were off.

Politico did a little dancing and showing off, probably for Jezebel's sake. Anna's comment from the day before mentally crossed my mind, 'men'. In the horse world, it was all too true. It made me wonder if my human counterparts had forgotten their more instinctual behavior after so many years of 'civilization'. The word 'domestication' came to mind as a suitable synonym. For Jezebel's part, she played the hard to get, hard to impress female, side kicking Politico a few times to establish her boundaries. Maybe my assessment wasn't so accurate after all. Women.

We were tracking the same route and my thoughts turned to what might lay out among the power poles that led to the highway. We talked about our plans for the morning and discussed an alternate route to the pool under the waterfall for the sake of our two equestrian lovebirds as they continued their mating rituals. By the time we finally approached the goat path on the canyon wall, they'd calmed down a bit. From the same vantage point as the day before, I looked hard down over the ridges where the poles led off into the distance. The air was clear of any of the circling birds I'd noticed the day before. Still, I reined in Politico and studied the area intently. Maybe it was just the workings of an overactive imagination. Anna misread my thoughts as she came to a halt beside me.

"We can ride a bit further along the ridge." She offered. "There is other path that is not so steep or narrow a few miles more. It will only take a while longer to get there."

"No, that's not it." I shook my head almost absently. "I was just…"

A bird suddenly popped into the air just where I'd seen several of them the day before. A moment later, two more joined it.

Anna followed my attention.

"What is it?"

"Those crows, or whatever they are down there." I was studying their activity as they played the air currents on their outstretched wings. What was bothering me was the position of their heads. They remained pointed down, reminding me of seagulls drifting over scraps of bait in a fishing harbor.

"What do you think they're doing?" Anna turned a bit concerned.

I broke my attention and looked at her.

"Anna, I better see what those things are up to down there."

"You said something dead was down there." She shrugged. "A coyote or something."

"Yeah, that's probably all there is to it." I looked back down the line of poles and then back at Anna. "But my curiosity is getting the best of me."

She looked at me with an inquisitive look, but didn't object.

"I'll just be a minute." I tried to calm her concerns.

"You forget." She half smiled. "Politico and Jezebel will not part."

I looked at the two horses and nodded.

"You're right. I forgot."

"I will go with you." She offered.

"Just a ways." I agreed, but conditionally. "When we get closer, maybe you can hold him while I walk down to have a look see."

"As you wish." Anna furrowed her brow. "But I have seen many dead animals before."

'What about humans?' I wanted to ask, but didn't voice my suspicions. Instead, I only nodded and we eased the horses in the direction of the soaring birds. They continued to dance on the canyon thermals during our long and gradual descent towards them, not noticing us until our mounts spooked at some unseen hazard. By the way their nostrils were flaring, I knew they'd found an unpleasant scent on the shifting breeze. We urged them on a bit more, but they finally protested and tried to turn back towards the house and the stables.

"Will you be alright holding them here?" I dismounted an agitated Politico and gave Anna the reins.

"He will stay, because Jezebel will stay." She nodded. "Be careful."

"Whatever it is, I think it's past the point of being a threat to anyone." I grinned a little, probably as much to relieve my own concerns as Anna's.

I walked on, side stepping the scrub oak and mesquite. The terrain was more forgiving than higher up on the ridge, but still challenging for anything less than a stout 4X. A picture of DeLaCosta's Hummer came to mind. The foul smell hit me as I walked over a small rise and I hesitated. It was the clear, overpowering stench of rotting meat. One could most often catch the smell at the rear of a market whose spoils section hadn't been picked up for a few days. My experience as a cop with it was much less pleasant.

The sound of swarming flies came to me next and I instinctively pulled my cap off and down over my face as a mask against the growing stench. Detouring down a small gully and around the next rise, I stopped at the sight of a pile of rocks. The flies were so thick it looked like they were consuming the small crag of land. Movement caught my eye just beyond and I recoiled a bit before catching sight of a retreating bushy tail. Coyotes. Whatever was dead lie in the pile of rocks not twenty feet in front of me. I took another step and froze. The sole of a man's shoe protruded over the rocks.

"Ah, shit." Was all I could muster as my shoulders sunk.

I looked around the area and then back where Anna was hopefully still holding the horses. Gratefully, she wasn't within line of sight of where I now stood. I took a few of the deepest breaths I could before walking closer. The cop in me searched the ground for any signs of a struggle, but constantly darted to the near horizons, unreasonably but instinctively for those responsible. It made no sense that whoever would dump a body out here would stick around for several days to watch it rot. But then again, the Lone Tree Hotel didn't have cable TV, so who knew what the sub-species living there did for amusement, besides maybe killing the guests.

I circled the rock mass and more of the body started coming into view. Both the shirt and pants strained to contain the bloating flesh within them. Parts of torn clothing were marked by red stains and jagged holes of raw flesh. I tried to get closer, but the flies and smell drove me back. The shirt was short sleeved and there were bloody gashes and gnaw marks on the black skin. The brown hair told me the dead body had once been a Caucasian male, but the flesh had turned charcoal from the lack of internal oxygen and the sun's heat.

The cause of death wasn't apparent, but the whole body couldn't be examined in its present position. Darting in for a better look, I saw there was no face left. It was just a mass of meat and bone, partially buried down in the rocks. Whether he'd been dumped like that or the coyotes had been busy I couldn't tell. Taking a sort of mental picture before darted away so I could breath again, I reviewed in my mind what I'd seen. I thought I'd detected the discoloration in his exposed arm that formed a pattern. I'd seen it before and recognized the man had gotten a tattoo sometime in his life. The skin was too crispy to make out what the pattern was, but it had definitely been a tattoo at one time.

His clothes were casual, slacks and what looked like a button down shirt. I immediately searched my memory for what Carl Stapleton had been wearing when we first met. I didn't recall a tattoo, but then remembered he'd been wearing a light button down long sleeved shirt. I had noticed it because the long sleeves had seemed unseasonable for the climate. What I could see of the hair color on the corpse matched Carl's, but again I couldn't see the remains clear enough to be positive.

Since Stapleton was easily the odds on favorite for the deceased, I didn't speculate much further on his identity. I took a few more breaths and darted back in, this time checking the pants pockets I could reach from his position on the ground. They all appeared empty and I had to retreat again for more air. As I stood and watched, catching my breath, I looked around the ground for tracks. I didn't see any footprints except for the four-legged variety, but I thought I noticed the faint tire marks of a vehicle in a patch of loose sand near the rocks.

I was bending over, looking at the tread marks when I heard her scream. I nearly jumped out of my skin. It was short, but very loud and I looked back up the ridge to find Anna holding her hand over her mouth, staring wide-eyed at the body. I ran up to her and turned her around, away from the remains. She seemed to be in mild shock, her eyes closed and arms shaking. I started leading her back up to the horses.

"I'm sorry you had to see that." I apologized, never thinking she'd tie the horses and follow me.

"Who was that?" She almost demanded through her fingers, still covering her mouth.

I debated a few moments before replying.

"I regret to say, but it's probably the guy I was supposed to work with up here on my assignment."

She stopped and turned in her tracks, looking up at me.

"Then it could have been you, instead of him." She looked me square in the eye.

"It almost was two nights ago in the hotel." I confessed. "I had a late night visitor who shot my sleeping bag and travel duffel full of holes, thinking it was me on the bed."

"Are you serious?" She looked at me, unbelieving. "Those holes in your jeans?"

"Yeah." I nodded and gently forced her further up the ridge. "Let's get up here where we can breathe without gagging."

"Who would do such a thing?" She demanded as we walked.

I didn't answer until we reached the horses. They seemed a bit skittish, no doubt from the uneasy scent they were still catching. The smell was now all over me, which didn't help.

"Let's lead them away and walk a bit." I suggested.

Anna followed my proposal and soon we were all walking four abreast, lead lines in hand.

"Anna." I started without knowing exactly how to put it. "I was sent up here to find your uncle and watch him."

"Uncle only told me you were visiting to do some business with him."

"In a sort of abstract way, he's telling you the truth. There's some attention being drawn you your uncle about some artifacts that have been missing for many years now." I gave her the skeleton thumbnail of the case, hoping she'd be able to fill in some blanks for me. "I've been sent up here to see if he's got anything to do with it."

"My mother told me he used to collect things." Anna shrugged. "She'd sometimes talk about him buying and selling artwork."

"How long ago?"

"A long time ago." She shook her head. "I was pretty young and didn't pay much attention to what my ma-ma talked about back then."

"Did he ever go by the name of Zontos?"

"Maybe." She shrugged. "For much of my youth we never visited him."

I nodded and looked around some more, before continuing.

"Anna, I have to get to a phone somewhere and call this in to the authorities."

"The police?" She seemed a bit alarmed.

"I can't let that body sit out there." I explained. "Whoever he once was, there's family and friends who need to know, along with explanations as to how he got there."

"You can phone from the house, of course." Anna volunteered.

"I think it might be better if I rode down to the diner and used the public phone outside."

She stopped and looked at me hard.

"You don't' think Uncle had something to do with this, do you?"

"I'm not sure." I stopped and looked back at her. "Look, Anna. I'll be the first to admit I like your uncle. I really do. I also think something's not right with that hotel down there. It's just…"

"Just what?" Her look turned accusatory.

"These missing artifacts are worth a ton of money and crimes may be involved here."

"My uncle is not a killer." She was defiant.

"And what about Tony?"

"What about him?" She crossed her arms.

"You think he's capable of something like this?" I watched her closely and her expression sank. I nodded slowly. "I'm not saying anything, but I can't let that corpse sit out there and rot."

"No." Anna seemed to agree, but then looked up at me very hard. "Would you ever hurt my uncle?"

"I've never been in the 'hurting' business." I looked at her a little surprised. "I've only been in the business of keeping people from being hurt."

Anna searched my eyes for a very long time, before she seemed to make up her mind. She bent down and pulled up her pant leg over her roper style, riding boot. When she straightened, she presented me with my 45 automatic. My jaw dropped and I looked at her for an explanation.

"I saw you had it at the pool yesterday." She admitted. "I sense you have no malice in your heart, but I could not take a chance."

"Chance at what?" I slid it from her hand and stuck it back in my rear waistband. "I only carry it for personal protection."

"For many years there's been talk." Her eyes softened in some sad memory.

"Talk?" I could see she was reluctant to continue.

"About others who wanted to harm my Uncle." She was holding back, but I couldn't read exactly why.

She fell silent and I thought better of pushing her, at least under these circumstances. I nodded and she came closer, putting her hand on my chest.

"I do not want anything to happen to either of you."

"You thought Tony was coming to my room last night to get rid of me?"

"I couldn't be sure." She shook her head and looked up at me. "I sense he has done things in the past without my uncle's knowledge, to protect him from what he thought were dangerous men."

I nodded and pulled her into me the rest of the way and we embraced for several minutes, both collecting our own thoughts of the past, problems for the present, and desires for the future.

I started to relive the door opening again in the middle of the night and remembered reaching for the gun. What if I had found it? I had been really edgy after the hotel incident. If Tony had really been armed with his silencer, there might have been a nasty scene, one with Anna caught in the crossfire. I gathered my resolve and gently pulled from our embrace.

"I better get down the hill and make that call." I advised.

"You forget." She forced the slightest smile. "We are together with the horses. They will not leave each other."

"Ah, darn." I cleaned up my response. "You know another way down, beside the driveway?"

"Yes." She smiled a bit more openly. "I will show you."

11

Lone Tree looked as if it had been caught in a perpetual time warp. Nothing had changed. The same cars sat alone out in front of the hotel and of course there were zero customers at the diner. Anna held the horses while I went in to get more change from Lorene.

"New color?" I nodded at her deep red nail polish while handing her a couple of bills.

"Yeah." She smiled and displayed the full set to me.

"Very nice." I smiled back. "I like it."

She handed me the change and I jingled it in my hand.

"You know, we need to get you a phone in here." I offered, suddenly struck by the odd circumstances of her existence. "How can a young girl live without a phone?"

"Tell me about it." She expressed her frustration, openly chewing a wad of gum. "I can't wait to get out of here."

"Anytime soon?" I stopped on my way through the door.

"Daddy says really soon, now." Her expression brightened. "Goin back to Vegas."

"Good." I smiled back. "That's real good."

Walking the short distance to the phone, I decided that this little rest stop could be something worth saving, if the right people came along and cleaned it up. The hotel would have to be gutted and of course the management would all have to go back to prison, but the place actually was kind of a time machine, one many people might come to just to get away from everything for a while. It certainly would make a good hotel for fly fishermen.

The same dispatcher answered my call at the Elko Sheriff's Office and I just said I needed to talk to Mitch. She must have figured it was a personal call and asked why I didn't call him direct. I played along and said I'd lost his number. She recited it with a heavy sigh and I promised not to bother her again. She patched me through, or whatever they call it, and Deputy Turley answered on the first ring.

"A call for you, Mitch." She said in an irritated manner. "You know, you should get your own switchboard operator."

She abruptly hung up on her end.

"Yeah, this is Turley."

"Turley, this is Jack Hollister."

"Mr. Hollister." He sounded surprised to hear from me again. By now, I was almost getting used to it. "I was by the DeLaCostas this morning like you asked, but the man said you'd left already."

"That would be hard to do without a car." I answered.

"That's what I thought, but he talked like you was gone for good."

"Well, I'm still here, but not from lack of somebody trying to make it otherwise."

"Huh?"

"Never mind." I dismissed the comment. "I've got some serious work for you up here."

"What's up?"

"I found a body up in one of the canyons off the highway."

"A what?"

"A body." I repeated. "You now, someone who used to be, but isn't anymore?"

"Where?"

"I'm not really positive." I shrugged from reflex. "I was on horseback and came across it from the opposite side of where the highway is."

"I need to know where it is." Turley now sounded anxious. I wondered how many dead bodies he'd handled out here.

"Does your department have a helicopter?"

"No, but we have a Med-Evac chopper that handles accidents and such."

"You might need it." I explained. "And some very serious four-wheel-drive vehicles. It's up in some pretty rugged terrain."

"Where are you now?" I could hear Turley's car engine working hard in the background. I took that to mean he was on the way.

"Where else is there a public phone for miles around this place?"

"I'll be there in just a bit." He advised. "I'll call it in and get the proper people on the way."

"Sounds good." I felt relieved for the first time since I'd left for this trip.

"Just stay where you are."

"Do I have a choice?" I shook my head and hung up.

I turned around and looked at Anna. She was still holding the horses next to the gas pumps with a worried expression on her face. Attempting a half-assed smile of comfort that could be described as weak at best, I started wondering what the full might of the Elko County Sheriff's Department looked like. I pictured a line of blue and red strobes stretching for miles, with military grade 4Xs leading the charge, supported by helicopters flying air support. In my mind, it was a beautiful sight.

"They're on their way." I assured Anna, but she didn't look the least bit relieved. "Would you like to wait in the diner?"

"I should stay with the horses." She nodded. "Will you be riding back with me?"

"They're going to want to know where the body is and I'm not sure how easily they're going to be able to get to it. I don't even know where to cut in from on the highway to get up that particular canyon."

"I can show them." She acted strangely defeated, like something inevitable was about to happen.

"It shouldn't be long." I assured her.

I had just wandered over to the soda machine to see what was offered when I heard a distant rumble. Looking up the road, I saw a line of vehicles across the whole highway coming our way, but there weren't any red and blue strobes over them. As they got closer, I realized it was the opposing team. It looked like a good two-dozen outlaw grade bikers on their choppers rolling in from the direction of Elko. I wondered how Turley could have missed them if he was anywhere on the main highway.

Anna backed away from the gas pumps with Politico and Jezebel and I walked over to help, trying to get them as far away from the noise of the oncoming bikes as possible. We watched as the full array of brightly colored, low-slung motorcycles slowed and made their massive turn into the hotel's parking lot. I mentally counted the bullets in my 45 and anguished for my extra magazines. I had buried them in the bottom of my duffel after taking my hiking boots out to ride in.

Our horses wheeled and fought against the lead lines at the deafening sound of the open exhaust, but Anna kept them under control and backed them up a bit more, until the diner wall was at her back. Dust rose and swirled around the slowing choppers as the leaders came to a stop in front of the hotel entrance. The others came to a grinding halt and killed their engines wherever they happened to end up behind them. Our horses settled down in the silence that followed, leaving us to watch the new tour group silently kick their old shovelhead Harleys onto their stands and dismount.

Every one of them looked hardcore, much like the three in the hotel the night I'd checked in. Most had the same crusty Levis with matching sleeveless jackets. There were bits of leather here and there, but mostly denim Levis and matching sleeveless jackets, everything signaling hard-core lawless gang bikers. I couldn't make out the patches on the back, but those that had them were all the same. They glanced over as they formed small groups and started walking towards the hotel entrance, but didn't seem the least interested in us, or the diner as they started filing through the entrance.

I thought we were going to be OK until I spotted Larry, Moe and Curly Joe in the pack. The tallest of the three, the one I'd dubbed Moe because he seemed to be the only one with half a brain, noticed me and nudged his two friends. When they started to walk over, it got the attention of a few others that followed. The ones I took to be the real leaders had taken the rest inside with them by now and the parking lot was quiet again. The approaching group gave Anna more than an appraising eye, but she was dressed down and covered up enough that they couldn't get a good look. One of the much larger, crustier new arrivals walked directly up to her and stooped a bit to look under her hat brim.

"Hey, darlin." He smiled with a mouth only half full of teeth.

"Let her be, Ace." Moe warned toothy with a side-glance as he squared off in front of me.

"She's nice." Ace looked over and smiled wider. "Like to take her for a ride."

"Not that one." Moe shouted with a shake of his head. "She's connected."

"Really?" Ace's smile faded, as he looked Anna up and down with a sober expression. "Too bad."

"You be that cop that was here couple days go." Moe stated as he stepped up to me, 'invading my personal space' as I'd come to understand the politically correct term for it. He was as tall as me, but had the wiry frame and lean muscle of a New York survivor rodent. I quickly decided that showing a weak front wouldn't work with these boys, but if I could start something personal with just one, maybe it would stay that way.

"My, Grandma, what a big memory you have." I stared back with a crooked grin.

"The one with the smart mouth." He spat, his anger rising. "You want to start something now?"

"Well, if I could borrow someone's harmonica I could probably get this little hootenanny going with a polka. Do you play the washboard or spoons?"

Moe made a move to close our distance and I backed a half step, calculating where I'd hopefully land the first punch.

"He's with me." Anna blurted out. "Please leave him alone."

Everyone stopped and stared at her, including me. Moe's eyes widened as he just stared. I wondered just how much juice Uncle DeLaCosta had here. I thought I'd test the waters as I turned back to Moe.

"That's right, Sparky." I smiled. "Since you're the one who does the talking for your clan, that must mean you're also the one who can count to ten without taking off your shoes."

"What?" He looked at me like a junkyard dog straining at the end of his chain.

"You heard me." I nodded at Anna and the horses. "See the horses? There's two of them. The black one there is the one I'm riding and that's Mr. DeLaCosta's personal horse. You didn't know that?"

"Fuck you." He spat, but didn't move a muscle more.

"Billie, get the fuck out of here!"

We all turned to watch Lorene stomping up to us. Not only did

Billie, formally Moe of the Three Stooges, back up, but also the entire group backed a few feet away from both Anna and me.

"But..." Billie started to protest.

"But fucking nothing." Lorene shouted hard and loud. "Get the fuck back in the hotel where you belong. I'm not telling you again."

I looked around at Lorene like someone had just performed a reverse exorcism on her. I thought she was going to walk up and start slapping every one of them like stepchildren. As she stormed in closer to the group, they all reeled away some more from her, like she just might.

"Get in here." We all froze and looked around again at the evenly given command coming from the hotel porch.

One of the bikers I'd seen leading the pack was standing just outside the entrance, looking at the ones surrounding us. His calm demeanor and evenly delivered vocal commands belied the look in his eyes. I'd have to get him and Tony together. That would be extremely interesting.

Every one of the bikers except Billie and his two shallow bookends immediately headed for the hotel entrance. The leader stood aside and watched as they all filed by him. As the rest fell into step, Billie reluctantly gave me one more look that said something like 'wait till after school' and turned to follow the rest. In a few moments, they had all walked through the hotel entrance and the leader gave me that same vacant look of Tony's before he disappeared behind them.

He had now left me standing between two women I absolutely did not know. I looked from one to the other without the foggiest clue what to say. I had at least a small handle on Anna, figuring something was going on between her uncle and these bikers whose hangout had just been confirmed as the Lone Tree Hotel. What I couldn't fathom was Lorene. Sweet, let me file my fingernails, can't make a decent cup of coffee, wish I were with my girlfriends at some Las Vegas mall, Lorene. I could only stare at her.

Before my very eyes, she transformed back into her former self, shrugging and smiling girlishly up at me.

"I couldn't let them mess with you." She tried to feebly explain. "You made me breakfast."

"I'll have to come by later and make you dinner." I didn't know what else to say.

The sound of a car distracted us and I looked down the highway in the opposite direction from Elko. Turley's cruiser casually approached and eased up to the gas pumps beside us. Lorene backed away toward the diner a bit and Anna moved up closer to me. Turley got out, straw hat and low-slung 44 on this hip, and sauntered up to us. He looked over at the sea of Harley choppers, but didn't comment on them. He gave Lorene a glance and she nodded without comment before walking back into the diner. That done, he finally turned to me.

"Can you show me where that body is?" He stated simply.

"I can try." I nodded and turned to Anna.

She looked from me to Deputy Turley.

"They must have used our old access, about halfway up, just before it turns steep and doglegs to the west."

"I know it." Turley nodded in understanding. "I have our homicide detective coming out in a Jeep with the coroner right behind him."

I watched their exchange and saw that personal touch again, that hint of history between them. When I first noticed it, there was nothing to be bothered about, but now there was. I studied Anna and then Turley for something that would tell me what was going on, but they gave no further clue. Deputy Turley gave Anna one final long look before turning to me.

"Hop in. I'll give you a ride to town so we can make a report."

"He's still staying as my uncle's guest." Anna interrupted and stepped to my side, putting her hands around my arm. "Surely there's nothing he could tell you except that we found him."

"I understand." He looked where her hands were and then at each of us in turn. "I better get over to the access before the detectives and coroner get past it."

"Will you let me know when you get an ID?" I spoke up as he started to turn towards the car. "Maybe I can talk to your homicide guy to see what he might have?"

"I'll let you know." He said with his back to us.

"I might have a lead on a couple dozen suspects." I tried to force his hand concerning the choppers parked next to us. "If you still have your notebook, the license plates are pretty handy right now."

He seemed not to hear me as he waved his hand and got inside the car. Starting it up, he eased back and then out onto the highway in the direction of DeLaCosta's old driveway. Anna and I were alone again in the diner's gas station lot. The horses had grown strangely quiet and even Politico seemed to say 'can we go home now?'

I turned to look down at Anna after Turley's car disappeared.

"Well, all things considered, that went well."

"We should return to the house." Anna became uneasy. "Uncle will be worried that we've been gone so long."

"I have to make one more call, first." I walked back over to the phone.

"Who to?" She seemed concerned again.

"My client." I commented over my shoulder.

"Who is that?" She stood her ground, but the phone was within easy earshot.

"I'm not supposed to tell anyone." I explained with a smile as I reached the phone and dropped a few coins in. I gave the operator the number and told her to make the call collect. Screw Melvin C. Croup. Surprisingly, he came on the line and accepted the charges.

"Where the hell have you been?" He demanded in his squeaky, trademark voice.

"Lone Tree, where you sent me. Remember?"

"Why haven't you reported in?"

"I was waiting for something *to* report."

"So, what have you got?"

"One dead PI."

"What?"

"Carl Stapleton."

There was a long pause.

"You do remember Carl Stapleton?" I said sarcastically. "The one you sent me out here to work with, but didn't bother to mention it?"

"I was going to tell you about that." I could actually hear him shrinking over the phone.

"Remember that office window I pointed out when you gave me this 'easy as pie' assignment?"

"Yeah?" He admitted meekly.

"I'd keep it open for when I get back." I answered. "I wouldn't want you to cut yourself and bleed to death on the way down."

"OK, OK, I should have told you. So what about Stapleton?" He tried to change the subject.

"Did he have a tattoo on his left arm?"

"He was in the Navy. They all have tattoos."

"Well, you better pull the file on his next of kin. I'll let you know when I have positive ID."

"Jeez, what the hell is going on out there?"

"I thought you knew."

"I sent you out there to find out. Stapleton sounded crazy with fear. Somebody had stolen his case file and things were going bump in the night."

"So you sent me out here blind."

"I had to get someone out there. Who would go if they even talked to Carl."

"Well, no one's talking to Carl anymore."

"What's DeLaCosta doing?" He tried to get back on track.

"Drinking lots of cappuccino and watching the sun set every evening from his terrace."

"Is that all?"

"As far as this case is concerned, it's about as far away as you can get from 'is that all'."

"Well, keep on him." He ordered. "Did he hear the news yesterday?"

"Not personally, but I heard."

"And what did DeLaCosta do?"

"He had an extra cappuccino."

"How do you know what he's drinking?"

"I'm having one with him."

"What!" He nearly screamed.

"I'd love to chat, but I'm out on a horseback ride with his niece and riding his prize stud."

"What the hell are you talking about?"

"Have to go." I smiled at myself. "I smell fresh cappuccino brewing."

"Hollister, you ass….." I hung up.

"Do you have *any* friends?" Anna was smiling from a few feet away, listening.

"He's a client and about as far from a friend as anyone could get." I walked over and we embraced with a kiss. "Besides, who needs friends when you have a lover?"

"Can we go back now?" She smiled warmly.

"We missed our swim."

"There's always tomorrow." The wicked expression was back.

"How will we explain another ride?" I grunted as I gave Anna a boost up onto Jezebel. "Is there another Politico I haven't met yet?"

"I'll think of something." She smiled openly.

"What's with you and Turley?" I tried to act nonchalant as I gathered my reins and mounted up on the black stud.

"What do you mean?" She suddenly wouldn't look at me.

"I mean there's something going on there."

"He… tried to court me." She seemed embarrassed.

"And?"

"Uncle would have no part of it."

"Is that all?"

"Yes, that is all." She turned and started for the road across the stream behind the hotel.

"Why do I not completely believe you?" I trotted up alongside her.

"But you must." She tried to put on a face.

"When will you tell me the rest?"

"Soon." She admitted and kicked Jezebel into a lope.

Politico followed and caught me off guard. Regaining my seat, I let the stud out a bit and we galloped over the bridge. We were heading for the driveway behind the crack in the mesa, but as we passed the ramshackle cabins I thought I caught a whiff of something familiar. I knew for sure it was out of place, but was so busy catching up with Anna that I let it go. I was letting too much go, lately. It was the price of being in love.

12

It was getting late by the time we got the horses unsaddled and brushed out. After everything was put away and all the livestock was noisily chopping on their alfalfa, Anna walked over to me and folded into my arms.

"I keep thinking about that poor man." She laid her head on my chest. "Did you know him very well?"

"I only spoke with him for a hour or so." I shook my head.

"It's scary how fragile life is."

"Tell me about it." I agreed.

"Nothing will happen to you." She cuddled closer. "I will protect you."

"I'd sleep a lot better at night if I thought you could."

She looked up and me and pulled me down into another kiss, before replying.

"I can, and who says you're going to get any sleep tonight?"

"Isn't that throwing gasoline on the fire?" I eyed her. "What if your uncle finds out?"

"I'm a grown woman and want a life of my own."

"You mean a life of *our* own, right?" I wondered if there was really any chance I could ever be part of it.

"Love me?" She looked up at me.

"You know I do."

"Want me?"

"In every way."

"Good." She said softly before we kissed again and slid apart. "Don't worry about anything."

What, me worry? I wasn't worried. I was scared shitless, but I wasn't worried. I had no doubt the same lot that had killed Carl had already picked out a similar rock pile for me in some neighboring canyon and I'd be next week's wildlife buffet. If anything could scare me more, it was the realization that I meant everything I was saying to Anna. It had been a long time since I'd felt so strongly about a woman in this way, but I really didn't know who she was. My feelings revolved around basic instincts and magnetic attraction, but I fully realized I didn't know anything about her.

I did suspect she'd want to clean up after what we'd been through and calculated Uncle Ray would be on his terrace about this time, waiting for his sunset with a carafe of his private stock. It might be a good opportunity to have a talk about why there was a dead PI in his old driveway.

So many questions had been building up in my mind over the course of this assignment that I scarcely knew where to begin. Aside from what DeLaCosta had already told me, it had all the appearances of a very simple case. Raymond DeLaCosta, aka Something Carlucci, Dimitri Zontos, had a history of dealing in artifacts of questionable origin. After visiting the French Riviera at the exact same moment an art thief happened to roll through from a heist in Paris, he'd simply disappeared from the face of the earth. A few months later, after resurfacing with a brand new name and buying half of Elko County, he'd built a nice little chateau on top of a mesa and become a recluse.

Everything I'd learned from the file supported what he'd confessed to the night before, but his statements about Carl Stapleton hung in the back of my mind. Like me, Carl had come into Lone Tree, thinking he'd hang out and buy a couple cups of coffee while he waited for DeLaCosta to show up. Maybe he'd snap some pictures and make a few notes on his comings and goings, but he'd certainly be no threat to DeLaCosta in doing so. Or would he? The one indisputable fact about Raymond DeLaCosta was he was hiding out. If Carl was perceived as a threat to Ray's anonymity, might not have Tony paid him an auto-a-la-silencer visit?

As far as I could tell in our brief meeting, Stapleton certainly hadn't found out anything about DeLaCosta. He seemed to know less about the case than I did when we'd met in Lorene's diner. So, why would DeLaCosta have Stapleton killed and thrown in a canyon? Why then, after taking a shot at me in the middle of the night, invite me up to his secluded Avery as a guest the very next morning? And why the hell was I calling it 'Lorene's' diner?

Something else had been gnawing at the back of my brain since I'd found Carl Stapleton's body. I was no forensic expert and I'd never worked homicide, but something seemed off about it. I couldn't put my finger on it what was amiss, but the absent tidbit lingered there like a golf ball on the edge of the cup, needing only a stiff wind to drop it in for a Birdie.

I mentally ticked off these disturbing little coincidences as Anna and I walked silently in from the stables. Once on the open ground between the barn and the house, she retreated from any signs of intimacy, apparently keeping up a masquerade of proper conduct between us for the sake of her uncle. Once inside however, she pulled me off to a corner in the laundry room for one last kiss before excusing herself to take a shower. I could see the invitation in her eyes to sneak in and join her, but I gave her a 'you behave' expression as she looked back with a seductive smile. After she disappeared towards the back of the house, I strolled out to the terrace, finding my host sitting exactly where I'd expected.

Disturbingly, DeLaCosta had switched to the hard stuff and I thought I detected the aroma of scotch in the air. He seemed to barely notice my arrival, as I casually sat in the chair next to him. Pretending to take in the view, I could see he was again deep in thought and something was troubling him. His moods had been seesawing over the length of my stay and it seemed to revolve around him either being in control of things or not. I suspected this was a 'or not' moment and with it, a change in the way he addressed me was eminent.

"How was your ride, Mr. Hollister?" It appeared I had grasped the situation correctly, since we were back to last names again.

"Eventful, Mr. DeLaCosta." I nodded to myself and looked over at him. After a moment he looked back and I brought my point home. "Look, let's get the name thing straightened out, OK? I'm Jack to my friends, all one, maybe two of them. My father's name is Mr. Hollister. To my bank I'm…never mind, but I'd appreciate it if you settled on one or the other."

"Our relationship does seem to be in a state of constant flux." He admitted with a deep sigh. "I apologize for that and would like to call you my friend, but you keep complicating my situation here."

"How do I keep complicating your situation, Ray?" I had no idea how he'd know about Stapleton's body so quickly, but then he seemed to know pretty much everything that went on around the place, almost before it happened.

He turned in his seat and looked back inside around the main room.

"Anna's in the shower." I assured him, guessing correctly who he was looking for.

"I am reluctant to broach the subject, because I have mixed feelings about it." He turned more in his seat, both towards me and to keep the slider in his peripheral vision. "As I've already advised you, I've been charged with looking after my niece."

"Is this what you wanted to talk about this morning?" It appeared that Tony had spilled the beans regarding Anna and myself, but it also appeared that Ray hadn't fully formulated what he was going to say about it. "I sense this has pre-empted that conversation."

"You are perceptive, Jack." He eyed me with a surprised look. "I do have something to talk to you about, but this is more important, for both Anna's and your sake."

"Sounds pretty ominous." I tried to play dumb.

"It has come to my attention that Anna has taken a liking to you." DeLaCosta searched my expression for any reaction.

"She seems to like me." I shrugged and colossally downplayed the truth. "We get along well and she's very good company."

"But that is all it is?"

"We're not picking out wedding rings, if that's what you mean." Apparently Tony had kept his report brief and omitted certain observations.

"That is well." He sighed again, this time in relief. "Anna's mother is extremely meticulous about the company Anna keeps and she was sent here specifically to keep her away from any, how would you say, romantic influences."

"Is this a residence or a convent?" I couldn't understand any of this.

"She's not allowed to talk to anyone but Maria out here?"

"Our family is very old world and strict about this." DeLaCosta advised with an expression that told me he didn't agree with it. "When the time is right, Anna will be betrothed to an appropriate gentleman with the proper credentials."

"Another race car driver?" I cocked my head.

"Race car driver?"

"The one she was engaged to. The one that died at LeMans."

"He was barely an acquaintance of Anna's." DeLaCosta shook his head. "She has only been engaged once and it was not to a race car driver."

"Who was it?" I was almost afraid to ask.

"A gentleman from another old and respected family."

"What happened?" I was trying to sound curious without appearing overly so. Someone didn't have the right picture of Anna's relationships here and I was hoping it was DeLaCosta.

"It was cancelled after certain facts arose."

"Facts?" I shook my head.

"My sister discovered his credentials were lacking and highly overrated." Ray looked away and took another sip of his drink.

"His credentials or his checkbook?" I replied.

"You are very direct, Jack." He pointed his finger at me and smiled. "That is why I like you."

"So, your sister is fixing to sell Anna off to save the farm." I shook my head in dismay. "An arranged marriage to save a bunch of grapes. What's she fixing to do, auction her off to one of Ernest or Julio's heirs?"

"You'd be surprised at just how close you are to the truth." Ray shook his head sadly.

"You seem well heeled." I looked at him with a wave of my arm. "Why don't you lend the money to your sister? It's all a family business anyway, right?"

"I have the bulk of my assets wrapped up in this residence and the surrounding property, Jack." Ray followed my arm. "The capital needed to revitalize our family business is much greater than I can afford."

"Where'd all your money come from, if you don't mind me asking?"

"I sold my share of the business some time ago." He stated flatly. "Since then, I've been investing my proceeds in certain ventures."

"Got out of it." I confirmed. "To go into art speculation."

"Among other things." He eyed me closely.

"Well, your sister sounds pretty mid-evil to me." I shook my head and determined that Ray's family might have to start getting used to some disappointments in life.

"Regrettably." Ray nodded slowly.

"So, I guess you haven't heard the news." I smiled a bit, thinking I'd actually be able to tell this guy something he didn't already know.

"What?" Something in his eyes told me he already did. Damn.

"The body of Carl Stapleton was found."

"That is most unfortunate." He tried to act surprised, even a little shocked. It didn't work. "How did it happen?"

"Well, either someone took him up in a hot air balloon and threw him out of the basket, or they killed him first and dumped him in your old driveway." I tried to look like a contestant on Final Jeopardy. "I'm gonna take a wild stab at guessing he was killed first and dumped there. What was that old line in the movie, buzzards gotta eat, same as worms?"

"I'm shocked and saddened by such news." Ray hung his head.

'I'm shocked and saddened that you already know'. I thought I might be pushing it to say that, so kept the observation to myself for now. "Kind of odd that he was dumped in that canyon you used to build this place with."

"It is remote." Ray nodded in agreement.

"Well, at least they didn't pollute the stream with him." I was fishing for any kind of reaction from him, no pun intended.

"I am sorry to receive such terrible news." He looked up at me. "Did you know him very well?"

"Since grammar school." I nodded, lying through my teeth. "Boy Scouts, through the police academy, Godfather to his first son, where do I stop?"

"Truly." His expression was starting to change to something more alarming, like maybe I'd take up a crusade to find his killer.

"No." I admitted with a knowing expression. "But I liked your reaction."

"You believe I had something to do with it?" His growing alarm turned more to hurt.

"I don't suspect anything." I shook my head, but kept watching him. "But, he did come up here to do the same thing I'm doing from his chair."

"Yes, apparently he did."

"But he couldn't cut it, as you said last night." I eyed him. "So, why is he laying on a bunch of boulders down your canyon and I'm sitting here drinking your liquor and smoking your cigars?"

"Believe me, Jack, I had nothing to do with his death." He looked serious, but I couldn't read him.

"What about Tony?" I cocked my head toward the main room just inside the door. "Would he do anything without you knowing about it, maybe like some unwritten Iran/Contra understanding between the two of you, like 'don't ask, don't tell'?"

"Tony would do nothing without my express instructions." Again, Ray gave me a serious look.

I eased back in my chair. It didn't make sense to me either. If nothing else, Tony seemed like a professional. A pro wouldn't drag a body down the driveway and leave it like that. Even a shallow grave out here would be a chore to dig, but a professional would dig it. Carl's body being left in the open only indicated two possibilities. Either the killers were too damn lazy to properly get rid of it, or they left it out there for a reason, like to send a message. Whichever it was, maybe both, it fit the breed and credo of the lawless biker. I looked at Ray and changed tact.

"I'd suspect there'll be some investigators snooping around up here for some answers to his death." I eyed him again. "Will that be a problem for you?"

"Certain aspects of my life I guard very closely, Jack." He regarded me seriously. "But anything dealing with their investigation would not be an intrusion. I have nothing to hide in that regard."

"And what are you two talking about?" Anna came bounding out the door, drinks in both hands as she handed them to each of us. She turned to me. "Maria is making my uncle's favorite tonight, Scaloppini in my ma-ma's special sauce."

"It sounds like you're buttering up your old uncle, my dear." DeLaCosta took the drink and smiled up at his niece.

"Maybe." She teased and looked over at me.

I did my best trying to send her eye messages for her to cool it regarding our relationship, but she wasn't getting them. I knew she wasn't about to blurt anything out, but at this particularly delicate moment, I didn't want to even allude to anything deeper than just riding partners between us.

"I should clean up." I took the drink from Anna and stood up. "We got carried away talking about this terrible business with the body and I forgot to make myself presentable for your supper. I apologize."

I sensed, more than observed, Anna giving me a strange look while Uncle Ray watched us closely for the first time. If he didn't know fully what was going on by now, he'd be figuring it out at the rate Anna and I were going. Part of me didn't give a damn, but the other part didn't know what was going on with the family tree and needed to know more before Anna got in some trouble with her mother.

"Don't be long." Anna watched as I moved towards the slider. "Do you need any towels or laundry done?"

"Thanks, Anna, I'm fine." I felt like a guilty lover stealing off in the middle of night while the woman slept. "I've got what I need for now."

"Excuse me," Tony was standing in the doorway, blocking my retreat. "Deputy Turley is at the front door."

I looked over at DeLaCosta, but he didn't react in the slightest.

"He's asking to talk to you, Mr. Hollister." Tony finished, looking directly at me.

"Me?" I asked and then realized he probably wanted statements from Anna and me about finding the body.

"Send him out, will you Tony?" DeLaCosta advised.

"Certainly." Tony left us looking at each other.

"Well, drink up." Anna motioned to the fresh drinks in our hands and we toasted nothing in particular before taking sampling the liquor, another scotch for Ray and a Greyhound for me.

"Thanks, Anna." I tried to sound proper. "You knew exactly what I needed. Perfect."

"Yes, I do." Her eyes openly darted from both of my own, flirting with a wide smile.

"Deputy Turley." I shifted the conversation at the appearance of

Mitch as he walked out onto the patio.

"Hope I'm not interrupting anything." He took off his hat, showing a seriously receding hairline.

"Not at all." DeLaCosta rose from his seat. "Would you care for some refreshment, a beer or something less alcoholic?"

"No, but thanks." Mitch held up his hand and looked away, like he'd be struck by lightening for even thinking about a beer while on duty. "I was just wondering if I could have a word with old Jack here. I got a couple of questions for him."

"What else can I tell you?" I said apologetically. "We found him just the way your people must have. Except for a few of my footprints you'll probably want for elimination, the scene is fresh and clean."

"That's kind of the problem, Jack." Mitch looked at me with a funny expression. "There weren't no footprints but yours."

"They probably used the solid rock face to walk on." I excused his observation. "I did see some tire prints in the loose sand and…."

"We've determined that he was shot several times with a handgun." Mitch blurted out. "About the size of a 38 caliber, maybe a 9mm."

"Yeah." I shrugged. "Sounds consistent. He was carrying a 9 mil when I met him at the diner. Probably taken from him in his room and then used on him."

"A 357 magnum makes the same size hole at a 38 and a 9, right?" He was still looking at me with an odd expression.

"Yeah, they do."

"And you were the last one to see him alive, right?"

"Right." I started seeing where he was going with this and started shaking my head. "But I also found him and reported his death to you."

"True enough." Mitch conceded with a nod. "But that way your footprints around the body could also be explained for another reason than dumping his body up there."

"Look, if you're even insinuating…."

"Ain't insinuating nothin, Jack." He held up his hand again. "Just being thorough in my investigation."

"Your investigation?" I looked around him. "Where's your homicide detective?"

"He's on it." Turley assured. "I've just been sent up here to collect your magnum."

"Why?" I looked at him incredulously.

"Only so we can do a ballistics test on it and rule it out as the murder weapon."

"You have a hotel full of bikers down there, the veritable who's who of ex-cons, and you're asking for *my* gun to do ballistics on?" My voice was starting to rise as Tony, Anna and DeLaCosta looked on with great interest.

"Just routine." Turley shrugged. "I'll have it back to you in a day or so, after the ballistics guys does the tests."

"Fine." I expressed forcefully. "I'll get it for you."

"No need." He held up a hand again, this time to stop me from walking by him. "Just tell me where it is and I'll fetch it."

"Under the bed in my room." I said in a deflated tone. "Unloaded."

"Unloaded?" Mitch restated in his own 'ain't that peculiar' tone'

"Unloaded?" I reiterated.

"That's kind of strange, ain't it?" Turley almost scratched his head in mock rumination. I expected Columbo to walk out any moment with his famous 'one last question'. Instead, Deputy Turley stood in for him. "Where'd the bullets get up and walk off to?"

"I really wish I knew." I looked at Mitch with a bewildered expression. "Just like I really wish I knew who shot at me in the hotel the other night."

"Somebody shot at you?" Turley looked only slightly surprised.

"Yes, with a silencer." I glanced at Tony who displayed no reaction whatsoever.

"Why didn't you report it?" Turley was looking at me again with that expression.

"I can show you the bullet holes in the woodwork and you can dig the slugs out to match them with your homicide victim." I looked squarely back at him. "While you're getting my magnum, feel free to inspect the bullet holes in my duffel and clothes. They look like 9mm to me."

"Someone shot your duffel bag?" Mitch was sounding more perplexed with every exchange.

"It was lying on the bed and in the dark. They thought it was me."

"Where were you when this was all happenin?" He studied me, now really curious.

"On the bathroom floor." I said, a bit exasperated. "Where I'd been puking my guts out for several hours."

"Why didn't you shoot back?" Turley shrugged.

"Because the magnum was in the duffel." I exclaimed with an open hand towards the direction of my bedroom.

"Mighty peculiar." He shook his head. "I'll have to check it all out."

"Please do." I nodded.

"Well, sorry for the fuss." Turley nodded to everyone else standing there. "Maybe Mr. Hollister should come with me while we do these tests?"

"That won't be necessary." DeLaCosta abruptly stepped up, almost between Turley and me.

I couldn't watch everyone, but it looked like they all saw Anna move towards me in the same way, almost taking hold of my other arm, opposite Ray.

Mitch looked at DeLaCosta, then at Anna's familiar movement in my direction. He glanced over at Tony before turning back to Ray.

"Well, if you'll sort of vouch for him and let him stay with you till the tests are done, I guess it wouldn't hurt none."

"I greatly appreciate your confidence, Deputy Turley." DeLaCosta became the gracious host again and smiled. "He'll be right here until you settle this matter and please do bring Mr. Hollister's firearm back when you've determined it isn't the one you're looking for."

"OK." He nodded his dismissal and turned to Tony.

"I'll show you Mr. Hollister's room." He led the deputy back into the house.

I looked at Ray and Anna, astounded and speechless.

"Jack, you look like you need another drink." Ray said openly, as a friend would. "Scotch?"

My stunned expression found Anna, but saw nothing but compassion in them. Numbly, I turned back to DeLaCosta and nodded.

"Better make it a double."

13

I spotted Anna this time before she was even in my room. It was dark and very similar to the night before, but tonight I wasn't sleeping. Current events were running rampant through my mind and I thought I'd go nuts if I didn't figure out at least one aspect of this mess I could only politely call a 'situation'. Staring out the slider into the darkness, Anna's approach caught my eye as she passed the light and threw her shadow into the room. I knew it was Anna immediately from the fast movement and behavior of her dancing silhouette, but it still shot a chill down my spine.

The sliding screen door made little noise on its tracks as she entered, darted across the room, and was in my bed within what seemed like the span of two heartbeats. She recoiled a bit when she found me sitting up with my back to the headboard, but pressed on and gave me a tender kiss. I gladly accepted it, as it seemed to be the only thing in this place that made any sense or was remotely friendly.

"Why are you sitting up so awake?" She put my face in her hands and examined it in the dim light. "Were you expecting me?"

"More like praying for you." I put my hands on her shoulders. "But I was also trying to put some things together. Things that haven't been letting me get much sleep lately."

"I thought I was the only one keeping you up." She smiled openly and cuddled in under the covers, putting her head on my chest. "I couldn't wait to be with you again."

"Is there any reason Deputy Turley and your uncle would be close to each other?" I tried to put it diplomatically. "I mean is there any business going on between them?"

"Why on earth would you ask?" She pulled back and looked at me again. It wasn't an alarmed look or accusative, but highly curious.

"Would Tony tell your uncle about us?" I studied her eyes. "Do you know exactly where his loyalties lie?"

"They are with my uncle, of course." She nodded. "But when such delicacies as my affairs are concerned, I do not believe he would say anything, unless he was deeply concerned for my safety."

"Huh." I nodded thoughtfully.

"Why are you asking such questions?"

"Because while you were in the shower, your uncle and I had a heart to heart about you." I looked closer at her. "And me."

"Does he suspect?" Again, she wasn't alarmed, but more curious.

"I don't think so." I shook my head slowly. "It was more like he was all-of-a-sudden worried there might be something going on between us."

"My love," She cupped my face in her hand again. "Believe me when I say the only reason I keep us from my uncle is so he won't worry about what he might have to keep from my mother."

"We talked about her, too." I conceded. "And about your engagement."

"My engagement?" She cocked her head. "They could not have known about it."

"To the winery heir, not the race car driver?" I narrowed my eyes at her.

"Oh, that engagement." She all but dismissed it.

"How many times have you been engaged?" My voice lifted in mock disbelief.

"Twice, my love." She stroked my face gently. "Alberto was my mother's fantasy that she could save our vineyards from bankruptcy, but Vincent was my attempt at freedom."

"Maybe next time you should go with a banker." I joked. "Better life expectancy."

"I think an ex-policeman would be a perfect love." She looked at me like she meant it.

"If we're still talking about life expectancy, you might want to reconsider." I shook my head. "There's even a good chance we might be consummating our marriage in a conjugal visit."

"What is 'conjugal'?" It was going over her head, but I hadn't intended to say it, anyway.

"More of my bizarre humor." I returned her gaze lovingly. "If I had my way, I'd handcuff you to me and throw away the key."

"I'd love that." She smiled widely.

"I'm still bothered about Turley, though." My face darkened with facts that wouldn't go away.

"Why, my love." She shook her head again, not wanting to see my mood change.

"I saw his reaction today when you grabbed my arm in front of him." I confessed. "Then, I'm almost certain your uncle knew Stapleton's body had been found before I told him."

"Why would he tell Uncle such things?" She seemed to be getting curious, too.

"If Tony told your uncle about us, he'd know *all* about us." I reasoned. "But he was only suspicious about something possibly happening. Your actions in front of Deputy Turley would only give that impression. Then, he seemed to know about Stapleton's body before I told him, and again, only the three of us knew because we were there. Unless your uncle has the Sheriff's phone lines tapped, it stands to reason one of you had to tell him before I could."

"I said nothing." She shook her head in confusion. "But, I was with you the whole time, also."

"For some reason, Turley told your uncle about us." I decided. "It makes sense, because I could see the jealousy, almost pain in his eyes when he figured out we were together."

"But why would he say anything to my uncle?" She seemed to be asking herself, as much as me.

"What happened between you and Turley?" I asked as clinically as possible, trying to keep any hint of my own jealousy out of my voice.

"He became interested in me." She shrugged. "I was driving back from that town up north and he stopped me in his big car."

"And?" I prodded, trying to keep a quizzed expression.

"He became interested in me." She seemed to shiver slightly at the thought. "He wasn't improper, but he was very, how you say.."

"Adamant?" I asked.

"Not forceful, but as a course of action you would not easily give up to." She searched her vocabulary.

"Adamant." I repeated with a nod.

"Yes, I guess that is it." She nodded. "He wanted to know everything about me, where I came from, where I lived, if I had anyone in my life…"

"I get the picture." I nodded.

"But then he learned that I was driving to my uncle's and he became very, how you say…"

"Concerned?"

"No, how you put it…."

"Frightened?"

"No…"

"Apologetic?" I was ready for her to start pulling on her ear to give me a syllable.

"Like wanting to know…"

"Inquisitive?"

"Yes." She exhaled deeply and smiled in relief. "He started asking me all kinds of questions."

"About your uncle?"

"No, more questions about me."

"What kinds of questions?"

"Mostly, my family."

"What about your family?"

"Where I was from in Italy, about the vineyards and my mother and uncle's relatives."

"Really?" I was out of ideas. Unless Turley had his pension invested in wine futures, why would he care? But then again, Anna was a natural for inviting curiosity, if not adoration.

"But when he tried to talk to Uncle, Mr. Turley was informed in no uncertainty that I was spoken for."

"Well, that might explain why he's calling your uncle about us." I nodded with a grim expression.

"Why?" She asked.

"Because we look like we're playing house after your uncle has ruined any chances for him to…court you." I put it in more tactful terms.

"Oh." She stared off a bit, considering what I was telling her.

"If he doesn't get you, why should I?" I restated more bluntly.

"Because him I do not love." She smiled dismissively at me and put her arms around my neck. "And you, I do."

"And you, I do, too." I said back with a smile.

"Good." She fell into my arms and we slid down under the sheets.

Our lovemaking was less frantic this time, as if we both calculated we'd have many other nights together. We slowed every aspect of it down, savoring every moment and committing it to memory. Every touch, every scent of our bodies mingling, every long gaze into each other's eyes lingered for what seemed like an eternity in our minds. Coming to our pleasures was agonizing, because we couldn't verbally express it. We held our breath rather than burst with the releases of pure bliss. It made me want to run out in the middle of nowhere and scream with ecstasy.

Instead, we'd melt in each other's arms between each orgasm, panting and drawing long breaths to release the energy it built up in us. Keeping our lovemaking quiet was actually more tiring than if we'd been allowed to howl at the moon. We'd sleep for periods of time, before one of us would wake and look at the other. When we couldn't watch any longer without touching, the touching would lead to fondling, arousal, more kissing, and the cycle would start all over again.

We would have felt seventeen again, but this was different. Having had the experiences of life behind us, having known what false feelings, betrayed trusts, and disappointment from higher expectations felt like, we both reveled in something solid and simple. With the experiences, came knowledge of how to please and where to touch, how soft or firm and where and when to kiss. There existed no book that guaranteed perfect intimacy, but if we could have written as we made love, we would have come close. In the end, our bodies gave in to sexual exhaustion and physical fatigue. Fully spent, we fell asleep in each other's arms, our combined essence making something completely new and different. I fell asleep thinking nothing could feel better.

~ ~ ~ ~

The sunlight woke me, but I felt lethargic. I wondered if there was such a thing as a lovemaking hangover, because that's what it felt like. The sheets positively swam with Anna's scent, along with the new one we'd made together during the night. I wanted to lay there for the entire day and just breath it. For a moment or two, I wondered why I couldn't. I was basically under house arrest, although if this was what it would be like, I wanted to be sentenced to it for life without parole. I eased back into the pillows and closed my eyes with a contented smile.

It was so quiet I could hear the water falling off the canyon some five miles away. My eyes opened and stared at nothing. It *was* quiet, wasn't it? No conversations, no smells or noises from the kitchen. It was deafly quiet. I picked my head up off the pillow and listened. Had everyone gone out for breakfast? For all intensive purposes, I felt like I was alone in the house. Growing more curious, I sat up in bed and listened for a good long period of time. After several minutes of strenuous eavesdropping, I still heard nothing.

'That seems awfully peculiar', to borrow a phrase from the good Deputy.

Moving over to the edge of the bed, I dug my hand, then my arm, down deep between the mattress and box springs. What the?? She'd done it again! I got up and tossed the mattress, not believing it. My 45 automatic was missing again and I'd buried it deep between the bedding just so I wouldn't lose it like the night before. Shaking my head in amazement, I tried to clear the cobwebs and think why she had taken it this time?

Forgetting about the silence I'd awakened to, I stumbled to the shower and turned on the water. If I had to face the new day, I was at least going to sit down to breakfast next to DeLaCosta with a clear head and not swimming in Anna's wonderfully personal perfume. I soaped up good and almost broke into song 'Oh, What a Night', but caught myself. I did mutter some lines from some old tune I couldn't remember the name of, much less all the lyrics. I fumbled and hummed as I cleaned up and shut off the water. Stepping from the shower I reached for the towel, but it wasn't there.

"Now what?" I said quietly to myself.

"Looking for this, Monsieur?"

"Shit!" I recoiled back in shear surprise at the man standing just off from the shower enclosure. I'd been so busy with my revelry that he'd walked right in on me.

"Meird indeed, Monsieur." He nodded with a crooked smile.

"Shit."

I looked down to see him holding my towel out in one hand and an automatic handgun in the other. Shit, indeed. The only relief I could muster was it wasn't my own handgun.

"I'm sorry?" I recovered, confused as to what he was saying, as well as to why he was there and where he had come from.

He looked down and then up at me again.

"I am too, but then you can only blame your mother and father for that, can you not?"

I looked down at myself and then back up at his somewhat cocky, smiling face.

"It…gets the job done." I was at a loss, but it was a bit unnerving that he seemed to be such an expert.

"I would think you'd want to cover that before we join the others." He advised with a slight wave of the gun towards the bedroom. "Unless you wish further embarrassment."

"Others?" I took the towel from him and started drying off.

"My, aren't we the inquisitive one?" His smile grew wide with raised eyebrows.

"Funny you should use that word." I frowned at him and recovered a bit. "It came up in a game of charades just last night."

He followed behind me as we left the room and I saw no way of escaping him for the moment. I had no idea what was going on, but his French words might be a good omen. What were the odds of holding a European convention out in the middle of Nevada? Of course, the word 'French' evoked the word association test with answers like France, Paris, the Riviera, and lets not forget my favorite, the Louvre.

I started breathing easier as I dried off and hastily got dressed. My best guess was that the Interpol posse had arrived and taken the whole house into custody. Once we got this all straightened out, I'd explain my part in it and after a quick call to my good buddy and bosom pal Melvin C. Croup, everything would be cleared up and I could be on my way.

By now, Turley must have run those tests and cleared my handgun of any involvement of Carl Stapleton's murder. Surely, the homicide dicks from his department had recovered those slugs from the hotel and would soon be hot on the track of the real killer. Perhaps a search of Tony's belongings would uncover the suspect weapon and the case would be cleared 'by arrest'. My spirits lifted as I slipped into my clothes and regarded my captor, still holding his gun on me.

"You don't have to point that at me with your finger on the trigger, my friend." I frowned a bit. "Didn't you go to some kind of academy and learn how to safely handle firearms?"

"Excuse?" He gave me a look that he had no idea what I was talking about. Perhaps someone else in his attachment spoke better English for all of them.

"Never mind." I shrugged him off and stood up, now ready to go. "Where?"

"The lobby, Monsieur." He motioned towards the bedroom door and I walked towards the main room.

DeLaCosta and Anna came into view as they sat opposite each other on the small couches there. Another man, armed much like the one behind me, was standing behind them. The TV on as it had been the morning I'd seen Ray and Tony watching the news about the paintings. Maria was in the dining room, sitting at the table alone. I noticed Tony was the only one conspicuously absent from the little gathering.

"Good morning, all." I addressed Ray and tried not to look too much at Anna, still thinking I'd give us away with a tale-tell expression.

They both looked concerned and serious, but not quite alarmed or desperate. Neither of them answered or barely acknowledged my entrance, so I looked at their guard and then around at my own.

"Well, you didn't exactly bring the whole army along with you." I smiled. "Who's in charge?"

"That would be me, mon ami." I looked up at the sliding door that led to the terrace. A middle-aged gentleman was just walking through it as he spoke. He had the same French accent, but more muted than my guard. I immediately found his face familiar, but couldn't place it. He saw my perplexed expression and seemed to find it amusing. "You know me, do you not?"

"I'm usually good with faces." I nodded. "You're not the French President, are you?"

"No, but one never knows what might happen in the future, does one?" He walked in and looked over his involuntary hosts.

I had a sinking feeling my initial assessment of who they were had missed the mark.

"Would it be a bit too optimistic to presume you're with Interpol?"

That got a laugh from the other two. I looked at DeLaCosta and now noticed his color was off, like quite pale. I wondered what condition his heart was in. I glanced at Anna and she looked very sullen.

"Allow me." The man cut off the low snickering from his men. "My name is Phillippe Mersant."

"Phillippe Mer...." I looked closer at the man and my face lit up. Shit, it was one of the thieves in the case file, the one who'd matched up with Ray's visit to the French Riviera.

I placed his face now. He still had that sleek French look about him, but he'd put on a bit of weight and now looked distinguished rather than roguish. I looked at the man standing behind Ray and Anna and thought I'd seen his picture in the file as well.

"Yes." He nodded with a smile as he read my thoughts. "And I'm most grateful that you have at long last helped in bringing me and my associates to this grand reunion with my old friend, Dimitri Zontos."

I looked at DeLaCosta and Anna and they both had just a trace of incrimination in their expressions. I put my hands up.

"I didn't take the picture." I offered my exasperated disclaimer to all in the room as I looked around it. "I just answered the phone and got this whole mess dropped in my lap. I didn't bring anyone to anyone."

"It is all right, Mr. Hollister." DeLaCosta spoke up in a sullen voice. "You are not to blame. Eventually, I knew this would happen."

"Indeed, you did." Phillippe spoke up. "As you have prepared quite well for any contingencies and have disposed of the asset very efficiently."

"I sold it along with the rest." DeLaCosta assured him.

"So," Mersant brought his index finger to his lips and pursed them, thinking as he studied the room and his situation. "Obviously, we have to know who you sold it to and formulate a plan for its retrieval."

"Hey, I'll go." I offered, having no idea what they were talking about. "Hell, give me the keys to the Hummer and I'll hop out for whatever you're looking for. I'll even bring back some burgers, with fries and milk shakes."

Mersant looked at me, as if he were actually considering it. The man behind me pushed me further into the room, a signal to shut me up as well as join DeLaCosta and Anna in another chair. He motioned to the man behind the couch to watch me and walked over to Mersant. Leaning close to his ear, he whispered something to him. Mersant nodded slightly and his eyes fell first on me and then drifted to Anna.

"My associate says there are a couple of lovebirds in this little nest." He kept looking at us both, but soon settled on me. "He says the bedding in your room positively stinks with perfume and sweat."

I licked my lips with a raw expression of guilt on my face before I even realized it. Damn, the only good thing about my life was I hadn't attempted to become a high stakes poker player. It would have been a very short career. Mersant was reading me like a billboard. I avoided looking at DeLaCosta, even though the prospect of Anna and I together was probably the furthest thing from his mind at the moment, I felt lousy about deceiving him anyway. Instead, I just kept looking at Mersant. I could see the wheels turning. I knew what was coming, but couldn't accept it until it was actually spoken. Slowly, Phillippe Mersant nodded and smiled at me.

"Perhaps stepping out, as you say, and running a personal errand for me wouldn't be such a bad idea, Mr. Hollister."

14

It was obvious that Phillipe was the leader of his little Corp of Thieves. As we all sat around in DeLaCosta's, Zontos', whoever's living room, our guards standing mute while he pondered in silence. I had no idea how he had found Ray after all these years, but speculated that the current open and freewheeling investigation Lloyds recently launched had shaken a lot of information loose on the streets. Figuring that something akin to my casebook had been distributed on an International level, Mersant had probably gained access to one and recognized DeLaCosta's picture. After that, it was only a matter of consulting his own European version of Mapquest and 'voila', if you'll pardon my French.

I couldn't say I was all that surprised, but I'd rather expected an angry buyer to show up on Ray's doorstep and not an angry thief. Ray seemed to be in the middle of something between two angry people and I just wanted to figure out a way to get him out of the equation. Maybe if I somehow could, Phillipe here and the buyer could go at it. Between the two of them, they could work things out, bullets or not.

Of course, the biggest question was why he had made the trip at all? Even if Ray could get all the paintings back, what was Mersant going to do with them? The jig was up and there wasn't anything to do but give the paintings back to the museum. Their only real value to anyone at this point was perhaps to give them back to the owners and negotiate the finder's fee. But nobody connected to the actual theft could hope to collect on them, lest they end up in the Bastille.

The only other reason Mersant might be here would be to exact some measure of revenge. Perhaps Mersant had discovered that DeLaCosta, aka Zontos, had sold one of the paintings as real and he'd been short changed on his share of the price. Then again, I wasn't sure from DeLaCosta's next statement, which threw me back into the dark.

"You got the money for all of them." He said evenly to Mersant. "I only took my commission as usual."

"Yes." Mersant's concentration sidetracked, he gave Ray an almost evil look. "That is what you've said."

"So, why are you here?" I had to second Ray's question on that one. If they had made a deal and it was settled out, why would he be here with guns pinted at all our heads?

"You know very well why I'm here." Mersant's gaze didn't falter.

I looked at Ray and could see immediately that he did know, but his silence wasn't exactly telling the rest of us. I glanced at Anna and she seemed to be trying to tell me something with her eyes. I couldn't imagine what it might be at the moment. Turning my attention to Mersant's associates, they acted like they were as much in the dark as the rest of us. As the room fell silent again, I figured someone should take a stab at it, even if it was a shot in the dark.

"Why don't you two sit down and formulate a plan to get the paintings back and negotiate the finder's fee between you." I looked between them. "You've worked together before, so why not put the guns away and get down to business?"

Mersant's stare shifted to me, but the expression and look in his eyes didn't. I took that to mean he had left his sense of humor in his other pants, perhaps the ones he'd left in France.

"Or not." I backed off any expectations of a peaceful resolution.

Mersant looked back at DeLaCosta with a fair amount of what I'd term as calculation in his eyes and slowly asked his next question.

"Ou est cela? Where is it?"

"I sold it to a collector in New York." DeLaCosta replied with a defeated look on his face.

"And the money?"

"I didn't get much more than the others for it." Ray shook his head and from where I was sitting, seemed to be doing a good job of convincing Mersant about the fee on what I suspected was the third painting. "I still only took the commission. The other buyers knew theirs weren't authentic. I'm sure they all checked the work out the best they could for themselves."

"All that aside, you're going to buy that one back, bien sur." Mersant said evenly. "I have my own buyer waiting and we will together resell it to him and make our fortune. He does not care if it is stolen or not. He only cares that it is what it is."

"It is what it is?" I looked at them both, completely confused over their conversation. "When you mix French with Italian, does it always come out Greek?"

"My client's not the type to sell things back." Ray ignored me, shaking his head at Mersant.

"I think he will." Mersant nodded back. "Especially when he is approached with the money to buy it back, no questions asked."

"I'm trying to tell you, Phillippe," Ray shook his head again. "This collector is not someone who sells things back, especially now."

"Indeed?" Mersant's eyebrows rolled up a bit. "But he still may not know?"

"I doubt it." DeLaCosta sounded certain. "It was all over the news."

"There is only one way to find out, yes?" Mersant turned thoughtful again as his attention fell on me.

"What?" I finally said.

"Who is this man?" Mersant finally came around to wondering about me.

"This is Mr. Hollister, a private investigator, sent here by the insurance company to monitor my reaction to yesterday's news." Ray explained.

"And you invited him up here?" Mersant almost laughed. "Tres Bien."

"I'm glad you're finding it amusing." I grumbled.

"Indeed," Mersant smiled as he regarded me. "It is fortunate you are here."

Our captor fell silent, as if playing some chess game in his head, looking at each of us in turn and even glanced over at Maria, sitting mute in the dining room. After a few minutes of silence while we all looked back and forth at each other, he turned to the man who'd collected me from the bathroom.

"Jacque, bring the other gentleman out here, s'il vous plait."

"Oui." My initial captor and expert on male anatomy left the room in the direction of the back of the house.

I locked eyes with DeLaCosta and noted the ambiguity in them. I saw regret, perhaps that he'd deceived me concerning his involvement in the case, but also saw disappointment, probably because of my affair with his niece that I had deceived *him* about. In my mind, I thought that made us even. But something else lingered there in his gaze that I couldn't decipher. I glanced at Anna and she was still trying to tell me something without showing it in an overt expression. Again, I couldn't figure out her look, either, but she acted like there was something she knew that might help our situation. At this point, I really didn't know what that could be.

A few moments passed before Tony was marched out with Jacque with a third guard that had apparently been keeping him company. He had duck tape around his wrists behind his back and then looped around his midsection for good measure. He didn't look happy. From what I'd perceived of Tony in the short time I'd known him, I was almost relieved for our captors that he was wrapped up like a liquor store clerk in a five and dime robbery. I would not want this man unrestrained and unhappy at me at the same time.

He didn't speak, but only looked intently at DeLaCosta. Looking between them, I couldn't read their faces, but after a moment, Tony looked away and stared at nothing in particular across the room. It was clear something had passed between them, but their signals were so good I couldn't see them.

Jacque and the guard who'd been watching him placed Tony on his knees and then on his stomach, making him face away from the rest of us. After that, they stood back and watched with their guns trained on him from a safe distance. Apparently, the signals Tony sent out in terms of his seriousness and capabilities were universally recognizable.

"Mr. Hollister," Mersant jerked my attention away from our predicament as he motioned to me. "Let us take a walk, si vous plait."

He opened the slider he'd come in from previously and stepped out. Jacque motioned to one of the third guard to follow us. As I left the cool house, the heat of the day hit me full force and I could see it was going to be another hot one. What I could appreciate of the DeLaCosta's lofty perch on the terrace at sunrise or sunset was lost during the middle of the day. Squinting into the bright sunshine with the tile work reflecting and intensifying it even more, we all felt the heat, but only Mersant commented on it.

"It is so hot in your country." He shook his head. "How do you live in such a place?"

"God given, I guess." I shrugged behind him. "Maybe He just wants us to get used to it for where we're eventually all going."

"And where would that be?" Mersant slowed and turned at my side.

"Where it's really, really hot and nothing smells too pretty." I smiled and squinted at him. "You should stick around and get used to it, too."

"You Americans," He allowed a slight smile. "Always with the jokes."

"We try not to take things too seriously." I commented, but let it drop, not wanting to push the envelope to see if he could actually laugh. I did find his lack of humor curious, though. "You must at least chuckle once in a while there, Pierre."

"Phillippe." He corrected.

"Whatever." A little antagonism might be useful, if not fun. "As a thief, aren't you ever curiously amused, thinking of what expression would cross one of your victim's face when they get home and open their door or safe, whatever, and see their treasured jewelry or art gone? That must bring some kind of smile to your face."

"I take no personal amusement in depriving others." Mersant shook his head in dismissal. "It is a living and nothing more. They are all insured anyway, so the only ones who really pay are the insurance companies."

"Thereby raising their rates, so we all end up paying more eventually."

"What your premiums are, my friend, I have no concern over." He shook his head. "Buying insurance is a matter of choice. Personally, I do not believe in it."

"What about your family?" I shrugged. "Your house, your car?"

"I have no family." He looked at me. "Women are for pleasure and the moment they become wives, they cease to be a pleasure. For the rest, I believe in room service and stealing transportation when a cab is not practical."

"Sounds like a fairytale life." I shrugged again. "Until you're caught and thrown in prison. How are those French prisons?"

"I have no idea, having never been in one." He mused, grabbing some far off memory. "But their visiting rooms are quite tidy."

"Me being here in Ray's, I mean Dimitri's house, seems to surprise you." I continued with the small talk, glanced around as I asked. We were walking in the direction of the stables.

"Knowing Dimitri's distrust for just about everyone, I would have expected you to be floating down a nearby stream."

"Disconcerting." I nodded as fresh image of Stapleton's body came to mind.

"In either case, there are more important issues to discuss and your unexpected presence may end up being of benefit."

"To who?"

"Believe it or not, to all of us." He looked at me. "Even you."

We reached the barn and Mersant signaled the trailing guard to stay put. Together, we walked into the shade of the breezeway. He looked around and I could see his thoroughly professional glance taking it all in, studying every detail and nuance of the interior. To watch a pro work, even under limited circumstances, was interesting. I pictured myself doing the same thing, only from the opposite end of things. I'd be trying to figure out how he did it and here he was trying to figure out how he'd do it in the first place.

His last comment hadn't gone unnoticed, but I judged this man to be one who'd speak his mind how he wanted, and when he wanted to. I turned and waited to see what Mersant would eventually propose as it was obvious this hostage situation would soon turn itself into some sort of twisted business arrangement. 'Benefit', in any thief's terms meant money.

"Now that Dimitri and I have become… reunited," He began. "I must keep him company while still attempting to retrieve a certain item.

"And that item would be what?" I turned my ear towards him slightly. "Some fake painting?"

Mersant regarded me with a slightly confused look and then an expression of understanding came across it.

"I see now." He smiled thinly. "You were sent out here without knowing why, were you not?"

"That's a pretty good assessment of my situation."

"Then you must not have seen the CNN broadcast yesterday." He mused.

"I was out on a horseback ride." I dumbly shrugged.

"I hope I haven't picked the wrong man for the job." He stared at me, as if he still trying to decide if I was that stupid or that much in the dark. He finally shook his head. "Bien. It will have to do. Perhaps someone can accompany you on your quest."

"Anna would work well." I offered.

"Monsieur," He smiled. "Please do not confuse me with a buffoon. To see one, you need only look in a mirror."

"Thanks." I couldn't argue.

I could see him forming the words for what he about to say very carefully. I knew it wasn't going to be a short story, so I waited for some hopefully deeper understanding as to why I was standing there… in Nevada… on top of a mesa… staying in an Italian's pueblo and talking to a French thief.

"A certain Tizano Vecellio painted one of his many works in 1538." He paused, looking around at the horses in their stalls. They were all watching us intently, probably wondering where breakfast was. Mersant hesitated, as if one of them might be taking notes.

"Don't worry," I followed his curious attention and dismissed his concerns. "They can't understand us, although I'm not sure about the black one over there. He might be psychic."

Mersant turned back to me, holding his breath before he released it with a sigh and another shake of his head.

"You Americans." He commented before returning to his story. "The work I am speaking of is known as Venus of Urbino. It is a loose rendition of Giorione's Sleeping Venus."

My mind raced over the preamble of the casebook that I now wished I'd studied better. Nothing he was telling me was striking a cord with what I remembered of it, so I showed little reaction and continued to watch Mersant.

"You might know the artist better as Titian." He read my ignorance easy enough.

I did remember the name in the book and nodded my recognition of it. However, I was still lost in a field I knew little, if nothing about.

"It was among the artworks we acquired in our little venture some ten years ago." He finished with a smile.

I could see his amused expression wasn't over his articulate summation, which was lost on me anyway, but on some fond memory of the job he'd pulled off so many years before. I felt compelled to correct him on the authenticity of the artwork he spoke of, but had a bad feeling about my assumption.

"You mean the echo of the famous painting, of course?" I took the shot, anyway.

I saw the answer in his eyes before he even spoke. In turn, he saw the recognition in mine, so didn't bother me with another correction.

"You should have watched the news broadcast." He shook his head in amusement again. "It is true that my colleagues and I relieved the museum of some precious forgeries they use to decoy the authentic works, but what they did not say until yesterday was that the real Venus had been on display with that collection of echoes in Florence around July of 1997." He explained. "There had been grievous concerns over security on the exhibit, but since Titian had been borne in Florence, someone in management at the Louvre decided to send the authentic Venus to the exhibit out of respect for the city."

"Somehow, I suspect that manager is no longer with the Lourve." I nodded slowly.

"Good assumption." He smiled a bit broader. "But another colleague of his has been a wealth of information for the right price. The mix up occurred in Florence and the real painting continued into transit with the other echoes after the exhibit. God bless the French work ethic. They have to be the most over unionized and laziest workers in Europe. They discovered the mix up a month ago when Lloyd's came in to inspect the Venus for a policy renewal. Then, the museum officials had to divulge the loss of the echoes as well."

"That explains a lot." I nodded in understanding, wondering why Ray hadn't told me the truth about the Venus.

"Of course, with a authentic priceless painting on the loose, Lloyds immediately put the full weight of their investigative resources to bear, employing hundreds of investigators around the world, usually working through third intermediaries to cushion themselves from publicity, to recovery the Venus."

"Me being one of them."

"That is correct." He nodded at me. "My colleagues and I had a good many paintings and split them immediately afterwards. I took my three and gave them to Dimitri. We had worked together before and I trusted him."

"But he's already sold it, like he says." I shrugged. "You got your cut and it must have still been a pretty one."

Mersant shook his head.

"He told me he sold it as a fake, but I now believe he already knew it was genuine. The price he gave me wasn't nearly what he owed. He disappeared from the face of the earth and that made me suspicious. I've been looking for him ever since."

"But you still made out pretty good." I argued for DeLaCosta without knowing why.

"A price on a forgery is nothing compared to the price on an original, Mr. Hollister." Mersant sighed again. "Besides, I believe he practically gave the painting away in haste at a fraction of what it is really worth, even on the black market." He looked over my shoulder to make sure his colleague was still out of hearing range and continued in a lower voice. "Right now, I have a buyer in Germany who knows the painting is real and is willing to pay a very handsome price for it."

"No doubt one of those collectors Ray, I mean Dimitri, told me about. Some rich bastard that puts stuff in a secret vault where only they can go and look at it."

"Exactly." Mersant nodded. "But I must retrieve it from this New York collector before I can sell it to my own buyer."

"Sounds like the guy who has it now isn't going to give it up so easy." I shook my head.

"That's why you're going to get it for me." Mersant looked at me and smiled. He did have a sense of humor. I just didn't like it.

"And why would I go?" I raised my eyebrows, absolutely certain I wouldn't like the answer.

"To keep Anna safe and happy." That grave, pardon the pun, expression returned to his face. "If you refuse to go or disappear on me, I'll have to eliminate her as a witness. However, if you do go and are successful, you and Anna might benefit well from your quest."

"What's to stop you from killing us all when I get back anyway?"

"I am not a killer by profession." Mersant expression turned incredulous. "I am a thief and a businessman."

"And Dimitri?"

"I'll admit I'm not pleased with him, but if he will come out of retirement and broker this one last deal for me," Mersant shrugged. "I will have enough money to forgive and forget."

"And his commission?" I looked at him.

"He already earned it with the first sale." Mersant smiled thinly.

"So, you're going to lounge around here while I go off looking for this collector." I shook my head, acquiescing to the plan. Did I have a choice? "Well, I can vouch for Maria's cooking, but good luck with Tony. You're holding onto a rattlesnake by the tail with that one. I'd expect to find you all dead by the time I get back."

"That is why he'll be going with you." Mersant shook his head seriously. "He knows I will be with Dimitri and that my old friend will sadly suffer the same fate as Anna if he does not do my bidding. Besides, I'd suspect he'll be a great help to you in finding this collector for you, since he never leaves Dimitri's side."

"You know," I shook my head before cocking it sideways to look at him. "I was just beginning to like this assignment. Then you had to show up."

"You love Anna." He regarded me and saw it was true. "I can see she loves you also. It is in her eyes."

"Not something you can put a price tag on." I shook my head.

"I think I just have." Mersant smiled widely for the first time.

15

I held onto the handrails inside the Hummer as Tony negotiated the steep driveway to the base of the mesa. He hadn't said a word since he'd returned from his own private chat with Phillippe Mersant. I thought it had looked a bit funny, him walking away from the house alongside the French thief, bound like a Christmas present with two guards flanking on either side of him. He reminded me of Hannibal Lector being escorted without the mask.

It had been a brief walk and when they returned, Phillippe and gone straight to where DeLaCosta was sitting, pulling his own handgun and standing behind him. Only then had Jacque had been instructed in French to cut the tape off of Tony's wrists. Again, there had been that unspoken communication between my host and his bodyguard, but once unbound, the man had remained docile and mute. One of the guards had thrown Tony the keys to the Hummer, while another had come out from the back of the house with hastily packed bags for both of us.

The real surprise had been Anna. Making a huge scene of my departure, she had rushed up to me and held me close to her, wrapping one arm around me as she kissed me passionately while the other had gone into my pants and under my shirt. Trying not to look shocked at the move, I felt something cold and solid drop into my waistband and then covered with my T-shirt. I knew what it was immediately, and mentally blessed Anna for returning my forty-five automatic. Pulling back from her lingering kiss, she seemed to search my eyes with another message, but again, I was finding her hard to read. It was somewhere between 'do what you have to do and come back to me' and 'nice knowing you, my love, good luck in your next life'. I wrapped my hopes around my first impression.

Now, we were tumbling down the driveway at a good clip and I could see the sharp corner at the bottom looming in the midday shadows. I tightened my grip on the handrail over the passenger window and glanced at Tony. He was expressionless as ever. At the turn, he kicked the wheel over and the Hummer's rear end swung out and lined us up perfectly with road leading towards the highway. We broke into the daylight and the hotel now loomed ahead. For some reason I started thinking of Lorene. At the moment, I'd be happy to watch her throughout the day, filing her nails and adding more polish above her demolished cuticles. That kind of day really appealed to me right now.

We made the highway and turned south, passing the hotel and diner. The bikes were gone and only the usual two cars sat out front. The diner was deserted and I decided I'd find a stray dog for Lorene to take care of. It would give her something else to do and add that finishing touch to Lone Tree, kind of an Ansel Adams theme in black and white. 'Last Stop' would be the perfect title for it and the mutt sleeping outside the diner's door would make it a classic study in still life. With the mesas in the background and maybe a full moon just above them, Ansel would have done the place proud. When we were past the buildings and Tony picked up speed, I got curious. Elko was the other way.

"Are we avoiding Deputy Dawg, or do you have a destination in mind besides an airport?"

"Driving will be quicker." He commented, one of many sparkling anecdotes I was sure to be in for. I started hoping it would be a short drive, wherever it was we were headed.

"OK. We go. Save tribe from Long Knives." I mimicked a Native Indian with a hand-sign that cut a path ahead of us. It suddenly reminded me of what Anna had said about the movie posters in his room. It was the only personal tidbit I knew about him "I hear you're quite the movie buff, Tony. You like any of the old westerns."

Tony didn't respond to any of the bait, but instead gave me the distinct impression he'd launch me out of the SUV when the road bordered some thousand-foot drop off along the way. I subconsciously started looking around the interior of the Hummer for a parachute.

"Sit back and relax." Tony finally said something, but didn't look over.

"Just trying to make conversation." I was becoming aggravated by his condescending manner. "Can I ask where we're going?"

"Yes."

"OK, where are we going?" I pronounced the words slowly for his benefit.

"Las Vegas." He answered simply.

"To catch a flight to New York, right?"

"No."

"No?"

"No."

"One of us is going to have to work on our vocabulary," I kept my words clear and distinct. "Because 'yes' and 'no' are going to get awfully boring as the day wears on."

"Don't push it." Tony's words were chillingly low key and casual. "If it weren't for Anna, you'd be scraping what's left of your face off the highway about now."

"Really?" I raised my voice, feeling the 45 under my shirt. "Well, maybe I'd have something to say about that."

Tony's fist was in my face before I knew it. There was a sharp pain and I was seeing stars, making me think for sure my nose was now pointing out from the back of my head. His hand was back on the wheel before my eyes could refocus from the Hummer's headliner.

"God damn…" My hand reached for the 45 handgun, but found only empty waistband.

"Looking for this?" Tony's other hand came up from the far side of his lap, holding my gun.

"How…" I looked at it and froze. Finding no words to finish my sentence, I instinctively wiped the blood now running from my nose.

"Shut up and enjoy the view." His hand disappeared with the gun as he placed it somewhere between his door and the driver's seat.

I had a lot of things I wanted to say right now, but none of them equated to living very long after I said them. I felt like someone trapped in a circle of prizefighters who were all daring him to keep up his remarks, promising a beating of a lifetime if he did. In that light, I did what came natural.

"Do we have anything resembling a plan?" My voice resonated from the nasal congestion.

"Have you ever had your nose and cheekbone broken?"

"My nose, once." I nodded absently, completely missing the threat.

I laid my fingers from both hands along either side of my nose and firmly pushed them together. It was a stupid gesture, having seen something like it in some movie, but it also seemed to be the thing to do, absent a nose splint. Tony didn't look over, but smiled slightly in amusement. I wasn't amused. I figured I'd look like a raccoon for the next six weeks.

"It's not broken, but keep it up and you'll need reconstructive surgery by the time this is over." Tony pushed the SUV up to around 80 mph.

"You know, Anna loves this nose." I tried to wrap her affection for me around my body for protection. All of a sudden I felt like a schoolboy threatening to tell on the class bully. "If I come back with a broken face, I'll make sure she knows it didn't come from running into a door."

"You'll be lucky if you come back at all." Tony said again in his unique simple way. "Besides, she's just using you."

"What?" I looked at him in surprise.

"Don't feel so bad." He glanced over with the first sign of emotion I'd seen on his face since I met him. "She uses everyone."

"What do you mean?" I couldn't believe what I was hearing.

"Oh, she likes you." He reassured. "But she's still using you."

"For what?" I said incredulously.

"She's been trying to escape her family for years." Tony shook his head slightly, as if it was the simplest plot in the world and only a nine-year-old could've missed it. "You're just part of another attempt for her to break free so she can have her own life."

"Yeah, with me." I defended.

"Suit yourself."

"What?"

"You believe whatever you want." He closed the subject.

I spent some time assimilating his comments, but still couldn't

The Carlucci File

believe it. Anna's passion was as real as my own. She was genuine and real, and if she had plans to break away from her family, I was clearly the path she had chosen to make that break with. I pushed the matter back in my mind, knowing our love was real. Perhaps Tony couldn't see it, or maybe didn't want to. Maybe he was jealous himself. I dismissed the entire subject and brought my thoughts back to the business at hand.

"So, what's in Las Vegas?" I pushed our agenda, heartened that he did have more than a two-word vocabulary.

"I think it would be better if you let me handle this." He advised, this time more reasonably. "If you even try to help, we both might end up in a lot of trouble."

"Oh, I don't know." My own inflection eased off a few notches and we started having what many people might term a normal conversation. "I've got some negotiation skills."

"Not with these people." Tony shook his head.

"You and Ray keep calling them people." I studied his face. "I thought he sold this painting to a art collector?"

"There are art collectors and then there are art collectors." Tony's face turned serious again.

"That's it?" I shook my head and offered an open hand. "That's the whole explanation?"

"Yes." He answered in such a way that it didn't invite more questions.

"Just checking." I fell silent and watched the scenery.

Wiping my nose again, I could see it had almost stopped bleeding. Feeling around it, there was little swelling and it still seemed to point out instead of off to one side, so I took it as a sign Tony hadn't broken it after all, just as he had said.

"The nose has a hundred and fifty nerve endings in and around it." Tony explained out of the blue, obviously watching me in his peripheral vision. "The shock of a light and sudden blow to it has the same effect as when you punch it full force and break it."

"Did you learn this in some bodyguard school?" I was still touching it lightly with my fingers, trying to assess the damage.

"You pick up things as you go along."

"Were you one of those institutionalized kids, orphaned and raised in the revolving door system of foster homes and reform schools?"

"No." Tony frowned, almost perceptively. "Just grew up on the streets."

"Where?" I eyed him. Tony looked over at me, as if deciding whether to keep talking of shoot me with my own gun. I thought better of asking and backed off. "Just curious, but if you'd rather not talk, I'd understand. It's just a long drive and I'm not sleepy, yet."

"South side." He turned back to his driving.

"Brooklyn?"

"Chicago." He shook his head slightly.

"How did you end up here?" He looked over at me again and there was that 'don't go there' look in his eyes again. "I mean, if you'd like to elaborate, but if it's going to be one of those 'I'll tell you, but I'll have to kill you if I do' answers, let's pass on the whole thing."

"Word gets around." He surprised me with the answer and I became hopeful I'd learn something about the man. "I fell in with some people who recognized my skills."

"Fighting skills?" My eyebrows went up.

"No." He gave me that look again. "'Keeping my mouth shut' skills."

"Oh." I took that as a hint and fell quiet.

We were clipping along at a good speed and I could see we were also dropping in elevation. I had no idea how long the trip to Vegas would be, but knew we weren't taking any major highways to get there, at least not yet. The landscape was slowly turning from higher altitude mountains and canyons, with its scrub oak and mesquite, to a sparser, desert floor and sandy terrain.

The road was a two-lane blacktop that wound its way out of the meandering canyons and then started to follow the low-lying desert floor. There were no rest stops and not very many smaller towns with gas stations for the first few hours or so. I could see the route Tony had chosen was well known to him from the way he knew just what speed he could use on the blind curves. I now realized this was their back way into Lone Tree from the more populated cities further south, like Vegas and LA. I probably could've found it myself if I'd studied my maps closely, but on a normal trip, a normal person liked to follow the established routes with an occasional Denny's or Village Inn for waffles in the morning and instant mashed potatoes at night. So far, I hadn't been able to describe anything related to this case, or anyone attached to it, as normal.

The drive was giving me time to reflect on my odyssey thus far and I had to admit it was anything but dull. So far, one man dead, one attempt on my life, one mysterious man with a past, maybe two, one beautiful woman who was becoming even more of a enigma as time went on, and one brazen International thief that had come out of the past with a definite agenda. Now I was teamed with what I could only describe as a seasoned 'professional facilitator' to recover stolen property, property as it turns out I'd originally been sent to investigate the disappearance of. But we weren't going to recover it, instead, we'd only be handing it over to the man who had originally stolen it. All to save a woman I was in love with.

I couldn't wait to try and write a report on this case. I did have to begrudgingly admit that some things were falling into place, but the loss of Carl Stapleton, the only casualty of this expedition so far, was still a complete mystery. Who had killed him? Had he gotten too close to Raymond DeLaCosta and been killed because he had, but if so, why was I still kicking? The thought crossed my mind that Phillippe Mersant may have somehow employed Stapleton to locate his long lost broker, Dimitri Zontos, and had eliminated him out of expediency. But, Mersant had already proffered himself as a thief and not a killer. If he had murdered Carl, he was lying and therefore disturbingly not to be trusted in his latest proposition.

The third possibility was probably the most viable. Perhaps Carl had just wandered afoul of the bikers and they'd killed him out of sport. The sloppy disposal of the body and manner in which he was murdered lent a lot of credibility to the scenario. It made me wonder about Elko County's murder rate and how many unmarked graves belonging to touring fly fishermen were dotting the countryside. What didn't fit was the silencer in my own attempted homicide. I doubted backwoods bikers used such sophisticated hardware, and if they did, why would they have to? The hotel was theirs. Why silence a shot in your own backyard?

The whole case was starting to take a circular pattern, folding back over itself whenever a part of it seemed to start making sense. I started longing for a mundane stockbroker's malpractice case, or maybe a tax fraud case spanning a couple of decades. Right now, either would be more desirable than this one. If nothing else, the danger of anything more serious than a paper cut would beat getting shot at and having your associates decorate the nearby canyons to feed the wildlife.

I pushed all these facts further back in my mind and started feeding a new fantasy to escape all this. It included clean sheets in a Maui condo with Anna by my side. Past that, I didn't care much what else happened, as long as it was far from here.

I must have dozed some, because the next thing I heard was a familiar soft beeping that brought me around. I looked out the window to get my bearings and saw it was turning dusk. We were still the two-lane blacktop, but I could now see a line of headlights and taillights stretching across our path on the not too distant horizon. Looking over, I noticed Tony hadn't moved a muscle except to turn the steering wheel or the re-angle of his foot on the accelerator.

"Where are we?" I stretched and looked around.

"That's I-15 ahead of us." He nodded at the line of lights and glanced in his rearview mirror. "We'll be making Vegas soon."

"Good." I answered without having any idea why it was, except for my stomach that was starting to growl.

"Your cell phone service just came back." He commented without inflection, nodding towards my lap.

"Is that what that was?" I searched around, feeling my pockets until I found the strange lump in one of them. "I'd completely forgotten I had it."

"Do you have roaming now?" He asked, strangely polite.

"Probably." I fumbled with it as I dug it out of the pocket and opened the faceplate.

"Here, let me take a look." He casually offered an open hand.

"I think it's on roaming, now." I squinted in the failing light as I tried to make sense of it. Without thinking, I handed it to Tony.

He looked at it and nodded.

"Oh, yeah, you're back on line now." He rolled down the Hummer's window and tossed it out.

"What the… Hey?" Was all I could manage.

"You're not going to need it." He looked over at me. "You're with me."

"That's anything, but comforting." I protested. "That was an expensive phone."

"Did it take pictures and all?" Tony was looking in his rearview mirror again as he asked.

"It even had Internet." I complained.

"Relax." He cut me off. "Ray will buy you a new one, provided we all make it out of this."

"I have a client to report to." I caught myself almost whining.

"Not until this is over, you don't." Tony shook his head. "If you say anything to anybody before we do what we have to do here, we all may end up dead."

"Is Mersant that dangerous?"

"No." He shook his head and even in the dark I could see a new expression I'd never thought I'd see on the man: concern. "But the people we're going to see are."

"Shit." I deflated as I watched the highway get closer. "Any chance of stopping for some coffee or something?"

"Soon." He nodded, looking up at his mirror again.

I finally noticed and looked behind us.

"What do you keep looking at?"

"We're being followed." Tony said simply.

"By who?" I searched the road behind us and now saw a lonely pair of headlights several miles back. There were no other cars on the road, but we'd come a long way and passed through a couple of small bergs during the portions of the trip I could consciously remember. "How do you know?"

"He's been pacing us since we left Lone Tree." Tony confirmed. "I wasn't positive until now."

"Why now?" I looked back again.

"He's closing, now that we're reaching the Interstate."

"Who is he?"

Tony looked over at me with that same serious look.

"Now that's really the million dollar question, isn't it?"

16

Las Vegas really never made sense to me. Why would someone go traipsing halfway across a desert wasteland to lose all their money when they could just as easily go around the corner to a convenient justice of the peace? Even worse, you could lose everything the first night in the gambling mecca, thereby royally flushing yourself without so much as getting kissed. At least with a marriage you got a honeymoon with lots of kissing before, some during, and then a little peck on the cheek just before the divorce when you really got screwed. Lets face it, both avenues were a roll of the dice, but I did have to give Vegas credit for recognizing these alternatives, since there were almost as many wedding chapels in town as there were casinos.

Interestingly, Tony only teased me with the bright lights along the Vegas Strip as we skirted that part of town on the Interstate during our arrival. It was early evening by the time we eventually exited onto a boulevard I'd never heard of and drove in the opposite direction of all the brightest lights. Of the few times I'd visited the city, I had to admit I'd never gotten off the Strip, except maybe for a quick trip down to Fremont Street to visit the older section of town with some of its original casinos. I was struck immediately by how LA'ish it looked. Same traffic lights, same street lighting, and the same asphalt any major city across the nation would have. I caught myself wondering why I'd expect anything different.

My musing over residency was cut short by a few turns Tony made, taking us off the main thoroughfare and onto some quiet side streets. The neighborhoods were anything but ordinary on the ones he had chosen. Large homes loomed on either side of the streets as we wove our way deeper into what looked like the 'Beverly Hills' equivalent of town. The biggest difference here in the desert was most of the front yards had no lawns. Colorful rock landscaping surrounded ground lit palm trees and other vegetation that didn't need large amounts of water to flourish.

I took it all in, noticing that Tony was keeping a watchful eye on the rear view mirror. He said nothing and signaled even less, but I glanced back myself occasionally to see if we had any shadows behind us. I saw none and took that to mean we'd lost our tail somewhere along our gradual descent into the hell of an August baked Las Vegas. There was only one possibility I could think of for who it could be, and that would be Jacque or another one of Mersant's men to keep an eye on us. It only made sense with so much at stake.

I thought about asking Tony where he was going and almost verbalized it, but he acted like a man on a mission and seemed to have an itinerary all laid out for us. I couldn't comprehend how such a plan could have been devised between him and his boss without a word, gesture, or expression, but he and DeLaCosta had seemed to manage just that, so I let him roll with it. The idea that they might have had it all worked out months, maybe years in advance, like some fail-safe device, did come to mind as Tony took more turns into the plush neighborhood.

I started to regret the use of such of an ominous phrase as Tony finally took a fast left onto a very short dead end street. Before us, a large gate loomed on a brightly lit cul-de-sac, while more lighting glowed skyward beyond the ornate iron barrier. It was obvious some sort of secluded estate hid behind a small knoll on the other side, but just who lived there only Tony seemed to know. Without hesitation, he drove straight up to the call box and pressed the button. Instead of a voice answering, a small green light on the device lit up, apparently signaling the line was now open and that if someone had something to say, now was the time to say it. It reminded me of a speakeasy where the eye would look out from the peephole and wait for the password.

"It's Tony." He said as he looked openly into the lens mounted on the gate frame.

After a considerable silence a male voice answered.

"Who's with you?"

"He's alright." Tony cocked his head back towards me, but kept facing the camera lens.

There was a pause before the green light went out and the gates started to slowly open. 'That was it?' I asked myself. 'It's Tony' is the password? As we entered the grounds and started weaving around the richly watered lawns that would make any golf course green with envy, I couldn't stay quiet any longer.

"Are these friends of Ray's?"

"It would be much better if you didn't say a word from about now, until the time these gates start closing behind us as we leave." He looked over with that very serious expression again. "Whatever you see or hear, or think you see or think you hear, don't see it, and don't hear it. In fact, don't even think it."

"Oh, OK." I nodded nonchalantly in understatement. "I feel better now. For a second there you had me worried."

"Sarcasm here is something that will get you planted much faster than anything else." He added. "You do not want to anger these people."

"Then I'm a dead man." I shrugged to myself.

"Not if you just shut up."

The house, if you wanted to call it that instead of a hotel, finally came into view. It was low-lying architecture with lots of sloping angles in earthen stucco. Lights blazed almost like a Hollywood premiere, illuminating the grounds in every direction outward from the house. There were several cars around the front door, most ultra-expensive with a Mercedes limo to round out the stable. The place signaled money in capital letters. In comparison, DeLaCosta's Hummer, which could easily be traded in for the whole cost of the town of Lone Tree, now looked like a Vespa on a Harley Davidson sales lot.

Tony parked the SUV as close to the entrance as possible and got out. I followed his lead, not knowing what else to do.

"You know, if it's going to be awkward for you in there with me along, I'll be happy to wait in the car." I offered.

"No." Tony signaled me to follow him towards the front door. "People sitting in cars make them nervous."

"You just had to say that, didn't you?" I shook my head and fell in behind him as we walked.

The front door opened before we could knock or ring a bell. Two men, looking every bit as competent and serious as Tony, walked out on the porch. Same stature, same look in their eyes, even the same dress code for the most part.

"Tony?" The older one addressed him in a questioning manner, while the other looked me up and down.

"Abe." Tony nodded back in greeting.

Both Abe and his partner turned their attention my way as if I were an unwelcome pest. The one who hadn't spoken started to move around behind me as Abe squared off in my face with a suspicious look on his eyes.

"He's clean." Tony shook them off and they both looked back at him with curious expressions. Reluctantly, they seemed to take his word for it and assumed their prior positions on the porch.

Abe turned his attention back to Tony.

"This is unexpected." He clasped his hands in front of him. "You know the old man doesn't like surprises."

"It couldn't be helped." Tony shook his head. "I'll explain when I see him."

"It's card night." The man frowned. "Depending on if he's winning or not, it might not be such a good time."

"Maybe we should see, before we go barging in on him like this?" I blurted out and turned partially towards Tony. "If he's having a bad night, we can always come back tomorrow."

All three looked at me like I was an alien. After the awkward silence, Abe turned back to Tony with an inquisitive look on his face and waited for an explanation.

"Nick's in trouble." Tony stated simply to the unasked question.

"Trouble?" Abe cocked his head.

"He's got some unwelcome guests up at his place right now." Tony admitted. "At the moment, he's collateral on a business deal."

"How'd that happen?" The man's tone turned strangely accusatory, as if they'd gone to the same bodyguard school and Tony had just flunked his final exam.

"Pre-dawn, four guns, and no perimeter security." Tony again reported flatly.

"Seasoned?"

"No, but they're all stealthy little pricks." Tony advised.

"I'm still surprised you let it happen." The man pursed his lips a bit, examining Tony with a critical eye.

"Complacency, old age, whatever." Tony shrugged off any further explanation. "I need to see the old man."

"OK." Abe nodded thoughtfully, as if to say 'it's your funeral' and looked suspiciously at me again. "What about this?"

"He can wait in another room." Tony answered without looking over at me.

"You're vouching for him, then?" Again, Abe looked a bit surprised.

"He's Anna's latest." Tony advised.

Abe looked at me again, this time with a bit of shock in his expression.

"This?" He said as if he was sadly disgusted, like I wasn't fit to even be speaking to her.

"You should've seen the competition." I couldn't let it pass. "Bikers, a rotting corpse, good ole boy deputies and a barn full of horses. It was rough, but I finally won."

Abe just kept looking at me as if *I* was a rotting corpse, but eventually regained his composure and nodded towards the open door behind him.

"This way."

The foyer was an impressive preamble to a house that was both sprawling and cavernous, without being opulent or palatial. The furnishings weren't antique, but surprisingly contemporary without being ultra modern. I could see a pool way out back equipped with a two-way bar, one facing in and the other stepping down outside to water level. I'd seen similar setups at the homes of Hollywood producers or successful attorneys. The layout wasn't that uncommon in the wealthier sections of LA and I'd seen enough of these mansions during my tour not to be overly impressed.

Abe left us standing just inside the door with his mute bookend sidekick while he disappeared further into the house. Tony didn't look around at all, which led me to believe he wasn't a total stranger to the place. I took the layout in like a cop on a radio call and it dawned on me what I was doing. Glancing at the sidekick Abe had left with us, I acknowledged that he was reading me like one of those neon billboards on the Strip. Still, he only kept stared at me, much like a cat would stare at a wounded mouse under its paws. I could almost see his metaphorical tail twitching anxiously behind him, slapping the floor occasionally in expectation of the kill.

"Fraternity brothers of yours?" I asked Tony as I cocked my head towards Abe's bookend counterpart.

Tony started to burn holes through me and then suddenly softened, like he'd given up. He shook his head and looked back after the disappearing Abe, his expression turning to some kind of Zen patience he'd probably practiced all his professional life.

"Something like that, I guess." He finally said in resignation.

"I must have missed Rush Week that year."

"No, you didn't." He glanced back at me. "You were just attending classes on the opposite side of campus."

I nodded with upturned eyebrows. Touché. Abe rejoined us and looked at his partner while pointing at me.

"Take this mutt into the library and stay with him." He then turned to Tony. "Come with me."

We paired off and walked in opposite directions. I followed the bookend down a long hall and through a set of double doors. As promised, the large room was lined with nothing but first additions from one end to the other, floor to ceiling. Wall tables with floral arrangements dotted the perimeter of the library, signaling at least some feminine presence in the house. However, the centerpiece ensemble was comprised of a couple of massive leather couches with matching easy chairs, all facing each other over a large rectangular coffee table. Four matching end tables filled in the corners of the set with carved wood table lamps centered on each. Except for the flowers in the vases, it all gave the decor a very symmetrical, very masculine look. Surprisingly, there were a couple of open books lying on the table with bookmarkers lying across the pages. Glancing back at my escort, he didn't register any objections, so I sat on one of the couches and examined them.

One was on the life and times of Napoleon while the other dealt with Alexander the Great. Someone was interested in the history of world leaders, or world dictators. I fingered across the pages and read a few paragraphs while my escort stood nearby, watching me intently. I finally found the attention unnerving and looked up at him.

"Come here often?" I asked.

He apparently shared his sense of humor with Phillippe Mersant and said nothing. Instead, he just continued to burn apathetic holes in me. I browsed some more and tried reading to escape the thought of being watched so closely. I nodded at a few of the passages I found and looked up again at my babysitter.

"Did you know Alexander swung both ways?" I shook my head while watching him. "He was acey-ducesy. Can you imagine that, the leader of more than half the known world jumping in and out of bed with girls and boys? Kind of makes you wonder, doesn't it?"

The bookend shifted his weight from one foot to another as a somewhat uncomfortable expression started to creep across his dour mug. I thought about adding a slight lisp to my speech and even braving a wink in his direction, but we were interrupted by another door opening behind us.

I turned in my seat and was mildly surprised to find a woman entering the room from another direction. She was closer to my age and looked like she was dressed for some high society gala. Her black hair was meticulously set on top of her head and the gown was white, with the style that signaled it might be out of a recent designer's collection. She had a stately beauty about her that reminded me of Anna. In fact, looking at this woman, I could almost picture Anna in a few years. She seemed to regard me with curiosity as she approached and moved around to the couch opposite where I sat. As almost an afterthought, she glanced at the guard.

"You can go." She dismissed him like a butler.

He nodded slightly and left the room the same way we'd come in.

I stood up as she reached the couch, taking her mature beauty in, along with her obvious authority that indicated she was undoubtedly the lady of the house. She acknowledged my courtesy with a nod and wordlessly scrutinized my looks and apparel, as if she were shopping at Sack's Fifth Avenue for a gardener or pool man. When she finished, she managed a barely audible 'humph' before sitting down. I followed suit, but neither of us said anything as we studied each other for a few moments. I couldn't read much from her eyes, except for the inquisitive nature of her expression that accompanied them. I half expected her to hand me some pruning shears or a leaf net.

"What's your name?" She finally spoke.

"Jack." I answered. "Hollister."

"Hollister?" She repeated with a slight narrowing of the eyes. "Is that Irish?"

"English." I shook my head and tried to smile. "But my family's from all over the place. Even have some American Indian in there someplace. My greater than great Grand-pappy was supposedly a mountain man."

"Well, Jack." She made a pretense of turning one of the books around to examine it while she processed the information. It didn't seem to matter much as she went on with what I suspected she had planned to say anyway. "I need to get out of this place for a while and you're going to be my escort."

"I am?" I inquired.

"Yes." She confirmed casually. "When you get to the hotel, please clean up and groom yourself accordingly for the evening. In one hour, I'll have you summoned to the men's shop and we'll get you something suitable to wear."

"We will?" I noted the rock on her third finger was about the size of Rhode Island and kept staring at it until she noticed.

"Your duties will consist of accompanying me and nothing more." She followed my attention and answered my unspoken question. She then looked back at me. "I'm bored and want some company. I'm also a bit curious and would like to know more about you."

"Curious?" I was glad she was curious, because I was completely lost.

"One hour." She repeated and rose from the couch.

I stood up with her, but didn't know what to say, so I simply watched her walk out the way she'd come in. As she left and the door behind her closed, my bookend guard slid back into the room on the opposite side, but now stayed by the door. He ceased to watch me as he'd done before and instead, absently browsed the titles on the bookcases. I didn't have the heart to tell him there was no comic book section, so sat back down and started to scan the book on Napoleon. I had been told once that my family crest had showed up at Waterloo, but hadn't fully explored the genealogy on it. Subconsciously, I looked for the coat of arms in the many photos that depicted various battles the Little General had fought.

Again, I was deep in thought when the door opened next to the guard and an older man strode through it. He waved for my sentry to again leave the room as he passed him and approached me. There was enough purpose in his step to tell me our conversation would be brief and to the point. He carried his weight well and was about my height, but thicker in the shoulders and chest. There was that familiar creeping midsection trying to peek through his expensive, but with a casual button down shirt, even for his advancing age it looked like he was winning his battle with it. From the tan, I suspected he watched his diet and swam frequently for exercise. His hair was graying, but was still thick and relatively close cut. The low brow-line suggested that if he died of old age, he'd take most of it with him to his grave.

Noting the heavy jewelry and fat cigar in his hand, it wasn't hard to figure out he was the owner of the house. Beyond that, while the two men on the front porch had signaled 'don't fuck with me' in their demeanor, this man signaled 'don't fuck with me, because those guys work for me' in his. What worried me most wasn't just the glare in his eyes that conveyed these warning signs, but the accompanying frown that clearly suggested he wasn't happy about something. I took that to mean that either he was losing at cards, or he hadn't taken the news about Raymond DeLaCosta too well. I stood up at his approach, hoping he wasn't going to hold me responsible for either.

"What's your name?" He curtly asked as he reached the coffee table and stopped.

"Jack." I replied.

"Your full name, genius." He barked dryly.

"John Hollister."

"You think you can find Caesar's Palace?"

"Sure."

"Drive the car there and check in." His orders were rapid fire. "A man will arrive with a package sometime tomorrow. When you get it, you'll return to that fucking dump in the mountains Nick calls a home and give it to that French prick Mersant."

"What about Tony?" All of a sudden I felt very alone. And who the hell was Nick?

"He's staying here with me."

"Here?"

"Good, you can hear." He glared at me. "You have a cell phone?"

"Tony thought it would be happier hitchhiking, so he threw it out the window."

"You trying to be funny?" He fired back as his nostrils flared.

"No." I backed off any further commentary, remembering Tony's admonishment.

"Good." He snapped. "You'll get a cell before you leave."

"I'd appreciate it." From his reaction, I immediately realized it wasn't a gesture of friendship.

"I'm not giving it to you so you can dial 900 numbers, Einstein. I want you there when the package arrives, Kapish?" He pinned me with a look.

"Oh." I nodded dumbly.

"It only takes incoming calls. You'll get further instructions as you go. Be at the hotel when the package arrives and don't talk to anybody." He pointed at me while boring holes through my brain, before repeating his order in a concise manner. "No one."

"Got it." I meekly shrugged.

"I sincerely doubt you've got anything." He leaned a bit closer, glaring at me before he turned towards the door and stomped towards it. "Fucking amateurs."

He muttered to himself as he left the room, swinging the doors open and letting them bang against their doorstops as he barked at my guard.

"Get him out of here."

"Let's go." The guard ordered me. "Now."

We stood in the foyer for a few moments before Abe approached, holding the keys to the Hummer and a cell phone.

"The room will be in your name." He advised as he handed the items to me. "I shouldn't have to tell you to be there when the package arrives. Obviously, you'll be watched closely from now on."

"I don't suppose you have a road map to help me get me out of your neighborhood here?" I took the items he handed me with an apologetic shrug. "Tony drove and there were a lot of turns."

"Two rights, a left and then another right will get you to the main boulevard." He informed me. "Then just drive towards the lights."

"Thanks." I turned towards the open door.

"Hey." He lowered his voice and gave me an inquisitive look, as he nodded towards the Hummer. "Your piece is still in the side pocket where Tony left it. I hope for your sake you know how to use it."

The unexpected comment caught me off guard and it took a moment to thank him again. Once outside, I jumped in the bright yellow SUV and started weaving my way through the estate grounds and then the neighborhood.

In three short days, I had gone from what was promised to be a simple case of knocking on a few doors and taking some quick notes. To date, I'd dodged bullets, found my luckless partner's murdered body, been suspected of his murder, squared off with an entire motorcycle gang, and then kidnapped by International art thieves. Now, I was playing mule in a multi-million dollar theft ring and dealing with people that seemed so dangerous I didn't even want to think about who they really were. Oh, yes, and let's not forget about falling in love with a woman who might be mixed up in all this and have her own agenda beyond them, and quite possibly me. Even with all this going on, there was only one question nagging at the back of my head at the moment: Who the hell was Nick?

17

Caesar's Palace wasn't the newest hotel on the Strip, but from the times I had visited the city, I'd always thought it was one of the classiest. I always expected Tony Bennett to be singing in the lobby as I walked in to the piano music that often played there. The hotel's smooth white walls and Roman style theme of architecture always struck me as simply elegant, giving it a clean and comfortable feeling.

I felt more than out of place walking through such surroundings while looking around for the registry desk. After being on the road all day and leaving with just what some miscreant had hastily packed for me, I suddenly felt a bit self-conscious with my holy jeans, unshaven face, and the bullet hole ridden duffel I was dragging behind me. My pocketbook was so light at this point, I wasn't sure I'd be able to tip the valet to get the Hummer back. The desk clerk seemed to read my financial status as I walked up to her, but covered it well with that Vegas 'your always welcome as long as you leave your wallet behind when you leave' smile.

"I believe you're holding a reservation for me?" I said in a resigned tone.

"Your name, Sir?" The voice behind the smile showed a trace of concern.

"Hollister." I sighed, looking around at the other guests. Maybe I wasn't that much out off the dress code. "Jack, I mean John Hollister."

She typed in the information and suddenly lit up like a Christmas tree.

"Yes, Sir." She stammered, trying to regain her composure, as if she'd just discovered I was an Emir just off a private jet from Saudi

Arabia. "Mr. Carlucci has a penthouse suite reserved for you."

"Mr. Carlucci." I looked at her with my best poker face, trying to hide mild shock. "Suite. Penthouse. Of course."

"The management has also set aside complimentary amenities for you at his request." She was typing at breakneck speed. "Just put everything on the room and it will be taken care of."

"What everything?" I was looking at her with a totally confused look, now.

"And here's a thousand dollars in chips, also compliments of the management." She pushed a stack of $50.00 casino chips over the countertop with a couple of keycards to the room. "You can use them at any of the tables or cash them in. Whatever you'd like."

"Thank you." I took the chips and the keycards and stuck them into my pockets, trying hard not to look too stunned. I searched my memory for the name Carlucci, until I recalled Anna giving it as her mother's maiden name. The way the clerk was acting, it sounded like the Carlucci's might own the place. I looked at the clerk, knowing my mystery date would be along soon. "Do you have a men's shop here that might still be open?"

"They've been asked to reopen for you within the hour." She advised. "Mr. Dumas will see to all your needs."

"Sure." I hefted the duffel, shrugging like I'd known that all along. "Mr. Dumas."

"Oh, we'll get that." She signaled a bellboy who was standing nearby.

"How about a restaurant or café?" I asked as I handed the bellboy my bag.

"If you know what you'd like, I'll take the order here and have it sent up to your suite." She punched a couple more commands in and then poised her fingers above the keyboard of her terminal.

"Ham sandwich and a beer?" I shrugged.

She took the particulars, rattling off a dozen brewery labels and almost as many options for the sandwich and condiments. We concluded the arrangements and check-in and I was soon following the bellboy towards the elevator. Partway there, I suddenly became conscious of a light feeling in and around my waistband. I gave the bellboy one of the keycards and a tip, telling him I'd be up as soon as I retrieved something I'd forgotten in the car.

Retracing my steps out the main entrance, I spotted the Hummer off to one side waiting to be parked in a line of other cars. I showed the valet my ticket and explained I'd left something in my car and he nodded in understanding. Making my way to the SUV, I wove my way through the small gaggle of cars that were also waiting to be parked. Before I could reach the Hummer, I stopped in my tracks and froze. A car I'd just passed had triggered recent memories and arrested my attention. I turned around and walked a few feet back to a light colored sedan. It was non-descript in every way, but still there was something very familiar about it.

Glancing inside, there was a bag of half-eaten sunflower seeds on the passenger seat and a paper coffee cup with a lid on it in the beverage holder. I immediately recognized the cup. I had one exactly like it in the Hummer from buying coffee at our last gas stop off the I15. I looked for any other clues that would confirm my suspicions, but found none inside the car. It was traveled in, but no extra clothing or maps, or anything that could identify its origin or driver. Slowly, I backed away from the sedan and moved around to the rear of it. The Hertz sticker was right where I'd seen it the first time I thought I'd noticed the sedan, but that wasn't here in Vegas.

Still, how may light colored sedans of this make did Hertz rent out? Hundreds? Thousands? I tried to dismiss the possibility as I continued on my mission to reach the Hummer and get my handgun. Once there, I used my body to cover the retrieval of the firearm from the door pocket on the driver's side. Valets were swimming all around me, going about their assigned tasks and I didn't want to alarm anyone by the sight of it.

"Mr. Hollister?" I jumped at the voice that came from right behind me, just as I was covering the 45 automatic in my waistband with my shirt.

I spun around, half expecting to need the gun, but found a valet standing within arm's reach. I acknowledged the fact that my immediate proximity alarm was malfunctioning, but exhaled in relief at the absence of any threat. I did register one curiosity and verbalized it.

"You know my name?"

"The front desk has advised us to extend every courtesy." The older than usual valet was smiling at me. "We'll get your vehicle washed and gassed for you?"

"OK, I guess." The services being offered here were a bit overwhelming, and I was growing disturbingly impressed by the juice Tony's friends were squeezing out of this town.

"I'll have it done within the hour for you, Sir." He jumped in the Hummer and started it as I watched.

"Thanks." I shrugged and tried to look nonchalant about all the attention. "I guess it could use a wash."

Scanning the Hummer's appearance I noticed the powdered dirt, almost like a fine red dust from DeLaCosta's driveway. It was all up in the wheel wells and sprayed behind them on the side panels. 'Shit' a voice inside me yelled. I turned back towards the hotel entrance as the Hummer drove off. Retracing my steps, I found the sedan again and immediately checked the condition of its sides and wheel wells. The same road dirt was splashed up on the doors and quarter panels.

The substance and pattern matched the SUV's perfectly. I had to remind myself that much of the soil right here in Vegas was the same find red dust I'd find in Lone Tree, but how many rental cars in Vegas ever drove off the pavement? I backed away from the sedan again and looked around me in a 360-degree search. No faces looked familiar, not that I was expecting to find one staring at me from the curb, but out of instinct, I had to check. I surveyed the interior again and noticed the keys were in the ignition. I nodded to myself as I slowly retraced my steps back into the hotel. Not only had I found our tail, the car that had followed us from Lone Tree, but I'd also found Carl Stapleton's rental sedan, the car that had been parked in front of the inn the night he'd been killed.

Reentering the hotel, I made my way to the casino where I cashed in a couple of the chips for some pocket money. Now, I was very conscious about everyone around me. Trying not to look obvious, I used my peripheral vision to sense more than see, anyone who might be watching or following me.

Whoever had followed us from Lone Tree was sticking to the SUV and probably didn't know Tony was no longer part of the equation. The Hummer's windows were tinted heavy enough that they never would have seen who was actually in it at any given time. Since Tony and I had parted company abruptly and under such secluded conditions, they wouldn't have known I was now alone until I arrived here at Caesar's.

So now the question was who was really following us? The most disturbing part of being shadowed by a dead man's rented car was how they had gotten it. Was I being shadowed by Carl's killer or killers? Now with Tony out of pocket, I felt increasingly vulnerable. It would be too much to ask for whoever was following us to backtrack to the mansion on the dead end street and try to find Tony. If they did, my problems with them would be over.

Not seeing any signs of being followed or watched, I made my way to the elevators and took in the first one that became available. A giddy couple of lovebirds got in with me and we started riding up together. I started getting nervous about reaching my floor, wondering who might be waiting for me there, when I noticed the 'P' button on the elevator panel was still not lit. I punched it a couple more times before realizing I needed my keycard to access the floor, as well as the room. I passed the card through the reader and punched the button again. This time the panel pinged and 'P' lit up for me. I sensed the lovebird's watching me in amusement, but they were polite enough not to comment.

They got off on their floor and left me alone in the elevator. I subconsciously held my breath and clasped my hands over the 45 as I continued my ride up to the penthouse. I tried to think of what I'd do if I were in this guy's shoes, the one that was tailing us. If he could've somehow discovered what room I was staying in, he might have figured out, as I had just done, that he needed a keycard to access the floor. To get to me, he'd then have to wait on the floor just under me, continually pressing the 'up' button so that every elevator going to the penthouse level would stop to let him in.

My heart stopped as the elevator paused at the floor just under my destination and started to open. I quickly pulled the 45 and held it behind me, clasping my other hand around that wrist to make the hand positions look more natural. The door cycled open and a serious looking man dressed in slacks, open polo shirt, and a sport-coat stood in the gapping hole looking at me. I'd never seen him before, but he looked somewhat kin to the two bodyguards I'd just left at the mansion, but then again a bit different. He did act a bit surprised to see me standing in the elevator and noted where my hands were before looking back to meet my curious eyes.

"Sorry." He said without inflection or pretense. He turned his empty palms toward me at his sides with the apology. "I wanted to go down. Must've pressed the wrong button."

"No problem." I smiled my Melvin Croup smile and pressed the 'close door' button on the elevator panel with my free hand, leaving the gun conspicuously behind my back.

If he was watching me, for whomever he might be working for, he now at least knew I wasn't going to be an easy mark. I kept my gun in hand till the doors opened on my floor and verified no one was waiting for me there, either. Feeling the sweat in my palms and armpits, I shook my head and almost ran to the room. This was getting unnerving and I was starting to think someone might accidentally get shot before it was all over.

The room was spacious, but not presidential, as it's name implied. Since it was Ray's well-connected friend that had requested the hotel, perhaps lacking any specific instructions, they had decided to roll out the red carpet. I wasn't going to argue. Looking at the duffel sitting on the closet caddie, it dawned on me that I'd lost complete track of time. I checked the clock on the wall and calculated that I didn't have much of it left before the mysterious 'lady of the house' would be calling on me.

I started stripping off my clothes as I headed for the bathroom. My shower was interrupted only by the arrival of the sandwich and beer and after I'd shaved and dressed in the only clean clothes I had left, I paused to eat and look out the window. The room afforded a spectacular view and the only thing missing here was some company to enjoy it with. Of course, my thoughts immediately drifted to Anna. I wondered what she was doing right now? I could only picture her as I had left her, sitting across from her uncle with Marsant's men positioned around them.

The room's phone rang and tore those disturbing images from my mind. I walked around the king sized bed, decorated a bit too pretentious for my taste, and picked up the receiver.

"Yes?"

"The men's store has been reopened and Mr. Dumas is ready to receive you, Mr. Hollister." The desk clerk announced.

"Thank you." I hung up the phone and looked at the gun on the bed.

Constantly changing clothes in a men's shop would be interesting with a firearm in my waistband, but just trying to get back down to the lobby in one piece without it might be even more interesting. Still, at this point, I had to remind myself that whoever was following me had to be more interested in the 'package' than me. Once I had it, things might get a damn sight livelier, but for now I should be relatively safe. I looked around the room, wondering where I could conceal the 45 and still get to it if need be. My eyes fell on the oversized lamp sitting on the far end table next to the couch.

After taking care of that, I slipped into my Nikes and left the room. The ride down was uneventful and I found the men's shop only after asking two bellboys and a casino waitress. The lights were on inside, but the shop was still locked up. Not to be deterred, I knocked on the heavy glass door and a man of slight build and feminine manner walked out from the back to open it. He looked me up and down is an expression I could only surmise was fashion horror.

"Please don't tell me you're Mr. Hollister." His lisp and soft voice matched his mascara and lip-gloss.

"OK, I'm not Mr. Hollister."

"Good God in Heaven." He exclaimed with his fingers spread across his chest to punctuate the statement. "I wish people would stop calling me the Miracle Man. It just keeps raising the bar to accomplish the impossible."

"Well, you don't have to worry about me." I said casually as he let me into the shop. "The only way I'll call you Miracle Man is when your pregnancy test comes back positive."

He stopped in his tracks with his hand still stretched across his chest, staring up at me. His eyes darted back and forth from mine for a couple of moments before he broke pose and playfully slapped me on my chest.

"Now that *would be* a miracle, wouldn't it?" He laughed and let his fingers linger on my chest. "Oh, I like you."

"Well, you can't have him, Pablo."

We both looked up to see the 'lady of the house' walk into the shop. She was still dressed in the same gown, but now had a feathered stow, or boa, whatever they called it, draped over her neck and loosely tied over her ample chest.

"Madam Sophie." Dumas gushed as he backed away from me. "How divine you look in that Ralph Lauren. I'm so glad you didn't go with that Coco Chanel number. It just wasn't you."

"I wish you and Donna wouldn't gossip about my choices." She pinned Pablo with a chastising glance and then walked up and stood close to me. While looking up and searching my eyes, much like Anna had done when we first met, she continued. "The fashion world is so close knit in this town, you can't window shop without everyone connected to the industry knowing about it."

"Makes me wonder how many people will know what color my jockey shorts are by the time I leave." I commented, staring back at her and thought about her husband. "Hopefully leave."

"I'll know." She eyed me as she slid her fingers down my jaw line and off my chin, before turning away and walking towards the racks of men's suits.

"That's disconcerting." I followed her movements.

"Not to worry. It won't be from seeing you put them on." She eyed me over her shoulder. "Or taking them off."

"Considering who, or what, your husband is, I'm extremely happy to hear that." I said as I watched her run her hand over the various selections.

"That would be the only reason." She started examining the suits more closely.

"Why would you be interested at all?" I had to ask. "You've known me all of two seconds."

"Why?" She echoed with a pause in thought. "I suppose Anna's choices have always fascinated me."

"You're interested only because Anna's interested?" I watched her continue her study of the suits on the rack.

She stopped for a second and squinted at a price tag.

"Does that offend you?"

"How do you know Anna?" I pressed.

"The question might be more properly phrased 'how do I not know Anna'?" She mused as she pulled a selection off the rack and showed it to Pablo. "Do you have this in his size?"

"Nothing here is his size until I make it his size." Pablo rushed over and examined the suit. "I have something close, but it will take a half-hour at least to hem the pants and nip and tuck the coat."

"That will be fine." She smiled and held her selection up in my direction, closing one eye as she lined it up with my face. "I like this color on him."

"Shirt, socks, shoes." Pablo shook his head. "And he'll have to put this on so I can mark it."

"Be a doll and try this one on for Pablo, darling." She asked me sweetly and turned back to Mr. Dumas. "Can you really do it in thirty minutes, Pablo sweetie? I'd like to catch the midnight show."

"Of course, Madam Sophie." He assured. "Anything for you."

"You *are* the Miracle Man." She beamed and turned back to me as she handed Pablo the suit. "I'll pick out a dress shirt and tie. What size shoes do you wear?"

"Elevens." I answered.

"Ooow." She cooed. "You know what they say about men who have large hands and feet."

"Yeah," I nodded as I started to follow Pablo to the fitting room and passed her. "They wear large gloves and shoes."

"You're too modest, I'm sure." She remarked as I disappeared behind a curtain with Pablo.

"Madam Sophie?" Pablo's voice called out from the dressing room where I was stripping down for the fitting.

"Yes, Pablo?"

"This hunk needs some fresh underwear and socks. If you can find some casual slacks and shirts, he needs a whole new wardrobe here."

"What's wrong?" She called back.

"Either there's some monstrous moths in his neighborhood or something's desperately wrong with his laundry detergent."

"Bullet holes." I commented as I stuck my fingers through the gaps in my jeans I now held in my hands.

"What?" Pablo made a horrible face.

The curtain swung open and Sophie walked in, first appraising me and then examining my protruding fingers wiggling from the holes in the fabric.

"My God, darling, who have you been playing with?" She said in a tone that was just short of alarm.

"It's a long story." I shook my head. "Thankfully, I wasn't in them at the time."

"Anna?" Her alarm started to grow.

"No, it happened before I even met her." I shook my head again. "But not very far from where she's staying."

"She needs to come back to town and stay with us until her mother returns." Sophie said mostly to herself. "That sad little place is not where she belongs."

"No argument there." I agreed as I pulled on the suit and Pablo started marking it up.

"I'll speak to my husband and make arrangements. Maybe you could bring her back here." She said in a voice growing with determination, before looking up at me. "Would you do that for me?"

"I'll do it for me." I nodded. "And the sooner, the better."

Sophie stepped up on the platform and placed her hand alongside my face as she studied my eyes.

"You are a good man, Mr. Hollister." She said with conviction. "Anna's always had a talent for finding the wrong men, but she has done well with you."

"There isn't much to choose from in Lone Tree." I admitted. "But I'm very happy we found each other up there."

"Please, Madam Sophie." Pablo was protesting from below us, trying to get his measurements.

"Of course, Pablo." Sophie kept looking up at me, but stepped back off the platform. "I'll find some clothes for you."

She retreated back out into the shop and asked for sizes from me. Pablo called them out before I could answer for myself and flat astonished me with his accuracy. I'd never had a personal tailor, but if I could ever afford one, this little guy would be it.

"How long have you known Anna?" I called out between the sizing questions.

"Since she was very young." Sophie answered. "I watched her grow up."

"Then your two families were close?"

"At first, yes, but now they are the same."

"Same what?" I called out.

"Family, silly." Came the answer. "Anna is my niece by marriage."

"Small world." I answered in a tone of complete understanding, hiding my complete lack of it. Still, I pressed on for some clarification. "The Carlucci Family."

"But of course, darling."

"Of course." I repeated quietly, looking down at Pablo who was crouched in front me, suit pants fabric in hand.

He was looking up at me, nodding his head vigorously with an assortment of pins fanned out across his wide, tight smile. His orientation, sexually and physically suddenly crossed my mind.

"Don't get too comfortable down there, Pablo." I admonished in a kidding tone. "These are the Carlucci's we're talking about."

18

My mystery date shunned any further questions about Anna while we shopped for my new wardrobe, or to put it more accurately, 'while *she* shopped' for my new wardrobe. Everything from socks and shoes to shorts and shirts were selected for my new fashion statement ala Madam Sophie, as the Miracle Man had dubbed her. Between the two of them, they sounded more like a tag team for a brothel catering to impotent men. But Sophie seemed to be having such a good time throwing different items of apparel onto the cashier's counter that I didn't have the heart to tell her how happy she'd make some homeless person who'd eventually dig through my building's dumpster.

It wasn't that I was ungrateful or unappreciative of her help in getting me out of my holy jeans. It was just that the Perry Como look wasn't me. I did most my everyday shopping around the corner from my flop pad just off of Venice Beach. That meant a lot of stone washed jeans and tie-dye t-shirts. My idea of dressing up was to wear Levis and tennis shoes. I had never thought of myself as an anti-establishment sort of guy, but at some point I'd rebelled where I could and my personal fashion tastes had been adopted as my own non-violent protest against the mainstream.

So, after being extensively nipped and tucked by that master of design Pablo Dumas, I stepped out of the men's shop at Caesars Palace in the company of my exquisite looking date at least looking good enough to accompany her somewhere. The suit was midnight blue and handsomely tailored, but even though I looked the part, I still felt like a caveman dragging his club into a Broadway musical. I regarded my companion and became aware of the looks she was getting from the common tourists and wondered just how necessary this whole trip down fashion lane had been.

"Did you ever think about just throwing on a sweater and going to a bistro?" I commented to Sophie as I tipped the two bellboys lugging the rest of my new wardrobe off towards the elevators.

"In Las Vegas?" She paused to turn to me. "In August?"

"Just a figure of speech." I explained. "I meant just go somewhere casual and let your hair down."

"But Darling, that's all I do day in and day out." She touched my chin again with her fingertips. "I was about to go out alone when I heard this perfectly interesting man had arrived. A man who had by all reports captured the heart of my sweet and beautiful niece."

"And being the naturally curious type..?"

"I had to take you out with me and see what you were all about."

"So, where were you heading out to?" I dropped the subject, seeing a woman's undeniable logic shining through. "Originally."

"Why the Bellagio is the place to be and be seen." She admonished. "Besides, I never tire of watching Cirque Du Soleil."

"Of course." I agreed with a shrug. "The only place."

"That suit looks marvelous on you." She looked me up and down.

"Thank you. I once heard somewhere that clothes make the man." It wasn't working, so far.

"We have just enough time to catch the last show if we hurry." She checked her watch and looked around.

"Do the words 'hurry' and 'Las Vegas Strip' really equate?" I cited from my experiences trying to drive on the main drag through the towns glitter palace.

"Tommy knows all the back streets to get there." She advised and started leading me towards the front entrance.

"Color me stupid, but why not just book me a room at the Bellagio? It would have made going to the show a short walk."

"Silly." She hooked her arm into mine and fell in step. "Frank made the arrangements for your stay and I'm just making do with them."

"Frank, as in your husband Frank?" I confirmed. "Frank Carlucci?"

"Yes, of course." She looked at me as if I should've known. "You did meet him, didn't you?"

"Briefly." I replied.

A Lincoln Towncar was waiting for us just outside the door and although it wasn't obvious, it looked like it had been slightly 'stretched' to limo specs. Tommy the Driver held the door open for us, nodding to Sophie and glaring at me as we slid by him and into the spacious backseat. He looked like any one of the men I might have met at the Frank and Sophie's mansion if I'd stuck around long enough. The expression he gave me said more than a mouthful. Without actually verbalizing one word of it, I understood perfectly that I was out with the lady of the house and I'd be expected to conduct myself accordingly. I did my best to convey back the simple comforting thought 'no problem'.

Tommy did know all the ins and outs of getting around town and his first turn was around the back of the Palace. After that, a series of back streets and alleys marked the progress to our destination. We seemed to join a small caravan of taxis and airport shuttles, bobbing up and down over speed bumps and parking lot ramps. The limo rode like a tank and I immediately suspected it was armored from the way it handled and rode. I stole a glance at the driver, who looked like he was busy with parking lot traffic, before dropping my question as nonchalantly as I could.

"So what does your husband do, if you don't mind me asking?"

The driver immediately made eye contact with me in the rear view mirror and held it just long enough to signal the message that I was treading in murky waters, if not quicksand.

"You don't know?" She really seemed surprised again for some reason.

"No." I admitted. "But then again I don't subscribe to the Wall Street Journal."

"Oh, Darling." She snuggled up at my side and hooked her arm through mine again. "If you haven't been told, just consider it a blessing."

"Really" I looked down at her. "That bad?"

"Really." Her expression turned a bit more serious as she ran her fingers down the lapels of my new suit and gingerly straightened the ruffled material out. "Have you ever heard the term 'ignorance is bliss'?"

"More than once." I admitted, glancing again at the driver. He had gone back to his driving, but he was listening so intently, I thought I could actually see his ears turning in our direction. Apparently, Sophie had given the party-line answer to my question, even if it had been laced with a few clues.

"Frank is nothing more than a businessman." She sighed, finally throwing a small bone to my question. "A businessman with wide and varied interests."

"But not a business I'd find on Wall Street?" I shifted my eyes from the driver to Sophie, seeing if anything I was saying would rate a reaction. "Would his interests happen to include art?"

"Darling." She drew out the word, as if the answer was all too dreadfully obvious. "If I can't pry him out of the house to see even the teensiest little show, how could I ever get him to even glance at a sculpture or painting?"

"I see your point." I thought I even saw the rare trace of a smile in the driver's eyes, as well. I'd been waiting for the opportunity to drop this name ever since her husband blurted it out earlier and figured now was as good of time as any. "So 'Nick' is the real art connoisseur of the family?"

"Oh, Nicky adores the arts." She gushed in admiration. "I only wish he lived closer so we could go out more often and enjoy the finer things this town has to offer."

"This town?" I said in a doubtful tone. Checking the driver in the mirror, nothing seemed amiss so far in my line of inquiry. Still, I took my time to angle around the things I wanted to learn for the sake of conversation. "You are talking about Las Vegas here?"

"Oh, of course we don't have the sophistication of New York here in the desert," She explained. "But a few of my lady friends and I have brought a lot of the fine arts into town over the last few years."

"Really?" I acted surprised.

"Oh, yes." She beamed and then suddenly hit me playfully again. "Why, the art gallery at the Bellagio right here is sponsored in part by us."

"No kidding?" I managed. "There's a gallery there?"

"One of the finest in the west." She nodded. "Artwork from all over the world and from some of the finest galleries pass through here on exhibit."

"Like works from that famous Museum in Paris?" She was now starting to get my full attention. "The Louvre or something like that."

"The Lourve?" She repeated and looked up at me. "Of course. The Bellagio often displays works from there and Nicky knows the director here quite well."

"Interesting." Certain possibilities were starting to bubble up and I wondered more and more how often that back way in and out of Lone Tree was used. "Does your husband know the director, also?"

That got a look from the driver.

"He just called him a couple of hours ago, while you were waiting in the library." She suddenly looked thoughtful. "That's a bit odd, too, considering I always have to twist his arm to call Maxwell when it's necessary."

"Perhaps it was necessary." I offered and she seemed to be willing to let it drop as I changed the subject. "I wish Anna was here to go with us."

"Me, too." She agreed and then pulled herself closer. "But then I wouldn't have you all to myself."

"You miss her." I confirmed.

"It's been a while, yes." She lamented. "And I love to take her shopping."

"Why is she staying with Nick and not you?" I asked.

"She loves her horses and Nick has so much land out there for her to ride on." Sophie shook her head slowly. "After Sean Claude died, she only seemed interested in riding alone for hours at a time."

"Was that the race car driver?" I cautiously guessed.

"We've arrived." The driver chimed in a bit too timely.

"Thank you, Tommy."

The Bellagio was both magnificent and opulent to the level of grandeur. It seemed that someone had constructed their vision of what the French aristocracy had originally had in mind and then added 20th Century lighting. What the American aristocracy of the 20th couldn't, or were unwilling to fork out on a daily basis, the slightly 'dumbing down' of the hotel in the 21st had brought in the upper crust tourists to enjoy a glimpse of what they normally couldn't afford.

The Cirque Du Soleil was one such expenditure most tourists were willing to shell out the big bucks to see and from what part I saw of it, the price of admission seemed well spent. What was even more amazing was the fact that these gifted performers completed these feats day in and day out, sometimes twice a day for the viewing audience. From our executive box, most likely reserved for last minute customers like the Carlucci's, we had a very good view of the show and I was surprised to see such a large attendance at such a late hour. I had to keep reminding myself that Vegas was very much one of the few towns in America where the clock was rarely watched, if even looked at.

Quiet cocktails followed the short night of entertainment in the lounge just off the main auditorium, where numerous locals who appeared to run in Sophie's social circle wandered by to say hi and chat for a few minutes. Most of them were women of distinction and many had younger men on their arm. I got the impression that these were neglected wives of powerful men who found acceptable substitutes as escorts so they could enjoy a night on the town, sort of what Sophia might consider a 'girl's night out'.

I could see the flip side of the escort industry at work, as a few the men standing off to the side of these overdressed ladies smiled courteously, but said very little. In fact, a couple of them regarded me with a questioning look, as if I were some kind of new competition in town. In reality, many of the male escorts that made up the parade of Sophia's gang of female friends were family friends and relatives, with even a couple of sons and daughters thrown in here and there. It made me wonder just how tight a circle of friends my date ran in; since it was more than obvious some of these escorts did more than just escort.

But, my glimpse into this bizarre little world was cut short by Sophia's need to get home before the sun came up. It seemed that for her, being out all night wasn't defined by how much of the night you spent out, but rather by merely ending it before the sun made its appearance in the eastern sky. Eventually, all the contacts were made and I'd been brought up to date on all the latest gossip via ease dropping. Indeed, there had been so much talking that Sophia had barely finished her one drink to my four. By that time, I was lubricated enough to stop caring who was buying what house and which marriages were in the toilet.

Once back in the Towncar, Sophia instructed Tommy to drive back to the Palace and I chimed in with slightly slurred speech.

"Yes, home James."

Sophia took a few moments to examine me as our metaphorical train left the station.

"Did you enjoy the Cirque?"

"Very much so." I tried to straighten up my vernacular and sit up in the back seat.

"Do you drink a lot?" She kept looking at me, as if she would fill out a report card later and issue it to Anna's mother for signature.

"Only when I'm trying to stop the ringing in my head."

"What ringing?"

"The incessant ringing to the melodic chorus of ladies too long without anything of real substance to talk about." I looked over at her with slightly vacant eyes. "You, know, gossip."

I thought I even caught Tommy's eyes smiling on that one in the rear view mirror.

"Yes," Sophia turned thoughtful before admitting to herself more than me. "We do tend to go on a bit."

"Present company accepted," I added. "Its no wonder Anna finds the company of horses more stimulating."

"I never thought about that." She brightened at the revelation as she turned slightly towards me in her seat. "She never liked the social events I planned for her. The more people she was around, the less comfortable she always seems to be."

"Maybe because she didn't know them." I offered with a slightly pickled expression. "Next time she's down, maybe try a day lying around your pool out back, just the two of you."

"She's never really liked being around Frank too much." Sophia admitted, almost thinking out loud. "Maybe a day at the spa or a short retreat in the mountains."

"I think that's what she's doing now." I eyed her.

"Yes, I see your point." She looked at me again and studied my face. "You are a perceptive man."

"Perceptions are elusive." I admitted. "And often false."

"Are you a false man?" She asked with a sideways glance.

"It pains me to admit I'm not the man in the brand new suit before you." I shook my head a bit. "I don't belong here and definitely don't belong in your circle of society."

"That's too bad," She was still looking thoughtfully at me. "Because you'd be a refreshing change to it."

"Anyone who didn't belong would be a refreshing change." I gently admonished.

"I suppose you're right." She nodded thoughtfully.

"People should stay where they're most comfortable."

"And you're not comfortable in our world."

"The bigger question would be: is Anna?" I raised an eyebrow.

"Anna is family." She explained.

"Sometimes kids have to run away from the family and find their own life." I explained with a shrug. "It happens in a lot of households."

"Some families are harder to run away from." She shook her head.

"I can fully appreciate that." I agreed. "But living a life someone else has chosen for you can break the spirit of the one being coerced."

Sophia seemed to take my comments under advisement for a few blocks before finally looking at me as we pulled up in front of Caesars.

"If Anna ran off with you, where would you take her?" She searched my eyes for any truth I might depart from in my answer.

I looked for a long time back into her eyes, searching for the answer and the truth of my eventual answer. I saw all the pitfalls. How could she be happy living off a California beach with cheap shops, runaways, goofy European tourists and lots of drug culture sleeping under our windows every night? I had long rejected the nine-to-five culture with its picket fences and two-car garages. Estates and nine-car garages didn't even compute. Anna seemed most comfortable with her horses and long rides in the wilderness, an introspective woman of mystery and quiet charm. I noticed Sophia still staring, waiting for an answer. She must have seen the conclusion I'd come to in the growing sadness in my eyes, but also some distance determination.

"I'm not sure." I answered solemnly. "But I'd make sure that wherever we ended up, she'd be happy."

"Happiness is a state of mind, not a place." She smiled sadly. "Someone can't be happy unless they decide they want to be happy."

"True enough, maybe." I admitted with a sheepish smile.

"There's a chance whatever you try to do for her won't make her anymore happy than being with her family and dealing with all the intricacies and, as you might guess, eccentricities of it."

"I guess the main thing is that she decides what's best for herself." I shrugged.

"We can spend our whole lives doing just that." A trace of personal sadness seemed to cross over Sophia's face with the comment. She realized her own self-reflection and snapped out of it, looking at me as Tommy got out and quickly moved around the car to open my door. "Whatever you both decide, please don't lose touch with me, OK?"

"We're just beginning to find each other." I assured. "But no one ever forgets where they came from."

Tommy snapped the door open, seemingly anxious to get rid of me, but possibly even more eager to stop the sappy conversation.

"Be careful." Sophia suddenly looked concerned. "And take care of Anna. Don't let anything happen to her."

"That's one thing you don't have to worry about." I assured her and stepped out of the car.

I was lost in my own thoughts while making my way to the elevators. On the ride up, I couldn't stop thinking of Anna and where she fit in my life. We'd found each other so suddenly and unexpectedly, I'd never considered the long range effects on both our lives, should our relationship blossom further into something more long lasting and serious. She seemed so out of place in the Nevada desert, more like a mirage than an actual human being. Still, my feelings were undeniable and I couldn't just walk away.

I was mentally trying to picture her at my side as we walked along Venice Beach, wondering if she could accept such a simple life. I worked the room's keycard for my suite as I reflected on how I had met her. The reason why I was here came rushing back to me as I entered the suite and looked around.

The room was a mess. I surveyed the disarray of couch cushions laying out on the floor and drawers pulled open. Cautiously walking to the door to the bedroom, I found the mattress was half off the bed and everything had been rifled through. My attention fell on the four bags of newly bought clothes, sitting untouched next to the bedroom door. It was a big clue as to who Goldy Locks might have been as I muttered the old fairy tale rhyme to myself.

"Who's been sleeping in my bed?"

19

I called down to the more than helpful desk clerk who'd checked me in and was actually surprised she was still on duty.

"Yes, this is Mr. Hollister in the... Penthouse Suite."

"What can we do for you, Mr. Hollister?"

"You know, I don't feel like I tipped those two bellboys enough earlier," I explained. "The ones who brought up my new wardrobe Mrs. Carlucci purchased in the men's shop?"

"Why of course," She gushed at the mention of Sophia's name, which is why I dropped it. "I can add whatever you'd like onto the bill for the room."

"I'd really like to thank them in person." I stood in the middle of my bedroom that had recently been tossed like a salad. "Are they still on duty?"

"I'll have to check to see who they are, but I believe so." She sounded a bit hesitant, but complied. "I'll send them right up as soon as I get their names from the bell captain."

"Thank you so much." I gushed back. "I'll certainly remember your name to the management and especially the Carlucci's."

"Oh, please," She sounded like she was going to have a panic attack. "It's just our job and no special mention of names is necessary at all."

"Well, if you really would rather remain anonymous?"

"Yes, please, that would be fine." She reassured.

"Well, thank you for being so prompt with my request."

I hung up the phone and looked around some more. I wasn't sure what my intruder had been looking for, but had a suspicion it had something to do with that item that hadn't arrived yet. 'Like I'd leave that unattended' I thought to myself. Somebody needed a reality check. I spent the next fifteen minutes looking around the suite, seeing if anything was missing. To be on the safe side, I checked the status of my handgun I'd left resting on the wire supports for the lampshade next to the couch and recovered it. Using it as sort of a pointer wherever I looked, closets, shower stalls, etc, I still found no one waiting for me, nothing missing, and no further clue as to why the place had been sacked.

When I heard the knock at the door, I dropped the gun back into my rear waistband and answered it. The same two fairly young men in hotel uniforms stood with smiling faces. I looked from one to the other as if I were a magician about to open the curtain on a trick and say 'voila', but instead let the door swing open slowly, gradually exposing the décor of carnage. As they surveyed the interior, their faces dropped like atom bombs. They went from 'we're ready for our fat tip' to 'oh, my God, are we in trouble now' in a record breaking two-point-three seconds.

"You know, that was my first thought, too." I registered their expressions and stood back to let them enter.

"Oh shit!" The one I took to be the more senior asked as he walked in and looked around. "What happened?"

"I was so hoping you could tell me." I looked at them both seriously.

"You don't think..." He started to deny any culpability and then read my face and fell silent.

"Well," I motioned to the bedroom. "The only thing in here that hasn't been treated like a snow globe is the two bags you guys carried in earlier tonight. Beyond that, there's no signs of a breaking in, so I'd take that as a clue that whoever did this already knew what was in those bags and had a keycard to the room."

"Believe me, we didn't have anything to do with it." The bellboy pleaded.

The younger one finally turned to me and blurted out.

"Did your friend know anything about what happened?"

I leaned on the edge of the door and regarded him with a long and serious look before I replied.

"Look, the only friend I had in this whole state is now the buffet

The Carlucci File

for the desert's food chain." I cocked my head sideways. "Did you mean *that* friend?"

"Sir." The senior of the two broke into our exchange, apparently ready to come clean. "What he means is the man who came in just as we were leaving."

"What man?" I turned to him with my drawn out question.

"He said he was your friend and called you by name."

"And for that you let him in and left him here?" I kept my voice even. After all, I was after information and the hint of retribution towards them was only an arm twister to get it.

"Absolutely not, Sir." He shook his head vehemently. "But he also mentioned Mr. Carlucci's name."

"Carlucci?" I repeated and then asked. "Which Carlucci?"

"Is there more than one?" The senior bellboy sounded like his life couldn't have ended any sooner until learning there was more than one Carlucci walking the earth.

"Apparently so." I said in a resigned tone. "Look, when he mentioned the name Carlucci, did he offer a first name with it?"

"Mr." The younger one nodded.

"Mr." I nodded slowly, suddenly realizing I'd been upstaged by a twenty-year-old, and an idiot at that.

"Yes, Sir." He nodded more adamantly, becoming more sure of his answer.

"So, what are you telling me, Sport?" I asked. "That the man didn't mention Carlucci's first name, or that there's no IQ test for becoming a bellboy?"

"Yes, Sir." The younger blindly answered as his older partner hung his head and shook it.

"Did this man offer his own name?" I asked.

"No, Sir." They both shook their head and the senior one added. "We've learned that when that name is mentioned, we aren't supposed to ask any questions."

"So at the mere mention of the name Carlucci, you assume everything is fine and leave?"

"Yes, Sir." The senior bellboy answered and added. "And we don't leave slowly."

"I get the picture." I nodded and waved any further explanation off. "So, can you tell me what my mystery guest looked like?"

"About your age, kind of overweight and he was losing his hair." The senior was trying to remember.

"The guy didn't look like he was from around here." The younger one added. "Looked like he was from New York or Canada or something."

"Why, did he have an accent?" I turned to him.

"Naw." He shook his head. "Just didn't look like he came from somewhere that had a lot of sunshine."

"Yeah, like Alaska or something." The senior one agreed. "We sort of thought he might be your bookkeeper or something."

"How was he dressed?" I catalogued the information, wondering why there was never a composite artist with his kit handy when you needed one.

"Definitely dressed for Las Vegas." The senior one shrugged. "Maroon slacks, green shirt, like the stuff we brought up in your bags."

"How would you know what I bought?" I eyed him.

"Well," He backed off at mach three and looked me up and down. "Like what we'd expect you to buy in the shop down there."

"OK." I waved him off again with a resigned sigh. "So the guy followed you up to the room?"

"No." The younger one shook his head. "He was just standing there when we opened the door to leave."

"Yeah." The senior bellboy nodded. "He said something like, 'Where's John?' and we said we were just bringing your clothes up. Then he said he was a friend of yours and he'd wait for you here, said he had some information from Mr. Carlucci that you needed to have. We heard the name Carlucci and…."

"Yeah, yeah, I get the drill." I nodded with a frown and looked around the room. "Can you at least get house-cleaning up here to tidy up?"

"Absolutely, Sir." They both seemed all too eager to leave.

"Look," I stopped their hasty retreat to the door while digging into my pockets. "If you see this guy again, I want to know where, when, who, everything but why. I'll find that out myself when I speak to him."

"Yes, Sir." They said in unison.

"Here's a retainer and I'll put another one on the room tab in both your names if you come through for me, OK?" I flipped them each a casino chip. "If he's dressed in stuff like my new wardrobe, he shouldn't be hard to spot."

"Yes, Sir." They looked at each other in mutual agreement before looking back. "We go off shift in a half hour, but we'll stick around and find him for you. If he's here, we'll bring you his room number and everything we can find out about him."

"Good lads." I shoulder-chucked the senior bellboy who'd made the promise and waved them out. "Don't forget housecleaning."

"They'll be here in a minute." They practically ran out the door, but the senior stopped and looked back.

"Are you going to report this so security, Sir?"

"Why?" I shrugged. "The secret password was given, right?"

"Yes?" His face pleaded.

"Keep your eyes pealed for me and it's forgotten." I assured them.

They both beat feet like Olympic sprinters, leaving me to look around the room for the complimentary bar. Since I was going to be up for a while longer, I thought a nightcap would be in order. As I poured the drink, I reflected on my conversation with the boys. It struck me as odd that the man had asked for 'John' and not 'Jack'. In fact, I was beginning to realize that more people had called me by my formal Christian name on this trip than on any other assignment I'd ever worked. I tried to enumerate those who had used my given name and decided it was everyone, everyone except Anna and Ray.

The maids appeared within minutes as promised. They propped the door open with their carts and gave me funny looks as they surveyed the mess. I followed them into the bedroom and watched as they started to straighten the mattress on the bed. They exchanged looks and glanced at me.

"Those showgirls." I offered a smile and a shake of the head. "They just can't get enough and when there's two of them, whoa, are you in for a ride."

One turned to the other, saying something in Spanish and they both laughed, probably to the effect of 'is this Bozo dreaming or what?' I was sure they'd seen worse.

I shook my head and walked back out into the main room,

highball in hand, only to come face to face with a man in a suit. By pure happenstance, it was cheaper than the one I was wearing, but still more expensive than any worn by the guys on my old job, at least below the rank of Deputy Chief. The look on the man's face was one I'd seen one too many times in my career. That look multiplied times two as his partner sauntered in behind him. The whole scene jumped-started an attitude I'd tried to bury long ago, the stuff reserved just for Department Brass and these clowns. It was a long story.

"Let me guess," I put a finger to my lips. "Hotel security."

"Agent Tandy." He flashed his ID. "FBI Organized Crime Taskforce."

"Well, you have to admit I was close."

"You John Hollister?" He ignored the taunt. This was going to be a challenge.

"Do you have an arrest warrant?" I asked back.

"No."

"Then I guess I can be John Hollister." I smiled my Melvin Croup smile.

"Can I ask what you're doing here?"

"Drinking?" My smile widened as I raised my glass and turned it in my hand.

His partner was the smart one. He moved off to the side and didn't say a thing. Instead, he busied himself looking around curiously in a way that seemed familiar to me.

"You'll have to excuse the mess." I started to say and then had a brain fart. "That is, unless you people made it."

"You have a little party here?" Tandy asked, looking around for himself.

"No, I paid extra to have them make the place up this way."

"I understand you're ex-LAPD?" Tandy said as more of a confirmation than question.

"Retired." I sipped from my glass.

"Well that at least explains the hostility." His partner chimed in with a smile and a nod. Now him I could get to like.

"You know whose suite this belongs to?" Tandy asked.

"Since its called 'Caesar's Palace' I'd suspect the obvious, but I heard he was killed some time ago." I kept the smile. "Knifed in the back by people who were supposed to be on his side. Sound familiar?"

"We also heard you had some history with us." He cocked his head. "And had quite a mouth on you."

"Right here, smiling at you." I held up my glass and giggled the ice in the nearly empty container. "Care for a drink?"

"No thanks." He waved off the offer. "Unlike you sorry ass PD dicks, we don't drink on the job. We prefer to conduct our investigations sober."

"That may work well enough for you," I drained what was left of the nightcap. "But us lowly PD dicks discovered early on that watching you guys work was so hysterical funny that knocking down a few helped us cope with the slap stick. So, in essence, we drank to remain sober."

"Very funny, wise ass." He nodded. "For your information, this suite belongs to Frank Carlucci."

"Then there must have been some kind of double booking." I shrugged. "Because there's no Frank Carlucci here and I've never heard of him."

"That's odd." He eyeballed me. "Since you were in his living room earlier tonight."

"I met some guy." I shook my head in all honesty. "But he never introduced himself."

"How about his wife?" Tandy shot back.

"How about her." I shook my head in mock adoration.

"She tell you who she was?"

"She only introduced herself as Sophia." I shrugged again. "I just assumed her last name was Lauren.

"What are you doing in Carlucci's private suite?" He switched to the

direct approach.

"At the moment, it would seem obvious that I'm talking to a clown in a cheap suit." I answered.

"Do you know who Frank Carlucci is, smart ass?" I think I was finally making some headway in my quest to piss off Agent Tandy.

"No, but I suppose you're going to tell me, eventually." I upended the glass one more time, figuring the liquor would be the last I'd taste for several days while I waited for Melvin to come and bail me out.

"Does the fact that we're assigned to the FBI Organized Crime

Unit suggest anything to you?" Tandy put his hands on his hips.

"Well," I squinted at him. "Given the pay you get from the American taxpayer for doing absolutely nothing, I'd suspect that title would have something to do with Internal Affairs."

"Look, smart ass." Tandy started towards me, but his partner grabbed him and whispered something in his ear.

Tandy's reddening complexion eased off and his face regained some normal color, but he pointed a finger at me, still restrained by his partner.

"We aren't through, yet, you understand?"

"That's dandy." I smiled back. "Agent Tandy."

"Mother…" Luckily, Agent Tandy's partner was slightly bigger and a lot younger. He pulled Tandy back and walked him over to the door.

"I'm sorry, what?" I put a finger to my ear and leaned forward, glass in hand. "What was that about your mother?"

After whispering apparently more good advice, the younger agent nudged Tandy out of the door and closed it behind him. He turned to me and pulled up his pants, I'd suspect to reposition his gun and holster, as he didn't look like the shoulder rig type. It was another promising clue that he wasn't cut from the same pompous bureaucratic cloth his partner was. He walked over to me and leaned up against the bar, close to where I was standing.

"Name's Osterholt. Bill Osterholt." He looked me in the eye and then took in the bar. "Doesn't look like the Shortstop, but a drink sounds pretty good right now."

I looked at him and my attitude deflated. The Shortstop was the main watering hole for every LA cop who'd ever worked downtown at one time or another. That meant at one time of another we'd patrolled the same streets.

"Shit." I sighed as I grabbed another glass and put some ice in it. "What division?"

"Metro." He confirmed with an almost apologetic shrug. "I'd just been promoted to Detective at Central when the agency's recruiters came around. I had no family and their pension was a hell of a lot better than ours."

"Turncoat." I accused in a half-kidding tone.

"What, I should stick around so I could eventually end up like you," He smiled with a chuckle. "Trolling the gutter trying to make last month's alimony?"

"You make it sound so romantic." I poured more Scotch for both of us and motioned to the seltzer. "Do go on."

"Isn't it though?" He waved off the mixer and took the glass, downing half of it in one slug. "When did you pull the pin?"

"At twenty." I nodded.

"Minimum pension." He shook his head. "Damn, that's not a lot to live on."

"You were smart." I said begrudgingly. "Get out and go for the fat retirement."

If the old Department had adopted a fight song for itself, I would have expected us to break out with a chorus of it any minute. Instead, we drank for a few moments in silence, dwelling in our separate melancholia over the same job. Everyone's memories were different.

"So, what's going on, Jack?" Osterholt finally looked at me for the truth.

"Just doing the deed to make a few bucks." I shook my head with outstretched arms, with glass in one hand and bottle of Scotch in the other. It was better if he didn't know, anyway. "You have me pegged. Just working on last month's alimony payment."

"Guys got to turn a buck, that's for sure." He nodded in understanding and backed off. The sound of the cleaning ladies chattering in Spanish filtered out to us.

"Who's back there?" Osterholt asked in a cautious tone.

"Housecleaning." I shook off his concerns. "Just tidying up after my latest orgy."

"Have any idea who it was or what they were looking for?" He glanced around the room.

"I'm trying to retrieve something for a client." I confided. "I suspect a wildcard player got froggy and jumped too soon."

"Then he didn't get it?"

"No." I shook my head and emoted Confucius. "But frog that jumps prematurely often finds no lily-pad to land on."

"Where does Carlucci fit in all this?"

"Damned if I really know, but sounds like he might deliver what

I'm looking for."

"What's that?"

"Something floating around that belongs in a museum." I chuckled at a sudden epiphany. "Like me."

He smiled and examined the glass in his hand. I knew he could let Tandy drag me in for a rousing tag-team interrogation, as well as muster a surveillance army large enough to know every time I sneezed if he wanted to, so he really didn't have to pressure me into saying anything.

"Then Carlucci's not your client?"

"No way." I shook my head.

"You know if you fuck around with this Carlucci guy you'll be taking an early and very permanent retirement, if you get my drift?"

"I'm beginning to get that picture in Technicolor," I lowered my voice even more. "But I had no idea who this guy was. Actually, I still don't."

"West Coast syndicate." Osterholt lowered his voice to almost a whisper. "Of course, they're probably hearing everything we say here, so I won't press you for details."

"Honestly, there's nothing to give." I shrugged. "I'm an errand boy and that's it."

"They don't hire ex-cop PI.s, Jack, unless the errand only calls for a one way trip." He looked at me with an upturned eyebrow and a wink.

"I've already gone the one-way and I'm still sucking wind." I eyed him back. "But like I said, I'm not working for them."

"We figured that after we discovered who you were." Osterholt advised. "We're just puzzled about what's going on."

"It's a job and nothing more from my end" I tried to turn the conversation in another direction. "So, what's a Frank Carlucci?"

"This really isn't the time or place for a seminar on these people, but he came out here about fifteen years ago from the east coast, sort of a forced reassignment. He's been trying to engineer his way back into the east coast mainstream with a deal, a sort of merger with the Vettriano family who's running things now."

"Sounds like a episode of the Sopranos?" I commented.

"That's the rumor and this ain't prime time, pal. This is real life."

The Carlucci File

He nudged his drink into my side. "I'll give you one thing, though. You must have balls of steel to go out with Sophia Carlucci right under Frank's nose."

"Does Frank have a brother?" I ignored the compliment. I think it was a compliment.

"Nicolas." Osterholt frowned and shook his head. "Dropped out years ago, way back when. Not a player. In fact, we don't have a thing on him other than an archived footnote in Frank's file."

"Good news." I said to myself thoughtfully.

"Frank does have a sister in play, though." He added. "Merciless bitch, from what I hear. Anyone gets around her she doesn't like, shit happens to them. Word is she's more dangerous than Frank. Some of the guys even think she's behind this power play merger to get Frank back in the driver's seat."

"Bad news." I felt that cold chill shooting down my back again and thought of Anna.

"Of course, you know we'll have you under surveillance when you leave." He was close to me now, almost whispering in my ear. "Our job is to keep tabs on Carlucci and fatten up his file."

"Of course." I affirmed as I whispered back.

"Answer one question for me, if you can, Jack?"

"What's that?" I shrugged.

"Why are you driving one of Frank's Hummers out in the middle of nowhere?"

"*Frank's* Hummers?" I asked back in a surprised tone.

"It's under one of his holding companies, almost untraceable, but we've got it in our book as one of his." He nodded. "It was caked with desert soot. Why it that and why are you driving it?"

"I'm beginning to wonder myself." I looked at him with a thin smile, remembering how mature my valet had been. "But I'm glad you guys are getting some valet experience. It's always nice to have another profession to fall back on."

"Glad you like the service." He handed me a business card. "You know, a few minutes ago I could've offered you some protection, but Tandy says he's going to throw you to the wolves. For some odd reason, he's developed a serious hard on for you."

"Jeez." I memorized the number before handing the card back to him. "All that anger he's carrying around and now you say on top of everything else, he's gay?"

"I'll tell him you said that."

"I'd expect no less." I smiled and he joined me.

20

I might have expected a sleepless night, what was left of it, with all the traffic wandering through my suite, but it was just the opposite. Osterholt's comment that the room might be bugged was well founded and it dawned on me that at the moment, I might be a valuable resource for Frank Carlucci. In the gray world were stolen objects floated from one pair of soiled hands to another, an uninvolved medium for such a transfer could be a precious commodity. It had never occurred to me that a private investigator, more aptly described as a jack of all trades with contacts in both the criminal and law enforcement communities, was an ideal facilitator for such movement. This was an aspect of my post-career vocation that I had never entertained or sought, but like the profession itself, it had chosen me rather than the other way around.

As for my intruder from the night before, he had gotten in on a fluke and I didn't think he'd be back in the same capacity, since he clearly had no independent means of getting in and hadn't found what he was looking for in the first place. It did make me wonder how he'd gotten onto the Penthouse floor in the first place, though, and that disturbing thought had landed me on the couch for the night, gun in one hand and a Scotch highball in the other. Not the best combination: lethal force and impaired judgment for using it, but like everything from my taking this case in the first place to the conversion of my suit pants and dress shirt as pajamas, it had just turned out that way.

The knocking at the door woke me with a start and my body twitched, sloshing some of the diluted highball I was still clutching onto my new shirt. It was strange that even in my usual morning stupor the knocking sounded familiar. Then again, I had to admit it was only the second time anyone had rapped their little rat claws on my door since I'd checked in. Everyone else had just helped themselves in without formality. Since the rapping did have the same tempo and vigor applied to it, I figured it must be the same person from the evening before, i.e.: the bellboy.

I got up, stuffing the 45 in my rear waistband out of habit and rubbed my eyes as I started for the door. Glancing out the room's large window for some sense of the time of day, I noticed the eerie predawn haze that always seemed to settle over the town just before the sun came up. I figured it must be somewhere around 5:00 a.m. and knew from experience that the temperatures outside had probably ebbed to a breezy 98 degrees, the coolest anyone could expect in Vegas this time of year. I walked to the door, looking out the peephole to confirm my suspicions. Sighing, I opened it.

"I just saw him." The senior bellboy said in an excited voice. "He just left."

"Just left?" I stifled a yawn.

"I caught him walking out the rear door towards the parking lot with his bag." My newfound friend and informant was breathing hard, as if he'd taken the stairs all the way up.

"So, he checked out."

"Must have." He nodded eagerly. "But that's not all."

"OK." I could see it was something the bellboy thought was intriguing.

"He gets in his rental and…"

"Whoa, what rental." I interrupted. "How did you know he was driving a rental?"

"I was a valet before I got the bellboy gig." He replied as if to say 'dah'. "I can spot a rented car a mile away."

"Let me guess, a cream colored Dodge Challenger."

"Yeah." He paused to look at me with a bit of wonder in his expression.

"OK, go ahead." I urged him out of his trance.

"Well, I tried to get close enough to like get the tag and the name of the rental company, but he stopped in the parking lot and got out with something in his hand."

"What?"

"I couldn't tell, but it was shiny and about the size of a pack of cigarettes."

"OK."

"He walked over to another parked car and put it under the rear bumper."

"A bright yellow Hummer." I nodded with an educated guess.

"Yeah, that's right." His eyes lit up. "Is that your car?"

"Good guess, Sherlock." I nodded with a frown.

"You think it's a bomb or something?" His eyes widened.

"Only if he's working for my ex-wife." I shook my head, trying to wake up and think clearer.

"Well, he lit out of there like it was going to blow up any second." His tone changed to apologetic. "I didn't get a good look at the rental sticker, but think it might be either Alamo or Budget. He was driving right at me and I had to duck behind a tour bus."

"Good work, anyway." I dug out another chip and flipped it to him.

"Thanks." He was beaming again. "Anything else I can do for you just let me know."

"I'll remember." I nodded and shut the door.

It wasn't too hard to figure out what my mystery guest had been up to and I knew he wouldn't be too far away from here on out. I reflected that my activities were starting to gather a decent sized audience. Maybe I should start looking for a publicist. I stretched and yawned openly, noticing I still had last night's drink in my hand. I shook my head and walked over to the mini-bar, pulling out the 45 and plopping it down on the counter while dumping the liquid from the glass into the small sink with my other hand. I found the fridge that came with the bar and dug out a single serving of orange juice that had been stocked as a mixer. I poured it into the glass and drank it straight. I anticipated drinking the liquor the same way sometime later in the day, but for now, I looked around for the coffee maker. I needed to get the cobwebs out of my head, because something told me this was going to be a busy day.

I ordered down for some breakfast and retrieved the Daily Sun from just outside my door. There were no clues in the headlines as to what was going on in my life, but I wasn't really expecting to see my picture with the caption 'Another dead body about to found in the desert'. Newspapers were more about Monday morning quarterbacking and less about psychic fortune telling. Instead, it was business as usual in the entertainment/gambling capital and no names in the news leapt out at me. At this point, I was becoming hypersensitive to any names with Italian sounds to them. The food came and I ate next to the bay window, forcing my mind to slow down and enjoy the sunrise over Mt. Charleston. Slowly, the day dawned with the large blinding globe that promised the town another fourteen hours of blowtorch weather.

Retreating from the growing heat that was penetrating even the heavy window tinting, I closed the shear section of drapes and headed for the bathroom. Once shaved and feeling somewhat human again, I picked through the clothes Sophie had selected for me. Settling on a pair of slacks and polo shirt that dated my taste by at least ten years, I was at lease grateful for the new round of socks, shorts and T-shirts she had been thrown into the mix of fashion leisurewear. She had even been thoughtful enough to grab a soft suitcase to take everything with me.

I looked at the bullet-ridden duffel and decided to leave everything from my old wardrobe behind, except my treasured Nikes. I looked at the shoes Sophie had picked out and then at the Nikes. Leisure didn't always equate to comfort, so I tossed the oxfords into the suitcase and slipped on the athletic shoes.

I was in the middle of sorting through my new set of threads when I heard the chiming of the cell phone in the next room. Whoever had purchased it had left the ringer on the distinctive tone that identified the service carrier. I followed the ringing out to the living area and immediately noticed the breakfast cart was gone. I also noticed a large metal carrying tube, approximately six inches in diameter and nearly five feet long sitting on the couch. It was fitted with heavy leather caps on either end and a stout matching shoulder strap clipped between them. Someone had been in the suite while I was in the shower. Probably disguised as part of the wait-staff, the courier had deposited the carrying tube and left with the breakfast cart, or more likely, brought it in under the cart in the first place and left it when he'd come back for the cart.

The ringing phone didn't leave me and time to dwell on it, as it was about to vibrate off the end table next to the couch where I'd put it the night before. I caught it just before it rattled off the table. Fumbling with the buttons, I opened the connection.

"Hello?"

"How was breakfast?" It was the man I'd met the evening before, the one with the short temper and big cigar, who also happened to be Sophie's husband and by all other accounts, the head of the Las Vegas mob syndicate.

"Good." I answered. At least he didn't ask how the date with his wife had gone.

"See the package?"

"Yes, I see it." I looked at the tube on the couch.

"Keep this cell phone with you." He advised in the same curt manner he'd used when we'd first met. "Check out of the hotel and start driving back to that shit hole up north, the way you came in. There'll be further instructions."

"I should probably tell you…."

"I heard about your visitors." He cut me off. "From the sound of your conversation, it almost appears that we have mutual enemies."

"Almost." Apparently Osterholt had been right about the place being bugged. "Am I going to…"

"Survive this?" He read my mind right through the unrelated question I was about to ask. "You see what was left for you?"

"The package? Yes, I see it." I looked dumbly at the container.

"That's not a package." He said curtly. "That's my brother's life. Do I need to say anything else?"

"What about the Feds?" I asked "They'll have me under surveillance. What if they jump me before I can get back to Lone Tree?"

"They won't." His reply was quick and confident, like he'd already read their game plan. "They know you're only the middleman and they're more interested in where you're going with the package."

"They got a hold of the Hummer yesterday." I advised. "They've probably got it tagged for GPS."

"Let me do the thinking, Einstein." He cut me off again. "You just drive and keep the cell phone handy."

"Yes, Sir."

"Anything else you want to say?" I could tell he was expecting something.

"Uh, thank you for the nice room?"

"About my wife, genius."

"She's a very nice lady, Mr. Carlucci."

"She's family." He stated adamantly. "Like Nick and Anna."

"Yes, Sir."

"This fuck Mersant has no idea who he's dealing with and some people are on the way there to enlighten him if anything goes sideways."

"I understand." I didn't want to. All I could picture was a ring of guys like Tony surrounding Mersant's band of hired thugs, then a larger contingent of Federal tactical teams parachuting onto the mesa to surround everyone. I didn't think DeLaCosta ever planned on so many guests all at once and Maria would have a bitch of a time trying to feed the ones that survived.

"What I'm saying is don't be a fuck up, Einstein." His voice rose just enough to get my attention back and make his point. "Nick wants it played straight, so we'll play it straight. Do your job."

"Yes, Sir." I couldn't help but be reminded of the bellboy and notice I sounded just like him now. The ocean was full of bigger fish feeding on smaller fish, ad nauseam. Right now I felt like a minnow.

The connection closed on his side and I looked at the cell phone long and hard before putting it down. My eyes wandered to the tube on the couch and I didn't want to think about what was in it. All evidence pointed to a priceless artwork that had been missing from the Lourve for a decade. It was something, really the last thing that I ever wanted to be responsible for.

My eyes wandered to the table phone on the complimentary desk set across the room and I recited Osterholt's number in my head over and over again. I was thinking very strongly of diving towards it and making the call, but wasn't sure they'd get here in time. Even if they did, I thought about what it would be like to live in some witness protection program and who'd administer my ex's alimony payments. Strange what goes through your head in times of stress? In the end, I thought of Anna and curiously Ray, or Nick, knowing I'd have to play this out to keep them safe. If it all went upside down and I survived, I'd have to try my best to explain my way out of jail time on the other side.

I grabbed the tube and what was left of my stale coffee and carried them into the bedroom. The artwork wasn't going to be out of my sight until this was over, that much was for certain. Hastily throwing my new clothes in the suitcase and taking one last look around the suite, I suddenly felt like some poor slug skipping town after losing a bet with the wrong people's money. Right now, I almost envied such a scenario. Shouldering the carrying tube and dropping my 45 back into my rear waistband, I cautiously surveyed the hall outside before letting the door close behind me and then headed for the elevator.

Pushing the call button incessantly, it finally arrived and I entered the lift, again pressing the 'lobby' button several times, impatient to get out of the hotel. On my repeated command, the elevator finally cycled and began it's decent, but stopped at the next floor down. I instinctively moved into the far corner and switched shoulders to put the tube behind me, hiding and shielding it with my body. At the same time, I rested my hand in the same area, which was also closer to the 45. I almost physically nodded in affirmation when I found the same man wearing the same suit standing outside the lift on the same floor. We made the same eye contact, but this time he got in. 'Surprise, surprise' I thought to myself in Gomer Pyle inflection.

"Going the same way, this time." He tried to smile, but it didn't work.

"Looks like." I tried to give him my Melvin Croup smile, but it didn't work, either.

"Having any luck?" His speech was casual and the statement seemingly innocuous as he eyed my luggage and the strap around my far shoulder. "Looks like you're heading out already."

"Thought I'd give it a shot somewhere else." I tried not to communicate too much of what was really going through my mind.

"I hear the odds are better up north." He smiled slightly as he made eye contact, not doing a very good job of concealing his real meaning, if there was one. As an afterthought, or disclaimer, he added. "I heard Reno has looser slots."

"I'll keep that in mind." I nodded as the elevator mercifully made the lobby and we were instantly barraged by the sound of falling change and clanging slot machines.

"Well, good luck." He nodded back and disappeared into the casino crowd.

I stood outside the elevator and watched him until he disappeared into the crowd, before looking around for the best escape route. If I had ever felt self-conscious in my entire life, this was the granddaddy of the feeling. My attention drifted to one of the smoked Plexiglas bubbles protruding from the ceiling. It was a given that casino security, probably owned and operated by Carlucci, was watching me from all the angles. Ironically, the Feds might be watching right over their shoulders, both doing the same job from the same monitors. I took a deep breath and started making my way cautiously to the front desk to surrender my keycards. The shift had changed, so the clerk I'd dealt with earlier had gone home. Lucky her.

That done, I stopped by the cashier's cage on the way out, exchanging what chips I had left for traveling expenses. Once outside, the full force of the new day's heat hit me like a blast furnace as I walked over to the valet's station, bag in one hand with the carrying tube over the same shoulder. I was leaving my 'business' hand free, given the cargo I was handling. I gave the claim ticket to one of the kids, who quickly disappeared towards the valet lot, and tried to find the one who'd surprised me the day before and offered the car wash. He was nowhere in sight. No surprise. He was probably sitting in one of the Fed's numerous chase vehicles, watching me through binoculars at this very moment.

The Hummer finally came around and stopped in front of me. I tipped the valet as he jumped out and waved off any further help with my luggage. Making a pretense of walking to the back of the SUV to put the suitcase in the rear area, I accidentally dropped my keys in the process. Oops. I bent down to retrieve them and inspected the undercarriage the best I could. It wasn't hard to spot the tracking device my mystery guest had tucked up behind the bumper assembly. I figured it was a cheapie, one that could be purchased from a junior private eye catalogue or Radio Shack. I shuddered to think where the Feds had concealed theirs and wondered if Carlucci hadn't installed one of his own for the occasion.

Shaking my head, I closed the back of the SUV down and walked to the driver's door and got in. Placing my precious cargo in the passenger foot-well, I looped the carrying strap around the shifter for good measure. I made sure the doors were locked and repositioned my self-defense tool under my leg on the seat before putting the SUV in gear and easing out of the Caesar's Palace breezeway. I had a full tank and the Hummer was spotlessly clean, so there was nothing to do but find the nearest street that would hook me up with the Interstate and head north.

Just under an hour later, I was approaching the turn off where Tony had connected to the Interstate, which was marked Basin Valley, with Ely as one of the destinations on the sign. We'd passed through it on the way in, so I figured it was the one I wanted. I hadn't been driving and it had been dusk when we'd been here last, but it all looked familiar.

So far, the trip had been uneventful. I had opened the sunroof headliner early on to keep an eye on air traffic through the tinted glass, but had seen very little. A private aircraft had flown overhead just after I left town, but it appeared to fly off west and I'd seen nothing suspicious in the air since. Likewise, on the highway, I had also caught a glimpse once or twice of a light colored Dodge behind me, very similar to the one driven by my mystery guest. But then again, I was also becoming paranoid about every Chevy Tahoe or Yukon with tinted windows that I spotted in my wake. I had to start wondering why I bothered to look. Besides the bright yellow paint on the Hummer, I was the equivalent of an electronic Christmas tree driving down the highway. It made me wonder what the SUV looked like on real-time satellite imaging.

I was just started to get over and slow down for the exit ramp when the cell phone rang again.

"Yes Sir." I expected it to be Frank Carlucci.

"It's about time you started showing a little respect." Tony's subtle voice responded. "How's the trip so far?"

"Other than feeling like the main float in a parade, I'm doing great."

"There's a truck-stop just past the turn off you're getting ready to use, exit number 75." He explained. "Keep going and get off there. Go into the rest room on the trucker's side and sit in the last stall."

"I hope they're heavy duty johns?" I replied. "Cause right now I could...."

"Save it." He cut me off. "Take the tube with you."

"It hasn't left my sight since I found it in the room."

"Good." He hung up before I could ask anything else.

His call had been so timely I knew the Hummer had me under their own close scrutiny, as I'd suspected. I resumed my highway speed and kept going. As promised, soon the truck stop he had described loomed off to the right and I took the designated ramp. I checked my gauge and thought it would be wise to top off the tank anyway, since I'd soon be heading into no-man's land. Turning towards the large complex, I noticed one side of the truck stop ,was for the large semi-tractor rigs, while other was for Ma and Pa Kettle tourists.

I drove into the isolated travel stop and idled slowly around the trucker's side, behind the main store and then back to the public pumps. This way, I was now facing the side road I'd come in from, giving me full view of anyone who might be following. Sitting for a moment at the pump island, I caught sight of the cream colored Charger driving up from the highway towards me. It drove on past, disappearing up the side road where I was certain it would turn around and wait.

"That's one." I nodded to myself.

The Feds would be much harder to spot and might not have any ground resources close at all. I scanned the skies, but didn't see anything. Getting out of the Hummer, I used my plastic to activate the pumps and started refueling. Watching the road while I held the trigger down on the nozzle, I reflected how hard it might be to spot the Feds. There were a few contenders, most notably a silver Suburban I watched take the off-ramp and stop at the bottom, before continuing right back onto the highway. I finished at the pumps and re-parked the Hummer outside the truck stop.

Making a dramatic scene of stretching for my unseen audience, I restrained myself from flipping off the Fed's orbiting satellite and walked into the main store. I found the trucker's lounge off to one side, complete with showers and everything else they needed for a short break, and walked back to the bathroom stalls. Not many drivers were using the facilities, but I could tell what few I did run across were real enough by the way they regarded me. I expected a couple of them to kick me out of their reserved space, but for whatever reason, they chose only to give me dirty looks and say nothing more.

I went to the rear stall in the bathroom and closed the door behind me. A minute or so later, the room was empty and fell silent. Shortly afterward, I heard the bathroom door open and the stall door next to me open and close.

"Open the tube." The voice from the other side of the partition was ominous and monotone.

"What?" I looked at the carrying tube between my knees.

"Open the fucking tube, asshole." He spat. "We haven't got all day."

"OK." I shrugged and worked the clasp on one end of it.

"Take the clothes out and slide the tube under the partition."

I dug my hand into the large tube and extracted a rolled up pair of jeans and a gray short-sleeve Henley shirt. Digging deeper, I found a NY Yankee's baseball cap with a pair of sunglasses and pulled them out as well. I scanned the interior of the tube, especially around the circumference and found it completely empty. No painting. You had to wonder where the trust was. I closed the tube and rolled it under the partition as instructed.

"Now get undressed and hand your shirt and pants over to me." He sounded like he was changing clothes while talking to me.

I obeyed his instructions while retaining my personals and a couple of minutes later he sounded like he was done.

"Slide the Hummer keys under the partition."

I did as instructed and a moment later another pair of keys slid back to me.

"Silver Avalanche with the visor down on the passenger's side. Wait at least ten minutes after you get dressed."

With that, the stall door again opened and closed. I stood up and peered over the partitions, but only caught a glimpse of a man stuffing a pair of work overalls in the trashcan before walking out the door. He was now wearing my polo shirt and slacks and from the back I actually thought I was watching myself leaving the restroom.

21

Strangely relieved to rid myself of the Perry Como shirt and slacks, I casually got dressed in the clothes from the tube while waiting the amount of time I'd been instructed to pass. Checking my image in the mirror on the way out, I pulled the baseball cap on and down low over my forehead as I left the rest room. Forgoing the sunglasses until I was ready to walk out the truck stop's door, I now felt like some sort of fugitive evading the authorities. Walking through the locker room, I got a few strange looks from the few drivers loitering nearby, but it was a mixed bag of expressions. Their demeanor suggested that somebody had probably 'closed' the restroom while my little quick-change was taking place. I smiled a weak apology and continued on my way.

Reentering the store, no one seemed to give me a second look, but I knew in the world of quality surveillance, that could be a sign that indeed I was being watched. Or maybe I was just being paranoid. I didn't have much time to check what few customers were loitering in the aisles, but I did force myself to stop at the coffee makers while glancing in the convex security mirrors. Everything looked business as usual, so I paid for the coffee, checked the time, and walked back out to the parking lot.

Outside, I found the Avalanche my contact had described, a hybrid Chevy product that amounted to a four door, four-wheel drive SUV with a truck-bed the size of a tackle box. I pressed the button on the key fob and the 4X's headlights winked at me like a hooker eager to leave the bar and make a few bucks. I jumped in and started it up, leaving the truck stop and heading back to the interstate. I got on going back south in the direction of Las Vegas, where my original exit was waiting for me not far away.

It was obvious that Frank Carlucci had engineered the vehicle switch to get the small army of Feds off my tail. I was hoping the ruse would work on my mystery guest as well. But now I had to ask myself where the painting was? It made me wonder if Frank Carlucci had actually ever possessed it at all? I tried to line up the days and estimate how long it had been between the time his brother Nick realizing he needed the painting and his brother Frank sending the carrying tube to my hotel room. It seemed awfully quick, given the news story about the arrest only a few days ago and Phillippe Mersant showing up even later than that.

Then again, Nick's description of this collector who'd originally bought the painting matched his brother Frank to a 'T'. Had Frank Carlucci been the original collector all along? What I remembered of him didn't fit any profile of an art collector I'd ever heard of, but people were all kinds of strange and the more rich and powerful they were, the stranger they seemed to get. Whatever was happening at this point, I felt relieved to be out from under Federal surveillance, but had no idea what part, if any, I had left to play in this game.

I took the exit towards Lone Tree and headed northwest, not knowing what I'd do when I finally arrived there. I attempted to formulate a plan as the two-lane blacktop eased around towards the northwest and into the low mountains. The day was clear with heat waves shimmering off the desert floor. In the distance, their effect was that of tranquil lakes inviting a refreshing swim. I guessed it was the thermal waves reflecting the blue sky above, but wasn't in the mood to entertain a science fair at the moment. My mind kept trying to wrap around what I should do next.

As if on cue, the cell phone rang again.

"Yeah?" I answered after opening the connection.

"There's coffee in a thermos and some snacks in the backseat." It was Tony again. "Drive straight through to Lone Pine and don't stop anywhere. You have enough gas to make it now."

"What am I supposed to do when I get there?"

"Deliver the car to Nick." Tony said in an assuring tone. "You've got the ball. He'll know what to do from there."

"What does that mean?"

"The package is hidden in the car with you."

"What?" I looked around behind me, but all I saw was the thermos and a brown shopping bag.

"You're the courier." Tony said. "Don't fuck it up."

"Where are you?" I glanced in the rearview mirror, suddenly feeling vulnerable again.

"Not too far away." I could hear him almost smiling in his response.

"Where is it?" I looked around again, this time at the rear floorboards. "The painting, I mean."

"That's not your concern." His business tone was back. "Nick and I know where it is. You know only what you need to know."

"Where's the trust?" I echoed my earlier thoughts, more to myself than to my caller.

"It's not a matter of trust." Tony replied. "It's a matter of not being able to give it up, no matter who else asks or how hard."

"Who would that be?" I surveyed the road ahead of me before it hit me. "What do you mean, hard?"

"If you're stopped by the Feds, you won't know and they won't find it without tearing the car apart." He answered. "If you're jumped by anyone else, you won't be able to tell them, no matter how much they beat on you."

"How reassuring." I nodded and I commented sarcastically. "I take it Frank Carlucci looked up 'expendable' in the dictionary and found my picture."

"Something like that." There was no humor in his voice. "But remember, we won't be far behind you all the way home."

"I hope Mersant's men haven't drained Nick's liquor cabinet." I shook my head. "Cause by the time I get there, I'm going to be very thirsty."

"Relax." Tony said. "We've got your back."

The connection went dead and I tossed the phone on the seat next to me, still shaking my head. I had to admit, having Tony on my team actually was comforting, but I had to remind myself he actually wasn't. I could picture myself lying on the ground, bleeding to death as he stepped over my soon to be rotting corpse to retrieve the package. I could even envision looking down at me before he walked away, telling me what a good job I'd done. Not a comforting thought, but reality usually wasn't.

The trip back to Lone Tree would have been uneventful, if it had not been for the appearance of Carl Stapleton's rented Charger. I had calculated that I was almost halfway to my destination, passing through a small berg consisting of a small Main Street with a dozen or so houses built in the late 50's. The coffee had gone right through me and I was starting to look for a safe place to stop long enough to relieve myself. I didn't want to chance stopping in any town, so I'd decided to get through this one and look for a turnout of sorts to do my business.

At the end of town, two gas stations on either side of the road invited what had to have been stale gas from their rusting pumps, all for inflated prices. I did a double take at the sight the Charger, sitting in the shade of one of the pump islands. I held my breath as I mentally tried to become invisible and slip by unnoticed. The car looked unattended, just sitting there in the shade with no one near it. I stared at the car long and hard in the rearview mirror until it disappeared around the first bend behind me.

Letting out a deep sigh of relief, I glanced at the cell phone on the seat next to me. It wasn't very reassuring, since I could only receive calls and not make them, that is if it worked at all out here in no-man's land. Still, I had to remind myself this wasn't the bright yellow Hummer and although there wasn't much traffic on this highway, my ride looked anonymous enough. It was a newer model, but that was the only thing that remotely stood out up here in the outback of Nevada.

I was just starting to breathe easier when the Charger suddenly appeared in my rearview mirror. He was taking on speed and coming up fast.

"Shit." I studied the car in the mirror and felt for the comfort of my 45, now lying on the seat next to the cell phone.

The car closed the distance and then just as suddenly backed off to follow me at a reasonable distance. It was obvious from the way he had come up and then leveled off that he was checking my vehicle out, but he couldn't have known it was me inside… right? The Avalanche's windows were tinted, although not as heavy as the Hummer, but enough that I was reasonably sure I couldn't be recognized in it. I eased up ever so slightly on the gas, encouraging him to pass and keep going, but

The Carlucci File

he wouldn't take the bait. Finally, it became obvious he had zeroed in and was blatantly tailing me. I slowly resumed my speed and nervously glanced at the cell with the automatic handgun lying beside it.

We drove tandem for several anguishing miles with me constantly glancing in the mirror, wondered what I should do next. My bladder was dictating the need for a bodily function soon, but stopping could very well put me in a terminally vulnerable position. I wondered if the guy in the Dodge behind me was armed, then wondered if he was thinking the same thing about me. We were the only two cars on the road for the most part, with only an occasional pickup or lost motorhome passing in the other direction.

"So, how long are we going to do this dance?" I asked the car in my rearview mirror.

We maintained our little rolling standoff for the next twenty miles or so when I decided I had to stop or sit in a puddle for the rest of the trip. I found a suitable turnout and picked up the 45. It was already in a safety-off status, but with the hammer down. The old design dictated the hammer be cocked all the way back to start the semi-automatic sequence of replacing one bullet after another as it was fired. I cocked it and carefully laid it alongside my leg. It had been a very long time since I'd even pointed a gun at someone, so naturally the adrenalin started to leak into my system and my heart began to pound in my chest.

I eased off the gas and pulled off the road in the dirt area that had been leveled and cleared for assorted roadside emergencies. My bladder was telling me this was one of them. I stared at the sedan in the mirror to see what it would do. It slowed and started to follow me into the turn out. My mind raced for some tactical advantage and somewhere in darker recesses of my mind I figured if all else failed I'd drown my assailant in urine.

With almost as much relief as I was seeking on the side of the road, I watched the Charger stop at the edge of the pavement and hesitate. I pulled around to my right, making a U-turn further off on the turnout before stopping. This would keep my SUV between the Dodge and myself when I got out. It was the only tactical thought I could come up with, which was really depressing. For several long seconds, our two cars sat with only the idling motors breaking the silence of the wilderness. I was about to open the door and take care of business when the Dodge turned back onto the highway and kept driving north.

I watched it continue out of sight before jumping out and taking care of my pause for nature, standing in the car's open doorway. As if Tony was out to torture me with his timing, the cell phone started ringing while I was quite literally in midstream. Trying to reach it and relieve myself at the same time was comical enough for a whole episode of America's Home Videos. Stretching over the driver's seat and slapping the vinyl seat, the phone only bounced further away. Cursing some more, I finally finished my emergency and stretched over the driver's seat to pick it up.

"Yeah?" I was so pissed, no pun intended, that I didn't even think to question how the phone was working out here in the middle of nowhere.

"What are you stopping for?" Tony sounded alarmed and I could hear the motor of his car in the background laboring under acceleration.

"Nature call." I explained, zipping up my fly. "By the way, I've picked our old tail again."

"Who?"

"I suspect the same guy who followed us into Vegas." I jumped back into the SUV and pointed it back onto the roadway. "I spotted the car in the valet area at Caesar's and a helpful bellboy told me the driver had planted something on the Hummer."

"Who is it?"

"I thought you'd be able to tell me." I shook my head. "All I'm relatively certain of is that the car used to be Carl Stapleton's rental."

"The other PI?" Tony's inflection sounded like for once he was in the dark as much as I was. "The guy you found in the canyon?"

"The same."

There was a silence, but I could hear his car motor in the background slacking back off to normal.

"Where's the car now?"

"Up ahead of me somewhere."

"OK." His tone was calm again and he was back in control. "Keep going, average speed and if you have to piss again, do it in an empty coffee cup or something. Don't stop again. Got it?"

"Got it." I replied in a resigned tone, but then it occurred to me.

"How is it our phones work out here in the middle of nowhere?"

"It's only the two of us that can talk and only if we're close enough to each other." Tony explained. "If you need to reach me, press the call button."

"It would've been nice to know that about twenty miles ago." I said sarcastically.

"Just keep driving." He instructed. "We've closed in on you a bit, just in case."

"Comforting." I replied just before the connection closed from his end.

I returned to my cruising speed, now wondering how Tony had known I'd stopped in the first place. It was becoming apparent my ride was just as tractable as the Hummer I'd given up back at the truck stop. It seemed reasonable for what I was carrying, but it made me wonder what other little surprises the big SUV might hold.

I kept an eye peeled for the Charger as I made my way further up in elevation, working my way north to where I hoped Anna was still alive and well, along with her uncle Nick, aka Ray, aka Dimitri. Thinking back now on my conversations with Anna, I remembered how she hesitated every time I asked her something about her uncle. At the time I'd thought it was because she was under some kind of instruction, but now it was becoming apparent she'd been reluctant to tell me the truth about him, and her.

I tried to keep my private thoughts of our time together out of my head and concentrate on the situation not far ahead of me. What would Mersant really do once he had the painting? Was he the professional thief he professed to be, or was he just another gangster who'd try to bury any possible witnesses once he had what he wanted? Then again, what did Nick's brother have up his sleeve if things went sideways on this deal? Tony wasn't far behind me and from the way he was talking he definitely wasn't alone. How many guys did he have with him and what was his plan?

On a more personal note, how was I going to go back into the house armed and not be discovered? Should I try? I quickly decided I couldn't risk it. I'd have to find a hiding place for the gun just before arriving at the house, as I was sure both my body and the car would be searched by Mersant's men when I got there. Things were winding up in my head and the spring was getting tighter as the miles stacked up and I got closer to Lone Tree.

Lone Tree. I shook my head at the thought of it. What the hell was going on there that Carl had been killed and I'd been shot at? From the way Tony was talking, Carl hadn't met his end at the bodyguard's hand. Instinctively, I hadn't thought Nick was involved, but I had lingering doubts about Tony acting on some auto-response to protect his boss. With that factor negated from the equation, the bikers moved up a notch as the responsible party. But the description the bellboys gave me of the guy driving Carl's rental didn't match any of the bikers I'd seen in Lone Tree. It actually didn't match anyone I'd come across at all, at least anybody that was still sucking wind. Mersant crossed my mind again and that possibility of it being one of his men did compute, but I didn't want to think about him being involved like that. It would mean my deepest fears about what was going to happen when I showed up at the house would probably come true.

There were so many things that had happened since I'd taken this case and so many possibilities of it's eventual outcome rolling around in my head that the life I'd known in Los Angeles now seemed like a distant memory. I wouldn't know where to start in a report to Croup, even if I wanted to be accurate about what I'd gone through here. I tried to think of what my stinky little flop pad just off Venice Beach looked like, but couldn't. There was no way of telling what I'd come out of this with monetarily, that is if I *did* come out of it at all. That triggered thoughts of Anna and what kind of life we'd have if she ran off with me. It wasn't anymore an encouraging scenario than my pending physical arrival at the mesa-top pueblo.

I still hadn't formulated any concrete plan by the time I started recognizing the landscape and knew Lone Tree would be coming up soon. No sign of the Charger had been seen since my nature stop and I wondered if Frank Carlucci's 'assets' had caught up with my mysterious shadow. If they had, I entertained a wrong, but vengeful form of dark hope that they'd meted out some form of justice for whoever was driving it. Since Carl was dead and this person was driving his car, it seemed a no-brainer that he'd been responsible.

When the diner and inn finally came into view, the daylight was just starting to fade behind the canyon walls. All seemed as I had left it. There were no signs of life and still only the one car parked in front of the hotel. It looked like the whole place was closed or deserted. It should've been a clue, but I had been so anxious to get back, yet so reluctant to do so without a plan, that my mind was still wandering and I missed the obvious.

I passed the hotel and turned in towards the mesa wall where Nick's bizarre little driveway lay hidden in the late afternoon shadows. Simultaneously, I started to look down for the four-wheel-drive controls I'd need to get up the steep grade. I glanced up and shock set in as I slammed on the brakes and come to an abrupt stop. Two cars were stretched across the road in front of the small conduit bridge that went over the stream. They were immediately recognized as those seen at one time or another parked in front of the hotel. I barely stopped in time and when the cloud of red dust from under my locked tires started to settle, I looked around for what the hell was going on.

No one was around the cars, but light from one of the cabins not thirty yards from the bridge came on and caught my attention. No, it wasn't a light coming on, but rather a door opening. Alarmingly, all the choppers I'd seen drive up the day before were now visible, grouped together behind the hotel where they couldn't be seen from the road. Even more alarming, the outlaw bikers who owned them were now pouring out the open cabin door, all holding rifles and shotguns of assorted description.

They were all walking towards me leisurely, like border guards in a Mexican town. I immediately recognized the leader of the group; the same hard case who had called in his flock from the hotel's porch the day before.

He had an almost evil smile on his face as his arms rested over the barrel and stock of the rifle he had perched over his shoulders. He looked like he'd escaped some strange form of crucifixion and taken his cross with him. Behind him, most notably, were the Three Stogies, as I'd dubbed them. I remembered Lorene's scathing admonishment to them, but couldn't remember the name she'd yelled at the one guy I'd dubbed as Moe. Had she called him Billy? I wondered where Lorene was now, not that she'd be able to help this time.

The hard-case walked up to the SUV still smiling but stepped slightly off to one side, allowing Billy, or whoever, to do the honors.

Billy had a similar smile on his face, but it looked stupid on him rather than evil. He didn't have the stuff to carry himself like his chief could, but he gave it his best shot. He pulled a cheap, chrome-plated revolver out of this waistband and leaned over a bit, knocking on the driver's window with its barrel. This had all the potential of getting very ugly.

22

A lot of questions had been answered in a heartbeat as I stared back through the car window, especially the one about where my mystery shadow belonged in all this. Besides Tony, the occupant of that car was the only one who knew what I was driving and my proximity to the mesa's pueblo. Since the car used to be Carl's, it pretty much cinched who was behind his death. But although some questions had been answered, others had taken their place. What did these guys want with me, or did all this have something to do with the painting? If it was that, how did they even know about it?

Of more immediate concern, at least a dozen dirty smiles were now facing me, smiles that would gag the most enthusiastic dental hygienist. Billy, as I was almost sure he'd been called earlier, was displaying his large revolver that he'd used it to tap on the window in greeting. His smile never wavered as the rest of the Boy Scout Troop of Lone Tree fanned out around the front of the Avalanche. I watched them as my hand started to wander towards the 45 on the passenger's seat. Another tap and I looked back at Billy. His smile had waned just a bit as he was now pointing the revolver at me and slowly shaking his head.

Tony's words about not being able to give up the package, even under a good beating, came rushing back to me. Was he clairvoyant? More important at the moment, was he nearby? What could he do if he was? How many guys did he have with him? If he was close, at what point would he intervene and how? It was obvious he had to, given my cargo. My mind shifted gears and instinctively I knew I only had to stall for time. My wandering hand came back to the steering wheel, while my other one slowly moved the to window controls on the driver's door. The electric window's motor hummed softly, but I only let it drop halfway, not enough for them to drag me out through it. The doors remained locked.

My innate inclination to purposely piss people off again suddenly overrode what common sense I had left.

"Yes," I smiled my signature Melvin C. Croup grin directly at Billy. "I'll take a cheeseburger, order of curly fries and a large coke."

Billy's face dropped like a rock, but instead of pulling the trigger or punching my face through the partially open window, he just hung there in confusion. Given his perceived IQ, it was the reaction I'd expected.

"What the fuck you talkin about?" His face jutted out, still trying to comprehend my mocking disposition.

The leader kicked Billy hard in the leg and the village idiot yelped as he looked up at him, a bit shocked and hurt at the same time. He skulked away from the window like a beaten dog and the evil one took his place. A lot taller and still cradling his long firearm, an over-under shotgun over both his shoulders, he had to lean over just a bit to talk through the window opening.

"Get out." His words rolled out in a manner threatening enough to be deemed serious.

"You know," I unlocked the door and opened it slowly. "This was the hospitality I had originally anticipated when I drove in a few days ago."

"You don't say." His voice was deep and slow.

"I figured you guys would be more straight up, doing something like this, rather than shooting at me in the middle of the night, supposedly while I was sleeping in one of your flee-bitten hotel rooms."

I slipped out of the driver's seat, but remained standing in the doorway, now looking slightly up at the chief who went well over six-feet. A distinct odor immediately invaded my nostrils and I repulsed a bit. It wasn't body odor, but it was coming from every one of the bikers in close proximity. I remembered catching a whiff of it sometime back while passing the cabins, but now I fully recognized it.

"What the fuck are you talking about?" The leader's head cocked sideways a bit, now curious about what I was telling him.

"My first night here." I began to explain slowly. "Someone murdered my partner and then shot at me while I was in one of your charming little rooms."

The chief looked at me hard, partially wondering if I was telling him the truth as he processed the information. When he saw I wasn't just running my mouth, he slowly turned to Billy. Surprisingly, Billy got that deer in the headlights look and shrugged his confession. Between the two of them, I was learning all kinds of things.

"It weren't us, Lyle, I swear." He shrunk from his leader's scowl. "Todd did it. We just cleaned it up."

"And you didn't even have the piss ass sense to tell me about it?" His voice rose about as far as I thought it ever would, just before he pounded someone into the ground, or worse.

"He said it was personal." Billy almost whined.

"I'll show that mother fucker 'personal'." The shotgun swung fluidly off his shoulders and he gripped it tightly in his hands, pointing it in the general direction of Billy.

"It was him, not us." Billy whined as he backed up and started to move around the front of the car, instinctively using it as cover.

"Get the fuck back over here, asshole." Lyle ordered sharply. "I'll take this up with that fat fuck when I see him."

"I'll be happy to deliver any message you have for him." I interjected. "He might even hear me over the gunfire I have planned for him."

Lyle's attention came back to me, but the scowl on his face didn't change. If anything, it just deepened.

"I hate smart-ass fucks, especially ones that are cops." The barrel of his shotgun inched my way. "I've had a belly full of you mother fuckers and I'm getting close to digging a grave big enough for all of ya."

"At least a grave would be better than feeding me to the buzzards." I was starting to pray Tony wasn't far away now. "Like you did my partner."

"What?" He spat and then looked over at Billy again. "You didn't even have the brains to bury the mother fucker?"

"Todd said there weren't time." Billy was whining and backing up again. "He told us just to dump him in a canyon and he'd bury him later."

"Todd doesn't run things around here." Lyle bellowed angrily. "I can't leave you in charge of a fucking shit-hole for ten minutes without you fucking it up."

"Wrong canyon, as it turns out, Lyle." I smiled a bit wider now. "I found his body. Deputy Turley and friends will be all over this place soon."

"Is that a fact?" He nodded seriously at me.

"Who is Todd, by the way?" As long as I had him talking, I thought I'd learn as much as I could, although the smell permeating all their clothing was now telling me volumes.

"He's none of your fucking business, that's who he is." Lyle drawled without taking his eyes off Billy. I was beginning to think his court clown might leave this world before I did. Lyle finally glanced back at me. "But I suspect you'll be meeting him soon enough. You can fucking ask him yourself."

"Is he the one who dropped a dime on me here?"

"You're not only a smart-ass, but you are actually a bit smarter than you look." He nodded at me thoughtfully. "Smart enough to get yourself fucking dead."

"Do you ever get through a sentence without using that word?" I shook my head in mock concern, sensing I'd stalled him long enough.

Lyle looked at me as if I'd lost my mind.

"You're pretty fucking cocky for a someone who's about to take a dirt nap." He pointed the shotgun at me.

"There's that unfortunate word, again." I shook my head slightly and then nodded at his shotgun. "Before you pull that trigger, you should tell Todd that I'm the only one who knows where it's hidden."

"Where what's hidden?" He studied my face.

"What's in this little buggy that Todd has you stopping me for. He did tell you to stop me and get the car, right?" I continued with my bluff, taking a wild guess these guys were partners with, but at the moment only acting as soldiers for Todd who'd dispatched them to relieve me of the SUV.

"What if he did?" His curiosity was worse than my own, but I was starting to think his business relationship with Todd, whoever he was, was starting to thin out.

"The point is if you mess with the wrong item in this ride, it'll blow big enough to take Lone Tree and spread us all over northern Nevada like some kind of fertilizer." I nodded at the highway with renewed

The Carlucci File

confidence. "So before you do anything rash, you might want to wait till old Toddy shows up and talk to him about it."

Just when I thought I was getting big Lyle turned around on this situation, the cell phone started ringing behind me. 'Finally.' I almost said out loud in relief. Lyle's finger teased the shotgun's trigger for a moment, but backed away from it and a look of doubt crossed his face. My Melvin Croup smile flashed once again, knowing the tide of this Mexican standoff was about to do a one-eighty.

"That's probably for you." I nodded to the phone and started to reach inside. "You want me to answer it for you?"

"You move another muscle and I'll paint this piece of shit car with your fucking brains." He pointed the shotgun at my head.

"Fine." I stepped aside from the open door with my hands going up in full surrender. "But I suggest you answer it."

"Move over further." Lyle jerked the barrel of the gun to one side and I slowly followed his instructions, sidestepping a few more feet from the open door.

I could see an added trace of curiosity cross the big man's face as he reached into the SUV. I suspected he was well aware that normal cell phones didn't work out here and must have been wondering why this one was ringing at all. First, he plucked my 45 from the seat and looked it over, before glancing at me and sticking it in his waistband. He reached back into the car and grabbed the ringing cell phone, then stood back outside the SUV examining it as he faced me.

"It's the button with the small green dot." I advised, pointing my raised index finger at the phone.

"Shut the fuck up." He drawled as he pressed the button. He put the phone to his ear, not saying anything. Instead, he continued to stare at me with the same intimidating expression and intense loathing. Slowly, his eyes narrowed and his brows furrowed as he continued to star straight at me. I slowly lowered my arms and folded them across my chest. Leaning against the SUV with a wide smile, I could see my actions were a complete mystery to the other bikers standing close enough to watch what was going on, but knew they couldn't hear what Lyle's caller was saying.

"Is that so?" The chief's voice seethed in response to what the caller was telling him. He started to scan the surrounding landscape, no doubt looking for Tony's perch.

A soft pop, followed by an abrupt hiss of escaping air suddenly made every biker attending our little party jump. Everyone, including Lyle, looked over at one of the cars blocking the bridge. The tire on one of them was rapidly going flat. The sound repeated itself and the other tire facing us on the same car suddenly met the same fate. Lyle looked back at me with pure hatred in his eyes and gave one last glance around the countryside. He finally tossed the phone at me and I scrambled to catch it.

"This isn't over." He spat in defiance.

"Good shot, isn't he?" It wasn't hard to guess what the big biker had been told on the phone and what example had just been shown to him.

"Fuck you." He replied in a low growl.

"We'll have to work on your vocabulary skills." I smiled. "Maybe I can send you a dictionary when you get back to Folsom.

"We'll be seeing you again, asshole." He started to turn away to leave.

"Excuse me."

I halted his retreat and forced him to look back at me. I pointed to the 45 in his waistband and he looked down at it, then back up at me.

"In your fucking dreams." He smirked.

I put the phone to my ear and waited, looking directly in his eyes. It took a moment, but he got the message. Just to make sure, I vocalized it.

"One word from me and you'll be in *your* friggin dreams, Lyle." I said evenly. "Permanently."

"Mother..." He mouthed the next word, but didn't say it as he pulled the 45 from his waistband and tossed it to me.

"I love your cologne, by the way." I caught the handgun and stuck it in my own waistband. "What do they call it, 'Aud De Ether'?"

Lyle stopped in his tracks and stared hard at me. At that very moment he wanted to kill me so bad even I could taste it. His hand tightened on his grip of the shotgun and I could see every muscle in his forearm straining to wring someone's neck. I figured he could practice on Billy until we met up again.

"You'll be in touch, then?" I smiled one last time at him.

His eyes narrowed even more as he turned away again, this time waving his arm at the others standing around with confused expressions on their faces.

"Move those cars." He barked the order without looking at anyone in particular.

Slowly, all of the bikers followed their leader back to the rear of the hotel, except for Billy and his two bookends. They split up and got into the road-blocking cars, backing them away to give access to the bridge. Within a few minutes, the collective sound of their Harleys rumbled to life and they poured out from behind the hotel.

They hit the highway and accelerated towards Elko, but I had doubts they'd ever ride that far. I wasn't sure where their main hangout was, but knew now that Lone Tree was quite literally their business office, while the cabins out back were their factory sites. I watched them disappear up the highway before turning to watch Billy and his friends frantically ride off to catch up with them. I glanced over at the hotel and spotted the desk clerk watching in morbid curiosity from the corner of the building. Beyond him, Lorene walked into view and looked over to see what was happening for herself.

I nodded to both of them and looked around. The two cars, one of which was now sporting two flat tires, were flanking the bridge, but all was clear towards the mesa and Nick's driveway. Realizing I was still holding the phone, I put it to my ear.

"Tony?"

"You do know how to push people's buttons."

"It's a gift."

"A gift isn't something that gets you killed." He replied. "They call that a death wish. You even had me debating whether you were worth saving or not."

"You love me and you know it." I said in newfound confidence.

"You need to lose the gun." He commented. "You'll be searched when we get to the pueblo."

"I figured." I realizing he'd been watching my exchange with Lyle closely through the scope of his silenced sniper rifle while listening on the open phone line. "We should meet, don't you think? I haven't got a friggin clue what I'm supposed to do here."

"The diner in five." He advised and the connection went dead.

"Good." I said more to myself as I stuffed the phone in my pocket and looked over the SUV. I tried to picture my gray matter as an accent color and shuddered. Tony was right. I had to cut back on the sarcasm.

Driving over to the diner, I parked right in front of the windows where I could see it from every booth in the restaurant. I got out, locked it with the key-fob, and went inside where I was met with now familiar smell of aging bacon grease mixed with Lorene's most recent manicure. Strangely, it made me smile.

"What was that all about?" Lorene automatically went for the coffee and came over to the same rear booth I'd always taken.

"Parking dispute." I gave her the short answer.

"You really shouldn't piss those guys off." She poured the coffee and I looked at it suspiciously, remembering how sick it had made me the first time I'd come in.

"You aren't having any?"

"Sure." Her face brightened and she grabbed another cup. We both drank in silence for a moment of two. She finally looked out the window in the failing light. "Where'd you get the new truck?"

"Nick, I mean Ray's Hummer had some problems, so that's kind of a loaner." I nodded in explanation.

"Oh." She shrugged and seemed satisfied with the answer.

Looking out the window, I spotted Tony walking towards the diner from across the highway. He was still some distance away.

"You have any idea what Lyle and Billy are doing over there in those cabins?" I studied Lorene's face closely for signs of any deception.

"I thought they just partied and flopped in them. Sometimes I get a funny smell that I think is coming from somewhere over there, but they never say and I never ask." She shrugged again without thinking and then looked at me curiously. "Why?"

"You use drugs, Lorene?" I looked at her closely, ignoring her question.

"I'm dying for some good weed." Her eyes lit up and rolled a bit. "You got any?"

"I mean the harder stuff, like cocaine or crank?"

"Crank?" She scrunched her face. "Where did you grow up?"

"Meth." I shrugged. "You know, speed."

"I tried some Ecstasy at a party once and didn't like it." She shook her head. "But I could sure use some good smoke right now."

"Does Billy ever offer any of that stuff to you?"

"When I first started working here, yeah, but then he found out who I was and I think that scared him." She sipped her coffee and glanced out the window. "Hey, isn't that Mr. DeLaCosta's friend walking up here?"

"Yeah." I confirmed offhandedly, but didn't follow her gaze. "Just who are you?"

"Shit, I thought you knew." She was still staring out the window as she headed back to the register. "That *is* Mr. DeLaCosta's friend."

"Who…" I sighed in exasperation as she walked away and finished the question to myself. "Are you?"

The screen door to the diner opened and Tony walked in. He was dressed just as he had been the last time I'd seen him at Frank Carlucci's house. I expected that he wanted to maintain the same appearance for Phillippe Mersant, so as not to arouse any suspicion. He spotted me and nodded to Lorene.

"Coffee?" She asked.

"No thanks." He passed her and walked back to me, taking the seat across the table.

"For once, your timing was impeccable." I lifted the cup. "You should try Lorene's coffee. It isn't half bad."

"We don't have that much time." Tony advised.

"Where's the Hummer?" I'd been thinking about that for the last few miles of my trip.

"By now, it should be leading the Feds around in circles somewhere in Salt Lake City." Tony consulted his watch. "If my calculations are right."

"Did you put this whole thing together?" I sipped the coffee. "Because, if you did, I have to say I'm impressed. You must be a fan of the old James Bond movies."

"Yeah, I helped some, but as far as cinema goes, I prefer the old classics." He shook his head and smiled momentarily, however, only allowed himself a few moments of personal satisfaction before regrouping for the plan. Glancing back at Lorene, he quickly got back to business and looked at me with a serious expression. "We'll have enough good shots around the house to take out anything that moves within a hundred yards. We'll go in together just like we looked when we left, but there'll be more assets close in if needed."

"You're going to take out Mersant?" A sudden concern for Anna and Nick's safety crossed my mind, not to mention Maria. Really good cooks were hard to find.

"No." Tony shook his head. "As long as he plays it straight, we'll let the deal go down as he's directed. The assets are in place only if something goes sideways."

"So, you trust Mersant?"

"He's played it straight ever since Nick and he teamed up for some jobs in Spain and Germany years ago." He nodded. "Mersant's always been straight up for Nick. It's the other mutts he's brought along that concern me."

"At least one of them sounds like a close friend of Mersant's, countryman and all that." I offered. "He sounds like he's second in command, not to mention possibly his boyfriend."

"He's probably worked with most of them a number of times, but you never know. One of them might get twitchy." Tony nodded at my waistband. "Which reminds me, lose the piece. They'll search you and the car for sure."

"You're really going to give him that priceless painting?" I asked, a bit wide-eyed.

"Something like that."

"You don't give out much information, do you?" I was becoming familiar of his favorite detached and irritatingly vague answer.

"Do I look like I'm in the 'information' business?" He pinned me with a brief look.

"Do I look like I'm in the 'stake me out like a sacrificial goat' business?" I countered, reflecting on my most current predicament.

"You are a PI, right?" Tony cocked his head as he brought his point home.

"Maybe I need a career change." I slumped in sullen resignation.

"Actually, it suits you." He looked me up and down.

"Can we change the subject?"

"We need to get up the hill. The rest of the assets can't get in place until we offer a diversion."

"What diversion is that?"

"Showing up." He gave me another look.

"So, you're going to come out and see what it feels like?" I nodded. "To be staked out like raw meat."

"Don't push it." He countered with a shake of his head as he edged out of the booth.

"Baaa." I bleated.

"Do you have *any* friends?" He asked, disbelievingly.

"Anna asked me that just the other day." I shook my head. "Is it that obvious?"

"Lose the piece and let's get going." He reminded me.

I looked around and got an idea. Checking to see that Lorene wasn't watching us, I slid off the booth seat and lifted it from its pedestal. Acting quickly, I slid the 45 out of my waistband and into the empty space under the cushion. It occurred to me I'd spent more time hiding the damn thing than using it. Replacing the seat cushion, I stood up and regarded the untouched cup of coffee. Tony stood up with me and followed my attention.

"You need to cut down on the caffeine, anyway." He advised. "It almost killed you once on the trip back already.

"Twice actually." I saw the curiosity in his eyes and shrugged. "It's a long story."

"Let's hope you'll be around long enough to finish it."

"My, aren't we optimistic."

We headed for the door and I threw a five down on the counter in front of Lorene before leaning over it to whisper to her.

"If I can score some good smoke, will you tell me who you really are?"

"Sure." She seemed excited at the prospect of some good weed.

"Let's go." Tony yelled from outside.

"It's a deal." I pointed a finger at her and followed Tony to the car.

23

The pueblo looked more like a ghost than a residence, isolated and sitting in the shadows of near darkness on top of the mesa. Tony pulled up short from the entrance, I suspected to give Mersant and his men more time to recognize us after we got out of the car and walked towards the house. Tony instructed me to open the rear door of the Avalanche and leave my own door open as well, as he did the same on his side of the SUV.

Some bright exterior lighting snapped on and Mersant himself met us at the front door, opening it just as we walked up.

"You took long enough." He commented to both of us.

"Not the easiest task in the world you gave us to in such a short amount of time." Tony shrugged as we walked inside.

Mersant's second in command was standing behind him and the professional thief turned to him.

"Jacque, check out the car send Simon to the mesa's edge to look around. Send Hans out back to look down the back ridge."

Jacque only nodded and walked back towards the living area. Mersant turned and looked us up and down.

"So, where is it?"

"In the car." Tony cocked his head toward it.

"Were you planning on leaving it there?" He raised an eyebrow. "Go get it."

"Where's Anna?" I interrupted, as Tony walked back out towards the SUV. "And Ray, I mean Dimitri."

"In the living room." He looked at me as if I thought he'd actually hurt them. "They're fine."

"You mind if I see for myself?"

"Not at all." He appraised the look in my eyes. "But first…"

He nodded to Jacque who was walking back to us with another man in tow. Jacque approached and spun me around, patting me down for weapons as the guard continued out the door and down the beaten path we'd drove up on.

"I'm clean." I advised, noticing Mersant's 2nd in command, who I suspected was more than a business associate, was taking his time to do his job. "But, by all means enjoy yourself."

"Shut up." Jacque glanced up at Mersant and hurried through the rest of the search.

Mersant displayed no indication he overheard our little exchange, as he seemed preoccupied with Tony's movements. I followed his interest and watched Tony dig around in the back seat of the SUV. After a few moments, he extracted a large tube similar to the one I'd been given in Vegas and walked back to the house. Mersant took the tube from him and nodded to his second, who gave Tony the same cursory search he'd given me. Mersant examined the tube in his hands and then studied Tony's face.

"This is it?"

"That's it." Tony nodded without flinching.

"We'll see." Mersant nodded to Jacque before walking back towards the main room.

We all followed Mersant as he carried the tube into the living room where we found Nick and Anna, dressed different, but sitting in relatively the same seats we'd left them in. They seemed happy to see us again, Anna smiling widely at me while Ray made the same expressionless eye contact with Tony. I suspected they were conveying to each other that their prearranged plans had been carried out.

Anna couldn't contain herself and leapt from her seat and was in my arms in a heartbeat.

"I'm so glad to see you, my love." We embraced and kissed long and hard.

"You OK?" I managed after our lips parted.

"I'm fine." She smiled widely up at me.

"You OK, Ray." I looked beyond her at the man I now knew as Nicolas Carlucci.

"Good, Jack, thanks." He nodded as he seemed to now half accept my relationship with his niece.

"Now that we've established that everyone is alive and healthy, can someone get me a clean sheet for the dining room table?" Mersant kept walking, heading towards the dining area with the tube. He looked at Nick. "If you'll do the honors?"

Nick Carlucci got up and disappeared in the back of the house for a few minutes while Jacque took the precautionary measure of taping Tony back up like a Christmas present again. Apparently, Maria was still being considered a neutral party and had been allowed relative freedom during our absence. I suspected it was so she could cook and clean up after the new arrivals.

While the rest of us sat around the living room, I exchanged a few stolen looks with Tony, wondering if his little X-force would be able to make their approach to the house as planned, especially with two of Mersant's men checking the area. His expressionless eyes seemed to convey that my worrying was pointless. They also slightly flashed a warning for me to stop looking at him at all, lest Mersant catch us and become suspicious. Anna had at least been allowed to sit next to me and she leaned against me for comfort, with her head on my shoulder.

"Let's see what we've got here." Mersant spoke as he walked into the adjoining room where Jacque joined him and spread a clean sheet across the dining room table. With that done, Mersant popped the end cap off the large tube Tony had given him and peered inside with a penlight.

Nick appeared with a small leather satchel and joined the two Frenchmen at the table. Opening it, I could see some small vials of liquid and various small metal tools, looking something like what a dentist or surgeon might use on a house call. Nick put on some latex gloves he also extracted from the kit and carefully extracted a piece of canvas from the tube, telescoping a corner past the end of the tube while leaving the main body of the painting inside.

He took a small microscope from the satchel and slid the cloth between the lens and the mounting plate. Using an eyedropper, he then took some fluid from one of the vials and looked in the eyepiece at the material. As he examined the canvas under magnification, he placed a drop of fluid on the edge of it and observed the reaction. Watching for several seconds, he finally looked up Mersant.

"See for yourself." He said, leaning away and giving Mersant room to look at the magnification.

"Bon." Philippe agreed. "It looks good."

"It's authentic." He assured the Frenchman.

"It does appear to be." Mersant replied thoughtfully as he continued to pull more of the painting out of the tube.

"I wouldn't take the chance of contaminating it in any way." Nick advised as he moved to stop the Frenchman.

Mersant looked at Nick and hesitated for a moment. He then looked back down at the work of art, now almost half out of the tube.

"It should only be extracted under the most controlled of circumstances." Nick continued. "Otherwise, your price might be affected."

I could see Mersant teasing the small frays on the edge of the painting with his fingers as he thought.

"We've already tested the canvas and know it comes from the right period." Nick pushed his argument. "What else could it be but the Venus?"

Mersant upended the tube and picked up his penlight again, turning it on and looking down the center of the tube.

"Careful Phillippe." Nick continued, watching the Frenchman. "The price may be affected."

Mersant cocked his head in all directions as he followed the flashlight's beam inside the tube. He finally turned off the light and put the tube down on the tabletop. After some further thought, he looked over to me to Tony, studying our faces for a few moments. When he was done, he glanced down at Nick for a few more moments before shaking his head.

"Not that I don't trust you, my friend." He pulled the entire artwork out and carefully spread part of it across the table.

From my angle, I couldn't see the painting, but the Frenchman's face lit up and an expression of awe seemed to cross it. He caressed the corners of the painting with loving strokes.

"True masterpieces are a rare thing of beauty." He nodded and looked down at Nick, sitting at the table. "You will make contact with my buyer and set up the final meeting between he and I. Explain you are unavoidably detained and cannot be there to conclude the deal in person."

"I can do that." Nick begrudging agreed as his looked upon the painting with his own expression of awe. "It is beautiful, isn't it?"

"I admit I prefer to conclude deals such as this quickly, before I grow to attached." Philippe nodded in agreement.

"I know exactly what you mean." Nick nodded with him before cocked his head towards us with raised eyebrows. "And now, what about us?"

Mersant carefully slid the painting back into the tube without answering. Once it was safely in the traveling container, he recapped it and shouldered it with the long strap that attached at both ends. The silence grew as we all watched Phillippe Mersant nod his head at Nick, signaling him to replace the various items back into the satchel. He then sidestepped around the freestanding fireplace hearth and walked into the living room where the rest of us waited. He let the suspense build as he looked from each of us, apparently waiting for Nick to join us. When he walked in, Mersant turned to him.

"You gave the buyer your code so that the deal will go down as planned, yes?" He explained.

"I did." Nick assured him.

"Then I will take the keys to your new vehicle and toss them at the end of your driveway. I'll have to relieve you of your computer, I'm afraid, so you won't have anyway of canceling the arrangement within the usual time period I know you usually set up for them."

"I understand." Nick eyed his old partner in crime.

"Then, we will be off and you can go about your business." He concluded. "I'm afraid your man here will have to remain tied until we leave, just as a precaution."

"Fair enough." Nick looked around the room at Mersant's men as they wandered back into the house.

"All clear." One of them reported.

"Bon." Mersant looked at Jacque. "Make the call."

Jacque nodded and left the house through the slider. His voice could be heard, speaking in French to someone outside, but I thought all of Mersant's team were now in the house with us. A few moments later, he walked back in and nodded to Philippe, while holding a phone not unlike the one I'd received in Vegas.

"A few more moments and we will leave your hospitality, mes amis." Philippe announced. He looked over at Maria, still standing in the kitchen. "I truly regret having to leave you behind, tres belle, I will miss your exquisite cuisine."

Maria responded by shrinking further back into the kitchen, nearly out of sight.

"Von Rothsted is a lucky man to be getting such a prize" Nick spoke up, voicing for all to hear the name of the man Mersant was taking the painting to.

"A prize for him means an early retirement for me." Mersant smiled back.

"He was the second in line to receive it the last time it came on the market." Nick nodded again. "He must be in his eighties by now."

"Eighty-seven." Mersant said in confirmation. "He wasn't happy when it went to your other buyer and he couldn't imagine who could have beaten him to it."

"Life's full of disappointments." Nick shrugged.

"Isn't it, though?"

Nick looked up at Philippe with a slight hint of sadness in his eyes. I could tell a long standing business relationship was coming to a close and Nick regretted it to some extent.

"No matter, now." Mersant sighed and looked at us all. "I wish this had occurred under more pleasant circumstances. I would have enjoyed all your company in a more amicable atmosphere. Cest domage."

"Maybe another time." Nick smiled.

"Maybe." Mersant favored Nick with a slight smile and then signaled one of his team just behind him with a nod.

The man disappeared into Nick's office. I noted that so far Mersant seemed to be doing things on the up and up, but I kept wondering what Tony's men were doing outside. Nothing had spooked Frenchmen as they checked the area outside, so whatever else Tony's guys were doing, they were at least staying well out of sight. I pictured them lying in the bushes, watching us through night-vision sniper scopes. If all this blew up in our faces, this house would be a mess. The only move I could think of if that happened was to cover Anna with my body and let the chips fall where they may.

In the distance, I heard the faint sounds of large rotors chopping though the night air. I instantly pictured three black Ranger helicopters equipped with as many tactical squads sitting in the open doors, all fitted with black BDUs, helmets and night vision goggles, carrying an assortment of automatic weapons slung over their shoulders. My mind started to race, thinking how Tony's crew would react to an all out law enforcement assault. In addition to that, I tried to anticipate what Mersant's crew would do. I looked at Mersant in near panic as the thumping blades became more succinct and their pitch started to change for landing.

He strangely did nothing. I glanced at Tony who had little reaction, but did seem to convey a small look of concern in his eyes. I suspected he was thinking of the men he had surrounding the pueblo. Perhaps he hadn't thought of giving them the means to conceal their body heat against airborne technology. Something about the approaching copter seemed off though. It didn't dawn on me until it got closer, but the noise and pitch of the rotor blades told me there was only one helicopter. I doubted that was SOP for FBI assaults and started pondering alternate scenarios.

Philippe's man appeared after a few moments from the back office carrying Nick's laptop and seemed be in a hurry. The blades from the helicopter were slowing and it was obvious it was landing on the mesa, but way too close for any tactical approach by the FBI. Mersant walked towards the slider while facing us.

"Time, I'm afraid is short, mes amies." Philippe opened the screen slider and looked outside just as a cloud of red dust billowed by the porch light outside. He looked back at Nick. "I'll drop your keys at the end of your driveway on the way out, as I told you. I'm sure you'll find them tomorrow in the light."

Mersant's team assembled in the living room as he opened the slider's screen door all the way and squinting directly into the blowing dust. The whine of the copter's turbine wound down to idle just a dozen yards or so off towards the stables. It became apparent Marsent had planned this whole project much more carefully than anyone had expected.

"I am sorry, but my companions have taken the liberty of relieving you of some of your jewelry and other valuables." Mersant shrugged.

"They were a lot more angry than I when they learned of your secret sale of the Venus."

The man with the SUV keys handed them to Philippe Mersant and he held them up for Nick's inspection.

"Until we meet again, mon amie." He nodded. "It was good to see you again, oui?"

"Oui." Nick wasn't smiling.

Jacque came back in the room, carrying two large duffels. He handed them to other members of their party and they all squeezed past Mersant, heading for the chopper.

"Bon chance." With a final salute, he exited the slider and walked into the stiff prop wash of the idling chopper blades.

We all sat on the couch, facing one another without saying anything as the sound of the helicopter's turbine started to wind up again. The dust storm blowing by the slider became intense and after a few more moments, the rotor blades thumped at a feverish pitch, grabbing all the air it could to lift the copter back into the air with its new cargo. The blade pitch changed and then started to fade as it left the mesa.

"What about your guys?" I asked Tony when the diminishing sound allowed me to talk again.

"They're fine." Tony nodded back. "Get a knife out of the kitchen and cut me loose."

"Be glad to."

I got up and walked towards the kitchen, but Maria met me halfway with a carving knife in her hand. I took it from her and went back to the couch, cutting Tony free. He quickly went to the front door as I rejoined Nick and Anna. Anna fell back into my arms and Maria rushed towards the kitchen and her living quarters just beyond, I assumed to start packing.

"You did well." Nick said to me as he stood up and checked outside.

"Thank you, *Nick*." I shot the name at him like a bullet. "If even *that* is your real name."

"It is." He frowned and nodded. "I've been hiding out from everyone for so many years and using so many different names along the way, that sometimes I have to think twice when I hear it."

"Well, now that I'm practically part of the family." I held Anna at my side with an arm around her. "A family I'd like to sever myself from as much as you did at some point, can you tell me what the hell is going on around here? Who did you originally sell the painting to, your brother Frank?"

"Frank?" Nick looked at me in mild shock. "He wouldn't know a Picasso from a Monet."

"Then who?"

"Someone Frank had to make certain arrangements for through the gallery manager at the Bellagio."

"Maxwell?"

"I see you're quick to pick things up." Nick stopped to look at me, no doubt wondering how I knew. "A good trait for someone in your field."

Tony returned with one man in tow, who was unzipping a black jumpsuit and carrying a silenced Mac 10, something akin to the famous Uzi. He nodded to all of us and walked throughout the house, clearing it to make sure none of Mersant's men had missed the bus.

"That's it?" I looked at Tony. "You brought one guy with you and that's all?"

"I have my sniper coming up in the Jeep now." He looked at me with a rare defensive look on his face. "We had it covered."

"It went exactly as planned." Nick offered as he looked at Tony. "Good job."

Tony nodded as his man came back from the bedroom area.

"We're clear." He reported.

"Check the grounds with Jocko, will you?" Tony cocked his head in the direction of the barn. "Just to make sure."

"On it." The man disappeared out the front door.

"So," I looked at Nick with a questioning expression. "You really got that priceless painting back just to give it to an old partner in crime?"

"Well," Nick looked back at me and smiled. "Yes, and then again, no."

24

"Exactly what does 'yes and then no' mean?"

"He got a Venus painting." Nick smiled at me. "Just not the real one."

"But you tested it yourself." I was totally confused again.

"A very small piece of some original canvas was provided for me on the one you bought out with you." Nick explained. "I knew right where to test for it."

"Man, I'm lost." I now realized confusion was a normal state for working this case. "Just how many Venus of Urbino paintings by Titan are floating around out here?"

"Please, Jack." Nick smiled and started towards the back of the house. "Follow me. It will be easier to explain if you see for yourself."

I glanced at Anna who had a slightly perplexed look on her face, then at Tony who only stared with that damned impenetrable expression of his. Dumbly, I followed Nick down the pueblo's hallway, all the way back to his bedroom. I'd never seen this part of his residence, but it was decorated much like rest of the house. The master bedroom was spacious and well appointed with a California King bed. It seemed obvious he had a female companion, probably the 'secretary' he'd mentioned earlier in my visit.

He kept walking through the room and turned into a doorway I thought would be a good place for a closet. It was. What surprised me most was how much of the clothing was dedicated to his live-in girlfriend. The walk-in could be more easily described as a small room with the walls lined by racks of upscale apparel. A light had come on automatically when we walked into the windowless alcove and I took the few moments to scan the interior. I couldn't imagine why Nick had brought me here, so I just stood in the middle of the room, letting my eyes wander over the small Sack's Fifth Avenue in front of me. All it was lacking was a few mannequins and a sales clerk with a dripping 'may I help you' smile.

"Mimi loves her clothes." Nick seemed to follow my attention around the room lined with trendy attire.

"Seems to." I nodded and finally looked back at him, expressing my only thought on why we were standing in a dead end room with one overhead light. "Not a lot of places to wear this stuff out here, is there?"

"No, but she keeps hoping for the time we'll be moving back to civilization." He smiled at me. "I guess she'll be pleasantly surprised when she returns."

"You're really getting out, then?" I asked.

"Much of the reason I've been living out here is gone now." Nick sighed, but then seemed to want to continue on with whatever reason had brought us into his walk-in closet. "It appears to me that I've been a terrible host."

He moved over to a line of men's suits he'd probably never worn and pushed them slightly aside. Behind them, imbedded in the wall there was a small panel. He opened it and pressed a sequence of buttons on the keypad.

"I've never shown you my wine cellar." He said cordially.

"Cellars are usually below ground, aren't they?" I gave him a puzzled look.

"Yes, they are." Nick smiled back at me as a motor softly hummed from somewhere behind the wall and keycard panel.

A portion of the wall, quite cleverly concealed by its border molding, swung open on unseen hinges behind the line of suits. An almost vacuum-like sound accompanied the movement of the hidden door, as if some hermetic seal had been broken as it opened.

"You must have some very rare wine." I eyed Nick, not sure where this was going, but started getting ideas. "This looks more like a bank vault."

"Indeed it does." He agreed. "And rarities come in all shapes and sizes."

"That comment you made about super rich collectors keeping their stolen works of art in hidden vaults." I guessed as I watched Nick's smile broaden. He swept the assortment of suits further aside on the rack to allow our entry through the hidden door. I looked at him with an unsettling realization. "You were talking about yourself, weren't you?"

"Tony is the only other person on the planet that knows what's down here." Nick confessed with an open hand, offering me the lead beyond the walk-in closet. "We finished it ourselves, after the workers had made what they thought would be a typical wine cellar."

A dim light shadowed the narrow staircase that descended beyond the thick doorway. It was easy to see in the passageway, but at the bottom there was still only darkness. A smell reached me that was almost antiseptic in nature, but not in the medical sense, but rather something like a new car. As I reached the bottom of the stairs, another dim light came on, probably activated by motion sensors. When my eyes adjusted to the diffused lighting, I found myself at the end of a small rectangular room. Heavy carpeting covered the floor, very rich and thick with a knap that made it feel almost solid.

Two easy chairs sat facing a thick red velour curtain, much like one would find in a theater. Behind the chairs, there were catacombs of diamond shaped portals with the necks of corked bottles visible in many of them. Unlike a typical wine cellar, there wasn't a single speck of dust on the bottles, or anywhere else in the room.

"It has it's own air filtration system." Nick said as he walked behind me. "The below ground construction and the ambient climate for the region makes temperature control much easier, one of the reasons I chose to move here, but the atmosphere down here is also monitored and controlled by it's own system, all backed up by a separate generator if the power fails."

"Very impressive." I nodded as I followed him to the leather easy chairs in the center of the room where we sat down. I looked over at the many wine bottles on the wall behind the chairs and then back at the curtain they faced. "I take it you don't come down here to sit for hours and stare at your wine collection."

"Hardly." Nick smiled broader and pushed a button on the end of his armrest.

Another soft humming and the curtains separated in the middle, like it was time for the matinee to start. But instead of light coming on from some projection room behind the seats, the illumination clicked on behind the curtain. Glass separated the room's atmosphere from the painting mounted behind it. Like an unveiling of some new product, the Venus of Urbino I'd seen in the file came to life at the vortex of the small floodlights. There was a bit of reflection from them, due to the full glass encasement of the painting, but the overall effect was spectacular, even to my laymen's eyes.

"There is ventilation for the Venus within the case, all monitored as all the masterpieces are in the finest galleries and museums, to protect it from any outside deteriorating effects." Nick continued to explain with pride in his voice. I wasn't sure what he was more pleased with, the painting or the room he had laboriously built around it.

"So, this is the read deal?" I eased into the far chair and looked slightly up at the Venus from that vantage point. "I'm no art expert, but it does look impressive."

"For many hours out of every day I've sat here and just stared at it." Nick sat in the other chair looked lovingly up at the artwork, as if it were the first time he'd seen it. "I've never ceased to be amazed by it."

"That's a long time for 'never ceasing'." I looked over at him. "Ten years."

"I think I know every brush stroke on that canvas." He said in almost wonderment, still admiring at it. "To the point I think I could see Titan painting it in my sleep."

"Maybe you should have taken up painting yourself?" I watched him as he stared in awe at the painting.

"The source of wonderment for any individual usually stems from the complete inability to create anything remotely like it, don't you think?" He said without looking away from the Venus. "I know art when I see it, but have no capacity for its creation."

"Maybe you should open up your own gallery and become a critic?" I looked away from Nick and regarded the painting for several minutes as we sat in silence. I finally had to admit. "I can't share your fascination for art like this, but really admire your passion for it."

"Neither could Tony, but he was always good about coming down and keeping me company with it." Nick glanced at me, before looking back at the Venus. "It's something I've loved ever since I can remember.

My parents house had a good collection. It provided me with a basis I just kept building on, like being an Art History major at Yale."

" I take it your brother Frank has never shared your interest."

"Absolutely not." Nick tried to laugh, but it almost came out as a fractured sob.

"Well, I almost hate to ask." I interrupted his trip down memory lane, lest we digress to a family dumping session. "But if this is the real painting, what is Philippe Mersant carrying with him to Germany, or wherever?"

"The echo from the Lourve." Nick stated with a trace of sadness.

"And just how did you get a hold of that?"

Nick turned in his chair, the sadness escalating in his expression and tone.

"I got wind of what was coming long before you were sent out here, Jack." He said is a heavy voice. "Since that time, I've been quietly setting the mechanisms in motion for the Venus and the two other echoes I sold to be returned to the museum."

"Returned?"

"I have enjoyed my prize for many years, but with age comes the realization of how selfish I've been." He glanced at the painting and a pained expression came over his face. "It's time to give back what all art lovers never should have been deprived of in the first place."

"Is this an anonymous return?" I looked from Nick to the painting. "Who else knows what's going on?"

"Since the news story broke, I've been quietly communicating with the Lourve and Lloyds of London through intermediaries." Nick nodded while studying the painting, as if he were trying one last time to memorize the brushstrokes. "But outside of Tony and my brother, only you know that I've had it all this time."

"Anna doesn't know?"

"No, I don't think so. Without knowing the specifics, my brother has arranged the return through these intermediaries." Nick looked back at me. "The only problem I had with my plan was logistical. Then I learned that a private investigator was due to come out and watch me."

"Don't you just love it when a plan comes together?" I commented with a touch of discomfort.

"I've arranged for you to return the Venus, no questions asked." He confirmed with a smile. "And the two echoes I got back from the buyers I sold them to."

"They'll know where it all came from." I offered with an open hand. "They know where I've been and who I've been watching."

"They only know that the man they sent you to watch discovered what was going on, made a few calls to certain contacts he had, and retrieved the missing artworks from the culprits." His smile widened a bit. "They only know me as one more intermediary."

"How do you explain Mersant, and what's going to happen when he gets back to Europe?"

"Philippe was a last minute rearrangement." Nick said thoughtfully. "My brother Frank arranged at my direction to acquire the echo that was already in Vegas and substitute it for this one. The authorities will unfortunately be waiting at customs when he arrives in Berlin."

"Very coincidental that the Venus' echo was sitting around in Vegas." I eyed him.

"Not at all." He shrugged. "It was awaiting to act in the capacity for which it was intended when this one made its journey home."

"So you think this will all work?" I asked. "You pretending to be this grand intermediary, as you call it, to return this thing, no questions asked?"

"It will, if you can sell it that way." He studied me. "A piece of the finder's fee will go to you, of course."

"That's incentive." I nodded dubiously and looked at the painting again. "I guess we'll find out soon enough."

"I've been spending all the time I can down here since I started everything needed to return the Venus." Nick returned his attention to the encased painting.

"Soak it up, Nick." I couldn't believe I was suddenly putting myself in league with this man, but it was just beginning to dawn on me how much I like the guy. Still, there were a few nagging questions. "What was Carl Stapleton's role in all this?"

"He was unfortunately already on his way when I started communicating with Lloyds." Nick explained. "Your employer didn't believe Mr. Stapleton was up for the task and was very concerned about his state of mind after he arrived and reported back about the conditions here. You were hand picked to come out and replace him."

"I'll remember to put that on my resume." I gave him a matter a fact look. "But Stapleton never made it back and as far as i know, didn't even know I was supposed to replace him. He thought I was supposed to work with him."

"I don't know what instructions he got from your client, Jack." Nick looked straight at me. "And I have no idea why he ended up in that canyon down there."

"So, Tony didn't pay him a visit?" I shook my head at him. "Maybe pumping my bedroom with bullets by mistake?"

"No," Nick looked at me. "Your client was instructed to recall him at the same time you were given the assignment and sent out in his place. From what I understood, you weren't supposed to even know he had been here."

"But I did meet up with him and he never made it back." I started mentally moving pieces of the puzzle around in my head, but nothing would fit. I asked the question more to myself than Nick. "Why the hell was he killed, then?"

"I've never had anyone 'tapped', as my brother so subtlety puts it." Nick shook his head and looked at me in all earnest. "I got out of the family's real business because I had an aversion to that sort of thing. I've always had a knack for wheeling and dealing, but steered it towards my love of artwork, so I could be around it as much as possible. I left the Family to my brother."

"And Tony?"

"He's been my personal protection since we were both quite young." He shook his head again. "I won't say he hasn't done some intimidation work for me when the brokering demanded it and he's protected me more than once, but never killed anyone while he's been with me."

"How close are you to your brother?"

"He wouldn't do anything like that on my behalf without consulting me, if that's what you mean." Nick dismissed any possibility of his family's involvement in the homicide and looked over at me with a shrug. "Jack, I can only suspect he was killed by those people down the hill."

"I had a chat, of sorts, with Lyle who's the leader of that motley crew." I shook my head. "He acted like he didn't know anything about it, either. A couple of his idiots claimed Carl was killed by some guy named Todd for personal reasons."

"After you found his body, I assumed Mr. Stapleton had stumbled upon the chemical lab they have down there and he had been killed to keep it quiet. I don't think that could be considered 'personal' though." Nick started to look a bit more thoughtful as he bit into my ruminations. "You know, that is a bit disconcerting."

"You've known about their meth lab?"

"Information is the number one commodity to survival, Jack." Nick confided.

"In that case, do you know who this Todd is?"

"No." Nick shook his head thoughtfully and looked at me. "But that kind of violence so close to my residence dictates that I find out."

"I'd like to know myself." I agreed. "The idiots who cleaned up the hotel after my attempted demise dropped his name on their grand Puba and he seemed to know him. You think Deputy Turley might know who he is?"

"He's never mentioned the name to me." Nick confessed and looked at me.

"Just what is Deputy Turley to you?" I kept trying to make some sense of this.

"He only knows I own most of the property he patrols." He shook his head. "Nothing more that I know of."

"Well, this Todd, whoever he is, was the guy tailing us to Las Vegas and then picked up on me during my return trip."

"I heard about your shadow going into Vegas." Nick nodded. "Tony hasn't had a chance to tell me about the ride back."

"I definitely had some company."

"Even after changing rides?" Nick questioned. "I thought Tony's idea of the car switch would pull any tails off, not to mention having the tracking devices go in another direction. That's very interesting and again, a bit disconcerting, given your upcoming task."

"I agree with you." I looked at Nick.

"I'm becoming very concerned for it's safety." Nick seemed deep in thought, then realized I was watching him and looked up with a hasty addendum. "And of course yours, as well."

"How very touching." I looked at him. "But then I've always taken a back seat where women were involved. Now I'm taking it for one in a painting? I think I'm the one who should be concerned."

"I don't mean to demean the value of your own life, Jack. I've grown to enjoy your company and glad your client chose you for the assignment." Nick explained before looking back up at the painting. "But she's been a bigger part of my life than just about anything for a very long time now."

"You're going to need some counseling." I shook my head at him. "And I don't mean just for separation anxiety."

"Perhaps." He had to smile a bit. "I hear there's more psychologists per capita in New York than in any other city in America."

"You thinking of moving back to the Big Apple?" I looked at him with a bit of surprise.

"I've been sitting on an offer for all the property, including the inn and the house." He smiled a bit sadly again, this time for the loss of his lifestyle, no doubt, before glancing at me again. "Some movie industry mogul has been after it for his own getaway hideout. Wants to renovate the hotel for additional guests. Now that I've been found, it seems like a good idea to once again turn over a new identity."

"I hope I haven't caused any additional problems there." I said sheepishly. "I had some unexpected visitors while I was staying at Caesar's and I mentioned your name."

"I suspect I'll hear about if from Frank." Nick shook his head. "No, my concerns center more around Philippe. I don't know how he found me, but I need to get unfound again."

"I can appreciate your concerns there." I glanced up at the encased artwork and shook my head slowly. "I really don't want to carry this painting out of here. I almost had a breakdown driving from Vegas with what I thought was the real one."

"You won't take charge of the painting until you get back to Vegas." Nick smiled in appreciation of the weight of responsibility. "You'll be carrying something much more valuable to my family."

"What would that be?" I looked at him.

"Anna needs to leave here." He shifted in his seat. "Too much is happening now to let her stay any longer. Sophia's requested that you drive her back to Vegas where she can stay until her mother returns from Italy."

"Ah, yes, Sophia." I nodded in understanding.

"I can't risk Anna being harmed in any way."

"What does Anna say about all this?" My attention shifted to a higher gear, a more personal one.

"She doesn't know, yet."

"What if she doesn't want to go back." I unconsciously turned a bit defensive.

"I can see that Anna and you have developed some genuine feelings for each other, Jack." Nick conceded. "But I'm afraid her driving force to separate herself from her family obligations will ultimately conflict with those feelings. Coming from where I've been, I understand her completely on that, but regret she's dragged you into her plans."

"Plans?" I squirmed a bit. "What if her only plan is to get lost with me and disappear from your family?"

"Number one, it takes a considerable amount of money to 'get lost' as you put it." Nick put his hand on my shoulder. "And number two, Anna is used to being around money, and having lots of it."

"You never heard of love conquering all?" My sarcasm was laced with just a glimmer of hope. "Aren't we talking about something that Anna should decide, not us?"

"I'll remind you of exactly what you've just said at a later time." Nick gave the Venus one more look before getting up from his chair. He cocked his head towards the painting as I rose with him. "Personally, I think we're looking at the perfect woman."

"You need that therapy more than I thought." I shook my head at him and glanced at the reclining nude in the painting. "But then again……"

"Come to New York with me, Jack." Nick sounded serious. "I'll have my therapist set aside an extra hour for you, to help you with your own future separation anxieties."

"You're that sure?" I shook my head in disbelief.

"OK." He smiled. "I'll make it two extra hours."

25

It was too late to leave that night, so we spent the rest of the evening recovering from our ordeal and trying to calm Maria down. She'd take her suitcase and put it just inside the front door, then return for more things. Nick would follow right behind her, picking up the suitcase returning it to her room. The entire time, Maria was rattling on in excited Spanish while Nick tried to dissuade her from leaving in a soothing Italian tongue. The rest of us watched their strange ballet, as if it were a stage production entitled 'Maria, Don't Go'. Finally, Anna intervened and convinced the frazzled cook to prepare one more meal, promising to take her wherever she wanted to go the next morning.

As could be expected, Maria was off her game a bit and we ended up with a sort of Mexican quiche, or soufflé, rather than her usual masterpiece of International cuisine. It seemed understandable to me, given her state of mind. Whenever I was severely rattled about something, I always retreated to my baseline instincts. Like a child running home to mama or a woman retreating to kitchen duties, men seemed to circle the wagons and load their muskets. Still, Maria's dish was the best meal I'd had since leaving the pueblo. After supper, we adjourned to the patio where Nick, and I enjoyed our coveted cappuccino, along with two of his best cigars. Anna joined us with her own cup, leaving Tony to start the first round of cocktails inside.

"You're going to have to give Maria a sizable raise if you're going to hold onto her." I advised Nick as Anna settled onto the armrest of my chair and nearly on my lap. We kissed, now growing more comfortable with our intimacy in Nick's presence.

"She'll calm down." Nick chuckled. "I had an irate buyer tear up my house once and she did the same thing. I had to practically pull her off the bus to get her to stay, but she eventually did. We've been together for so many years, I'd expect her to outlast any other woman in my life, with the obvious exception."

"You'd never let Mimi go either, Uncle Nick, and you know it." Anna jumped into the conversation unaware of the 'woman' Nick was alluding to.

"Maybe you need a new line of work?" I changed the subject. "Like that art gallery I mentioned."

"Then I might not be able to afford her." Nick's laughter grew. "Maybe I should marry her?"

"Who, Mimi?" Anna looked a bit surprised at her uncle.

"No, Maria." Nick replied and we all laughed.

"She's scrubbing down every surface of the kitchen now." Tony emerged with a small tray of mixed drinks, advising on the name he'd just heard. "I have no idea what she's babbling on about to herself, but I'm not so sure she'll be with us much longer."

"I'll have to convince her I'm retiring." Nick shook his head. "Again."

"That's how you got her to stay last time." Tony slid a fourth chair and in what seemed to be a rare moment, joined us. I suspected he felt more comfortable doing so, since he now had a couple of assistants lurking around the grounds, one with a metal detector who was looking for the SUV's car keys.

We all sat in silence with the three of us men stealing glances with each other, leaving Anna on the outside of what was going on with the Venus. She didn't appear to be picking up on the clandestine atmosphere leading me to believe Nick had kept her in the dark in regards to the priceless artwork he'd been hording all these years. I thought he was on the verge of confiding in her when he put down his cup and addressed Anna in a fatherly tone.

"Anna." Nick looked a bit stern at her.

"Yes, Uncle?" Anna slid closer to me and buried her arms around me. I could see where she thought this was going.

"Sophia called just before dinner." Nick said a bit gravely. "Your mother is coming back to the states shortly and Sophia asked if you'd visit her for a while before you had to fly back to New York."

Anna's expression was mixed as a trace of dread and glee at the same time. I suspected the mention of her mother's return flashed with almost child-like glee, but clashed with the dread of family obligations. She turned to me immediately.

"Would you like to go to Las Vegas with me?" She put on her best face. "You haven't met my Aunt Sophia yet. I'd love to show you off."

"They've met." Nick confessed on my behalf. "The recovery of the painting involved Frank and Sophia and they met Nick while he and Tony were there."

"Oh." Anna looked at Nick and back to me, a look of concern crossing her face. "I didn't know."

"It was her idea that Jack bring you back to Vegas." Nick raised an eyebrow slightly.

"She must have been very taken by you." Anna kept looking at me with an expression that turned almost suspicious. "Did she take you shopping and then to a show?"

"She was kind enough to open the Palace's shops to me for some things and then asked me to accompany her to the Solis at the Bellagio." I shrugged innocently, wondering if Anna wasn't something of a psychic.

"Where she no doubt showed you off to all her friends." Anna's body temperature actually turned up a few degrees next to me. "Did you enjoy your evening?"

"It was educational." I admitted with more understanding of the dynamics between these two women. "At least in the politics of your unique family."

"As long as that's all it was." She studied me like a suspicious housewife confronting a wayward husband's arrival home at dawn's early light.

"She's the wife of Nick's brother." I replied with an air of disbelief. "You *have* met your Uncle Frank, right?"

"Well, I guess." She softened a bit, tightening her grip and pulling herself closer to me. "I can see there will be no letting you out of my sight."

"Jack will take the Avalanche and drive you back to Vegas tomorrow morning." Nick interrupted, eyeing both of us as Tony looked on with his typically unreadable expression.

"What about the...?" I had it halfway out before catching myself. I I stumbled for a question that wouldn't break the confidence Nick had placed in me over the Venus. "I mean, uh, what about that body we found in the canyon the other day?"

"All remaining matters will be handled in time." Nick telegraphed that his plan for me to return the artwork would go off as scheduled.

I looked over at Tony, who had the exact same message in his eyes that Nick had. It was rare to come across two separate people that could constantly be on the exact same page at every turn, with the possible exception of some long time partners I'd known on the job. I realized Nick and Tony had the plan completely worked out, but I had no clue as to how and when they had done so. I looked between the two of them and shrugged in surrender.

"If you say so."

Nick set his delicate cup down and picked up his highball glass.

"I'd like to propose a toast." He announced.

We dutifully picked up our drinks and turned to our host who waited with his outstretched arm, glass in hand. When we had assumed the same posture with all our glassed presented to the imaginary center-point, Nick continued by gesturing with his glass slightly in turn towards Tony, myself and then towards Anna.

"To old friends, new ones, and to family. I am the richest man in the world."

I had to admit, I felt like one of the family now, sitting comfortably with two, albeit reluctant, members of the mob world and one of their enforcers. I wondered what Bill Osterholt would say if he could see me now. It wasn't like I had turned Goodfella or something. The occupants of this household all seemed to have a distain for their family business and had gone to great lengths to escape its influence. All but Tony, but his allegiance was squarely with Nick and I had no doubts that if ordered by those in power to do any harm to his present charge, he'd go to war with them on Nick's behalf. At this point, they seemed more bonded than Nick's blood brother in Vegas.

We spent the rest of the evening chatting about the future. Nick was contemplating another hideout, someplace in upstate New York. He laced his plans for another place with ways of convincing Maria to stay in his employ. Anna countered with suggestions of a European tour, taking me on a whirlwind vacation that sounded more like a honeymoon than a trip. The word 'marriage' wasn't uttered, but her plans definitely sounded long term and exclusive only to me. I thought about the fat finder's fee I should be up for when I returned to LA with the paintings under my arm. It wouldn't be a fortune, but it would finance a lot of travel. The now distant memory of my flop pad in Venice flashed past me and I decided it wouldn't even be worth stopping there long enough to grab my toothbrush.

As the pitch black night was again invaded by a rising half moon, our conversation wound down to the silent puffing on cigars and deep sighs over what we'd all been through. Tony excused himself to check on Maria and handle some lingering security matters, while Nick eyed Anna and me in turn with a final puff on his stogy. Excusing himself to retire for the evening, I took it as a sign of surrender, accepting that Anna and I would be together for some time to come and then maybe some.

Anna and I openly adjourned to my room and slowly undressed each other, falling into bed in a passionate reunion of intimacy. Every time we made love, it seemed like the first, but somehow just got better. In the furious throws of making love, we chorused vows of love in our joys of physical ecstasy. In the intoxicating aftermath of our combined chemistry, we finally fell apart to let our soaring temperatures subside.

"I had fears I'd never be with you again this way." I confessed as we finally caught our breath.

"There was never any doubt in my mind, my love." She put her hand over my mouth. "I knew you'd be back."

"I heard disturbing rumors about your mother while I was in Vegas." I looked at her in the dim light coming from the open patio door. "Things that don't sound conducive to our continued happiness, or my good health if she knew we were here together like this."

"She is single-minded." Anna admitted, laying on her back and staring at the ceiling fan above us.

"I also heard some rumors that she might be behind some power-play with rival families back east." I looked at her closely. "That wine guy you were engaged to. Was he just a wine guy or was he someone else in the 'Family'?

"It was a failed attempt my mother made to save our own family."

Anna conceded. "She still believes she can put my Uncle Frank back in power there, but under all her plans is revenge."

"Revenge for what?" I looked over at her faint profile on the pillow beside me.

"Uncle Frank came out to Las Vegas to take over things there and most of the West Coast after the man who was already out there was killed."

"Killed?" The drawbacks of being involved with the underworld came home to roost.

"Yes, by some competing families and another one from the Ukraine." Anna continued in a matter-of-fact tone. "My mother has plans to eventually exact her retribution on them."

"Why?"

"That man they killed was my father." She said quietly.

"I'm sorry, Anna." I watched a tear stream down to her cheek.

"In some ways, you're a lot like him." She didn't look at me, but continued to stare at the ceiling. "He had a passionate, loving side to him, mixed with this strange sense of humor I never understood. He was the oldest son to an old world Don, my Mother's father, of course, but like Uncle Nick, he really didn't have that cruel, mean streak in him to do the work his father had given him to do."

"And your mother?" I brought the conversation 360 to learn where I stood with her family.

"After my father's death, Uncle Frank stepped in and took our family's power back. Some of the conspirators disappeared, but other more powerful members of rival families just stepped back and disavowed any part in my father's death." She looked over at me. "My mother is the second oldest on our side of the family. Women have no standing in family rule, but they can do much behind the scenes. My mother inherited, or adopted, that ruthless side that my grandfather and Uncle Frank have. To her, I'm like a chess piece, to be bargained away so the family can get closer to the real prize."

"A chess piece." I admitted. "Like a queen."

"At this time and place, perhaps." She agreed. "If she knew I was here with you in this way….."

"I'll end up like your racing car fiancé." I nodded to myself.

"My family never knew about him." She insisted.

"Sophia did." I countered.

"What?" She choked her reply and sat partially up in bed.

"She mentioned it during our evening out." I nodded in confirmation. "If your mother is like you says she is, I'd have to wonder if someone didn't loosen the lug-nuts on his car or something."

"Oh no." Her tears started to flow openly. "She couldn't have."

"I'm sure she didn't." I suddenly realized the possibility had never occurred to Anna and it wasn't my position to suggest different. "I'm sure she probably found out somehow after the accident happened, maybe because of your open grieving."

"It would be just like her." I could see a hatred replacing the sorrow in her eyes. A trace of what I'd seen in Frank's face crossed hers and I tried to conjure the same look in her mother's eyes. The image was something right out of a Stephen King novel, complete with a bloody axe poised in both hands above her head.

"Why won't she let you go?" I offered. "What good are you to her if your hearts not in the family's affairs?"

"Jack," She turned on her side towards me and stroked my face, searching my eyes. "She's now promised me to Sonny Vettriano. They're the family in power on the east coast right now, where the real authority rests."

"This whole concept is just nuts." I drew a bit more away from hers to study her whole face. "That people still do this?"

"Family is the strongest bond our families know." She replied. "Blood is everything to us."

"Unbelievable." Was all I could manage, but my brain jumped into overdrive, considering where I was lying at this very moment and what I was feeling for this beautiful woman in my arms.

"If we have enough money, we can disappear like my Uncle Nick." She renewed her agenda.

"What money." I looked at her. "I'm not exactly a Rockefeller, you know."

"I have enough." She affirmed with a hopeful look. "At least I will soon."

"What, you have some saving bonds that are about to mature?" The doubt in my expression matched what was in my tone. "What money?"

"You have to trust me." She pulled herself closer to me and wrapped her legs around mine. "We'll have a beautiful life together soon. Warm beaches and white sand, with water so blue it will hurt your eyes to look at it."

"Sounds inviting." I resigned as I held her in my arms.

"You'll see." Her voice drifted off until all I could hear was steady breathing coming from her lips.

I studied her angelic face in the dark, her lips slightly parted as she slid into what looked like a blissful sleep. I could almost see her dreaming about those beaches under a warm and inviting sun. Her touch and the aroma of her womanhood, her delicious taste and breathtaking beauty completely hid the reality that she was a walking, talking, ticking time bomb. Worse yet, if she went off, the only one who'd be turned into a mist of blood and bone was me. Still, I couldn't help but just stare at her, dismissing all the gruesome possibilities that seemed to be waiting outside. The term 'fatal attraction' crossed my mind.

Finally, I rolled onto my back and took up her vigilant stare of the ceiling, with the fan slowly rotating and moving the air inside our room. Its hypnotic effect seemed to have helped Anna drop off and right now I really needed to sleep. To put it more accurately, I needed any escape I could find in light of the reality staring back at me. Anna was at the fulcrum of a major underworld merger, a sacrifice offered up to the mob Gods. I wondered why the two Dons of the family couldn't just meet and cut their hands, shaking and becoming blood brothers? Hell, it worked for the American Indians, didn't it?

I had spent a good majority of my life chasing people who didn't want to be caught. I knew the odds had always been heavily in my favor. Something always happened. Even the most perfect crimes were solved by a single loose end, or slip of the tongue. Where the most careful planning, executed flawlessly with the precision of a Swiss watch could be put into play, there was always that one factor that could never be calculated or foreseen. In the world of crime, it usually meant some jail time. If I became Anna's running mate and that inevitability came to pass, the results would be a bit more terminal than a couple years in prison.

In the shadow of where I found myself, the mystery of Carl Stapleton's death and the bikers waiting for me at the bottom of the mesa were completely eclipsed. Ending up like the hapless private investigator I'd found in the canyon seemed to be a promised certainty, rather than just a remote possibility.

It now made sense that I'd find Anna out here in the wilderness, being protected by the remoteness of the high prairie and her albeit reluctant satellite, mob-serving uncle. Nick could posture himself as a self made black market art dealer to his heart's content, but he was driving his brother Frank's car and dealing his stolen art deals through him. Hell, they were probably silent partners in all of Nick's dealings. In return, there was no doubt in my mind that my host was acting as a 'holding company' for the signing, sealing and delivering of his family's future merger with the Vettrianos, aka Anna.

If Nick had really been my friend, he wouldn't have let this all happen. I reflected on my past conversations with him and Anna's secrecy over our affair. Nick hadn't really known about Anna and I until Mersant had showed up. I begrudgingly had to admit he'd done his best to dissuade me from any involvement with her before that. Even Tony had tried to warn me off.

Now, I could imagine Sophia on the phone with Anna's mother ten minutes after getting home from our evening engagement at the Bellagio. There might be something of a bounty out on me as I lay here thinking about it.

Squirming at the thought of it, I rolled back over and stared again at the enchanting creature lightly snoring next to me. Was she worth risking death for? I closed my eyes and curiously smiled at myself. If she loved me as much as I loved her, and was committed to escaping her family's influence as much as she said she was, then I'd run with her. What else was there to do for two people in love?

26

Lone Tree looked strangely quiet, almost deserted, as we turned onto the main highway and drove by it. Anna followed my attention on the isolated looking structures while I expected a flood of rumbling Harleys to emerge from behind them any second. I quietly held my breath and gratefully, nothing happened. The setting remained an Ansil Adam's still life with the usual two cars parked out in front of the Inn and none if front of the diner.

I abruptly pulled up to the diner's entrance.

"What's wrong?" Anna looked alarmed at my sudden move.

"I've felt naked since I left here yesterday." I shrugged as I started to get out. "I'll be right back."

I could picture Lorene inside the café, sitting alone behind the register while quietly committing carnage on her nails. I wasn't disappointed as I rushed by her towards the back booth where I'd stashed my pistol.

"Morning, Lorene." I intoned as I strode to the booth and retrieved the firearm from under the cushion. Tucking back in my waistband, I reversed my direction and gave Lorene a second look as I rushed by. "Who are you?"

"Got the weed?" She teased with a smile.

"Guess it'll have to wait."

"Later." She called after me with a snap of her gum.

"Not if I can help it." I was out the door and getting back in the car.

"Is anything wrong?" Anna finally spoke as she looked back at me.

"Just wanted to say good-bye to Lorene." I scanned the remaining area and checked my rearview mirror, feeling my 45 automatic imprint my back in its usual perch. Any other time, the dull pain of its positioning was a nuisance, but I had to admit this morning it felt quite comforting.

"You're so sweet." Anna moved closer and rested her head on my shoulder. "We're going to be so happy. Of course, I'll be pulling the girls off you constantly."

"I seriously doubt that'll be a problem." The thought made me laugh to myself, but helped lighten my mood and think of the more promising times ahead of us. "Besides, we'll be off alone on some small island, testing tanning lotions and sunglasses, right?"

"But of course, my love." She reassured, glancing up before settling in to watch the road with me.

I kept nervously checking my rearview mirror, not believing this was going to be that easy. I didn't think Todd, whoever and wherever he might be, was going to let this pass. He'd most certainly be lurking in some turnout off to the side of the road, hiding in the morning shadows of the tall canyon walls while he waited for us to drive by. I knew instinctively that Tony wouldn't be too far behind. He might have left one of his two soldiers with Nick, but I knew he'd be following with the Venus and a one-way ticket from McCarran Field in Vegas to LaGuardia. How soon this would all come about I had no idea, since secrecy was very much a part of Nick's grand plan. Not even Anna knew what was going on. The thought of her in regards to our immediate future prompted more curiosity.

"Tell me more about your plans to finance this little escape of ours." I prodded, still glancing in the mirror and into every turnout we passed.

"Philippe Mersant has put enough money away for us to last a life time." Her voice beamed with confidence. "At least a lifetime in Greece or somewhere similar."

"How very generous." My head snapped over to look at her so fast I thought I'd break my neck. She was still looking at the scenery, so I tried my best to recover with an off-handed tone. "This has already taken place?"

"It's on its way." She rubbed her head against my shoulder for a more comfortable fit. "As soon as the transaction is completed with his buyer in Berlin, he'll wire it to my numbered off shore account."

"Why would he do all that?" I eyed the top of her head, the possibilities multiplying by the second.

"A sort of finder's fee." She sighed as the familiar phrase echoed in my head. "He needed to know where my uncle was so he could obtain the real Venus of Urbino and sell it to his own buyer."

"How did you know about the painting?" I barely looked at the road. Instead, I craned my neck to watch her in the rearview mirror.

"I heard my Uncle Frank and Sophia talking about it while I was visiting them, just before I came out to stay with Uncle Nick. I did some of my own snooping around and learned about Nick's avocation, as it were, and heard about Philippe." She shrugged. "I knew a lot of money was involved from their conversation, so I contacted him."

"And told him where Nick was." I finished her sentence.

"There were conditions, of course, one of them was that no one would be hurt." Anna explained. "He knew Uncle Nick might not be too happy about recovering the painting for another sale, so the men and guns were necessary to convince him he was serious."

"It would have been nice to know, Anna." I said with a trace of exasperation. "I worried about you and Nick the whole time I was off running around Vegas, trying to get the Venus."

"I'm sorry about that." She snuggled closer. "I didn't know when they were coming and after they did, I had no way of telling you."

"I guess." I could see her point and remembered the looks she was giving me after Mersant had showed up. Perhaps that was what she was trying to convey with them.

"Besides, you played your part beautifully, not knowing."

"Who else knew about your plan?" I was shaken from our conversation by the appearance of a familiar car in the rearview mirror.

"No one." Her voice shook just a fraction as she looked up at me. "Why?"

"Because we have company." I tightened my grip on the steering wheel, while considering my options.

"Who?" Anna followed my attention and looked back through the rear window.

"Turley." I said in trepidation, checking my speedometer to confirm we were legal. Maybe he was just getting closer to check the car out. I was sure he'd never seen it and doubted he knew we were the occupants. The possibility he was responding to something else and would pass us also crossed my mind. I shrugged in dismissal and tried to joke about it. "Maybe he just wants to return the gun he took from me."

"Damn." Anna said quietly as she watched the car behind us.

"Then again, maybe not." My hopes sunk with my voice as I glanced down at her, reading her expression. "What is it?"

Whatever Turley's motives were as he aggressively gained on us, it was obvious there was something going on between him and Anna. By the way I'd caught him looking at her on past occasions, it seemed personal, but that didn't make sense. Anna hadn't been visiting Nick long enough for anything to happen between the two of them.

Any wishful thoughts about simply checking the car out or passing us for another call evaporated as the County Sheriff's unit abruptly slowed behind us to match our speed and the red and blue strobes lit up. For effect, he even hit the siren for a couple of seconds. A look of resignation finally appeared in her expression.

"He might know about the Venus." She blurted and looked up with an almost pleading expression in her eyes. "He stopped me on the road about a week before you got here and recognized my father's name from my license. He'd worked in Vegas as a cop and my father was well known there. He threatened to expose Uncle Nick and the only way I could think to stop him was tell him about the Venus."

"Quick thinking." I was being sarcastic, but she didn't catch it, at least not entirely. "Anything else?"

"I don't have time to explain." She gave me a look that seemed to ask me not to believe what I was about to hear, not from her, but from Turley.

I took my foot off the gas, still staring suspiciously at Anna, and let the Avalanche slow to the side of the road and stop. Anna moved from her position next to me and slid over to the more formal center of the passenger seat.

"Please." She let go of my hand as I watched her retreat in amusement. "I'll explain later."

My attention shifted to Turley as he made his approach. It was déjà vu from my first encounter with him and now it made me wonder where he'd been during Nick's captivity and my absence. I rolled down the driver's window as he arrived at it.

"Hey, Mitch." I squinted into the morning sun off his shoulder. "Where ya been?"

"Takin care of some last minute business." He nodded and looked past me at Anna. "Good morning, Anna."

"Good morning, Mitch." They locked eyes long enough to make it noticeable and I looked from one to the other.

"I'm not interrupting anything, am I?" My accusing expression towards Anna melted to one of curiosity as it came back to rest on Turley.

"I have some bad news for you, Mr. Hollister." He frowned and opened the driver's door and grabbed the keys from the ignition. "Ballistics matched the bullets in Carl Stapleton's body to your 357 magnum."

"That's a bit hard to believe." I gave the deputy a critical look and what had been nagging me about Carl Stapleton's corpse for so long just popped out on its own. "Since he was killed a day or two before I even got here."

"Does your experience extend to forensics as well as private investigations, Mr. Hollister?" Turley gestured for me to get out of the car.

"Not formally." I slid out of the Avalanche and faced him. "But I've seen enough crime scenes to make pretty educated guesses."

"You guessed wrong on this one, Amigo." Turley spun me around so I was facing the car. I heard the familiar sound of a leather pouch unsnapping and metal-to-metal sound of handcuffs. "Ballistics lined your pistol up perfectly with the slugs taken from Stapleton's body at the time of the autopsy. The coroner took his sweet time opening him up, so I just learned about it earlier this morning."

"And you just happened to run across us driving in the opposite direction of your beat." I nodded as he snapped the cuffs on behind my back. Strangely, he didn't even bother to search me. I could only surmise he'd bought my story on our first meeting that the revolver was my only gun.

"This is all my beat, Mr. Hollister." Mitch tapped me on the shoulder to signify he was ready to escort me to his car.

"Is this necessary?" Anna finally spoke up. "If this is about our arrangement, I'll be glad to cut you in for a piece of it."

"You'll need to come with us, Anna." Turley said through the open driver's door. There seemed to be what I interpreted as a tone of jealousy in his voice.

"You know he didn't do anything, Mitch." Anna was being more assertive now. "How much do you want?"

"We can talk about that when we get to the substation." I heard Mitch reply behind my back. "Bring the keys and lock it up."

"This is ridiculous." I turned to face the deputy. "I want to talk to somebody in Homicide."

"The detective in charge of the case is already on his way." Mitch nodded. "I radioed him to meet us as soon as I saw your car."

"How'd you know it was even us in this car?" I cocked my head slightly. "You've never seen it."

"A little birdie told me." Turley smiled slightly. "I have a good collection of informants."

"Like Billy and his two yard-bird friends?" I was beginning to wonder why Turley was giving Lone Tree such a wide birth. Maybe it wasn't just because of the large hostile presence of bikers.

"No, in this case it was the little birdie who runs the Lone Tree Inn." He turned me around again and we started walking towards his cruiser. "He's a slime-ball, but he doesn't mind playing both sides of the fence when it's profitable."

"How profitable?" I remembered the desk clerk walking out after my run-in with the bikers and I had to admit it made sense. It might have even explained why the silencer was used in my room the night I was shot at. Still, the choice of words was disturbing. "How much do you guys make a month out here in Elko County?"

He ignored the question and as we reached his car and opened the back door for me to get in. I looked back at the Avalanche and watched Anna strutting towards us, looking very angry as she approached the cruiser and got in the passenger door. Turley guided me into the backseat and then got in behind the steering wheel next to her. She slammed the car door hard for affect and glared at the deputy. The wire mesh cage between the front and back seats limited my vision a bit, but it couldn't hide the dynamics between the two of them.

"OK, I'm sorry I cut you out of the deal." She said angrily at the deputy.

"It wasn't the deal, as much as it was the promise you made to me, Anna." Turley replied in a surprisingly soft voice.

I detected considerable pain in his tone and knew he was more hurt than angry about whatever was going on between them. I started to wonder if this little fiasco over Stapleton's murder wasn't a pretext for something else. My stainless steel magnum hadn't been out of my possession until Turley had taken it from me. That had been well after Carl Stapleton's death was discovered.

Turley put the car in gear and got back onto the highway. Curiously, he passed the Avalanche and kept going straight. I looked out the rear window at the SUV as it shrunk in the distance and then back at Turley.

"Have they moved Elko since I was last there?" I inquired.

"We're going to the area's substation." Turley replied in a somewhat annoyed tone.

"Where is that?" I glanced at Anna who'd become mute, sitting in her seat and staring out the window.

"Up here a ways." Turley replied. "Not too far."

"Funny. I was up and down this road twice in broad daylight and never saw any substation." I cocked my head at the deputy. "How many guys do you have working there?"

"You should know that you have the right to remain silent." He began.

"Yeah, yeah, I know my rights." I nodded dumbly.

"No, just the one." Turley glared in his rearview mirror at me.

"Very funny." I frowned with a shake of the head.

"Mitch, this isn't necessary." Anna spoke up and repeated her original comment. "I told you I'd cut you in and you can trust me."

"Just like I trusted you that we'd be leaving this place together." He looked over at her. "That we'd be going to Europe and living on the Greek Isles. Tell me, where were you two headed just now?"

Needless to say, that got my attention. I looked at Anna for some kind of reply, but nothing came.

"I hear its lovely there this time of year." I tried the keep their conversation alive to learn more. "The brochures make it look inviting."

It didn't seem to work. Anna wouldn't look back at me or at Turley, but kept staring out the passenger-side window. Some time passed in silence as we made our way further down the highway. Turley finally slowed the car in the middle of nowhere and turned onto a small dirt road. I was becoming concerned for both Anna's safety and my own, but her reaction was only to look over and speak up with a confident tone in her voice.

"It wouldn't have worked, Mitch." She said almost apologetically. "It was an arrangement for the money and nothing else."

"What about us? You made it sound like…" He looked over at her, unable to continue.

"Yeah, what about us?" I took it from there, leaning forward to look at Anna and then the deputy. "What did it sound like, Mitch?"

"Where is he in all this?" Turley's anger flared as he nodded towards me in the backseat. "Is he my replacement?"

"And here I thought I was the first string." I looked back at Anna accusingly.

It was becoming very apparent that I was being played, just as Turley was now accusing he had been. Anna had suckered both us into her plans to make a small fortune on the sale of the Venus and escape her family with either one of us in toe. What plans she'd have for me, or Turley, once she'd gotten out of Dodge was still a bit muddled, but perhaps an innocuous name change by marriage might have helped her blend into the fabric of foreign travel and helped her disappear. Perhaps a boating accident after that would make her the widow Hollister, or the widow Turley. I wasn't sure, but found myself falling out of love with Anna just about as fast as I'd fallen into it with her.

"Why, Anna?" Mitch looked over at her, choked in pain.

"Yeah, Anna." I parroted his questions again as I looked at her. "Why?"

"I'm in love with him, Mitch." She ignored me as she looked sympathetically at him. "I'm sorry, but I am."

Now I was falling back in love with her. Or should I be? I looked over at Turley, strangely for some guidance in the matter. He appeared to believe her, as he almost seemed to fight back tears. Empathizing, I could only do what I did best.

"Sorry, Mitch." I smiled my Melvin Croup smile. "She's in love with me."

Our surroundings sidetracked my attention as we bounced in and out of a ditch in the rough terrain, forcing me to look around and back at the dust-trail roostertailing into the air behind us.

"This substation you we're saying we're going to." I looked back at Turley. "Is it an actual structure or something carved out of a mountain?"

"Shut up, asshole." Turley's disposition had turned surly, although I couldn't imagine why.

"You know, I could lodge a personnel complaint against you for that." I was being factious of course, because I didn't expect to find a personnel office where we were going.

In fact, I was starting to harbor considerable doubt I'd ever go to trial on my homicide charge and didn't believe any detective was coming to meet us out here in the bushes. I wondered how many shovels were in the trunk of his police car and if Anna was going to help dig the grave. I had to offer some hope for escaping my predicament from this hapless deputy, but could only think of one angle to play as I turned to my captor.

"You do realize if you kill me, it will only martyr me in Anna's eyes?" I argued, trying to picture Melvin Croup talking his way out of his carjacking on Wilshire Boulevard. "I've got a better idea. Let Anna and I run off to Greece and after a couple of months of living with me, I can almost guarantee she'll call you and tell you to bring two shovels and bottle of champagne to break over my tombstone."

"You thing you're funny?" Turley glanced in the rearview mirror and tightened his grip on the steering wheel.

"No." I sank back in my seat and shook my head in resignation. "I think my luck with women is that profoundly bad."

"Don't do this, Mitch." Anna suddenly caught onto the possible scenario and looked at him, shaking her head. Strangely, it sounded more like a warning than a plea.

"Without you, I've got to stay here and look after my personal interests, Anna." He shook his head in weak determination. It was clear he'd rather be with Anna on a flight to anywhere rather than driving down some dusty road with me in the backseat.

"What personnel interests?" I asked.

The narrow dirt road opened up before us and I realized our conversation had eaten up at least a couple miles off the beaten path. Our destination revealed a small ranch of sorts, complete with a simple framed house and neglected barn. Turley drove up to the front door and stopped, turned off the car and got out.

"Your substation looks more like home-sweet-home, Mitch." I peered out the window at the structures and surroundings. "I wonder: If a pistol shot is fired and no one's there to hear it, does it make a sound?"

"Get out." Turley's veiled anger flared again as he opened my door.

"Do I get my phone call now?" I exited and looked around. "Maybe a collect-connect smoke signal?"

I looked over the top of the car at Anna as she got out on the other side. She finally looked over at me. Her expression was pleading with me for some understanding. I wanted to believe her, but the handcuffs were blocking my decision-making capabilities. I could only return a look that said the jury was out for the moment. Behind the expression was a feeling that a jury would never hear the case at all.

"Inside." Turley's mood was darkening by the minute and watching Anna look at me was only accelerating it.

The deputy opened the door and Anna led the way, with me following, and Turley bringing up the rear. The inside reflected the outside: simple, spare and dusty. The only curiosity was a trace of a woman's touch here and there in the décor. Not much, but either Turley had an effeminate side or he wasn't the only one who'd taken up residency out here. From the depth of the dust sitting on everything, I surmised there'd been a woman living here sometime in the past. Whether there was a divorce or the possibility that my grave wouldn't be the only one on some real or imagined Boot Hill nearby was up for debate.

Anna seemed to miss my observations completely as she looked around making her own. It was clear this was the first time she'd been here and that was a good sign that their relationship hadn't gotten too far before I'd come along. I started to take the 'short tour', seeing some pictures on the fireplace mantle, but Turley's directions cut off my impromptu excursion.

"Sit there." He pointed to the couch just inside the door.

"Do you even have a phone?" I complied, but sat on the edge of the cushion, feeling the comfort of my 45 in close proximity to where ironically he'd handcuffed my hands.

"I doubt you'll need one." He took off his hat and placed it on the long counter that separated kitchen from the living room we were left in. His pattern baldness reminded me of our age difference. "My partner will be here in a few minutes and he'll take over."

"Partner?" I looked over at him. "I thought you said the homicide detective was coming here?"

"He *is* my partner." Mitch nodded and grabbed a beer from his refrigerator. He looked at Anna as he twisted the cap off. "Would you like something to drink?"

"Mitch, this is silly." Anna ignored the offer. "You and I both know Jack didn't kill anybody."

"Sorry, Darlin." Turley paused to rest his shoulder against the fridge and drink from the bottle. "Ballistics says otherwise."

"Don't waste your breath, Anna." I interjected. "He has no intention of taking me in or anywhere else for that matter."

Anna looked at me and finally a look of alarm registered on her face. What was just a possibility before we'd arrived was starting to look more like a reality for the future. She looked back at Turley.

"You can't seriously be thinking of doing that?"

"Doing what?" Mitch looked weakly defensive at her. "I'm just going to turn him over to the detective when he gets here. This is just more comfortable than waiting out on the side of the road, don't you think?"

"Just don't even think of..."

"That's all, honest." Mitch looked mock hurt. I knew, because I was a master of the expression. "You can stay and watch if you'd like to. Then, I'll take you back to your car or anyplace else you'd like to go."

"Like Greece?" I interjected.

The sound of a car approaching the house outside ended the conversation as Mitch smiled sheepishly and took another drink from his beer. Anna studied his face and then mine. I could see she doubted the sincerity of his claim, but seeing no alternative at the moment, she fell silent and waited.

The car outside stopped and the motor died. The sound of a car door opening and closing was clear and distinct in the silence of the surrounding wilderness. I was heartened at least to hear only the one door open and close and not more. I only had seven shots in the 45 and when the time finally came, I knew my accuracy would be off, trying to shoot with my hands cuffed behind my back.

The door opened and I braced myself for the worse. What I got instead was complete shock and dismay, as I watched Carl Stapleton walk into the room.

27

Or was it? Oh, it was the guy I'd met in the diner, of that, there was no question. My mind took a giant leap and all the remaining pieces of the puzzle of Lone Tree seemed to start falling into place. I looked at our latest arrival with a new understanding.

"You must be Todd. The one Lyle and Billy were talking about." I looked up at him. "Aka, Carl Stapleton, or at least the guy who probably killed him and took his place for my benefit at the diner when I first arrived. That would also make you the guy who followed me to Vegas and back in Carl's rental, tagging my ride with that Radio Shack quality locator."

"Wow, you really do have an IQ above the temperature of sea water." He regarded me with an amused grunt. "Too bad it wasn't high enough to catch on before it was too late."

"How many days did you have to wait in the diner for me to show up?"

"You know, I was really getting tired of eating that food." Todd smiled at me and glanced over his shoulder at Mitch. "No offense, but Lorene can't cook worth shit. I was so happy when you got word to me that this jackass was finally on the way."

"How'd you know I was coming at all?" I got his attention back.

"Your Carl Stapleton, the real one, had a habit of hooking up with local law enforcement and giving them a full briefing on his cases." Todd explained as he walked further into the living room. "You know, I really liked that about him."

"So, you really are a cop." I looked him up and down, J C Penneys all the way, probably from the catalogue. "You're at least dressed like one."

"Guilty as charged." He bowed slightly.

"Homicide?"

"And narcotics, bank robbery, felony assaults, pretty much all the serious stuff."

"You sound overworked." I mused.

"And underpaid," He nodded in agreement. "Which brings us to our current dilemma."

"You've been working us all from the shadows since day one, haven't you?"

"At first, I didn't believe Mitch when he came to me with this bullshit Mona Lisa fantasy about missing art from some French museum, but then Carl showed up in my office and confirmed it all, just before he headed out for Lone Tree."

"Then schoolboy Mitch here had confided in you in what was going on between him and Anna before Carl even showed up?" I looked at Mitch and then at Anna.

"We're partners." Todd shrugged. "He tells me everything."

"Partners in the Methamphetamine business also, I presume."

"No, in the protection business for those who do produce it." He corrected. "There's a big difference."

"Not as far as DEA will be concerned when they bust that lab and all your biker friends roll on you." I countered.

"That's the 'protection' part." He smiled. "We make sure there *is* no DEA in the picture."

"How'd you stumble onto that racket?"

"Mitch came to me some time ago with suspicions about Lyle and his gang out there. Seems some tourists were disappearing in the area and Mitch had smelled the chemicals from their lab." Todd explained freely. "I saw a chance to make a few bucks and convinced Mitch this was our best bet for fattening our retirement."

"You can't exactly quadruple a saving account in a town the size of Elko and expect it to go unnoticed." I looked around the room. "Where've you been stashing it all? It certainly hasn't been in real estate."

"Mine's far away and the account number is right up here." Todd tapped his temple with an index finger before looking at his partner.

"Mitch here is less trusting. He has it all buried someplace real close by, don't you, Mitch?"

"That's none of your business." The deputy turned defensive. It appeared that old Mitch had been lured into all this for the money, but now was having second thoughts, a lot of second thoughts.

"Mitch has beneficiary issues, so he's staying solvent." Todd explained as he regarded the deputy.

"So, you killed Carl after he got a whiff of the lab. He probably came straight to you about it, didn't he?" I voiced my suspicions. "But not before he told you I was coming out to replace him."

"He knew about the lab, but not enough about the missing art, so after I had to shoot him, I decided to take his place and stick around to see if you knew anything more." Todd shook his head with a sad expression. "But you didn't."

"So you gave me the silencer treatment like you did Carl on some previous night in the Inn, nice and quiet like."

"You know, I've been wondering about that since that first night. What the hell were you wearing in bed when I came calling?" Todd furrowed his brow at me. "I could have sworn I plugged you three times dead center."

"Kevlar pajamas. It's all the rage now in fashion." I replied sarcastically. "Actually, you killed my duffel bag, genius. I was too busy in the bathroom puking my guts out on the coffee you doped."

"I didn't put anything in your coffee." He looked perplexed. "I know Lorene can't cook, but her coffee's usually OK. You sure?"

"Yeah, I'm sure." I nodded. "I was so sick I was almost sorry I wasn't in the bed when you dropped by."

"I'm sorry, too." Todd's smile was back, looking a bit more evil this time. "You screwed up our plans to snatch the painting by playing along with sweet little Anna. Before I could get another shot at you, pardon the pun, you hooked up with DeLaCosta and then she cut us out of the loop all together. It forced us to work in the dark from then on."

"So you started playing it from the outside, shadowing me to Vegas in hopes of grabbing the painting and collecting the finder's fee for yourself." I gave Todd a knowing smile. "You set it up for Lyle to intercept me and take the painting before I could get back to DeLaCosta's."

"I knew something wasn't right when your Hummer kept driving north, so I turned around and waited for you up the road, actually not too far from here. When I saw the fancy pickup, I knew it had to be you."

"Nice try, but your biker friends bungled the intercept and now the painting's gone." I smiled.

"That was very disappointing." He shook his head. "How'd you pull that one off?"

"Friends of mine in high places." I riddled. "With quality optics."

"You seem to keep resisting my attempts to get you out of the way." There was considerably frustration in his voice. "So where's the painting?"

"Philippe already has it." Anna broke in. "He hired a helicopter, but there was no way you could've stopped him even if he'd driven out. He had a dozen men with him and stopping them would've been suicide."

Mitch looked at Todd.

"I told you we would have made more if you'd of just let me go along with Anna and collect on a percentage of the sale."

It looked like Anna had played Mitch the way she'd ended up almost successfully playing me, but Mitch had gone to his partner and Todd had convinced him to help highjack the painting and collect the finder's fee instead. Todd apparently hadn't trusted Mitch to wire him his share from halfway around the globe after running away with Anna. He was probably right.

"So, what brings us all here?" I asked as I looked at the two of them. "It can't be about the frame job on Stapleton."

"We were hoping to gain some control over you with that, maybe play ball with us." Todd explained. "At least we got your gun away from you."

"Your department doesn't even know Stapleton's dead, do they?" The revelation hit me as I said it.

"When you found Carl in the canyon where those three nitwits dumped him, you called Mitch and he called me." Todd's smile widened in victory. "I simply cleaned it up and relocated the remains."

"OK, so what now?" I repeated my question.

"Just some more clean-up, my friend." Todd pulled a handgun

from under his coat and turned to Anna and me. "Now let's all of us take a nice walk."

"Is that the same piece you killed Carl with?" I stayed where I was, eyeing the 9mm automatic. "Looks like your duty firearm."

"No reason to worry about ballistics when you're the homicide detective."

"I hope you do a better job of burying us than you did Carl." I nodded at Anna and eyed Mitch on that one, letting him know what plans Todd had for his would-be girlfriend. I could almost see the wheels turning and figured he'd intervene on Anna's behalf any second.

"Now, he's buried good and proper." Todd eyed us both. "Actually, you'll be a family plot with him soon."

"Not Anna." Mitch declared as he stepped between Todd and Anna, pulling his own old world six-shooter and pointing it at Todd. "That's not going to happen."

I almost visibly sighed in relief as I watched Mitch square off with Todd, who had a slight look of shock in his eyes. With any luck, they'd shoot each other and Anna and I'd make Vegas by dinner.

Todd looked from Mitch to Anna and back again and I could see him weighing his options. Finally, his attention rested on his partner.

"Can we trust her?" He asked in a suddenly cordial tone.

"Absolutely." Mitch looked back at Anna and then at Todd again. "I'd stake my life on it."

"I'll remember that." Todd's gun came down and he put it back in its holster under his coat. "Because our lives are going to depend on it."

"I'll be with her every second till we get our cut on the painting." Mitch promised as he re-holstered the hog-leg.

"Then what?" Todd asked.

"Then she'll get on a plane and be halfway around the world, while we'll be a million bucks richer." Mitch pressed his argument. "We can retire and get out completely."

"OK." Todd said in resignation. "If you say so."

"Are you really buying this?" I looked at Mitch in mild shock. "Your buddy here is about as sincere as a Louisiana real estate agent."

"Shut up." Todd spat at me.

"I know what I'm doing." Mitch added. "So, shut up."

"It's your life." I shrugged, watching any prospect of dinner at the

Bellagio fade.

"I said shut your pie-hole." Todd pulled his handcuffs and started to walk towards Anna.

"Wait." Mitch blocked Todd's advance. "What the hell are you doing?"

"You're going to help me bury this asshole after I shoot him." He explained, nodding in my direction. "Unless you want her to be a witness, we'll need to leave her here."

"Why the handcuffs?" He said defensively.

"To make sure she's still here when we get back." It was Todd's turn to be sarcastic.

Mitch rubbed two of his remaining brain cells together and nodded, letting Todd proceed to cuff her hands behind her back. He then pointed to a heavy easy chair next to the couch I was sitting on. Anna nodded and sat down while Todd looked around for something to secure her to the chair with. Finding nothing that would work, he wordlessly turned to Mitch.

"I've got some rope in the shed." Mitch nodded and left the room through the kitchen.

"I can give him a hand." I offered as I started to struggle to my feet. "I'm pretty handy with knots."

"You've helped enough already, Sherlock." Todd pulled his gun out again and pointed it at me.

"Careful." I eased back in my seat. "That goes off in here and there'll be blood all over the place. Blood that one of you will eventually have to explain."

"If it weren't for the cash in those floorboards, I'd burn this dump to the ground right now." Todd stamped his foot on the rug he was standing on.

"How do you know all this?" I smiled knowingly at him. "Have you been spying on him for some reason?"

"None of your business, dead meat." He shot back, realizing he'd said more than he intended.

The back door opened and Mitch reentered the room with a pair of tie-down straps in his hands.

"These should work better and they'll be more comfortable." He walked over to Anna and put one over her lap, then looped the other one under her breasts and around the backrest of the chair.

"Careful there." I spoke up, seeing the proximity of the strap.

"You're making it that much easier on me to pull the trigger, you know that, asshole." Mitch paused and looked over at me.

"No offense, but you don't look like the 'pull the trigger' type." I offered and then glanced at Todd. "But then again, neither does he."

"Shut the hell up." Mitch shook his head and returned to his efforts to secure Anna to the chair. When he'd pulled the straps tight enough with the buckles out of her reach, he walked around and tested the snugness with his index finger. "I'm sorry about this, Anna. Is it comfortable enough?"

"Mitch, don't do this." Anna repeated her plea.

"Maybe, after you've had some time to think about it, you'll see that I'd treat you right." He leaned a bit closer to her face and spoke softly. "We could still make that honeymoon in Europe."

"After we split up the our shares." Todd reminded him with a not-so-comfortable tone in his voice.

"Sure." Mitch looked over with an apologetic expression. "After we do the split."

I could see Todd's anger starting to churn and his stolen looks at Anna seemed to have some private issues going on as well. He found some release from it all as he turned to me.

"OK, tough guy, let's take a walk."

"Oh good." I struggled to my feet and looked at each of them in turn. "I could use some exercise."

"You're a piece of work." Todd looked at me in wonderment. "You know that?"

"Yeah." I smiled my Melvin Croup smile and leaned closer to Mitch. "Anna's been telling me that every morning, lately."

"Well, now you can tell her good-bye." Todd said through his teeth.

I looked over at Anna and winked.

"I'll be right back."

"I don't think so." Mitch angrily grabbed me by the arm and pushed me towards the door as Todd led the way out.

We got as far as the front porch before Todd stopped and looked suspiciously at me.

"I have to admit you're acting really confident for a man whose about to take a very long dirt nap. Is there something you know that we don't?"

"Well, let's see." I looked around him to make sure we were out of Anna's earshot. "For starters, you just tied up the grand-daughter of a founding mob Don, promised in marriage to the Vettriano family to seal a high-level merger of Mafia families. Would that little tidbit interest you?"

"We know her father was whacked in Vegas years ago." Todd shrugged. "So what?"

"So, the guy who took her father's place is Anna's uncle, Frank Carlucci. Does that name ring a bell?" I eyed them. "Who do you suppose Raymond DeLaCosta really is?"

"Some rich asshole who lives on top of a mesa." Todd shrugged.

I turned to Mitch.

"You *have* met Tony, haven't you? Does he look like a valet to you? Raymond DeLaCosta is actually Nicholas Carlucci, Frank's brother."

Todd paused and looked at Mitch who was flanking me. Mitch's expression of uneasiness couldn't be ignored. Todd caught it and they both looked around anxiously.

"Oh yeah." I smiled confidently. "You didn't think the mob would entrust my scrawny little ass to protect Anna all my myself, did you?

My full explanation finally registered on Mitch and he turned to me, ignoring my question.

"What marriage?"

"I guess you were left out of the loop on that one as well." I smiled a bit. "I met Frank Carlucci and had a brief chat with the Feds and it's all too true. She does seem awfully anxious to skip the country, doesn't she?"

"Why is she out here, then?"

"She's basically on ice while the deal is being hammered out." I nodded and looked at Todd. "You think that painting was priceless, you just tied up 115 pounds of TNT in there and I'll guarantee you I'm not alone out here with her. And neither is Tony. He brought back some of his own help from Vegas."

They looked at me and then again took in their surroundings. I could see my pitch was starting to work on their nerves, so I kept going.

"You were wondering why Lyle didn't mash me up into little tiny biker meatballs outside the hotel? It was because Tony was right behind me, like he has been today."

"What are you talking about?" Mitch put his hands on his gun belt and studied me with a confused look on his face.

"I'm talking about snipers, dumb-ass." I looked from him to Todd. "Don't take my word for it, call Lyle and ask him."

They looked around some more and then at each other. In unison, they seemed to dismiss my whole yarn and pushed me off the porch and towards an old windmill pump rusting off in the distance.

"Nice try, Sherlock." Todd pushed me again for effect. "You're so full of shit we're going to have to bury you deeper, just so you don't stink up the rest of the county."

"Suit yourself." I shrugged in confidence, wondering just what Tony was doing at the moment. If he was around, I was hoping he wouldn't wait too long to intervene. We walked into the tall scrub-oak and passed the windmill, further out and down a slight draw. The ground was relatively soft and it reminded me of something else I could needle them about. "Either of you two geniuses remember to bring a shovel, or is this going to be an Indian style fresh-air grave?"

"Let us worry about the remains, jerk-off." Todd pushed me again.

"You know, if you buried Carl in some soft gully, the runoff will probably wash him right out of it and he'll end up in some culvert next to the highway." I looked around and then up at the cloudy sky. "Oops, looks like rain."

"Like I said, let us worry about that." Todd pushed me again, this time with the muzzle of his gun.

"Just trying to help." I muttered more to myself as I looked up at the surrounding high ground. "Tony, jump in anytime you feel comfortable."

Our short hike took us partway down the shallow draw and then up and over a small ridge. We ended up in a secluded opening with tall brush all around us. It would have made a great campsite, except the vegetation was a little too close for wildlife comfort. There was freshly turned dirt in the middle of clearing, darker than the surrounding earth. A lone shovel sticking up at one end of the fresh earth was Carl Stapleton's only grave marker.

"Rest in peace, Carl." I offered the graveside blessing.

"I dug the last one." Todd moved off to one side and looked at Mitch. "Your turn."

"Me?" The deputy stopped and looked at the detective. "Why me?"

"You want to un-cuff him and give him a shovel?" His expression helped make his point.

"OK." Turley grabbed the spade and started digging.

Todd settled in, but kept his 9mm trained in my direction.

"You got any prayers, I'd start saying them." He smiled at me.

I looked skyward while I worked the 45-caliber automatic from my rear waistband.

"Almighty Tony." I exclaimed. "Deliver me from evil and dispatch this plague from their earthly bonds."

"He's lost it." Todd looked over and laughed with Mitch.

I had the gun in my hand now, waiting for the right moment. Soon, all hell would break loose and in expectation, my heart started pounding in my chest until I was sure they could both hear it. I tried to keep my breathing even, but it was becoming more difficult with the adrenalin creeping into my system. I wasn't up for 'moments of truth', preferring more to work things out in the absence of flying hollow point projectiles. Still, I had little doubt that this particular situation wouldn't end with the smell of cordite in the air. All I could do to control the trembling rush of adrenalin was watch them and keep talking. I really must've looked like I'd lost it.

"Thy kingdom come, your work isn't done…..yet."

Todd's edginess at the slow progress Mitch was making on his digging and my confident remarks were beginning to get the best of him. Finally, he took a deep breath, his nerve catching up with his resolve as he brought his gun up much faster than I'd anticipated.

"I can't wait all day for this shit." He said as three shots rang out from his 9mm. They seemed to echo forever into the nearby canyons, but in their wake, he continued to explain. "I've decided to dissolve our partnership and have some fun with your little girlfriend before I kill her, too."

I stood wide-eyed in shock, gun in hand behind my back, while staring at Todd. Slowly, reality set in as I looked over at Mitch Turley, a bloody corpse who stood there like a statue, moments before he fell face down in his own shallow grave. I looked back at Todd just in time to see the barrel of his gun swing my way.

28

We stood in the clearing, mille-seconds seeming like lifetimes as we both staring down at the body of Mitch Turley. Slowly and deliberately, Todd brought the muzzle of his 9mm up from the luckless deputy and towards me. Seeing the same fate coming, I swung the 45 automatic pistol I'd been holding behind my back around to hopefully shoot Todd before he could kill me, too. As luck would have it, my panicked reaction overextended the movement and the handcuffs on my wrists sudden halted the gun's progress halfway around my waist towards its intended target. My gun hand jerked to a stop and with it my finger, which was unfortunately on the hair trigger of the cocked 45. Todd and I both jumped in surprise as the premature gunshot kicked up dirt halfway between us.

The shock on both our faces must've been classic, as we stood staring at each other for the longest, most awkward moment. When the moment broke, all Hell broke loose as we simultaneously exchanging volleys of poorly aimed gunfire while scrambling for cover. Finding only the dense underbrush that surrounded the clearing for concealment, we eagerly dove into it in opposite directions to escape one another. It had been a long time since I'd experienced bullets being fired in my direction. They made a completely different, yet disconcerting sound than when they were going the other way. The concussion of air displaced by their approach sounded more like a sharp crack than a rolling boom.

Then there were all those stories about everything slowing down in times of stress. It always worked the opposite for me. It was almost like someone hit the fast-forward button on the player. In what seemed like a fraction of a second, we were crashing through bushes and falling over their exposed roots. Once on the ground and relatively safe from Todd's barrage, I rolled over and carefully looking back. What I could see of the clearing was now vacant except for Mitch Turley, who wasn't feeling anything anymore.

"Fuck!" I heard Todd scream as branches crunched under his body weight somewhere on the opposite side of the clearing.

"Did I get you?" I yelled hopefully.

"No, you asshole." He angrily yelled back.

I righted myself and fired two more shots into the brush towards his voice.

"How about now?"

"No wonder you were acting so cocky." From the sound of his exasperated voice, I estimated he was still direct across the clearing, probably sitting in a similar manner while taking stock of the new situation. "Where did you get that gun, you little prick?"

"Your incompetent partner..." I started looking around to get a feel for the new game that had just started. "I'm sorry, I mean your incompetent ex-partner. The one who never bothered to search me."

"Jeez, well if you want anything done right...." The sound of the brush crackling and snapping under his feet signaled he was already moving around the clearing towards me.

"He would have come in handy right now, don't you think?" I sensed his movement and looked off in the direction I'd need to go to keep away from him and still keep the clearing between us.

I started making my way through the tall brush, but the stiff branches immediately started hitting me in the face and blinding me. It was obvious I'd never make it with the handcuffs behind my back, much less be able to competently defend myself when the time came. I stopped and bent over, stretching my arms to slip the handcuffs under my backside. Rolling back into a large bush, I slipped the handcuffs to the back of my knees, gun still in hand. Hoping I wouldn't shoot my own foot off in the process, I attempted to slip the cuffs under my feet so my hands would at least be in front of me.

"He would've fucked this up, too." Todd's voice sounded resigned, but different. I could hear a degree of calculating in it, as if he were trying to guess where I was or which way I was moving.

"Having trouble finding me?" I paused to fire one more round blindly into the brush towards his voice. Maybe I'd get lucky and hit him. In any case, it would give him pause if he entertained any ideas about rushing me from across the clearing.

"You're not going to hit me like that." He almost laughed. "You're just going to run out of ammo sooner."

"I have plenty." I lied and added some wishful thinking. "Anyway, I'm not trying to hit you. I'm only signaling Tony so he'll know where we are."

"Give it up, jerk-off. Tony couldn't find this place with a helicopter." Now, it sounded like he was stalling for time. His voice seemed closer, but I couldn't tell exactly how close. "Why didn't you shoot us both when we were back at the house?"

"I figured I'd wait and let you both dig your own graves." I hoped he couldn't hear me grunting as I almost had one foot under the cuff chain. "No pun intended."

It was clear Todd was making some progress through the dense foliage. I estimated he was staying about ten feet from the edge of the clearing as he circled it in my direction. He was now moving slower and making less noise as he did, much closer than I had originally estimated. I needed to move, but was still hog-tied and helpless in my present position. I strained to see anything among the thick scrub oak, but nothing moved. We were both using the sound of our voices and crunching vegetation under our feet as a kind of a sonar. The only question was who would be better able to use it to their advantage?

"You city cops might do OK in warehouses and back allies, but out here in the bush, us good-old-boys know how to get around better." He was reading my mind and I was sure he was closing the distance between us. His voice had even returned to normal volume as he spoke.

"The only thing you good-old-boys are good at is stepping in your own bullshit." I struggled and finally got the one leg through the cuffs. "Careful, I can smell you getting closer. Or am I just downwind?"

"I can't wait to snuff your ass." The proximity of his voice now alarmed me and I abandoned my attempt to get the last leg through.

"Oh, I bet you're an ass snuffer from way back." I struggled to my feet as quietly as I could and backed away from his voice. "I'd bet you could only smell the manure when you walk through a rose garden."

Now I was 'crab-walking' straddling the handcuff chain between my legs. The overall position of the 45 auto would have looked obscenely comical if not for the seriousness of my current predicament.

"You know, when the time comes, I think I'll just wing ya so I can watch you die slow."

I put some quick and quiet distance between us and all of a sudden stumbled onto the path we'd probably walked in on. Looking back towards the clearing and seeing a portion of Mitch's body lying face down in the dirt confirmed it. I was wearing his handcuffs and he had the keys to them. If I had any expectation of getting out of this alive, I needed to get to him and get those keys. I looked back in the direction I'd come from, but couldn't even figure out where I'd broken through the dense shrubbery.

I couldn't see anything, but more worrisome, I suddenly couldn't hear anything, either. That was even more disconcerting, because it meant Todd had stopped moving too and was now listening for me. Hopefully, he was thinking I'd gone to ground and was hiding from him. I studied the corpse in the clearing and tried to calculate what Todd would do next. None of my options seemed very promising, but getting out of these handcuffs had to be a priority.

I kept low and crept towards the clearing, praying my pursuer wouldn't catch on to my plan. On the path, I at least made no sound, but the naked silence had me unconsciously holding my breath and I nearly passed out before realizing it. Sucking in a deep volume of air, I made it to the edge of the clearing.

"Hollister?" Todd's voice came as a cautious question from the dense vegetation. He sounded like he was facing in the direction where I had been, rather than where I currently was. It was the first promising sign since Mitch had stopped us on the highway.

I watched in the direction of his voice as I crab-walked into the clearing towards Turley's body. Once there, I rolled him over slightly to get the keys from his belt. I found them and winced as they clinked slightly on their large ring. I palmed the keys to silence them and as an afterthought, rolled him the other way to expose the holster for his six-shooter. It might come in handy if this kept going.

Limbs and branches started to move and snap from the direction I knew only Todd's voice had come from a moment ago. I could tell he now knew where I was and what I was doing. His progress sounded swift and decisive, like a bull elk charging straight through the woods towards a perceived threat.

"Shit." I grabbed for Mitch's gun and froze.

The holster was empty. I rolled him back the other way, wondering if it had come out of its holster and was lying in the dirt under his body. I couldn't find it. I looked up and could see the bushes moving with a form separating them as it approached. I backed away from the deputy's body and brought my 45 up from between my legs. There was no time left, so I aimed the best I could and waited.

My brain was doing the math, trying to divide how Todd had acquired Mitch's large caliber handgun by a quotient of how much it was going to hurt when he shot me with it. The remainder was attempting to recall just how many rounds were left in my own handgun. Forty-four divided by major pain equaled a dead duck with three rounds remaining. Or was it two? Funny what goes through your mind when think you're about to die.

Suddenly, my overtaxed mind relaxed as I waited to unload whatever was left in my 45 auto at Todd when he broke through into the clearing. Just as his shape became distinguishable, he cut to his left, staying behind the closest bushes as he circled me just outside the clearing. It was a ploy to get me to empty my gun at his moving target, a ploy that unfortunately for me, worked. Three shots later the slide on my trusty 45 auto locked open, begging me to feed it some more bullets.

I collapsed on the fresh mound of dirt that was meant to ultimately cover my grave, which now seemed a poetic prediction for my immediate future. It didn't take long for Todd to sense the same thing and he stopped running. He stood for some time just outside the clearing, studying me through the thinner layer of leafy branches. When he finally decided I wasn't playing possum, he relaxed and his smug confidence returned.

"Not a bad run, as runs go." He stepped into the clearing and walked a bit closer to me, where he'd be able to end the game and not miss.

"Fuck you." Was all I could muster for a reply.

"Don't feel so bad." He pursed his lips in mock sympathy. "You were just outmatched."

"I'm really sick and tired of this case." I said to myself, my gun limp in my hand, dangling between my legs. I could feel the handcuff keys in my hands and wondered if I could've made it if I hadn't paused to look for Mitch's gun.

Looked up at Todd, I saw the 9mm in his hands, pointing straight at me. I found it odd that he wasn't going to use Mitch's 44-caliber six-gun. It wasn't in his other hand either. 'Must've just thrown it in the dirt,' I thought to myself.

"You won't be sick and tired of anything in a second." He shook his head slightly as he took aim. "You'll just be dead."

A cannon-like shot rang out and the deafening roar made me jump so hard, my backside must have cleared the ground by six inches. The single shot echoed down the nearby canyons like a thunderclap as I watched in strange fascination as Todd jerked backward. It almost seemed like an invisible truck had slammed into him as his arms and legs went limp and he fell face up in the soft earth, eyes staring vacantly skyward. Once there, he never moved again.

I stared at him in troubled confusion, cocking my head like a Cocker Spaniel watching at his master do yoga for the first time. The echo finally rolled off and died, leaving me partially death in one ear, while shrouding the area in an almost eerie silence.

"Do you have any idea how ridiculous you look?"

I looked around as Tony walked into the clearing, holding Mitch's missing six-shooter.

"You didn't have to cut it that close for my benefit, you know?" I looked up at him in disgust. "I would've been happier if you'd jumped in towards the beginning of this dance, instead of waiting for the last one."

"I'm really surprised you didn't drill him dead center." Tony looked at where my empty auto dangled limply in my hand. "You seem to hit everything else you aim at from that region."

"What took you so long?" I ignored the remark, which I'd really be impressed with after a few months of reflection. "This is one version of hide-and-seek I never want to play again."

"We found the Avalanche, but you'd cleared out before we got there." Tony walked casually into the clearing and gestured to Todd's newly lifeless body. "We parked in the bushes and luckily, this goofball wasn't too far behind us. I remembered what you said about the rented Charger, so we just tailed him to the ranch. Once he was off the highway, the dust trail wasn't too hard to follow."

"You should be a detective." I commented as I used Mitch's keys to work the locks on the cuffs and free myself.

"Well, don't even entertain the notion to taking up my profession." Tony shook his head as he looked down at me. "You're pathetic."

"I'm just out of practice." I said defensively.

"You're out of your mind, that's what you're out of." He shook his head as pulled a handkerchief from his pocket. "Whoever gave you a license to carry a firearm should be shot. It's a wonder you didn't blow your own dick off."

"Are you through?" I got the cuffs off and stood up.

"Toss those to me." Tony now had Mitch's handgun in his linen sneeze-rag, motioning for me with his free hand to throw the cuffs over to him. What kind of bodyguard carries a handkerchief?

"I don't think anyone else is going to need them." I looked at Todd's remains and back over to Tony, who was now standing next to Mitch's body. "They both look pretty arrested to me, now."

"Just toss them over." He motioned again. "And the keys, too."

I did as he instructed and watched him wipe off both items, almost as if he were polishing them. As he worked on them, he slowly walked around Mitch's body. My tired brain started connecting the dots and I slowly nodded. Tony bent over the deputy's body and put the handcuffs back into their pouch, then re-clipped the keys onto his belt. After he was satisfied with that, he worked the six-shooter into Turley's hand, using the hanky to close it around the grip of the firearm without leaving his fingerprints on anything. 'That kind of bodyguard'. I answered my own question.

"Wait a second." I walked over and bent down with him.

"What?" He hesitated, but allowed me to approach the body.

I worked the gun further into his hand and the cocked it with my thumb, being careful not to leave any trace of my fingerprint. I aimed the gun off into the distance and put the dead man's finger on the trigger. Discharging the firearm with another deafening roar, I then let the hand and pistol rest in a position in a way it would naturally fall.

Looking back up at Tony, I shrugged.

"Paraffin." I remarked. "When they finally find them, now there'll be powder residue on his hand, making the case that they shot each other that much stronger."

"Hmm." Tony pursed his lips thoughtfully. "My opinion still stands, but as a technical adviser, you're not too bad."

"I also play a mean harmonica." I smiled and we both stood up.

Tony looked around at our handiwork and then up at the clouds.

"With any luck, it'll rain enough to cover all our tracks."

"When they're declared overdue, someone will come out here looking for them." I nodded in agreement as I looked at the two dead cops. "They'll see the cars at the house and then start a looking around."

"Time for us to go, I think." Tony nodded in agreement.

"Anna?"

"She's with Jocko." Tony confirmed. "At the house."

"The house." I repeated thoughtfully.

"This is as far as you go with her, I'm afraid." Tony remarked as we started down the trail towards the house.

"I know I screwed up…" I started to explain and then remembered the keys to the Avalanche were in Turley's pocket. I backtracked and retrieved them, tossing them over to Tony. "You'll need these."

"Actually, you did pretty good." Tony caught the keys and nodded his approval. "It'll just make her departure at McCarran easier on both of you."

"You know where she's going?" I looked at him in mild surprise as we walked side by side.

"Oh, she's going to make it to the Greek Isles all right." Tony confirmed. "It just won't be with the money from the painting, obviously, and her stay won't be very long."

"How long has Nick known about her and Mersant?"

"From about the beginning." Tony smiled. "Frank Carlucci routinely audits his phone records and Mersant's number came up. The rest was referencing the dates and simple addition."

"You guys play it way too close for my comfort." I shook my head. "So what's next?"

"We swap out." Tony advised. "I'll take Anna to the airport and you'll take the Venus back to LA where Lloyds is waiting for it."

"If I had a choice.." I looked at him.

"They're both Venus'." He agreed. "But the painted version won't break your heart."

"Wise beyond your age, but Nick might disagree." I looked over and frowned at him. "She really seems to love me."

"As much as she's capable of loving a man, yes." He smiled back in a rare display of emotion. "The problem is she's manipulative, incapable of sustaining any relationship, and if that isn't enough, there's that little matter of already being spoken for."

"Sacrificed to the mob." I nodded as I watched the ranch house come into view. "I'm envious and feel sorry for the young Vettriano at the same time."

"She'll try to run from the inevitable, but she won't get far without her finder's fee." He nodded and surveyed the area with a professional eye. "When she's finally caught, you won't want to be anywhere around her, believe me. If her mother knew about you now…"

"The Carlucci's know." I argued weakly.

"We'll keep it in confidence." Tony affirmed.

"I appreciate that." I shrugged.

"It's not for you." Tony again gave me a thin smile. Two times in one day? It must have been some kind of record. "We can't be delivering damaged goods to the Vettrianos. What you don't realize is Frank Carlucci is a pussycat next to Anna's mother."

"Jesus." I shook my head.

As we reached the front porch, Anna burst through the door and fell into my arms.

"I heard the shooting and thought I'd lost you, my love." She held me tight around my neck, burying her head in my shoulder. "I couldn't bear the thought of you dead."

"Me neither." I held her close and stared at Tony over her shoulder. "Tony here saved my bacon."

"Thank you, Tony." Anna turned to look at the recently reassigned bodyguard.

"My job." His usual demeanor was back.

"Anna." I pulled her back to look in her eyes. It wasn't easy to continue, knowing it would probably be the last time I'd ever do so.

"Tony's going to see you to the airport. Nick needs me to close out my case and keep the wolves off his back."

"When will you come over to meet me?" She was suddenly concerned, looking from me to Tony for some understanding.

"I'll follow you over in a week or two." I smiled and kissed her. "I'll bring a case of suntan lotion, whatever your favorite brand is."

"As long as you're bringing it, it's all I'll need." She hugged me again and burrowed into my chest.

"We might have some company soon." Tony interrupted as he looked up the dirt road towards the highway. "We need to get back to the Avalanche before it's noticed."

Jocko emerged from the front door and nodded to Tony, who turned to me.

"We'll take the Charger back to the highway and dispose of it after we pick up the Avalanche. Jack, we've got a Cherokee down the drive here a ways." He eyed me. "You'll find everything you'll need in it and enough gas to get back to Vegas. From there, you'll be able to head back to LA and finish up."

"Got it." I nodded and squeezed Anna one more time before pealing her off my chest. "I'll see you in a few short weeks."

I hated lying to her, but it was the only way to expedite our delicate situation. As if on cue, a mist started falling. I knew it would soon turn to rain.

"I will be waiting for you, my love." She kissed me long and hard, before drifting from my embrace.

"Here are all the keys." Tony handed me a key fob for the Jeep. He nodded to my hand that now held them. "If you have a flat, there's a special key there for the compartment in the back."

"I understand." I smiled and tossed the keys up and caught them again. "I'll make it OK."

"We'll give you a lift to the Cherokee." Tony started walking towards the Charger.

"I'll be OK." I hesitated and looked at the house. "I have a couple of odds and ends to clean up here."

"Don't be too long." Tony cautioned.

"Be right behind you." I smiled again.

They got in the Charger with Jocko driving and drove off towards the highway. The smell of the moisture in the air was a welcome relief to the heat I'd lived with the entire time I'd been here. I paused to look up and felt the moisture on my face, thinking how good it was to be alive. I'd had close ones, but this one ranked pretty far up there. I looked down and watched the large sedan disappear down the road and thought of Anna. She'd been the love of my life, even with her faults, which I doubted she was even aware of. For her, it was just the way she lived, a sort of family legacy.

Finally shaking myself from a brief melancholy, I walked into the house, making sure I wiped my feet off good before doing so. Inside, I took the short tour Mitch had deprived me of when we'd first arrived. As I suspected, I found what I was looking for in a picture frame on the fireplace mantel. That mystery solved, I turned to the rug in the center of the room. Pushing it aside, I found the loose boards Todd had referred to and pried them up with my pocketknife. In the floorboards between the framing, I found two large gym bags full of cash. It would be enough, I decided.

On the way out, I spotted a composite bow and a quiver of aluminum-shafted arrows. There were game tips in a box next to the outfit, but I left them. The practice tips would work just fine.

29

The Jeep Cherokee was right where Tony had said it was. I put the items I'd liberated from the house in the back and noted the compartment he'd mentioned in the floorboard. The keyed lock for it was round, like something an alarm box would use. Checking the key ring, I found one that looked like it would fit. I tried it and the compartment opened easily. Under the floor panel were two travel tubes very similar to the one I'd brought out from Vegas. I figured one held the two echoes while the other held the original Venus. Locking it back up, I only hoped this time it was the real Venus of Urbino as Nick had promised it would be. I got in behind the wheel and was relieved to find my bag from the Avalanche sitting on the backseat. Tony had thought of everything.

After pulling a U-turn, I drove the distance to the edge of the highway where I paused and checked for traffic. It was deserted as far as the eye could see in either direction. Looking down south where Anna and Tony were now hopefully driving towards Vegas, I gave pause to consider the situation. I had a priceless artwork in my possession and by all rights had a primary obligation to drive straight through to Los Angeles and deliver it to its long lost owners. I knew by now they'd be waiting for it, hopefully with a handsome finder's fee I'd no doubt have to arm wrestle Melvin for a piece of. It was the job I'd been hired for and my main responsibility was to turn left and continue on my homeward leg of this little odyssey.

I looked up the road in the other direction and the cop in me argued otherwise. I had already compromised my ethics by helping Tony stage a shootout between Mitch Turley, an Elko County Deputy

Sheriff, and his partner, another Deputy Sheriff whose full name I'd never even learned. Even though they'd been partners in what the literary community would term a 'criminal enterprise', they were still cops and their Department deserved to know the truth about them and what had actually happened. I even had a couple of gym bags full of proceeds from their little venture sitting in the backseat. I knew initially it would be considered evidence, but eventually it might go towards the Department's pension plan or better equipment for the honest deputies.

Armed with the information I could supply them, they could round up a search warrant with enough deputies to close the drug lab and arrest the outlaw bikers who'd been running it. Lyle and Billy might even get some jail time out of it, but I knew from past experience that they'd probably make bail and have another lab going full throttle by the time their case came to trial. Such was the law of supply and demand, illegal or not. Many realities of the criminal justice system I'd been a part of for so many years had never really appealed to me, but since I'd been employed as part of it, I'd been obligated to play their game.

But now, in my retirement where I was free from the burdens of legal responsibility, a third option was beckoning me from Lone Tree. It wasn't any distain I felt for proper authority or some innate desire to rebel, but more of a need to see things through for some sense of closure I could live with. Nodding to myself, I pointed the Cherokee north and skidded onto the damp pavement. The mist was still holding back any real rain, requiring only an occasional tap the wipers to keep the windshield clear. I kept the speed down to a temperate pace, gathering my resolve with every mile I gained on my destination.

~ ~ ~ ~

When Lone Tree finally came into view, it looked exactly like I'd left it. Only the two near derelict cars sat in front of the inn with no signs of life outside any of the structures. I slowly made the same U-turn I'd made on my first arrival and parked in the same place next to the gas pumps. Twisting in the driver's seat, I reached around to my bag, digging deep into the side pocket where I pulled out my extra magazines for the 45. Loading up, I regarded the firearm before returning it to my rear waistband. I had fired it in self-defense, but felt strangely grateful I hadn't hit anyone with it. I only hoped that my luck would hold for the next hour or so. Getting out and carefully locking the SUV, I turned to the lonely looking diner and walked in.

Lorene was right where she'd been the first day I'd met her, painting her nails while listening to some AM radio station playing AC/DC.

"I imagine you don't get too many stations out here." I nodded to the dusty ghetto-blaster on shelf behind her.

"Tell me about it." She grimaced with a bored expression. With a pop of the gum she was chewing, she displayed her latest fingernail color for my approval. "What do you think?"

"I think you need a vacation." I surveyed the empty diner. "A permanent one from this place."

"I wish." She re-examined her nails and sighed. "Just waiting on my dad to say when."

"If he could, he'd be saying the time is now." She looked up and began to pay attention, noticing the look in my eyes.

"What do you mean?" Her reply had a definite edge to it, hinting that maybe her female intuition had been telling her something hadn't been right for a long time, something that would possibly culminate in this very moment.

I'd made notifications of this nature to so many people, so many times that the words flowed out like a well-worn script in a bad play. Still, it was never easy to start with the opening line.

"I have some bad news about your father, Lorene."

"What?" Her eyes widened and started to moisten.

"Your last name is Turley, isn't it?"

"Gibbons." She shook her head slightly with an expression of wary surprise. "Mitch is my step dad."

"Stepfather?" The correction set me back a moment.

"My mom passed away a few years ago, just before we moved out here." She nodded very slightly. "How'd you find out?"

"The picture on your fireplace mantel." My eyes must have conveyed what I was about to tell her, because she read them clearly.

"I...." Her fingers crept up to her lower lip that was now slightly trembling. "I need to check the coffee pot."

"I understand." I nodded as I watched her walk back to the coffeemaker.

She made no attempt to work with the appliance, but only stood in front of it with her back towards me, shoulders slumped and arms limply dangling at her sides. After a few moments, she quietly spoke.

"He's dead, isn't he?"

"I'm sorry." I offered in sincere empathy, knowing how hollow it still must've sounded.

"I knew something would happen."

"You did?"

"He hadn't been acting right for a long time, like something was bothering him that he couldn't talk about." She picked up a dishcloth and absently wiped the chrome base of the coffeemaker. "He'd been hanging out with that shit head detective, Todd Banning and we argued about it. We've argued a lot since Mom died. He said he had an obligation to Mom to take care of me and it would all work out OK. He said we'd get out of here soon and go back to Vegas. I knew that asshole Todd was bad news."

"'Was' is the proper term." I advised. "He's dead, too."

She turned towards me.

"Did you kill him?"

"I found out what they were doing and Todd grabbed me." I lied, not really knowing if Mitch originally knew what Todd had planned for me and Anna. What would the truth serve now, anyway? "He took me out to the ranch and got into it with your step father over what to do with me. Todd wanted to shoot me and bury me out back with another PI he'd killed, the guy I'd been sent here to replace. Your father wouldn't have it. The arguing turned into a confrontation and they both started shooting at each other. I dove into the bushes and when I finally came out, they were both dead."

"He saved your life?" There was a distant trace of pride in her voice as the tears started to roll down her cheeks.

"He sure did." I replied with the most sincere look I could muster. "He got caught up in something that wasn't Kosher, Lorene, but in the end he stood up for what was right."

Lorene quietly nodded and looked around the diner.

"He leased this place from Mr. DeLaCosta. Thought it would give me something to do. Billy and his bunch always left me alone, because they knew he was the deputy on this beat."

"There were other reasons they left you alone." I nodded.

"It *did* have something to do with Billy and those jerk-off bikers, didn't it?" She spat. "I knew it."

"Well." I looked around. "It's still their territory and now the gloves are off. We need to clear out."

"Are you going into Elko and tell them what happened?" She asked as her tears began to dry.

"Your stepfather and Todd are....gone." I hesitated and changed my terminology for her sake. "Bringing the Sheriff into it would only drag out the facts on what they were doing and muddy his reputation."

"What are you going to do, then?" Her expression turned to one of curiosity.

"I'm going to destroy some evidence and put Billy and Lyle out of business for a while."

"How are you going to do that?"

"With your father's old hunting bow and some arrows al la flambeau." I smiled a bit broader. "Have you got some greasy rags in the back?"

"This is a diner." Her expression turned to 'duh'. "That's all I have in the back."

"Get some and meet me out front, OK?" I turned towards the door.

"Sure." She seemed to get right on board with the plan, probably thinking it would keep her dad's reputation cleaner if she went along with it. Maybe it even would, who knew?

I exited the diner and walked over to the corner of the building where I could see a portion of the hotel and the two cabins across the stream in back of it. All looked quiet. I turned back and went to the pay phone in front of the diner. Lorene came out with a bunch of greasy rags in her hands.

"Do you know the phone number for the hotel?" I asked as I dug in my jean pockets.

"Not by heart, but if you can believe it, they're in the book." She shook her head.

I went through the white pages in the phone directory that dangled on a chain under the phone kiosk and found it. Taking some change from my pocket, I thumbed it into the slot and dialed the number. I could picture the clerk inside the hotel looking curiously at the ringing phone, before finally putting down his magazine to answer it.

"Hey," I didn't wait for him to say anything when he finally picked up. "Would you guys be interested in the convoy of DEA vans heading your way?"

"What?" He replied in dismay.

"Turley came clean and dropped a dime on you. I figure you've got about two minutes max to clear out." I advised. "They're coming up north on the highway from Vegas and they look like they mean business. I think I even hear a helicopter coming with them."

I hung up the phone and looked at Lorene. Her expression told me she was in the dark about the lab I knew was sitting not fifty yards or so from where we were standing. I nodded for her to walk back the short distance to the front door and followed her so we could stand under the awning and out of the light drizzle. Once there, we looked back towards the parking lot of the hotel where the entrance to the highway was the only part we could see from our angle. Within thirty seconds, both cars that had been parked in front of the inn peeled out onto the highway and sped off in the opposite direction towards Elko.

"What was that all about?" Lorene looked up at me.

"I needed to get them out of the way." I said little more as I took the rags from her and walked over to the Cherokee.

"I don't understand." She followed me.

"That funny smell you've told me about." I opened the rear of the SUV and took out Mitch's bow and quiver of aluminum-shafted arrows. "That's ether. A highly volatile component used to make methanphetamine. Billy and his crew have been making it in those cabins back there."

"Ex?" Lorene looked at me and then down the highway at the disappearing cars.

"Ecstasy, crank, speed, whatever they call it now." I nodded and took a fistful of arrows out of the quiver. "I suspect that your father became aware of it and told Todd so they could do something about it, but Todd had better ideas and dragged him into a sort of protection racket for Lyle and his gang."

"That's why those bozos were always looking at me so funny." She nodded to herself. "And why they always backed off whenever I yelled at them."

"Yep." I took one of her greasy rags and tore it into smaller ribbons, then wrapped them tightly the arrows I was holding, making sure much of it was over the actual practice tip so it wouldn't slid off in flight. I looked at Lorene and smiled. "Got a match?"

She smiled back as she got the idea and handed me her lighter. I snapped it to life and put it to the arrow tip, now wrapped with the rag. I'd seen it in movies, but in reality it wasn't as easy. Some wire of something to hold the rag on tighter was sorely needed, but this wasn't metal shop 101 or the movies, so I'd have to go with what I had. I walked to the edge of the diner and around the corner, making my way down the path until the cabins were fully in view and just across the stream. I propped the flaming arrow onto the bow and took aim at one of the cabin's windows. It was the cabin I'd seen the bikers pour out of the day before when I'd almost gagged from the smell of the heavy fumes on their clothes. I pulled back on the bow and after careful adjustment of aim, let the arrow fly.

'Wow', I thought to myself. 'It really works.'

The flaming arrow made a fast shallow arc and struck the cabin wall five feet from the window.

"It's kind of wet out here." Lorene observed from over my shoulder. "Maybe if you get one through the window?"

"That's where I was aiming." I looked back at her and took another arrow.

"Oh." She offered with a look of consolation. "Why don't you make a torch or something and just get close enough to throw it through?"

"Ether isn't just flammable." I offered in reply. "It's highly volatile, like an explosive. You don't want to be anywhere around the cabin when it goes off."

"I understand." She handed me another arrow and I lit it.

Taking careful aim, I let it fly in similar fashion from the bow. Unfortunately, it landed in similar fashion, about three feet further away from the original one that still smoldered on the exterior of the cabin wall.

"Well, Robin Hood you ain't." Lorene shook her head. "Give me that, unless you want to be out here all day."

"You could do better?" I gave her a doubtful look.

"Mitch's father taught him to hunt with a bow when he was just a kid." She stepped forward and took the gear from me. "When he found out he couldn't have his own kids and married my mom, he taught me. It was the only thing in gym class I was ever any good at."

I shrugged and lit another arrow for her, handing it over and stepping back. She adroitly slipped the flaming arrow onto the bow and drew the line back, taking a moments aim before letting it fly. It went straight and true, breaking the window as it penetrated the cabin's interior.

Red flame immediately belched from all the windows, shattering them and took the door right off its hinges. The exploding fumes expanded within the cabin, buckling the walls outward like in a cartoon. The sides held, but the roof didn't fair quite as well as it lifted some two feet from the framing before settling back down, slightly askew from its original position. Lorene and I brought our hands up and turned away from the explosion, which rolled into the sky and ended up as a mushroom shaped cloud of black smoke laced with red flame. When the initial concussion passed us, we straightened and looked at our handy-work, a cabin now completely engulfed in flames.

"You weren't kidding, were you?" Lorene commented.

"One down and one to go." I nodded toward the other cabin.

"OK." She loaded another arrow and I lit it for her.

She let that one go and it flew through the window of the neighboring cabin. Nothing happened, but after a few moments, a red glow started coming from the interior.

"Must be living quarters." I commented with a nod. "Or maybe a storehouse."

Lorene was busy loading another arrow. When she was ready, she adjusted her aim at the hotel.

"Light me." She commanded with a set jaw and new strength in her voice.

"It's just a hotel." I offered an argument to save the structure. "Maybe someone can come in and turn the place around."

"Light me." She repeated in a tone that couldn't be argued with.

I shrugged and flipped the lighter to life, touching it to the wrapped arrow tip soaked in kitchen grease. She aimed quickly and let it fly. It disappeared through the front window of the inn and soon another dull flicker of flame started growing inside. I watched the fire progress inside the cabins and then the hotel, before turning to Lorene.

"You have the makings of a first rate arsonist."

"You think so?" She gave me a promising look.

"I wouldn't put it on a resume." I shook my head, making it clear I was being sarcastic.

"Too bad." She shrugged as we both started back towards the diner. "It seems to be the only thing I'm good at."

"You're not thinking of quitting the manicuring business, I hope." I gave her another look.

"You're a bit of a smart ass, aren't you?" She looked up at me.

"Funny." I smiled back at her. "No one's ever said that to me before."

We exchanged glances and I could see the sorrow trying to creep back into her eyes. We'd just torched an outlaw biker gang's main source of income. Although there'd been a small measure of twisted revenge meted out, there was no time to either congratulate ourselves or mourn. I tried to keep her mind off the loss of her stepfather by changing the subject.

"Where do you think you'll go now?"

"I'm not sure." A shiver ran down her body as she came to a sudden awareness she was on her own now.

"Well, if Venice Beach sounds appealing, I'll sublet my place out to you." I offered as we reached the Cherokee and looked around. "I've been thinking of moving up a bit and need someone to rent it till the lease is up."

"Venice Beach, really?" Her eyes lit up with the possibilities.

"Your father, I mean Mitch, set up a kind of trust fund for you." I nodded, thinking of the gym bags in the back of the SUV. "I know an attorney and we can set something up so you won't have to work for a while, maybe even get some college experience on that resume. Might round out the arson and beautician entries."

"That would be great." She nodded eagerly and looked at the diner. "What should I do with this?"

"Lock it and let's get out of here." I nervously looked down the highway. "I don't know how much time we have before Lyle's gang regroups."

"I have to go by the ranch and pick up a few things." She gave the diner a dismissive look and pulled the line on the bow to test its strength. "As far as this dump goes, you can light another arrow and I'll take care of it."

"You know, I think you've had enough practice for one day." I shook my head and took the bow from her. "I'll take you to the ranch, but we can't stay long. Lyle probably knows where you live. In any case, I have an appointment in LA I'm already late for."

"Just drop me off." Lorene walked around the car and got in the passenger side. "I'll grab a few things and be right behind you."

We got into the Cherokee, kicked it onto the highway and I ran it up to 70, anxiously looking behind us. Putting some quick distance between a flaming Lone Tree and us, we soon found ourselves close to the turnoff. Lorene started squirming, as we got closer.

"Is he... in the house?" She started to shake a little.

"No." I shook my head. "He's out past your well, over a small ridge and in a clearing."

"Oh." She got quiet again.

"They won't be there long." I saw the anxiety in her eyes. "They'll be missed soon and your step-father's cruiser is in front of the house. It'll only be a matter of time and they'll find them."

"OK." She seemed more comforted.

"Do you have another car you can drive out to LA in?"

"Yeah." She looked at me sheepishly. "Yours."

"Mine?" I looked at her.

"Todd drove your rental out and put it in the barn the day after you got to Lone Tree." She shrugged. "He said he was going to impound it for evidence or something."

"Well, I'd appreciate it if you brought it back with you, then." I shook my head and slowed down for the turn into the ranch's entrance. I noted that the sky was finally opening a bit and letting some heavier rain fall. Slipping the car into four-wheel-drive, we pushed on until the ranch house came into view. I stopped at the front door and looked at Lorene. "Better take Mitch's bow in with you."

"Right." She nodded and took it from me before getting out of the car. Before she shut the door, she looked back and hesitated.

"What?" I asked. "You're getting soaked out here."

"I like you and I'm kind of one of those people who don't like to lie or be lied to by friends." She looked at me straight. "You don't look like the 'dive into some bushes' type of guy and I know you picked up your gun this morning from under the seat cushion. I also know my step dad never opened anything with either of our names on it in his life, especially a trust fund."

"I might have embellished a bit, but overall, it's true enough." I studied her a moment and shrugged. "And maybe it's not exactly a trust fund, but I know for a fact he was putting it away for you."

"Good enough." She gave a decisive nod and smiled a bit before looking at me with a grimace. "I'm sorry I poisoned you."

"What?" I wasn't sure I heard her right.

"That first day when you came into the diner." She shrugged. "I put some cleaner shit in the coffee, hoping that asshole Todd would drink some and end up in the hospital for a while. He'd been hanging around and making me nervous. He ended up not drinking any that day, but when you came in, acting all friendly and shit with him, I figured what the hell, if you knew Todd you must be just as big an asshole."

"You know," I pinned her with a look. "Just a suggestion, but when you come out to LA, you might think about working somewhere besides a restaurant. Actually, anywhere besides a restaurant."

"I hope you didn't get too sick." She scrunched her face.

"Sick as a dog." I nodded. "But, you saved my life."

"Huh?" Her face contorted even more.

"It's a long story." I shook my head and gave her my business card with a few hundred-dollar bills folded around it. "Call me when you get to LA, and don't forget to bring the car."

30

Anyone growing up and living in Los Angeles all their life could never realize how vast and sprawling it is until they spent some time out in the country or in some small town. For me, returning from this trip was somewhat of an eye opener. The air now made me cough and traffic was as dense as a Brazilian forest. It was like being a long distance runner, jamming along on the open road, free and easy, and then all of a sudden finding himself ankle deep in tar with a plastic bag over his head. This trip was forcing me to give pause as to my living conditions and choice of residency. Still, there was a certain comfort about getting back into my original social environment with the hustle and flow of so many things going on at once. I shelved my contemplations and aimed the SUV towards the Wilshire district.

I was tired and needed a shower and shave, but my cargo weighed heavy on me and I wanted it out of my life, the sooner the better. The car's interior was littered with coffee cups and fast food wrappers, but at last some decent tunes were bleeding through on the radio. I swore if I heard one more country western song, I'd go postal and assassinate the car stereo. It wasn't that I hated the music genre, but when it was all you could listen to for several hundred miles, it was enough to push someone like me over the edge.

After three near collisions and two incidents of road rage from my out-of-practice city driving, I pulled into the familiar parking structure of Melvin Croup's law firm. I found a parking space and popping the cargo door, pushed the gym bags aside, unlocked the compartment, and retrieved the travel tubes from their hiding place. Concerned for security of the gym bags, I looped the tubes holding the paintings high over my shoulder and hefted the bags of money in both hands. They were pretty heavy and I hadn't looked too closely at their contents, but I figured the bills were probably rubber banded in lumps of a grand and tightly packed.

After taking the ride up to the 12th floor and walking into the reception area, I found Miss Timberlake behind the counter and smiled at her.

"Hi."

"Mr. Croup has been expecting you." She gave me a repulsive look, holding her finger to her nose against the clothes I'd lived in for the last two days.

I had to admit, after rolling around in the Nevada outback, dodging bullets and playing arsonist, I figured I must have looked and smelled like a poor man's version of Indiana Jones without the hat or whip. Still, seeing her reaction, it only made me push on.

"You should have come with me to that gambling Mecca I mentioned last week." My smile broadened as I opened one of the gym bags towards her. "You could have helped me spend some of my winnings."

"Oh, my God." She lit up at the sight of the money inside the bag and looked at the one in my other hand. "Is that one full, too."

"I spent most of it already." I nodded with a slightly bored air. "I would have bought you a fur coat or something, but you weren't there for me to take your measurements."

"Six." She replied off-handedly, still staring at the bag's contents. "I wear a six."

"Maybe next time." I pushed the smile and bit before zipping the bag shut again. "That is, if you're free."

"I might be." Her eyes drifted to my disheveled attire.

"Car trouble." I explained. "I lost a wheel on a hairpin coming back down out of the mountains."

"Really?" Her tone told me she was catching on.

"Have you ever tried to repair a Ferrari in the middle of nowhere with a pocketknife and duct tape?"

"It must have put up quite a fight." A knowing smile now crept across her face as she picked up on my game.

"Brutal." I concluded.

One of Miss Timberlake's eyebrows did its high sign and her expression turned dismissive. Like most California beauties, she was a veteran of advances. Hell, she did work in an attorney's office. Regaining her composure, she picked up the phone and buzzed Melvin.

"Mr. Croup? Mr. Hollister is here." Still pinning me with an icy stare, she nodded at the response. "Yes Sir, I'll send him right in."

"I'll probably just buy another one tomorrow." I offered casually.

"Go right in, Mr. Hollister." She whispered as she hung up the phone. "Mr. Croup is waiting."

"OK." I hefted the bags with a grunt and one last look her way. "Heavy."

Inside the office, Melvin was surprisingly not behind his desk. Instead, I found him sitting at his rarely used clutch of easy chairs that surrounded a large round coffee table at the far corner of his work place. The sound of conversation told me he wasn't alone. I walked past his desk area and the length of his office, approaching the attorney where he sat with his guest. Melvin jumped up and greeted me like I was some kind of son, coming home from a military tour in Iraq.

"Jack, my boy." I thought he was going to hug me, or something.

"Melvin." I smiled my signature smile named after him and held up a hand, just in case he had any notion of an emotional embrace. I looked over at his guest and recognized him right away. "Mr. Elevator."

It was the man I'd encountered in Caesar's Palace, the one I'd kept meeting at the elevator on the floor just below mine. He'd ridden down with me after I'd received the echo from Carlucci's courier. I noticed he was even wearing the same sport coat and open polo shirt. Either he was a creature of habit or it was some kind of insurance company uniform for their detectives.

"Theodore Hatchet." He stood and offered his hand. "Regional Investigator of Lloyds of London, West Coast Branch."

"Jack Hollister." I took the hand and glanced at Melvin momentarily. "West Coast investigator for anyone who promises to pay, but usually doesn't."

"Nice to meet you." He smiled knowingly and nodded at the travel tubes slung over my shoulder, then at the gym bags. "I see your luck turned for the better. What's in the bags?"

"Laundry." I gave Melvin a wary look and decided I'd set something up for Lorene on my own. Putting the bags down, I slipped the travel tubes off my shoulder and handed it to the investigator. I rolled his name around and, of course, had to vocalize my question. "That's your real name?"

"The Theodore part or the Hatchet?" He smiled back as he took the tube from me.

"Take your pick." I shrugged.

"Unfortunately, they are both real." He turned the first tube over in his hand as if testing it by weight. "This feels like the echoes."

"Your guess is a good as mine." I shrugged.

He opened one end of the tube and peered inside.

"Yes, very nice." He nodded and recapped the tube shut, before turning his attention to the second one. "And let's see what we have here?"

"You must be a real professional to take this thing in alone." It suddenly struck me as odd he was alone, so I looked around the office. "Where's your help?"

"No need." Hatchet shook his head with a slight frown as he worked the clasps on the second tube. "We negotiated the return of the original and it's already on its way back to France with other investigators."

"Original?" I froze, watching him pop the end of the tube off and pull out a large poster.

It was obvious from the quality of the paper it wasn't anything remotely valuable. Hatchet unrolled it and snickered as he examined it. He noticed me watching and turned the article towards me. It was a movie poster of Humphrey Bogart from "The Maltese Falcon".

"Shit." I shouted in frustration.

"What the hell is this?" Melvin jumped into the revelation.

"A movie of similar plot, I'd suspect." Hatchet laughed a bit as he rolled the poster back up and stuffed it into the tube. Once done, he looked at me. "You never did have the real one, but we kept an eye on you when you were transporting the echo. Unfortunately, the finder's fee will be split a bit differently than Mr. DeLaCosta, a.k.a. Dominic Zontos, had originally intended."

"Tony pulled a switch." I offered in disgust, but with a small trace of envy. "He said he always liked the classics."

"Along with some woman who was staying with DeLaCosta."

Hatchet nodded with a wry smile and started for the door. "Had to tie these loose ends up and retrieve these echoes, but you played a crucial part in the Venus's return and you'll be compensated. It just won't be the finder's fee for the Venus. Thanks for the help."

He was out of the office carrying the echoes before either Melvin or I could respond, leaving us standing together looking at one another. After a long pause, I hesitantly addressed my soon to be ex-client.

"So, you got the second half of my fee?" I tried my signature smile, but it faltered.

"In your dreams." Melvin sadly shook his head and walked towards his desk, shoulders slumped with a hangdog expression. "Nice work, Hollister."

"How could I of known?" I answered limply.

"I'll call you next time I need trace on a license plate." He reached his desk and fell into his chair. "Maybe you can handle that."

"Yeah, right." I headed for the door carrying the gym bags full of Lorene's money and wondering if she'd give me a loan.

~ ~ ~ ~

A couple of weeks later I knocked on my old apartment door, just off Venice Beach, but there was no answer. I'd helped Lorene settle into my old place by scooping up almost everything that belonged to me and placing it in the nearest dumpster out in the back ally. I reflected that most the apartments along Venice Beach should be built on some sort of hinges so they could be tilted up on end to expedite evictions.

Predictably, the dumpster out back that I'd thrown everything into had been picked clean and the old worn out furniture had been reclaimed long before the trash truck had arrived. The new coat of paint on the door I was now standing in front of should've given me a clue, but I was still surprised after finding the door unlocked and walking in.

"Lorene?" I called out, but there was no answer.

The interior had been completely redone with new paint, carpeting, the works. It looked so different I had to check the number on the door twice to make sure I had the right apartment. It was decorated somewhat contemporary with lots of posters and cozy furniture. I could see through to the kitchen with its typical clutter and shook my head, remembering the similar disposition of the diner's kitchen in

Lone Tree. I called out Lorene's name again, but there was no answer. I backed out and shut the door again, turning down the front path to the walkway leading to the beach.

Strolling along the concrete easement next to the sand was like visiting my old high school: It was nice to come back and walk around, but it now offered only strange, distant memories. After receiving my cut of the finder's fee for the echoes and renting minimal office space just off of Sunset Blvd., I'd settled into a modest condo in Brentwood with some rented furniture. Unfortunately, there was already a struggle to make the rent and I was looking for other cases to work.

Now dressed in my comfort attire of khaki shorts and tie-dye T-shirt, I walked into the sand and sampled the cool salty ocean air. The day was bright enough for my sunglasses, but a tad brisk, as August had now turned to mid September. Most the kids were returning to school and the European tourists were following a warmer sun, wherever they went this time of year to do that.

It left only the residents and hardcore sun worshipers laying out on their blankets, catching the last rays of the sun before it tracked further north and forced them to put on jackets instead of suntan lotion. The surf was flat and the gulls soared on the warmer currents coming off shore, calling to each other as they maneuvered randomly in the sky.

I walked out into the sand, halfway to the waterline before stopping to look around. It had been my home for a long time and I knew just about everyone, residents and shopkeepers alike. I wasn't positive I'd be comfortable where I was now, but this wasn't very far away. Maybe I'd end up finding someplace a bit closer or just visit more often.

The salty air forced me to think what the ocean smelled like in different countries, particularly the Mediterranean ones. I was deep in thought and trying to remember the intoxicating scents of the recent past when a voice brought me back.

"Jack?"

I turned to a woman lying on a colorful blanket, propping herself up on her elbows to study me. She was wearing an almost non-existent two-piece and blonde hair piled up and away from her neck. All that along with the deep tan and large framed sunglasses made her a mystery to me. Lying next to her in the sand was a young guy in utility shorts and windbreaker jacket embroidered with 'Speedo Delivery' on it.

"Yeah?" I squinted down at her, glancing at the young man as well.

"Did you see what I did to the place?" She smiled, knowing I hadn't recognized her.

"Lorene?" I lifted my sunglasses and looked closer.

"How do you like my hair?" She smiled broadly.

"Jeez." I shook my head and walked over to her. "I didn't expect you to go completely native on me."

"Like the tan?" She displayed her one arm, turning it so I could see there were no tan lines. "I joined a salon to catch up on the late season."

I stood over her and cocked my head, trying to recognize anything of the Lorene I'd invited out from Nevada. She was now an eyeful and the 'California' treatment she'd given herself made her fit right in, almost too good.

"No tan lines." I acknowledged her demonstration, still stealing glances at the stranger lying next to her in the sand.

"Anywhere." She smiled a bit wickedly. "This is so great. Thank you so much for bringing me out here."

"Don't thank me yet. You don't know LA like I do." I shook my head and smiled back. "You called and said an urgent delivery had come for me."

"Yeah." She tilted her head towards the guy lying beside her. "This is Rudy the Courier. He brought out a certified letter for you and I had him wait when you said you'd be right over."

"Hey, dude." Rudy nodded in greeting and pulled an envelope out of one of his utility pockets. "You got ID?"

I showed him my license and he nodded again, producing a clipboard he'd been using as headrest and dusting the sand off it.

"Sign here." He gave me a pen and pointed it to the line on his delivery log.

I signed and exchanged the clipboard for a large manila envelope.

"Guess I gotta go back to work now." He sighed, eyeing Lorene as he got to his feet.

"Tuff job." I watched him openly admiring the girl.

"Sometimes." He shrugged and looked back down at her. "Maybe Saturday night then?"

"Call me." She squinted up at him and made a phone receiver gesture with her thumb and pinky finger.

"Definitely." He turned to me as he started walking back towards the boardwalk. "Later, dude."

"Later." I laughed slightly and looked at Lorene. "Dude?"

"Stay for a late lunch or maybe dinner?" She looked up at me.

"You cooking?" I eyed her.

"Sure." She bubbled.

"Tell you what." I shook my head again. "Get dressed and I'll take you out."

"No, let me take you out." She sat up and started collecting her things.

"The fund I set up for you will only keep going if you don't touch the principle." I warned. "Don't go Hollywood on me. You'll never make it."

"OK." She stood up and gathered her blanket. "But I'm going to get really bored just sitting around here, especially with winter coming."

"Sounds like you're doing OK." I chuckled and cocked by head towards Rudy as we started walking towards the apartment some distance behind him.

"I think I need to look for some work." She looked up at me. "Got any ideas?"

"A job that doesn't include restaurants or making coffee." I eyed her back. "Right?"

"Sure." She agreed with a knowing smile.

"I'll keep my ears open." I promised with a nod.

"What about working for you?" She squinted up at me as we walked.

"Me?" I did a double take. "Doing what?"

"Whatever." She shrugged. "Doesn't your office have files and shit?"

"I'm working on it." I shook my head at her. "I need some cases for the files and shit."

"Let me know, OK?" She beamed. "Where we going for dinner?"

"I was thinking maybe the Charthouse." I looked around the beach and then remembered the envelope in my hand. I examined the array of addresses before tearing the end flap open.

"What is it?" She looked on in interest.

"Don't have the foggiest." I pulled out the largest item. It was a photograph.

"Isn't that Anna?" She looked over my arm at the picture in my hand. "And that friend of Mr. DeLaCosta. What was his name?"

"Tony." I frowned as I noted they were standing on a rocky beach.

"Yeah." She nodded as she studied the photo. "Jeez, they look happy together."

"Thanks for noticing." I shook my head and frowned deeper.

"What else is in the envelope?"

I handed her the photo and numbly pulled the next item out and examined it.

"Is that a check?" She watched me unfold it.

"Certified." I read the amount and nodded in mild shock, displaying it firmly in both hands for her to read.

"A Hundred and Fifty thousand?" Her eyes got as big as silver dollars.

"That explains the certified delivery." I folded it up and stuffed it in my wallet.

"Wow." She handed the photo back to me and grabbed my arm. "I guess I'll let you buy after all."

"I guess." I dumbly looked at the snapshot and Anna's bright smile. There was that hint of sadness in her eyes that she couldn't hide even from the camera. It made me rethink the whole idea of ever seeing her again. What had happened had probably been for the best. Probably.

The reality of the photo started to permeate my brain. Suddenly, it dawned on me that Nick might have planned this whole thing out, beating Anna to any plans she might have had to escape her family obligations. Perhaps, Tony had played Anna's game on his boss's behalf and taken my place, after I'd taken Mitch's, just to keep her on a leash until it was time to tie the knot with Vetrianno. I nodded to myself, preferring to believe that rather than what it looked like staring back at me in the photograph. I started to put the picture back in the envelope, but noticed something else inside it. I pulled it out and looked at it.

"What's that?" Lorene craned her neck to read the faded typing on the sheet of paper.

"Itinerary." I strained to read it. "Airline confirmation."

"To where?"

"Athens."

"Greece?" She questioned. "Who's in Greece?"

I held up the photo.

"They want you to join them?" She exclaimed. "Wow. Are you going to go?"

"Don't think so." I'd been on that ride and wasn't anxious to get back on the roller coaster named Anna. I started to stuff the itinerary and snapshot back inside the envelope, but noticed something else. There was writing on the back of the photograph. Hesitantly, I turned it over and read Anna's handwriting, 'I'll be holding the other half for you, my love'. I looked up at the beach around me and nothing else in particular.

"Ah shit."

Made in the USA
San Bernardino, CA
01 September 2013